PROLOGUE

January 2012

Dublin, Ireland

The last blow had sent her crashing to the floor. With his back turned he took another swig from the bottle and cursed; his left arm radiated with pain – a poorly aimed punch. With his guard down, he did not notice her stir.

Gripped by terror, the naked young woman moved surprisingly fast and raced out of the room, through the empty house, desperate to escape.

Backdoor, she thought in a panic, *the kitchen* …

'No!' she cried out, finding the door locked with no key.

Cornered, she held her breath as the heavy footsteps drew nearer.

Her eyes darted to the cluster of knives neatly stacked in their wooden stand; she grabbed one. The polished steel handle of the boning knife felt cold in her hand. It was too small! For a moment, she was filled with doubt.

Rushing at her, he tripped and knocked the piled crockery off the worktop. She lurched and swung the razor-sharp blade wildly. She did not feel the soft skin part as the knife sliced across his throat, severing the pulsating artery, vanishing in a gush of blood.

Her eyes remained riveted on the dying man clutching in

1

vain at the gaping wound. His knees buckled. He crashed to the floor.

Leaving the kitchen, she turned and took one more look; the dark stain had spread alarmingly quickly across the marble floor. She had to get away, as fast and far as possible.

Anxiously, she paced up and down - her slight figure barely visible in the hazy dark. Evgeniya blew into her cupped hands, trying to soothe her aching fingertips. Noticing the bloodstained nails, she shrugged her shoulders indignantly as her eyes flitted between the traffic and the overnight bag discarded on the pavement – her only earthly possession.

Her attempt to thumb a ride on the M1 north of Dublin made no impression on the few cars travelling at such an ungodly hour. She shivered and pulled the cardigan tight over her flimsy evening dress as the freezing weather sliced through her frail body. She wheezed and coughed, her chest ached, her breathing laboured. Drained, the temptation to curl up in a heap next to her bag was overwhelming. She was tired, too tired to carry on as the rivulets of water ran freely off the tip of her nose, the steady downpour plastering her blonde hair to her anaemic skin.

But the fear of being caught drove her on. At the most, three hours remained before the thugs would roam the streets and hunt her down. The fact that her last customer was dead was unforgivable.

Well, he got what he deserved, she thought, remembering Shirley, butchered by him in the dungeon! She lifted her chin and once more waved at the traffic.

A huge articulated truck hissed to a stop. She did not hesitate and climbed inside. 'Thank you. Sorry about the seat ... it's going to get soaked,' she apologised, removed her wet cardigan and slumped back into the seat.

The driver reached into the rear of the cabin and fished out a towel. 'Here, dry yourself.'

Massaging her scalp with frozen fingers, she focused on the glow of the truck's bright headlights cutting a swathe through the darkness. The large wipers swished reassuringly.

'Where're ya heading?' he asked.

'London.'

'Lucky day. What's your name?'

'Aoife,' she replied in a heavy Russian accent. 'I have no papers ... can you get me there? I'll pay,' she said, digging €200 out of her bag.

'No problem, *Aoife*. And I'm, *Jesus the Messiah*,' he mocked. 'Where're you from?'

'Kerry,' she replied bluntly, in no mood to talk.

'Okay, got it, no more questions,' he said and turned the music up. Loreena McKennitt's voice filled the cabin, enchantingly. As the lyrics flowed, "... a mystic land to dream of …" she felt a longing for shelter, for the comfort of her home and family. She did not bother to wipe the tears which rolled down her cheeks. Plagued by the haunting image of the dying man - his lifeless eyes and the soundless hollow gaping mouth - made her sick to her stomach, shocked at what she had become.

Engulfed by the throng of pedestrians crowding the pavement of Soho, she felt safe. Not even the powerful mister McGuire can find me here, she thought.

By the time she crossed the small hotel lobby off Kensington Gardens Square, it was past nine o'clock. Exhausted, she climbed the creaking stairs to the third-floor bedroom, shut the door and sat down on the bed. She reached for the phone. Hearing her sister's voice, she mustered a cheerful, 'Svetlana, it's me!'

She dodged a tirade of questions and twisted the truth to avoid being judged by her family, but mostly to avoid hurting them: fired from work, and while sulking in the park, someone had stolen her passport and money. She had to be repatriated home and promised to go to the Russian Embassy first thing in the morning.

With a curse, she jumped up realising she had overslept. She threw on her clothes, applied some make-up, scrutinised her haggard face in the mirror, grabbed her bag and left the small room.

Ten minutes later Evgeniya stood opposite the Russian Embassy. She sighed as the emotion of finally being free washed over her. Concentrating on the building she stepped into Bayswater Road, drawn forward by the white, blue and red banded flag adorning the entrance.

A silver BMW crawled to a stop next to her. Two men jumped out and surrounded her as a large hand clasped over her mouth. The next instant she was tumbled into the car. The doors shut. With a powerful roar the vehicle shot forward and raced through the traffic. Craning her neck, she caught a glimpse of the Embassy disappearing behind her.

It took the London Crime and Operations forensic experts several days to establish the identity of the mutilated body discovered in a skip in London's East End.

A name and dental records were supplied by the Russian Embassy; their involvement being prompted by a deeply concerned family reporting their daughter as missing – the last they had heard from her was the night before she was to visit the Embassy. The nameless victim was ultimately identified as Evgeniya Nikolaeva; deceased 12th January 2011, age twenty-six.

Instead of the hunt for her killer commencing, her file was filtered to the bottom of the pile – no one would miss another Eastern European prostitute, a heroin addict.

In the so-called *Free West*, Evgeniya had never existed.

However, condemnatory footage retrieved from the surveillance cameras at the Russian Embassy in London, recorded on the day of her abduction, was couriered to the head office of the Federal'naya Sluzhba Bezopasnosti (FSB) – the Federal Security Services – in Russia where Evgeniya Nikolaeva's name was added to the ever-increasing list of girls who turned up dead in the West, their silent screams forever hushed.

CHAPTER 1

The Present
Dublin, Ireland

Smiling, Sinead toyed with her food and ignored his hungry stares. She had no appetite. Another time, another life, maybe then the delicately flavoured black sole, a crisp and refreshing Sancerre, romantic music, seductive lighting and décor might have been perfect for the occasion. But these were all wasted on her. Tonight, like all the others, was filled with regret.

Her well-rehearsed repertoire was nothing special. The same banal routine. Meeting her client at the bar; tonight, it's Paul – *And last night, what was his name again ... Eamonn? Oh well, so, who cares* – exchanging insincere smiles, sipping sweet cocktails, and delving the profane depths of idle conversation, interrupted every now and then by spontaneous hollow laughter. A typical Friday night. A typical night in the life of an escort.

She did as they expected.

But from the moment she had laid eyes on him, she had struggled to suppress her contempt. It took an enormous amount of willpower to make her client feel at ease, stroking his over-inflated ego. His smooth middle-aged looks, his blatant arrogance, flaunted by the impeccably coiffured hair and meticulously clipped nails, gave her the creeps.

He seemed blissfully unaware that too many dinners and pleasures had long ago taken their toll. The mere thought of having to put up with his feeble attempts at foreplay repulsed her. He was nothing more than just another overweight, egotistical old fool, relying on his money to secure a few moments of pleasure – to rekindle his long-lost manhood.

Recalling the countless number of men she'd endured in the past was a subjugation which made no sense.

Why continue? she asked herself. *Why? And why, in God's name, did I throw away my dreams, my hopes? Why did I allow Lydia to twist my arm? So much for friendships,* she sighed, disheartened.

The urge to end this madness, to jump up and flee, was hard to resist. But she stayed. Yet again, she chose the easy way out, playing the obedient girl, bowing to her master's wishes.

Embittered, she watched the perfect red rose in its crystal vase diffuse into a million fragments – the icon of love – an emotion she would never embrace. She was destined to remain a lonely woman, as no man would love her. Love, a word that would never appear in her epitaph. The only word etched in bold letters above her grave would be 'WHORE'.

The innocent laughter of a young girl, reminiscent of the calm hypnotic resonance of a small brook washing over smooth, rounded pebbles, stirred emotions she thought she no longer possessed. Flustered, she stole a glance at the child with large, blue eyes – a soul with nothing to hide – not unlike herself, now, so many years ago.

Annoyed, she swiped at these memories; a life which belonged to someone else. Despite her inner turmoil, she managed to continue her role as seductress, the *perfect* companion.

After dinner, she reluctantly got up and followed him. She remained distant, not interested in what he had to say. Entering his suite, he flung his jacket on to the antique Victorian chair, along with his earlier charm and courteous manner. Grabbing her arm, he demanded what he had been waiting for.

She refused to budge.

'Look, I don't know and I don't care what your problem is,' he said. 'All I want is what I have paid for, for you to do your job. You've tried my patience long enough. All night I've watched you drift off to cloud cuckoo land. You must take me for a complete fool! Well, missy, game's over. You shall oblige like a good little girl.' He tightened his grip. 'We can either do this the easy way or the hard way. But know this – I'll have you, even if I must rape you. Stupid fucking whore!'

'Take your hands off me, you pig!' Sinead shouted and ripped herself free. Lashing out, her nails clawed at his face, lacerating the paper-thin skin. Stunned, she watched the red liquid ooze over his puffy white cheeks, mingling with the black and grey moustache.

The man wiped his face with the back of his hand and exploded at the sight of the blood. 'Jaysus, I'll kill you!' Snarling like a rabid dog, he launched himself at her.

Sinead ducked below his outstretched arms, raced out of the bedroom and slammed the door with a sickening crunch in his face. Ignoring his yells, she fumbled with the door to the corridor. Throwing it open, she dashed outside, tripped, and careened into the opposite wall. Regaining her balance, she plucked off her high stilettos and ran.

As her bare feet pounded the thick carpet, the sound of Paul's huffing faded behind her. Turning the corner, the emergency escape was on her left. She flung the door open and sprinted down the stairs. With her heart drumming in her ears, she reached the bottom. Pausing, she slipped her shoes back on and grabbed the push-bar. She was alone; no one was chasing her.

Where are they?

Unsure of what lay beyond the door, Sinead took a deep breath and stepped into the cool night.

The alley was clear.

She started to run.

Out of nowhere, hands seized her and lifted her into the air.

'Well, well ... where're you off to in such a hurry? Not leaving, by any chance?' a male voice ridiculed her.

Ciarán!

'Seeing it's so chilly, I suggest we go inside before you catch a nasty cold dressed like that. Shame on you, what would your parents think? Shall we go, *dearie*?' His sarcastic voice dripped honey sweet.

Sinead turned her head away, not wanting to challenge him.

'Have you forgotten the last warning I had smacked into your empty head? Or do I have to visit your little brothers before you'll listen? Whaddya say?'

'Stay away from my—'

Ciarán's open hand struck her cheek, leaving a mixture of blood and spit smeared across her face.

'Let's go. Niall's waiting!' he ordered and turned away. On impulse, he swung around and swore. 'You know what you've done? I don't care about the weeping fat boy, but you might have cost me my job!'

Gripping her shoulders, his fingers dug into her skin. He jerked her towards him and, with a loud clunk, their heads banged together.

Her knees buckled. She crashed on to the pavement. Despite the pain, she burst out laughing, recalling the look of dismay on Paul's face with the blood gushing from his wounds.

'You find this funny?' Ciarán hissed. 'Maybe you won't think so after the boys and I have rolled you over a few times. Believe me, Lydia won't mind.' He grabbed her breasts, squeezing with all his strength.

Screaming in pain, she spat in his face. He did not respond.

With a cruel penetrating stare, he seized her flowing black hair and wiped the spit off his face, struggling not to put a bullet between her eyes. Had it not been for Niall, he would have. Through clenched teeth, he scowled, 'Take her before I do something, we'll all regret.'

CHAPTER 2

Niall's Estate
Wicklow Mountains

Paul, you bastard! I'll make you pay! Niall fumed, seated in the semi-dark home theatre, tempted to smash the phone against the wall. He didn't need this. The two calls could not have come at a worse time: first Ciarán's and then Paul's. *Not good, not good at all …*

The swing of the door made him look up.

Irina!

'Mind if I come in?'

'Please do. Glass of wine?' Niall offered, swallowing the bitter taste in his mouth.

'*Spasibo* (Thank you). What are you watching?' she asked in her Russian accent, taking in the frozen image on the four-metre wide screen.

'The Last Samurai, oldish movie. You know it?'

'*Nyet* … sorry, I meant, no,' she corrected herself. 'Any good?'

'I like it … but maybe not everyone's taste.'

'Can I watch with you?'

'Of course, please. Although you'll have to excuse me. I just had a call from some friends. They're on their way over, need to discuss something urgent. Sorry,' Niall replied, heaving his shoulders apologetically, his mind preoccupied.

Sinead, you little hussy, why the hell did you refuse the bugger ... and attack him? Niall seethed. *You must be deranged!*

Unlike most girls, Sinead had joined his agency willingly, couldn't resist the money. And for wanting out, well, that would never happen. She knew far too much ... also, too good a prize to let slip away – plenty of miles still left on her.

And, Paul ... well, he's a real problem. The twaddle about Sinead being the reason he's pulling out of the deal sounds like a bloody convenient excuse and nothing else. What's he up to? Well, whatever the hell it is, it can wait. I'll deal with him later. First things first, before this deal blows up in my face, Niall thought. *If this goes south, the consequences will be disastrous.*

Niall struggled to keep his composure.

His head throbbed – not a good sign.

Best I'm out of here ... time to be alone.

The last thing he wanted was for Irina to see him like this, to experience one of his black moods. It would be a deathblow to any meaningful relationship he had in mind.

Next to him, the soft light danced inquisitively in Irina's deep-gold, hazel-green eyes, patiently waiting for him to speak.

He looked at his watch and stood up, unwilling to entertain her curiosity. 'Right then, I'm off. I'll be downstairs. Best you don't wait up for me. Please continue with the movie, and if you need anything to eat or drink, just buzz the kitchen.'

'You sure ... I don't mind waiting.'

'No. I have no idea how long this will take. I'll see you in the morning. Goodnight.'

'*Spokoynoy nochi* (Goodnight),' Irina said, nodding understanding. She took the remote control, pressed play and watched the frozen image jump to life. Taking a sip of her red wine, she wondered what was amiss. One thing she had learned in the few weeks since her arrival: her host was a real dark horse.

With the pain drumming in her ears, Sinead did not notice the car slip quietly in between the two grey limestone pillars.

Neither did she see the pair of heavy iron gates swing shut behind her. Looking up, the dark silhouette of the manor house etched against the treeline, loomed ever closer. Realising where she was, the thought of never leaving this dreaded place alive, tormented her. She cringed deeper into her seat.

To the passer-by, the sprawling Georgian manor house with its perfectly manicured green lawns huddled close to the lush backdrop of tall oak trees seemed nothing less than a haven of peace and tranquillity. The well-camouflaged security cameras, motion sensors, infrared alarms crisscrossing the lawn, nor the armed guards unobtrusively patrolling the grounds, were visible. The only hint of security were the guards and dogs stationed at the gate. The distant glow of a single light hanging motionless over the front door completed the picture, adding a quaint touch of innocent country nostalgia.

As soon as the car floated to a halt, the doors were flung open. Without fuss, Sinead was shoved out into the dirt. Groggily, she picked herself up and straightened her short, black cocktail dress. Marched towards the front door she tried to resist. A futile effort. A well-aimed punch tumbled her on to the vestibule's black and white marble floor. Dazed, she looked up, unaware of the gravel embedded in her hands and knees.

With his feet planted firmly apart, Niall towered over her, dressed in his all too familiar black casual-fit wool suit, designer white shirt, and thin black tie.

Dragged into the study, Sinead was dumped on the settee.

The study door shut.

In silence she watched as Niall's incensed gaze shifted between her and Ciarán – Ciarán's presence was somewhat reassuring. *Also, in trouble, I guess? No wonder he's peeved*, she mused.

A bead of cold sweat rolled down Ciarán's temple as Niall spoke. 'This is your final warning, my boy. I'll not tolerate any more mistakes, nil, zero, zilch, nada. Got it? Good ... good.' The measured words were spoken calmly, too calmly.

Impatiently, Niall continued to pace up and down, rubbing the day-old stubble on his strong chin. His full, black hair, with a hint of grey at the temples, was slightly dishevelled. In his current frame of mind, he was not to be provoked.

Breaking the silence, his deep voice resonated in the room, 'Remember how you had dangled off the roof at Great Windmill Street, peeing in your pants like a little boy? And how I had saved your puny skin? Did you not swear allegiance to me, to be my Rottweiler, to jump when told ... roll over when told, kill whom, when and where, as told?'

'Yes, I do,' Ciarán said.

'And so, you did. Until recently, I've had no complaints. But of late, I've come to regret my decision. A splat on the pavement might have been better. What's going on, my boy? Why this change of heart? Did someone get to you?' Niall asked, his voice rising a few decibels.

Without warning, he reached out and gripped the lethally sharp letter opener lying on his desk. He pointed the shiny tip at Ciarán's neck, ready to plunge the blade into the soft flesh.

Sinead watched the stand-off as Ciarán raged. She turned away, wanting no part in their idiotic muscling. The less she heard and saw the better, if she were to survive the night. As far as she was concerned, the sooner they killed each other, the sooner she would be free.

Staring into the darkness, she focused on the gentle sway of the tall trees in the distance. Ignoring the haunting reflection in the small glass pane of the two men, she nervously waited her turn, for Niall to do his worst. Blocking out their voices, she wracked her brains for a plausible excuse for her earlier actions.

'Why did you attack Paul? Oy, I'm talking to ya!' Niall snapped, having dispatched Ciarán.

'Oh, right ... OK,' Sinead replied confused, absorbed in her own world. 'The truth is, I don't know.'

'Come on, you can do better. Think. You've been warned. But it seems you're too stubborn for your own good. Question is, what to do with you now? Either I send you to the Ranch, or deal with you myself.'

The mention of the infamous brothel made Sinead wince. It was a place few returned from intact, if at all. 'Kill me, I don't care. I've told you, I cannot do this anymore. I've begged you. Please Niall, why can't I go?'

'You know that's not possible.'

'I promise I'll keep my mouth shut. You know me. I just want to live like everybody else. I want my old life back, please.'

'Exactly! I know you only too well, and you are trouble,' he said. 'Last chance. Give me one good reason why I should ignore this incident.'

Sinead knew she had nothing to offer. 'I can tell you what happened. Not that it'll make a difference.'

'I'll be the judge of that, so please hurry. I haven't got all night,' he snarled, infuriated by the wasted hour, time he could have spent with Irina.

'After dinner, back in his suite, he started shoving me around like a piece of meat, demanding what he had paid for.'

'My dear, is that not what you are - meat? And, I may remind you, one for which he has paid handsomely. So, what's the problem?' Niall insisted, unimpressed.

'All I'm saying, he has a really ugly side. Do you have any idea what he's like? He gives me the creeps, a real slimy worm. If I were you, I'd be very wary of doing business with him. I don't think he's to be trusted,' Sinead warned, hopeful to win some favour with Niall.

Her words rang true, confirming Niall's suspicion that there was another reason other than her little fit for Paul to have cancelled their deal.

'Please continue.'

'He had forced me to the bed, shouting and cursing, threatening to rape me. I don't know ... I must have snapped. I remember seeing black and lashing out. Next thing I saw was blood smeared across his face.' Having spoken the words, she realised they meant nothing. After all, Niall was right; to them, she was nothing other than a whore, a piece of meat.

'Do you have any idea what your little tantrum has caused?' Niall scowled. 'Being scarred is his problem, but because of you, he has cancelled our deal.'

'Surely, you can find a way out of—'

'Shut up!' Niall cut her off. 'The other problem I face: what if word gets out? What if your little friends copy you? Sorry, my dear, you leave me no choice. But know this, your sacrifice will spare many others the same fate. Let this be a lesson to ye all. I shall not tolerate any dissent.'

With an expression of death on his face, he wrapped his hands around her slender neck while mulling over the broken deal. Paul was to deliver the shipment of drugs to Crete, receive and assess the diamonds and *wash* the stones in the strictly regulated diamond market.

Niall's dilemma: It was far too late to postpone the operation with the shipment of cocaine due in Ireland within twenty-four hours. And with Paul out of the picture and no one else to trust, he would have to step in, use his private plane and conclude the transaction with Dimitris.

The mere thought grated against his better judgement.

It could be a trap. He was under no illusion about Paul's hunger for power. Anything was to be expected.

Being compromised made Niall's fingers twitch, aching for revenge. Incensed, he ignored Sinead's sorrow-filled gaze as his hands tightened their grip.

'Please Niall, please, no,' she whispered.

He paused. The long-forgotten memory of his dear sister Maura sprang to mind, the night she had killed herself, her look of utter despair. Slowly his forceful grip relaxed, unwittingly replaced by a tender caress. Confused, he brushed Sinead's tangled hair.

Daily, despite his enormous wealth and power, the emptiness and anger consumed him, fuelling his lust for revenge; an emotion which was still as strong as that day which had changed everything when he was only sixteen.

Jolted back to reality, he swore under his breath at this

unexpected attack of pathetic sentimentality. 'Ciarán!' his voice boomed.

As Ciarán charged into the study, Niall said, 'Drop her off at Madiba's. But warn him, I want my merchandise back intact. She still has work to do.'

'My pleasure boss,' Ciarán smirked and marched Sinead out of the study.

'No, no, not him. Please Niall, please. I promise I'll do as you tell me ... I'll behave,' Sinead snivelled.

The pair of eyes peering from the upstairs window did not blink. What Irina saw, infuriated her: three men forcing a beautiful young woman into the waiting car, her head rolling from side to side.

Irina did not turn away, studying the faces of the men. Next, a heavyset man with a crewcut joined them. Her stomach turned seeing the evil face. The curtain slipped from her fingers back into place.

CHAPTER 3

Niall's Estate
Tuesday

The early morning sun's rays filtered through the glass roof of the spacious conservatory. The sweet fragrance of blossoms hung heavy in the air. Irina tried to relax, tried to enjoy the warm ambience, the delightful view of the flowerbeds and rolling lawns. But the dark moods which ebbed and flowed out of Niall like the tidal sea made such a notion impossible. The deep frown creasing his forehead was a clear indication that he was not enjoying his breakfast. He was in a foul mood.

Today nothing was going to be easy ... will it ever? she wondered.

Contemplating her stay, she was mindful of just how long she would be able to remain detached, mind her own business, not speak her mind – something she was quite capable of. Her father had always teased her about this ingrained stubbornness, apparently taking after her mother, strong-willed and independent. These traits had manifested strongly over the years, faced with the usual tribulations life so keenly dealt each and all. As soft-spoken as she was, she never kept quiet or stood back for anyone. Having learned from a young age, she had kept the schoolyard bullies at bay with a few well-aimed punches. But this was a very different game. Niall was not some schoolyard bully.

Niall glared at Anne, the young chef who served his meal.

Her hands trembled noticeably.

Good, just the way I want it. Pathetic snowflake! Due to her continuous display of incompetence, she was restricted to prepare breakfast and light meals only. *It's time she quits. If not, I'll make her.* Niall chewed his food in silence, forced it down and nearly choked. His tanned complexion turned a shade darker, about to vent his anger on the cook.

Irina idly pushed the rubbery egg around her plate and asked, 'How are your friends, the couple who came to see you last Friday?' It was the first time she had broached the subject, even though she was filled with deep concern for the woman driven off into the night.

Niall looked at her, for a moment caught wrong-footed. 'Right, right, Sinead and Ciarán. They're fine. What a palaver over nothing. She was a bit upset over her fiancé's little indiscretion with a barmaid, which is understandable considering their wedding is in two weeks' time. Of course, this had meant nothing to him. He got a bit drunk and wanted to get a leg over – a last fling – before getting the noose round his neck. After a few harsh words on my part, she forgave him. Thanks to my intervention, they're both happy, ready to take their vows,' Niall said, rather like a cat licking the cream.

'What is, "to get leg over"?'

'I'll explain when we're alone.'

'Maybe you do that.'

'Explain, or get a leg over?' Niall asked and laughed.

'Oh, I get it. Funny, very funny.' Her face lit up, playing along.

'Sorry, hope I did not offend you?'

'No, it's fine. I am pleased that your friends are happy now,' she said, having no interest in pursuing the matter any further. *Of course, Mr McGuire, I believe you; Sinead really did look "ecstatic".*

Clever girl, Niall mused.

Again, he was delighted that Irina had found his company's advert on the internet and landed in his lap, so to speak, trusting she would not disappoint him.

Of course, the advert, like hundreds of others, was a sham enticing would-be secretaries, students, translators, nannies and housekeepers longing to escape their miserable lives in Eastern Europe or the Third World. What awaited them was nothing other than Hell. With their passports confiscated on arrival, they were thrown into brothels scattered all over Europe. Forced to earn their keep in the most dreadful way imaginable, they were kept in line with severe beatings, violent threats to their loved ones and a constant diet of drugs.

Irina was just another one plucked from this endless stream of women who made Niall's alternative businesses thrive. Not forgetting the valuable contributions made by those sold to North Africa and the Middle East. What happened to them was none of his concern. They earned him lots of money. After all, they were all grown-ups, old enough to open their legs when they felt like it, vote, and travel on their own. Therefore, if they had bought the wrong ticket, then so be it.

Niall felt no remorse.

For now, Irina had been spared such a fate. But if she disappointed him – off she'll go as well.

From the moment her photo had landed on his desk he had been drawn to her. Beneath the playful frivolity in her eyes there was a hint of sadness, of longing, not unlike himself. The long faint scar hidden in her hairline, he had only noticed the day she had arrived – the result of an accident aged seven when she had crashed through a glass door. He found her companionship enchanting, unlocking a part of him which had been suppressed for most of his life.

Once more, he studied Irina's Nordic-Slavic features, the shiny auburn hair, her slender arms and delicate hands with perfectly manicured nails. No sign of biting or ripping of cuticles, habits he found extremely distasteful and irritating. Thank God, he thought – not that he cared much for either God or beast – for women like her!

He wanted her. But notwithstanding his best attempts, she was playing it cool, very cool indeed. She was not like most girls who would simply bend over and dance to his every tune.

Boys-o-boys, he heaved, frustrated.

'Niall, when will I get my own place?' Irina asked, interrupting his flight of fancy. 'I'm very happy with what you do for me. But am I not in your way?'

'Not at all,' he replied reassuringly. 'Anyway, what's the rush? Don't you like it here?'

'Yes, I do. *Spasibo*. And when do I start work?'

'Don't worry, your flat will be ready in a few days. It's all arranged. Once you've settled, you can move in,' he lied, having made no such plans. 'The place is perfect, overlooking the sea, near the shops and the office in Blackrock. I don't think you'll be disappointed. Although you are welcome to stay here as long as you want. There really is no hurry.'

'I must start work or my money will finish soon,' she said warily, not wanting to sound too keen to leave.

'Fair enough, I understand. In the meantime, how about joining me on a short trip to Greece? A bit of business, a bit of pleasure. Time permitting, I may introduce you to some of my colleagues, people you'll be dealing with in the future.'

Up to an hour ago, he had still been in two minds whether to take her along as there was a real chance they could end up in trouble with the authorities – his gut warned him. When the idea had surfaced that her company could serve as cover – a couple on holiday in case they ran into the police – his mind had been made up.

'Are you sure? Maybe I must stay and work,' she said.

'Nonsense,' Niall laughed. 'You come with us. It will be fun, I promise.'

'*Spasibo*. How long we stay?'

'Pack for three days. We'll leave around six and should have you safely back by Thursday evening, latest. Don't forget your bathing costume. You do have one?'

'No, I do not. I am a bit scared. We do not have many seas in Russia, only Black Sea. Only lucky ones go there. Very expensive,' she explained.

Regardless of her little display of reluctance, she was looking forward to escaping the old house for a short while, for a change of scenery and to get to know him better.

Fresh from rural Russia, she found the mansion with its priceless pieces of art and antiquities stifling. Her stay was to be temporary – apparently, there had been a delay with her accommodation – but, he had assured her she was more than welcome as his guest.

This arrangement suited Irina perfectly. It had saved her a great deal of time.

CHAPTER 4

Blackrock, Dublin

'Bitch, wake up!' Ciarán shouted. The noise thundered in Sinead's ears. She stirred, tried to focus. His smug face stared mockingly at her, fascinated by her injuries.

She could smell his stale breath, his cheap cologne. Incensed, she wanted to tear at his face. But all she could do was muster a feeble, 'What do you want?'

It had been nearly four days since Madiba and his four friends had raped and assaulted her. She looked dreadful – one eye nearly swollen shut, the whip's red welts crisscrossing her face with the skin of her slender neck severely discoloured, bruised by strangulation. Her wrists and ankles raw where she had struggled to break free, chafed by the manacles which had held her spread-eagled in the middle of the room for most of her six-hour ordeal.

'Get out and leave me alone,' she whispered.

'Yeah, right,' Ciarán replied. His open hand shot out and slapped her across the face.

'My God, what are you doing, are you mad!' Vera screamed as she tried to grab hold of his arm.

With the greatest of ease, Ciarán shoved her aside and pulled out a silenced pistol. Pointing the menacing weapon at Vera's head, he threatened, 'Come on, go for it!'

'Don't you push me!' Vera shouted, unable to do anything more.

Sinead ignored Ciarán, and said, 'If you think you'll stop me, then you're wrong. I shall never do this again! I shall never allow any of you to touch me … ever. Just get the hell away from me. Get out … **GET OUT!**'

'Shut up and listen. I haven't got all day,' Ciarán growled as he pushed the barrel of the gun against Sinead's temple. 'The only time you'll quit is when Niall lets you. And that, my dear, will only be when you turn into an old frump.'

'What are you waiting for? Kill me if it'll make you feel better. Come on!' Sinead tested him, shaking with anger, willing him to end her life.

'Please, *moi kotenok*, don't,' Vera said, trying to calm her friend, not wanting to antagonise the maniac. 'Forget the *svinia*.'

'That's better,' Ciarán said, unaware that Vera had called him a pig. He eased the pressure of the pistol. 'It's quite simple. Niall never wants any trouble from you again, ever. And neither do I. I'm sure even you with your pea brain can understand that? And if not, you'll be on your way to South Africa. Your new lover, Madiba, said he'll welcome your contribution in his whorehouse. Maybe I should enlighten you on what goes on in sunny South Africa – the lawless world of the machete – not the one in the fancy brochures. A country where women, children, and babies are beaten and raped at will. And women burned with hot irons, boiled water poured down their throats and then slaughtered like cattle. And for *muti* – witchdoctor's medicine in case you don't know – decapitate and castrate little boys. Imagine a life working in his *fancy* establishment in Soweto. His buddies would most probably love to give ya another workover. Whaddya say, you up for it?' Ciarán paused, catching his breath.

About to continue his diatribe, Sinead asked, 'Have you quite finished?' Not waiting for a reply, she said, 'Then let **me** tell **you**, do not for one moment think you scare me. How many times must I repeat myself: I shall never work for you

22

again. Quit wasting time, send me right now. Send me, go on, send me, please I beg you!'

Ciarán raised the barrel and aimed at Sinead's head.

Defiantly, she looked at him, ignored the black cylinder and shouted, 'Shoot, just **SHOOT!**'

He hesitated.

Slowly, he lowered the weapon.

'Sinead, you don't seem to get it; this is no joke. I warn you, you'll do as we tell you. And you'll never disappoint me or him again.' He shrugged his shoulders, turned and left.

'Who do they think they are? I'd rather die than give into them. Vera, we have to get away as we've always wanted.' To escape had been a dream they had cherished since moving into the luxury penthouse in Blackrock south of Dublin.

'We shall, *moi kotenok*, we shall. Now you must rest and I must pack. He's waiting. I'll be back in a few days and we'll find a way, I promise.'

With Vera's encouraging words, she closed her eyes and prayed for a miracle.

CHAPTER 5

Night Sky
Crete

Irina reclined in comfort in one of the sixteen seats of Niall's Embraer Lineage 1000E jet, flitting through the night sky. Below the flickering lights of Chania hugging the Crete coastline winked invitingly. The small yachts dotted on the still waters of the old harbour lay motionless. The tavernas strung along the quayside were all quiet after a night of frenzied activity – forgotten were the hordes who had feasted on local delicacies, dancing until the early hours to the rhythms of Greek bouzoukis.

In the distance, a solid grey wall reached up into the dark sky, protectively guarding the slumbering villages scattered amongst olive and fruit groves at its feet. As the eerie gloom of the White Mountain raced towards them, the plane plummeted steeply and levelled out. Skimming the dark surface of the Chanion Gulf, the pilot made his final approach and touched down with a soft bump.

The secluded private airfield located thirty kilometres west of Chania ended more than five hours of travel including a stop en route in County Wexford where four passengers had boarded. Their large amount of luggage had filled the bedroom cabin. Although curious, Irina had known better than to ask awkward questions. She would wait – see what unfolds. The few days on the Greek island promised to be interesting.

Preoccupied, she did not sleep for most of the flight. The customised interior of full grain leather and walnut panelling, exhibiting all the latest creature comforts imaginable, had done nothing to seduce her to sleep. And her attempts at making light conversation with the only other female passenger, Vera, a compatriot, had been coolly brushed aside. Why, she could not understand.

Who was she? What was she to Niall? Competition?

Neither did she have much success in engaging Niall's attention. He had remained cooped up in the cockpit for most of the time.

As the plane finally rolled to a stop, Irina reset her watch to the local time, 4:10 a.m. With the first hint of daylight on the horizon, she hoped nothing was planned for the morning; she craved a soft, comfortable bed. Her childhood dream of one day dipping her toes in the warm Mediterranean could wait.

Once more, she peered out of the small window. Except for the two figures emerging from the cluster of buildings cloaked in semi-darkness, the place was deserted. Behind them, a private jet and helicopter sat idle inside a dim-lit hangar.

She saw nothing of interest. Patiently she waited her turn to disembark.

Irina was not the only one studying the small airport.

From inside the cockpit, Niall scanned the area, looking for danger signs. After a few minutes, he mumbled, 'Well, let's get this over with. Karl, keep the engines running.'

Next to him, the pilot nodded dolefully, going through the motions of checking the instruments in case a quick departure was required.

'You know the drill. If you spot any funny business, you smell a rat, you see that Greek as much as sneeze in our direction, you get us out of here.'

Niall was on edge; where the hell was Dimitris?

Despite his efforts en route, he had failed to reach him.

Nevertheless, he had to assume everything was still on track as arranged. Any notion of returning to Ireland with the contraband or dumping the valuable load in the ocean for some fisherman to enjoy, was out of the question. He was determined to get this deal done and be on his way to Ireland as soon as he had his diamonds.

Having brought Vera along – his only reliable agent operating in Crete – he hoped introductions would go smoothly. He did not know any of Dimitris' men, or who to trust. She did.

Niall felt the comforting weight of the .38 revolver in the palm of his hand and spun the fully loaded chamber. Satisfied, he pocketed the weapon, stood up and made his way through the cabin.

Pausing next to Irina, he smiled and greeted her cheerfully, 'Good morning. Hope you managed to get some sleep?'

'I did, thank you.'

'Good. Just sit tight for a minute longer while I go and meet our host.'

'Fine by me, I'm not going anywhere ... take your time,' she replied, relaxed.

'Good, good. Back in a sec.'

Turning to Vera, his smile vanished as he ordered, 'Let's go!'

Approaching the two figures on the runway, a deep voice boomed, '*Yassou,* daughter of Aphrodite whose beauty surpasses that of the goddess herself!'

'*Yassou,* Stavros. Be careful what you say. The goddess may strike you down or make me spin a web for all eternity,' Vera replied good-humouredly.

Before she knew what had happened, the Greek had closed the gap and lifted her into the air. 'I hope you're here to make me the happiest man alive!'

Stavros was a big man; one she knew only too well. He was a rogue whose sense of fair play was measured equally by his tendency for violence – a docile lion with the instinct to kill engrained in his soul. Despite her hatred of what Stavros represented, she planted a loud kiss on both his cheeks and said, 'Sorry, maybe next time.'

Lowering her to the ground, he replied laughingly, 'Shame on you.' Shifting his attention to Niall, his mood turned sombre; the little flirtation with Vera was forgotten. 'Where's Paul?' he asked.

'In hospital. He had a heart attack ... last night,' Vera said.

'Uh-hum,' Stavros huffed, rubbing his chin sceptically.

'Stavros, this is Rob,' Vera said, using the alias as instructed. Niall did not want exposure, although she could not care less what the consequences would be if people discovered his identity. All she wanted was to get this over with as quickly as possible and return to Ireland, to her friend.

Stavros seemed wary. '*Nai, nai* ... I understand, my dear, but I think we might have a problem. You see, I don't like surprises, especially when people disappear without warning. Very fishy. And can I trust you, mister Rob? Not so sure ... For all I know you could be a pig,' he said as his hand disappeared inside the folds of his jacket, his eyes not wavering from Niall's.

'Trust me, he's one of us; I've known him long enough. And he's most definitely not a cop, I guarantee,' Vera said, struggling to keep a straight face, finding Stavros' concerns hilarious.

'I hope you're right. My boss will have to decide when he's back. Now, please hurry. We've wasted enough time in the open. Tell the pilot to taxi inside the hangar,' Stavros ordered. 'There are too many nosy shepherds in these mountains.'

'Where's your boss?' Niall asked.

'Mr Spandidakis is in South Africa.'

'You're joking,' Niall snapped. Incensed, he turned towards the plane, wanting to leave – waiting on foreign soil with a planeload of drugs would be a huge mistake.

Vera tugged at his sleeve and flashed him a warning. Her gaze slowly shifted past him towards the open hangar door. Niall's eyes followed hers. At first, he did not spot anything odd. But then, there it was, a slight movement inside the stationed helicopter – a sniper adjusting his aim.

Niall paused and cleared his throat. 'Right mister, to sum up: you want us to have a nice time sunning ourselves while our plane, loaded with drugs, sits in this godforsaken outhouse with no guarantee it will remain here. Or worse, that we won't find ourselves behind a steel door surrounded by four white walls. Really, is that what you suggest? Well, you can scrap that idea!'

'Yes, my friend, that's exactly what I mean. You'll do as I say. End of discussion,' he scowled and shoved his face under Niall's nose.

Niall's arm shot out and grabbed Stavros by the throat.

The next instant a bullet whizzed past Niall's head, the silenced cough of the sniper's rifle muffled inside the helicopter.

'Let go or none of you'll leave here – that was a warning. Be careful my *friend*, be very careful,' Stavros cautioned.

Realising they were outnumbered and outgunned, Vera wedged herself between the two big men and said, 'Please stop this! Fighting won't solve anything. Rob, let's just do as he says.'

Glaring at each other, Stavros was first to speak, 'Look, she's right. This will get us nowhere. I suggest you show some trust. You're welcome to leave as many of your men here as you wish; it's up to you.'

Slowly, Niall released his grip and lowered his arm. 'When will Mr Spandidakis be back?'

'Friday morning.'

'Fine, so be it. I'm sure my boss will agree. Now excuse me, I have to brief the others.'

'*Parakalo* (you're welcome) ... and relax, you'll have two days to enjoy our scenic island,' Stavros said, his face hard as stone.

Pretending ignorance, Irina descended the few steps on to the concrete hardstand. The early morning warm air took her by surprise; it was like walking into an oven – a welcome relief after the cool Irish weather. On the horizon, the sun's first rays drew a veil of warm colours across the vast blackness.

In silence, she followed Niall into the waiting 4x4. Leaving the small airfield, she asked him, 'Is there a problem?'

'Not really, just a slight change of plan. My business has been delayed until Friday.'

'Oh, I see.'

'We'll make the most of it. You won't be bored, I promise,' Niall said, his mood lifting despite his concerns. In the confined interior of the vehicle, his 1.88 metre, 110 kg bulk pushed up against Irina with every muscle tight like a high-strung horse ready to bolt the gates.

'I would love to see a bit of the island if possible. Do you know any places we can visit?' she asked, trying to distract him.

Racing towards Chania, they zigzagged their way out of the deep valley. Reaching the coast, they veered westerly towards the luxurious Alexandria Village Hotel.

At the reception, the mood of the small party was not that of usual holidaymakers – people glad to be away from work, looking forward to a well-deserved rest. Instead, they stood in silence while Stavros completed their registration under aliases. No documents were required to verify any of the guests' names.

With formalities out of the way, Niall led them to their suites, traipsing over the stone-cobbled path.

The layout of the hotel had been meticulously planned, imitating a traditional Greek village with a mixture of single, double and three-storey stone buildings linked by narrow alleyways and small vine-covered courtyards. Passing underneath yet another archway, they arrived at the more secluded luxury two- and three-bedroom suites which lined the beachfront. Sheltered by two-metre-high natural stone parti-walls, total privacy was guaranteed to the intimate courtyard with its swimming pool and private spa. An unobstructed sea view had been achieved by elevating the suites nearly two metres above the adjacent sandy beach.

Entering her room, which she shared with Vera, Irina gazed out at the still waters. It looked irresistible. A quick nap and then she would most definitely fulfill her dream and jump into the Mediterranean. Maybe Vera would join her, and if not, so be it.

Unpacking her few items, Irina gave Vera a disarming smile, still puzzled why she refused to talk to her. After all, they were both Russians and by circumstance had been flung into the same room thousands of kilometres away from home. Strange?

'Hi, I'm Irina, nice to meet you,' she said, hoping for a positive response.

'And I'm Vera,' came the curt reply as she looked nervously around while hanging some clothes inside the wardrobe. Nodding in the direction of the open door, she mouthed, 'Not now.'

'OK, got it,' Irina said, beginning to understand why Vera had ignored her up to now – Niall's doing. She would wait.

Despite his anxieties, Niall was pleased with the unexpected opportunity offered for a possible romantic interlude. It may just be what was needed to sway Irina. Although for the moment any romance would have to wait; an urgent call had to be made. Trusting no one – the room was most probably bugged – he traipsed outside.

A few minutes later Niall sat alert, upright, in an overstuffed leather couch in the hotel's main lounge, empty at such an early hour. He fidgeted with the buttons of the hotel's sleek phone, being far too small for his large fingers. Finally, he managed to dial the correct number.

'As expected, we've run into a problem,' he said as he glanced up at the wall-mounted clock above the reception desk. It was 6:15 a.m. The fact that his employee had most probably been asleep did not bother him in the least.

'Please continue,' the calm voice replied – Michael, the

recently appointed head of Niall's security.

'It's green for go,' Niall said. Thoroughly briefed for such an eventuality prior to departure, there was no need for further explanations. Michael and his men knew what to do.

'Anything else?' Michael asked.

'We're staying at the Alexandria Village Hotel, west of Chania. I'll fill you in when you get here. And hurry, things may spiral out of control,' Niall said and ended the call.

Well, that should even the odds …

Within the hour, Michael's team of eight ex-mercenaries would board a company jet and head for Heraklion International Airport, Crete.

CHAPTER 6

Johannesburg, South Africa
Wednesday

Dimitris roared and banged his fist with fury on the car's dashboard. 'Enough! Are you going to be there or not?' he shouted into the phone.

'Of course,' came the indifferent reply.

'If you know what's good for you, you'll quit stalling, playing stupid games! You better not disappoint me again, mister Cohen.'

Dimitris was at the end of his tether trying to conclude the purchase of diamonds with the shady dealer – five times he had tried to meet with him but had failed. Known to be sneaky bastards, he had expected as much. But this was becoming childish. If the man had a problem then why not just say so?

Preoccupied with Mr Cohen and events in Crete, he had the least bit of interest in Johannesburg's rundown buildings which surrounded him. Many of the once shining high-rise office buildings, hotels and apartment blocks were ramshackle and burned out. Windowless openings gaped forlornly at debris piled high on broken pavements far below. Nevertheless, a glimmer of hope shone on this chaotic city, with some evidence of newly refurbished buildings popping up – reclaimed, hijacked structures with stringent security measures now in place.

The news Stavros shared was not good.

What really happened to Paul? Are we being set up? And who is this Rob character?

And now this cat-and-mouse game with Mr Cohen! Was this Paul's doing, warning him not to get involved with trouble brewing in Crete? Waving a red flag was the surest way to chase this vermin into the sewer he had crawled from.

I'll get to the bottom of this … find out who's responsible, Dimitris vowed to himself.

But for now, he would just have to dance to the man's tune – the last consignment of diamonds was vital. Deals with Niall were not to be broken.

So far it had been plain sailing with all previous shipments smuggled along the usual route – pilots in service of big national airlines rewarded handsomely for each package delivered in Greece. And then inexplicably this batch had been cancelled, forcing Dimitris on an unscheduled trip to the southern tip of Africa.

The problem he faced: time was running out fast; he had orders to meet and a rendezvous to keep.

With utter disgust, Dimitris looked at the makeshift shacks, the hordes of loiterers, and pockmarked streets. 'Hard to believe that not too long ago this used to be a nice place. And look at it now … real shame. Well, thank God, noon tomorrow and we'll be out of here.'

The three Greek bodyguards, squashed into the back of the chauffeur-driven car, nodded their heads in unison.

All of a sudden, the car swerved violently, flinging Dimitris against the door. With a dull thud, his head banged against the bulletproof window.

'Watch out you stupid tjotsis!' the driver shouted, barely missing the four hooligans racing across the road in hot pursuit, guns firing.

'Damn it, man!' Dimitris scowled, rubbing his head, relieved it was only a hard bump and not a bullet.

'Sorry sir,' the driver apologised, staring straight ahead at the two men fleeing around the corner.

None of the people crouched behind the piled-up rubbish on the pavements interfered. Terrified, the whites of their eyes were exaggerated by their dark skins.

'Welcome to Hillbrow,' the driver said. 'If you stay long enough, you'll get used to it.'

'No, my friend. Not my idea of fun, thank you,' Dimitris replied.

CHAPTER 7

Chania, Crete

Irina was last to join Niall on the patio for brunch, the table decked with platters of tasty cheese-filled pastries, smoked meats, sweet melon, figs and grapes. Sheltered in the shade of an oak tree, the warm morning breeze, fragranced by sweet honeyed-blossoms and ripe summer fruits, languidly massaged their bare arms and legs.

'I'm going for a swim. Anyone care to join me?' Irina announced, having purchased a bathing costume at the hotel's boutique.

Vera, who spotted Niall fretting, did not hesitate, anything to spoil his day. '*Da*, count me in!' she volunteered.

Not wanting to take unnecessary risks, Niall said, 'Why bother? We have everything we need right here. A private pool, a spa and room service. And this is much safer than the sea, not so Irina?'

'Yes, you're right. But don't worry, I'll be careful. I can swim in a pool anywhere, but not the sea,' Irina replied adamantly. 'Vera, you ready? Let's go.'

'Right, you win,' Niall conceded. There was not much he could do until Michael made his appearance. For now, he would play the holidaymaker and keep an eye on the girls. Fortunately, everything seemed quiet at the small airfield with no unwanted visitors nosing around. But one could never be too careful.

Sunbathing on a sandy beach was a pleasant distraction, notwithstanding his nagging unease. To his own surprise, he was having fun. He could not remember the last time he did.

Looking up for the umpteenth time – his eyes never strayed far from Irina – she emerged from the clear water. As if in a dream, fresh droplets of water rolled down between her supple breasts. Without pause, she floated across the warm sand like a weightless feather carried along by a gentle breeze. Enthralled by the sensual movement of her hips, her lithe legs, her bosom, he remained oblivious to the mischievous flames which danced playfully in her eyes. Spellbound, he gazed at the wet costume which clung revealingly to her porcelain skin.

His self-control floundered …

His nostrils flared …

His pulse raced …

His throat tightened as his desires coursed through his veins …

'Enjoying yourself, Niall?' Vera asked, ending his lusting.

Next, she turned on Irina and said in Russian, 'Be very careful what you wish for!'

But the warning had no effect on Irina who continued her seductive stride.

'What did you say to her?' Niall asked, annoyed. 'And no Russian in my presence.'

'Sorry, old habit. I told her we better get out of the sun before we end up looking like boiled lobsters.'

'Right, of course, you did.'

Ignoring him, Vera said, 'Irina, I suggest we go for a walk in the old town. It really is worth a visit. There's the ancient Venetian harbour, OR the popular Municipal Market, OR we can enjoy a light meal of freshly caught fish and some local wines, OR—'

'Cut it out!' Niall snapped, his temper fraying fast.

The fact was, Irina's advances disturbed Vera immensely;

the girl had no idea who she was dealing with. With the image of Sinead's battered body fresh in her mind, she would not permit Irina to suffer the same fate. She needed protection from this vile man. Filled with concern, Vera watched as Irina wrapped herself inside a large beach towel, and with her gaze holding Niall's, threw her head back, letting her long, silky, auburn hair tumble free below her shoulders.

But the instant Niall looked away, Irina's pupils sharpened, hostile, cold.

Vera did not miss this sudden flash of anger in Irina's eyes, leaving her confused. *What?!*

'Okay, Vera, maybe you're right. Too much sun is no good. Let's go and see what the old town has to offer,' Niall said, his voice hollow.

'Yes, Mr McGuire, good decision,' Vera replied, knowing the last thing on his mind was to waltz around some boring tourist attractions. For now, she had managed to stop their flirtations. But for how long, she had no idea. It was imperative to speak to Irina, alone. She must be warned.

CHAPTER 8

Heraklion Airport
Crete

Heraklion Airport terminal was packed. Tourists arrived from all over, eager to exploit the milder early summer weather and nibble on the Greek culture of lazy days and long drinks at sunset. Amongst this fortunate group was Michael and his men. Having arrived on schedule, they jostled their way through customs.

Inside the main hall, three men followed the signs towards Car Rentals – three 4x4's were required for the planned operation. The rest of the men converged upon the pickup zone in front of the terminal building.

Michael checked his watch as the first off-road vehicle pulled up; thirty-five minutes had elapsed since clearing customs.

Not bad, he thought. Jumping into the front seat, they sped off in the direction of Chania. Adhering to the frustratingly low-speed limit of hundred kilometres per hour, they arrived in the old town a few minutes past one o'clock.

Five minutes later the second 4x4 appeared in the sprawling town and then the next. Edging through the traffic, men were dropped off at various locations – each to make his own way to the designated rendezvous point at the Old Municipal Market.

Two men continued to Dimitris' private airport – the weapons concealed in Niall's plane had to be collected.

By 14h10 the remaining men were all in position awaiting further instructions.

Michael liked punctuality and order, aware that one missed beat could jeopardise any carefully planned operation within seconds. And the truth was, theirs was anything but a carefully planned operation. It was nothing other than a ripped hiking boot held together by some worn sock thread. No, they would have to rely on their extensive experience to see them through this.

Being in a hurry he pushed these concerns aside; Niall was waiting.

CHAPTER 9

Old Harbour
Chania

Aided by a few glasses of chilled white wine, the earlier tensions amongst the three diners had evaporated in the midday heat. By now an air of lazy calm hung in the shade of the large canvas awning.

Vera resigned herself to being there, as the last place on earth she wanted to be was in Niall's company.

The quayside was quiet except for a few boats bobbing up and down on the ripples of a passing yacht. Slap … slap … the water splashed gently against the old stone quay. Above, the squawk of a seagull pierced the stillness. Surrounded by an array of intricate buildings – quaint red-tiled roofs, balconies and tall French doors framed by colourful shutters – Irina relished the lingering flavour of the delightful light lunch. The freshly caught sole had been barbequed slightly crisp and sparsely basted with lemon butter, complemented with a hint of Mediterranean herbs.

The sudden ringing noise stopped Niall's lethargic daydreaming. He took one look at his phone, stood up and excused himself.

At the small reception desk of Nikos Taverna, Niall held the greasy phone a few inches from his ear. After only two rings Michael answered with a simple, 'Hello.'

'Glad you've made it. Trust everything went according to plan,' Niall greeted.

'Affirmative. We're in position.'

'Good. We'll rendezvous in thirty minutes as agreed.'

'Roger that and out,' Michael replied.

Returning to his seat, Niall ordered some sweet Greek coffee; the injection of caffeine was badly needed to counter the effect of the wine and soothing heat.

Sipping the sweet warm liquid, he wondered what Irina's reaction would be if she knew the real reason for their visit to Crete.

By 15h15 the three companions found themselves yet again seated in some eatery – this time outside Arias' small coffee shop opposite the Old Municipal Market's north entrance.

Niall turned and gawked at some young girls – their naked bellies and long legs were hard to ignore. Accidentally, he knocked the adjoining table over, catching the shell-shaped ashtray just before it hit the floor. For a second, he examined the cheap ceramic object and mumbled an apology to the patron before replacing it with great care.

During this little charade, he had never lost sight of activities in the street – expecting one of his men to appear at any moment somewhere in the crowd.

A lonely tourist, his face shaded by a wide-brimmed sun hat, camera slung over one shoulder and map in hand sat down at the adjacent table. Studying the drinks menu, he mumbled a few incomprehensible words which Irina could only interpret as open disgust at the outrageous prices.

He got up in a huff and sauntered off.

Neither Niall nor Vera showed any interest in the stranger. But Irina noticed the small folded piece of paper, craftily placed underneath the ashtray by Niall, missing. Amused by the secrecy, she kept this observation to herself.

Ordering soft drinks, Niall glanced at Declan, who turned the far corner, convinced no one had noticed the pickup, not even the Greeks if they were watching. His men's arrival on the island had to remain a secret.

The note Declan had lifted contained detailed instructions on what was required; the success of the operation was now in their hands with the advantage of surprise on their side.

Nevertheless, Niall fretted, hating the prospect of having to stroll through the imposing Old Municipal Market – an alternative form of entertainment would have been preferable.

Michael crumpled the piece of paper and shoved it into his pocket. Time was not on their side. He looked at the eager young faces surrounding him, wondering whose death he would have to report to a wife or parent this time tomorrow.

Without the benefit of real reconnaissance, they would have to raid the airport blind – a target which was guarded by God knows how many men – retrieve the planeload of drugs and secure the contraband in a safe house – still to be found – on the island. And all by daybreak tomorrow!

Undeterred, Michael set the plan in motion.

By 21h00 a set of car keys and an untraceable mobile phone were dropped off at Niall's suite.

Fifteen minutes later, Niall answered his newly acquired phone and attentively listened to Michael's brief. 'I will call latest 06h00 to confirm the all clear. Failing that, retreat to location "B". For this purpose, a car is parked approximately half a kilometre to your left on exiting the hotel.' No further details were shared.

Niall did not need, nor want, to know more in case he might compromise his men if he were to be interrogated. If all were to go south, he and his party were to escape in the parked jet at Heraklion International Airport – Location "B".

As promised, Niall received the all clear at six in the morning. With the element of surprise on their side, the operation had been a success. There had been no casualties except for a few bruised egos amongst Dimitris' men. Having disarmed and immobilised the guards at the airport, the consignment had been transferred to a safe house.

What consequences the clandestine operation would have on relations with the Greek was the least of Niall's concerns, although an immediate reprisal could not be ruled out. Therefore, to counter any such an offensive, six of Michael's men were dispatched to the hotel, increasing security substantially.

Niall discarded his clothes and lay down on his bed. He waited for sleep, but preoccupied with Irina, he could not.

Was he reading too much into her flirtations? Was she just humouring him? It was most frustrating being led on at every opportunity, only to be offered a cold shoulder for his troubles. He had heard many stories of Eastern European girls playing this little cat-and-mouse game with Westerners, especially men like him who were knocking on their fifties and more, a category of losers he never thought he would fall under. And yesterday had been no exception, teasing him at the beach, at the market, at dinner, and at eleven o'clock excusing herself and going to bed on her own.

With her an enormous amount of patience was required; a word which did not exist in his vocabulary, especially where women were concerned. Also, he was far too old for such infantile behaviour.

CHAPTER 10

Chania, Crete
Thursday

His strong athletic arms dipped rhythmically into the water, pulling back, five strokes, a fluid tumble-turn followed by a powerful kick-off, propelling him forward at speed. Niall hated the minute pool, regretting not having opted for a swim in the open sea where he could have struck out with purpose. Nevertheless, the refreshingly cool water had the desired effect in clearing the cobwebs, the result of a nearly sleepless night.

Breaking the surface for yet another turn, he heard someone call out, 'You want some juice?'

Vera, offering him a drink!? Surprised, he gulped down a mouthful of water. 'Thanks,' he spluttered as he climbed out of the pool and draped a large beach towel over his broad shoulders – his tall muscular frame lean and fit. At forty-nine, he still looked good.

He took the drink and studied the glass in his hand, wondering whether a pinch of some lethal substance had been added.

Reading his mind, Vera said, with some degree of regret in her voice, 'Now why didn't I think of that!'

'I believe you would, wouldn't you? Careful what you say, *my dear*,' Niall warned.

The drink was never meant for him, but for Irina, thinking it was her in the pool. Vera had hoped they could slip away for

44

a private chat before Niall would be up. But he had beaten her to it. Ignoring his threat, she drank her juice in silence and stared into the distance.

Good. At least by now she knows when to stop, he thought.

Her subjugation had not come easily, one beaten into her over the years. On the surface, she might look like she had simmered down, but he knew she hated him with a vengeance, unable to forgive him for what he had done, and was still doing to her.

Can't really blame her, can I now, he smiled to himself.

As the silence lingered, Vera recalled how they had met at the strip club, La Chérie, in Brussels. As an exotic dancer, forced to socialise with customers between routines, their first brief encounters were harmless. He had chatted openly, enquiring about her life, her past, her family, and her dreams. Soon an invitation to dinner was made.

At only twenty-one years of age, she was already extremely wary of men, refusing to socialise with customers after hours. Their boasting of successful careers with enough money to pamper her for the rest of her life, no matter how tempting, had been shunned as nothing more than false bravado. The promises of heavenly bliss were endless. Sweet talk, telling her to forget the club as she deserved far more – "with your looks, the world will be your oyster", etc., etc. Having heard and seen it all, she did not believe a word said by any. Neither did an evening go by without a marriage proposal made by some fool. These were kindly brushed off. The stories told of the many Eastern European girls trapped by such charlatans were seared into her brain – once lured into marriage, most were sold to brothels.

Although this time, charmed by his looks, open-face, and warm smile – having misinterpreted the sanguine look in his dark eyes as doleful – she had capitulated and allowed him into her life.

Niall.

Later that evening he had tried his best to persuade her to come to Ireland, to end this awful life she suffered. What she had found even more confusing was the lack of sexual advances. Except for a fleeting stroke of her hand during dinner, he had expressed no such desires. It had seemed all he wanted was companionship, a friend.

On the fourth night she had finally accepted his offer. He had been delighted, promising to obtain her an immediate release from her contract at the club. He further promised her she would be trained as a PRO in his company. She would be free to do as she pleased and would never have to return to this seedy world. "Believe me, there are no strings attached, I swear," he had said. "I really like you very much and I hope in time you'll learn to feel the same about me."

Putting his money where his mouth was, he had given her a beautiful diamond necklace. Vera could not believe what was happening. It was like a fairy tale come true: a new life, a new beginning.

The next day, she had met Niall as arranged, albeit with some apprehension; uncertainty had crept in during the long lonely hours of the night.

Sadly, her dream had been a very short-lived affair.

Never would she forget the day she had discovered his promise of a better life in Ireland was nothing but a hoax. She was to be his personal plaything. And when he had tired of her, she had been forced to work as an escort. With the passing of time, she became a mule, a smuggler. Now thankfully, entertaining men was limited to the odd *special* client.

Her castle of dreams had crumbled into dust, blown away by the brutal winds of reality.

'Is Irina still asleep?' Niall asked, interrupting her thoughts.

'No. I haven't seen her this morning,' she replied curtly.

'What do you mean?'

'She wasn't in her bed when I woke up.'

'Do you think she might have gone for a swim or a walk?'

'How would I know? I'm not her babysitter,' Vera retorted bluntly.

The thought that Stavros, despite the additional security

since the midnight raid, might somehow have managed to abduct her, spurred Niall into action. He slammed his glass on the table, donned the white beach gown, and ran down the steps on to the nearly empty beach. Passing by the two men posted at the bottom of the stairs, he ordered, 'Come, Irina's missing!'

On the double, they crisscrossed the area in front of the hotel. She was nowhere to be found. Accompanied by four more men they swept the hotel reception, lounge, pool area, restaurant and gardens. But with no success.

Hoping she might have returned to their suite Niall rushed back to the patio and asked, 'Any sign of her?'

'No,' Vera replied.

Entering Irina's bedroom, he noticed the patio's lock had not been tampered with, nor was there any sign of a struggle inside. Looking for some clue which could explain her disappearance, he rummaged through her belongings. The only obvious item missing was her bathing costume.

Once more outside, he asked Vera, 'What time did you wake up?'

'I guess an hour ago. Why?'

'It looks like she might have gone for a swim. But she's not on the beach. Which means she has either gone for a very long walk with barely anything on or has been in the water for … no, it's far too long. Nobody swims an hour unless they're a marathon swimmer, which she's not,' Niall stated as matter of fact. 'I won't be surprised if Stavros abducted her, wishing to trade.'

His mind was made up. Enough time had been wasted. Action was required and fast.

Phoning Michael, he ordered an immediate search and rescue operation. He should know what to do.

Ending the call, he turned on the row of blank faces staring at him. 'What the hell am I paying you for, you bunch of fuckin' cretins! Can any of you explain how she could have given you the slip; which for your sakes I hope it was? Or worse, how some slimeball could have sneaked in here and kidnapped her from under your noses! How is that possible?'

No one offered an explanation.

'Declan, you're in charge, therefore I hold you responsible. Pray nothing has happened to her. You better find her and quick. Is that clear?' he bellowed, furious. 'Now get them out of my sight and don't return without her.'

Next, he turned on Vera. 'What are you standing around for? Phone your friend Stavros and tell him I want her back, immediately.'

Furious, Niall disappeared down the steps on to the beach once more. Fifteen minutes later he returned to the patio and sat down, frustrated. 'I'll kill that Stavros if he as much as touched her! And where the hell is Michael?' he asked Vera.

The last thing Niall wanted was a gang war, but if forced to, he would not hesitate. This was unfamiliar territory for him; never in the past did he care for anyone who went missing. So why her? Why was she special … different? But deep down he knew the answer; he was infatuated.

Vera spoke quietly, suggesting an alternative explanation, 'Niall, maybe she did go for a swim … and something terrible has happened. She could have—'

'Good morning,' Irina's cheerful voice chirped.

Vera and Niall looked up at Irina who looked relaxed and radiant after a punishing swim.

'What happened? Did someone die?' Irina asked, sensing the tension in the air.

'Where the hell have you been?' Niall scowled.

'Why?' Irina snapped. 'I did not know I need your permission to go for a swim.'

'I'm sorry, that was uncalled for,' Niall offered. 'Of course you're free to do as you please. I was merely worried about your well-being. You may not be aware of the many girls who go missing on these islands, never to be heard of again.'

Vera nearly exploded in anger, wanting to scratch his eyes out. *You of all people, an expert in making girls disappear!*

'Thank you for the warning but you do not have to worry about me,' Irina replied glumly, keeping her thoughts to herself. The two-kilometre swim to the adjacent resort had been completed in under twenty-five minutes. An hour or so was spent relaxing, enjoying a soft drink while making the call to Russia. Reporting her findings since her arrival in Ireland, she was listened to attentively, and the response was positive. 'Sounds good so far. You should receive the make-up kit by courier, next Monday. It's all arranged as planned. But be careful; we can't afford to lose you. Goodbye.' The warning had been superfluous. She had no intention of being compromised.

For now, Irina had as much as she could stand of the doom-and-gloom face gawking at her. 'Niall, I promise I'll be a good girl.' Lazily, she dabbed the towel against her skin. 'My goodness, I'm starving! Have you had breakfast yet?' she asked.

'Good idea! Vera, you do the honours,' Niall instructed, leaving her little choice but to oblige. With his mood greatly improved, wanting to make amends for his earlier outburst, he asked, 'Irina, would you like to go for a sail?'

'Love to! Vera, will you be joining us?'

'No, she can't. She has work to do. Not so, Vera?'

'You heard the boss. Sorry, maybe next time. Thanks anyway,' Vera replied. Her heart sank, knowing perfectly well what was install for Irina.

CHAPTER 11

Chania, Crete

It was early afternoon. The sun had passed its zenith as the yacht scythed a steady path through the gentle swell, spraying a fine mist of salty water across its bow. On the horizon, the headland of Akrotiri simmered in the heat – a mythical temple perched upon Mount Olympus.

Two bottlenose dolphins frolicked alongside, challenging the sleek yacht to a friendly race. Irina, dressed in white shorts and a strapless marine-blue cotton blouse, leaned over the rails as her hair flowed freely in the warm breeze. With ripples of laughter, she cheered the playful mammals on. Their uncanny agility and speed saw them race ahead, emerge with perfect somersaults and splash down, soaking her to the bone. Grinning with high-pitched squeals, the two performers swam off into the distance.

Niall stood by her side, taking great delight in her young spontaneous spirit. Unexpectedly the yacht lurched, throwing her off balance into his arms. The touch of her skin against his sent a shiver of pleasure through his body. For a fleeting moment, he was tempted not to let go.

An hour later they dropped anchor in a secluded cove, quiet, and away from prying eyes. It was precisely as the skipper had promised. Apparently, it was also an ideal spot for snorkelling. Niall, regarding himself as an experienced diver, went to great lengths in explaining the basics of diving and spearfishing to Irina. Being the eager student, she tittered playfully. With the required introductory lesson out of the way, Niall helped her into the lukewarm water.

Submerged, his lusting grew tenfold as the sun and water transformed her into a sensual heavenly creature with the smallest imperfections airbrushed into oblivion. He fought the temptation to reach out and hold her. To Niall, the spearfishing was all but forgotten.

Irina turned, looked at him and smiled to herself as she reeled him in.

He moved closer.

With a quick flip of her ankles, she kicked clear of his grasp. Pointing at a shoal of fish, she took aim with the speargun and fired but missed.

The spell was broken.

Irina smiled and continued the hunt, toying with him, spinning her web ever tighter.

Having had no luck in harpooning any fish they dumped the empty nets and diving gear on top of the polished wooden deck, neither bothered by their lack of success.

'Thank you, that was wonderful,' Irina exclaimed. 'Now I can do with a nice soothing drink. Can I get you one?' she asked, heading for the galley.

'Yes, a Mojito, thank you.'

Having placed their orders, Irina re-joined Niall reclining on a luxuriously padded double sunbed.

'Hope you don't mind?' she asked. Sitting down next to him, she kept her distance, allowing the sexual tension to build.

Tired of her little game Niall took her hand in his, entwined his fingers in hers, and said, 'Why would I mind!' He felt content. For the first time in many years, the suppressing cloud of loneliness started to dissipate.

'Cheeky! And what are you thinking … hmm?'

'Sorry, can't tell.' Trying to move the attention away from

himself, he said, 'Right … make you a deal. Tell me about yourself: your family, your friends, the town you grew up in, etc., etc., and I'll tell you my deepest darkest secrets.'

'No, it's boring,' she giggled. Seeing the grave expression in his eyes, she asked, surprised, 'Are you serious?'

'Absolutely. And all about your boyfriends. On second thought, scrap that.'

'Okay. I was born in St. Petersburg where I spent most of my childhood.' Irina spoke softly, telling him about her past. As her melodic voice drifted up in the late afternoon air, she focused her gaze on the emptiness in the distance. Unknown to him, most of what she was saying was a slight deviation from the truth as names and places changed, re-invented. 'And that's my life in a nutshell. How about yours?'

Revealing his deepest secrets, he had no intention of doing. But there were events he could share, and with her, he found it remarkably easy, even the loss of his family many years ago. Under very tragic circumstances his father had died in a terrible accident, and then shortly thereafter, his younger sister. Devastated, his mother had abandoned him when still a teenager.

His words filled her with empathy; this was not what she had expected to hear. To break the melancholic mood, she kissed him on the cheek, jumped up, and said, 'This is too sad. Come.'

Slightly embarrassed, he got to his feet. With his hand in hers, she led him to the edge of the yacht. The next instant she dived overboard in one fluid motion. With a splash, he followed. Emerging for air, he struck out, trying to catch up with her. But whenever he thought he was gaining, she pulled further ahead with the greatest of ease.

Irina was enjoying herself. After a few hundred metres, she paused and turned on her back, waiting for him. Hearing his splashes close by, she rolled over and pulled him towards her. Embracing him, their bodies merged beneath the surface. Her soft, full lips touched his. As sudden as it had started, the moment of intimacy ended. Pushing him away, she said, 'Race you back!'

This time, she struck out forcefully and sprinted ahead. No matter how hard he tried the gap increased. He had no hope of catching her; she was gone.

Panting, out of breath, he clambered back on deck, exclaiming, 'Bloody hell, you're fast! Come on, out with it! Where did you learn to swim like that? And scared of the sea? Rubbish!'

'Did I not mention I used to be a gold medal champ at university?' she said cheekily.

'No wonder!'

This news to some degree explained her lengthy absence in the morning. *And what else did you not tell me?* he wondered.

'Excuse me, sir, miss, would either of you like a massage,' Ling, one of the petite Chinese crew members, asked.

'Wonderful idea. Don't you agree, Niall?' Irina said without hesitating.

'Why not?' he replied and followed her below deck. He could wait; the night was still young.

An hour later, Irina emerged from below deck, her flowing auburn hair tinted by the gold setting sun. Barefoot in a white sleeveless cotton dress, accessorised by a loose-fitting, wide, brown leather belt, she seemed to have stepped off the front cover of a fashion magazine.

'My dear, you are a vision!' Niall exclaimed.

'Thank you, you are most kind,' she replied modestly.

'No, I'm just being honest. Champagne?'

Watching the sun sink below the horizon, Irina let the tiny bubbles dance over her tongue, savouring the light, fruity dryness. Her thoughts drifted to a distant world thousands of kilometres away–

'What's wrong, Irina … why so quiet?'

'Nothing, I was just thinking how happy … how lucky I am to have met you,' she said. 'Thank you for a wonderful day.'

Underneath an umbrella of endless glittering stars

stretching far beyond infinity, they enjoyed a meal of fresh oysters, lobsters, and other delicacies freshly harvested from the sea. Sharing pleasant tales with someone special in this idyllic setting, with its unrivalled calm and ambience, made Niall wonder if this was not what life was all about. Maybe, being alone, fighting for power and wealth, were all just a waste of time?

Soon they found themselves transported from their private world. Snuggled together on the back seat of the car, Niall hummed to himself, reliving the moment he had taken her into his arms and glided across the deck with the soothing music their only companion.

Entering their hotel suite there was no need for words as Niall opened his bedroom door and led her inside.

CHAPTER 12

Blackrock, Dublin
Thursday Midnight

Tossing in bed, Sinead could not sleep. *Midnight*, she sighed. Her nerves were on edge. Feeling vulnerable without Vera, she aimlessly drifted through the spacious apartment. Despite the strong tranquillizers, the ordeal suffered at the hands of Madiba and his friends haunted her. Her body ached all over. The ugly bruises inflicted by the psychopaths had by now turned a yellowish brown. The only positive outcome of the encounter was the fact that she was still alive. Or was she? She prayed the AIDS vaccine administered on her arrival home, would work – convinced the pigs were riddled with disease, AIDS being one of them.

Once more she passed by her dressing room and paused as her eyes flitted over the rows of designer clothes, shoes and accessories – inconsequential trivia paid for at an extraordinary price. She rolled her eyes in self-disgust.

How could I ever have been so stupid? What was I thinking?

Amongst her clothes, the old shoebox protruded slightly from beneath a pile of jumpers.

My little box of memories … ha, ha!

Filled with trepidation she sat down on the edge of the bed, removed the lid and flipped through the pile of photographs, untouched for years.

The familiar faces looked up at her; ghosts from the past.

It seemed unreal as if it had never happened.

But she could not deny the once happy family: her mother, father, brothers and sister.

A snapshot captured in Hinterglemm, Austria eight years ago on a bitterly cold February day, their last holiday together.

Distracted, she rubbed her bruised cheek. The sudden sharp pain felt like the biting chill which had stung her face as she had hurtled down the mountain slope across a never-ending sea of pure white snow. With a vivid sense of reality, the treasured memories flooded back.

Exasperated by her blurred vision, she had regretted not having a pair of ski-glasses. Blinking, wiping the tears, she pushed forward with legs bent, determined to beat her two brothers.

Towering above her into the clear blue sky, the majestic white-capped peaks were like impregnable citadels of granite. And far below the quaint resort nestled snugly amongst the snow-laden pines adorning the valley floor. Ignoring the splendid scenery, her skis swished rhythmically, gliding across the snow. Without warning one ski slipped! Fighting to stay upright she shifted her weight, allowing the other ski to grip into the snow. Bringing her knees together, she regained her balance.

But despite her best efforts, she failed in her goal. By now her brothers were only red and black dots in the distance. To her dismay, arcs of snow sprayed into the air as they came to a grandiose stop at the bottom of the *piste*.

The race was over. They had won!

Not disheartened, she flew over the last hill and landed gracefully and glided to a stylish finish with a victorious smile.

'Fantastic, Sis. Shall we call it a day then?' Sean, the eldest, asked. Impressed by her performance, he gave her an almighty hug, nearly snapping her spine.

'Wow, not so fast! This is our last day or have you forgotten? Come on, one more, the big one over there,' Mark insisted, pointing at the looming mountain, at a dangerous slope riddled with moguls.

To Sinead, the incline looked difficult enough to walk down, let alone ski down.

'Come on, what do you say? Don't be a whoosh!' Mark challenged.

Petrified, Sinead shifted her gaze from the black run to her brother. 'Stop messing! Not in this life, nor the next, forget it! I opt for a nice mug of hot chocolate with Mum and Dad, thank you,' she said, not about to be goaded or bullied into something she knew she would regret. She would rather leave the resort with fond memories. The idea of wearing a lovely designer cast supplied by the local A&E to serve as a reminder of her own stupidity did not appeal at all.

But her brothers were set on conquering the mountain. Shaking her head in disbelief, she waved them off. Fifteen minutes later, two familiar specks appeared against the white, near-vertical cliff. Anxiously, she waited.

Their ability to attack the black run left her speechless. In quick short turns, they swerved in and out of the bumps, jumping, descending at an alarming rate. Then it happened, Sean fell. Head over heels he hit one bump after the next, tumbling down the mountain. Sinead stood with her mouth open. At last, his body came to a stop.

From all directions, concerned skiers raced towards him. She feared the worst. Her heart ached as the seconds ticked by. A fist shot up from the seemingly lifeless body, punching Mark in the stomach. With some help, Sean got to his feet, shook his arms, his legs, and rolled his head from side to side. Gingerly, he stepped into his skis and steadied himself with the poles, ready to take up the challenge once more.

She had seen as much as she could stomach and left, choosing the warm comfort of the restaurant over this male idiocy.

Opening the solid oak door of the log chalet her nose tingled, the air heavy with rich aromas of smoked meat. Famished skiers packed the semi-dark restaurant. Lit by the hearth's dancing flames idly consuming the logs, their faces glowed a warm orange.

Seated at the corner table next to the welcoming fire, which crackled pleasantly, her parents huddled together. Above them the walls were adorned with stuffed animal heads and two-toned pictures illustrating winters of long ago: images of two-metre-deep snowfalls obliterating chalets, of skiers posing in fashionable skiwear, and the latest paraphernalia of yesteryear.

Planting a kiss on both their cheeks she sat down and admired her mother's beauty, still untouched by the years. And her father, stout, rugged and weather-beaten, with the ever-deepening lines on his face becoming more handsome with the passing of time. How fortunate she was, blessed with such wonderful parents, still very much in love.

Maybe I'll also get it right the first time, finding my soulmate?

With an exaggerated expression of dread, she launched into a terrifying version of her brothers' escapades. According to her, they had clearly gone mad, gripped by the dreaded snow-fever.

Her mother's eyes grew huge, moaning, 'Oh no, no …'

Sinead ignored her flustering, allowing her to fret some more. 'Don't worry, Mum; they're fine. Well, they were the last I saw … come to think of it, I'm not quite sure. Sean did not move after his fall … and he did give his head quite a bang. Maybe I should go and check?' she added and winked at her father who was not in the least worried, well in tune with his daughter's tomfoolery.

She had welcomed returning home after the exciting holiday. However modest, she loved the place; it was the only home she'd ever known. As comfortable as the hotel had been, it could never replace her own bed, hidden in the cloud covered hills of New Ross. The view of the sweeping river with its timeless ebb and flow, of the old gnarled oaks, was immensely reassuring. It filled her with calm. It was her source of strength and nothing would change that.

Sean, the ever conscience student, was about to finish his last year of full-time education as a structural engineer. By contrast, Mark, aged twenty, struggled to apply himself to his studies. Reckless by nature, his pledge to make a considerable

58

effort did not convince anyone. But then, he had the Irish gift of the gab, always able to worm his way out of impossible situations, never backing down. He was his father's pride and joy.

Sean's old Opel, filled to the roof with their mum's special treats, had finally set off just before dark.

Sinead sighed. Her finger caressed the small coloured photo of Mark. He looked so young. They were all very close, a family everyone had admired.

And then it all had to change …

That terrifying sound which had pierced the night, making her jump up in bed, had remained with her ever since. It was a death-wail which had permeated every part of her soul – a cry of immense pain and sadness, her mother's heart being torn apart. Without hesitating, Sinead had rushed to her mother's side where she was cowering on the floor with her father stooped over her, his face glistening with tears. The news of Mark's death had ripped through the house like a powerful hurricane, tearing the once happy home apart in one furious flurry.

Thankfully, Sean had survived the accident.

But that was only the beginning.

First, her mother had withdrawn into her own world, unwilling to accept Mark's death. Her father was next, taken by a fatal stroke six months later. And after three years of suffering, her mother had finally given up the will to live.

The responsibility of taking care of the younger siblings and contribute financially had rested with Sean and Sinead. With her dreams obliterated, her life put on hold, she had jumped at the first opportunity which had come her way, hoping it would make life more bearable.

Furious, Sinead flung the shoebox across the room, scattering the photographs through the air. She looked at the teddy bear sitting forlornly on the recliner, its glass eyes staring vacantly into emptiness. If life could only have been so simple, void of emotion, of feelings, she thought bitterly. But the reality was very different. And she was not an overstuffed toy!

She had emotions, feelings. She felt pain.

Well, it's time to stop this self-pity and move on. The past I cannot change, but the future I can. I shall have my life back!

Having retrieved the pictures, she placed the box on her bedside table and reached for the phone. With steady fingers, she punched her brother's number in.

CHAPTER 13

Santiago, Chile

The room was dark, the curtains firmly shut, blocking out the chilly night. Outside nothing moved. The vast parkland was deserted. The only hint of life was the faint drone of city traffic. The shrill ring of the phone shattered the peace. Trying to grab the noisy contraption in the dark he dropped it. Retrieving it from under his bed he looked at the time, 4:45 a.m.

'Hi,' he answered, unimpressed.

'Sean, is that you?'

It took him a few seconds to recognise the voice. 'Sinead … Sis! I don't believe my ears! Where are you?' he asked, jolting upright.

It had been years since they had last spoken. For some obscure reason, she had broken off all contact with him. To this day he had no idea why. Nor did he know where she lived or what she did. Their relationship had been put on hold and being stuck in some far-flung corner of the world, did not help matters either.

Sinead was like a machine gun, firing questions, unstoppable. 'What's Chile like? Are you enjoying it there? How's work? Have you made lots of money … and friends? Was it easy to adapt? Any plans to come home?'

As the euphoria of hearing each other's voices receded,

their chatter turned more solemn, reminiscing about their early years, their losses, their pains. The sudden grave tone in her voice made Sean pay closer attention. Not totally insensitive, he realised the call was far more sinister than just catching up on old times. There were far too many questions about Chile and South America.

'Sis, you're not thinking of moving here?' he asked.

'No, what gives you that idea? I'm just curious about what's keeping you there. Maybe you have found love, that's all.'

'You sure?'

'Cross my heart.'

'You may be able to pull the wool over someone else's eyes, but not mine. Come and visit, have a good look around. You may like it.'

'Yeah, I may just do that. I'll let you know, so.'

Her deflated tone raised his concerns. 'Are you all right, Sis?'

'I'm grand. Everything's just tickety-boo!' she replied, trying to sound upbeat.

Sipping a mug of steaming coffee, Sean stood in front of the panoramic window and stared at the flickering lights beyond the woodlands. He could not sleep. His suspicious mind could not rest, far from convinced that, "everything's just tickety-boo". Her whispered goodbye had sounded too much like a final farewell. Incapable of doing anything about it, other than fret or board the next available flight, he decided to phone his youngest sister, Laura. She could find out what was going on.

CHAPTER 14

Chania, Crete
Friday Morning

The previous night's passionate memories had been forgotten. Any intention of leisurely preparing for his meeting with Dimitris vanished. His pulse raced. 'Repeat that,' Niall hissed, keeping his voice low, not wanting to wake Irina by his side.

'He said, Paul sold you out to the cops. The Greeks are coming for you!' Ciarán repeated, unable to hide his pleasure in bringing bad tidings.

'You think it's funny!' Niall snarled. 'Listen, my boy, if I go down, so shall you. You find that fucker!' He was livid, wanting Paul dead. Not wasting another second, he phoned Michael.

'Paul has ratted me out. Do whatever you think necessary to cover our tracks. Sterilise the plane,' Niall ordered.

'See it as done.'

No one was to be trusted. He had been set up. Who else was involved was anyone's guess. He wiped his brow, contemplating all possible scenarios to avoid capture. Careful not to disturb the slender arm protruding from under the sheet, he slipped out of the bed. Having donned his dressing gown, he entered Vera's room at precisely 6:20 a.m.

'Wake up! We have a problem,' he snapped, shaking her roughly by the shoulder

'Okay … okay!' Vera protested.

'On the patio, fifteen minutes,' Niall ordered and rushed back to his room.

Irina was still sound asleep.

Good, the less she knows the better.

The slight shift of her body, as well as the slight frown creasing her forehead, he did not notice.

The mood on the patio was tense. Drinking strong sweet Greek coffee, they faced each other. They were indifferent to the calm sea, the white sandy beach and the few early bathers.

Niall's gaze was fixed on Vera's large blue eyes as he spoke, 'I need you to do something.'

'What?'

'You must take out a safe-deposit box at your local bank. I need to store my diamonds there.'

'What bank?'

'I don't have time for games. Do you want the balance?'

Vera's face turned pale.

'Did you really think I'll let you waltz around the island without keeping an eye on you – one of my prize possessions?'

'Why?' she asked puzzled.

'Paul has ratted me out to the Garda!'

'You're joking, right?'

'No. Enough said. If you want to leave this island today, you better hide the stones.'

'What's in it for me? Will you let Sinead and me go free?'

'No, and don't ask me again. But I'll give you a nice fat bonus for your trouble and let ye both live. Don't forget, if I get caught, you'll all be in trouble, including Irina.'

Vera nodded her head in understanding.

'Good. I'm meeting Dimitris at ten. Should be at the bank by eleven-thirty. You store the stones, and we get out of here. By the way, Michael will accompany you – purely for your protection of course,' Niall smirked.

'Yeah, sure, "purely for my protection", of course.'

'And not a word to Irina.'

'Mum's the word … goes without saying.'

Her tone left him under no illusion that she was not to be trusted.

Niall, groomed and dressed, entered his bedroom carrying a breakfast tray of fresh fruit and pastries, adorned with a red rose. 'Good morning,' he greeted Irina cheerfully.

'Good morning to you too!'

'Here you go, my lady, breakfast in bed, delivered by your devoted servant.'

'Thank you, my dear. So very kind of you!' Pulling the sheet up under her chin, she patted the bed beside her for him to sit down.

'You'll have to forgive me for not joining you. I already ate. I didn't want to wake you.'

'*Spasibo*,' she said and kissed him.

'And now I have to run, or I'll be late for my meeting.'

'You don't want me to come?'

'Of course I do, but you'll be very bored. On our next visit, I'll introduce you to my colleagues. We'll make it a proper holiday and I'll be at your beck and call. I promise.'

'Sounds wonderful,' she replied, knowing a brush-off when she heard one.

'In the meantime, please order anything you need from room service or better still, go for a treat at the hotel spa; it's supposed to be excellent. On one condition: you don't run off with one of these Greek charmers,' he said. Moving closer, he whispered, 'How I would love to stay.'

Her hand briefly stroked his cheek. 'You better run before I tie you down!'

CHAPTER 15

Chania, Crete
Friday Morning

'What do you mean, "You must get off your fat lazy arse," and do what?' Chief Inspector Vasilis Kalivas roared in his office at the Chania police station.

His Friday morning coffee tasted vile having listened to a tirade of abuse hollered by Chief Superintendent Michaelis from police head office in Heraklion. Fortunately for the chief superintendent he was out of reach or he would have been choked to death. Instead, Vasilis' only resort was to slam the phone down. 'Who the hell does that upshot of a half-breed Aegean think he is?' he ranted.

The situation was serious – smuggling drugs into Crete – with the Irish demanding their cooperation. Well, that created quite a problem. This was his territory and he would decide what was to happen. He would not allow some nosy foreigners to sniff around on a holy crusade.

Drugs? Right. Then it must concern my friend, Dimitris.

And if not him, then Vasilis would permit his men to have a field day in apprehending the criminals who want to cut him out of his share. The upshot for him, Chief Inspector Vasilis Kalivas, was, that if he successfully eliminated an international smuggling network, he would shine in the limelight of the international press, a hero.

66

But then again, why get someone locked up if one can make new friends. The wise option would be to stall matters and scupper the investigation. He was not a man who would let an opportunity to make easy money slip by.

The search for the contraband would fizzle into thin air as nothing would be found – time and taxpayers' money wasted because of false information. He would remind his foreign colleagues and his superiors to be more careful before launching a full-scale international investigation the next time they receive a tip-off.

The problem was, his superiors were involved and they would expect proper procedures to be followed, reports on all actions to be filed correctly. They would insist that all possible points of access to and from Crete be watched. Vasilis knew his powers were limited. Nothing would stop the inevitable thorough search by the Coast Guard, airports' customs, and the apprehension and questioning of all likely suspects.

It was imperative to talk to Dimitris.

CHAPTER 16

Dimitris' Estate
Varipetro Region, Crete

Niall's car geared down, dropping revolutions fast as they turned into the kilometre long lane of tall cypresses, marking the entrance to Dimitris' estate. Racing up the hill they arrived at a cluster of buildings fortified by two guard towers. At the gate, eight armed men let them through. Circling the courtyard's fountain, they stopped next to Stavros waiting outside the front door.

Friday, and still no sign of Dimitris. Not good; trust he's back, Niall thought. *Or is something more sinister going on?*

The perimeter of the enclosed yard consisted of tall garrison towers linked by a three-storey-high sandstone wall. It all resembled a fortress rather than a private dwelling. To the north and east, the house opened on to olive grove terraces and rolling lawns, offering a panoramic view over the countryside below. No security precautions were required for these areas. The sheer drop of sixty odd metres to the valley floor below formed a natural insurmountable wall. Any attack on the Greek's palace would require a small army.

Getting out of the car, Niall was greeted with a frosty, '*Yassou.*' Stavros' face remained impassionate, displaying no warmth. Instead, it was cold, hard, obviously still smarting from the incident at the airport. 'Follow me,' he said and turned away. Without waiting for Niall and his men, he disappeared into the cool sumptuous main foyer.

Beyond the entrance, they passed through an even more splendid hallway containing a majestic sweeping staircase. Traversing the room with its shiny black colonnade they entered the centrally located atrium, basked in sunlight. Its pristine white Carrara marble floor, contrasting dark pond and decorative fountain smacked of opulence. The slightly diffused rays filtering through the huge overhead skylight three storeys above revealed a scattering of bawdy ebony sculptures depicting various stages of debauchery. The carefully placed lush green palms created an atmosphere of tranquillity. On the far side, the internal courtyard opened on to a covered patio with a vast wall of glass stacked to one side. Warm, sweet air, fragranced by summer scents flowed past the swaying white silk curtains.

'Not bad if you see yourself as a Greek god. But not for me, no thanks, buddy!' Niall scoffed in the direction of Michael who responded with a hint of a smile.

Dimitris, seated outside in the shade on a plush cream sofa, spotted Niall and jumped up with a loud, 'Welcome, my friend! It has been a long time.' His greeting sounded sincere, his handshake firm, but not overly so, having nothing to prove.

'Hello, Dimitris. Delighted as always,' Niall replied, wondering how much his host knew.

'Likewise, likewise, my friend, or shall I say *Rob*?' Dimitris joked.

Regardless of the friendly overtures, his dark beady eyes studied Niall. The broad smile was as spurious as the Greek god sculptures surrounding the oversized swimming pool nestled in the green lawn.

'Please come, sit, sit,' Dimitris said indicating to a sofa opposite him.

Niall's men fanned out and took up strategic positions on

the green. Being under pressure, he had no time to waste on formalities. Nevertheless, he would have to play it cool.

'Some Greek coffee, or Turkish, as those barbarians maintain. Well, screw them!'

'That'll do fine. And, may I?' Niall asked, indicating to the tray of syrupy baklava on display.

'*Parakalo*, please, help yourself,' Dimitris replied before returning to business. 'Sorry about the delay, although it was worth it. I have the whole consignment. Thanks be to Zeus.'

'Great, then shall we get on with it,' Niall said with a faint smile, concealing his eagerness to get away as soon as possible.

'Not so fast, my friend. What's this I hear of someone trying to scupper our deal?'

The question was like a well-aimed punch, hitting Niall in the midriff. Casually he brushed his brow, a signal for Michael to get ready, to expect trouble. It was time to placate the Greek, to ease his concerns before a bloodbath erupted. Niall's voice was steady as he spoke, 'Yes I'm afraid it's true. It seems my partner Paul wants me out of the way. When I return to Ireland, I'll take care of him. This will never—'

'Sorry for butting in,' Stavros interrupted, ignoring Niall's look of disapproval. Whispering in his boss's ear, Dimitris' body tensed. A deep furrow appeared on his forehead. His eyes turned an ominous deep black. He mumbled something in Greek. Stavros nodded and rushed off.

Affronted by Stavros' impertinence, Niall demanded, 'What was that about?'

'I can ask you the same,' Dimitris retorted. 'Is there anything you want to tell me before we continue?'

'Nothing specific that I can think of except for finishing this business so I can get back to Ireland.'

'Then we have a serious problem. I think you know that's not possible. Are you absolutely sure there's nothing you may want to share?' Dimitris tried again.

He knows, damn! The only way out of this mess was to come clean. 'If you're referring to the rumour that Paul has informed the Garda, then yes, maybe I can. But I was waiting for confirmation before raising the alarm. I only received this information on my way over here,' Niall lied, deadpan. If the meeting had taken place as originally scheduled, he would not be sitting here now explaining himself like some luckless employee.

'Thank you for finally sharing such an important development,' Dimitris said, his voice dripping sarcasm. 'Maybe that explains why you seem to be in such a hurry? The way I see it: you want to dump the drugs on me, slip away with your diamonds, and leave me to deal with the police creeping all over my house. Am I right so far?'

'Whoa there! That's quite an accusation …'

'My friend, to be frank, I'm deeply disappointed. I would have preferred you telling me this yourself. Nevertheless, I'm a forgiving man and won't waste time quibbling. Let's rather concentrate on finding a solution. But know this, under these circumstances I will not take the drugs.'

'Understood,' Niall said, 'and do you have any update on this rumour?'

'Yes, I do. Fortunately, the police have no specifics: no names or locations. As we speak, they are organising themselves to start the search. Luckily, I have someone who will stall procedures if possible. But for how long, who knows? Therefore, we better be quick. Any suggestions on how to outsmart them?'

'I have an idea,' Niall started, hoping to come up with a solution acceptable to them both.

For the next thirty minutes, huddled together, they argued intensely until reaching a consensus on how to avoid the authorities. With the new deal in place Niall was presented with the diamonds for valuation, a task which lasted half an hour.

Nodding, Niall let the stones trickle through his fingers. 'Good, good, this will do nicely. Thank you. Right, let's get to work,' he said getting up.

In a cloud of dust Niall, Dimitris and their entourage arrived at the isolated holiday villa, the newly acquired safe house. The Greek was anxious to test the purity of the merchandise, destined to make him a fortune if their quickly constructed plan worked. And Niall was even more impatient, wanting to get off the island.

The white powder supplied by the Russian Mafia in Columbia had started its journey two weeks previously. And only by some miracle had the 750 kilograms of cocaine made it thus far. Thanks to the tenacity of Niall's men the drugs had not been lost in a violent storm during the transfer – working on the cold treacherous waters of the Irish Sea south-west of Rosslare was no easy feat. From there the boat had been sailed into the calmer estuary beyond the famous Hook Lighthouse, making landfall five kilometres north of Cheekpoint. The last forty-seven kilometres to Niall's international equestrian centre by an unmarked delivery van had remained unchallenged. The private landing strip which officially served horse-lovers and foreign visitors was the perfect spot for flying contraband in and out of Ireland. The flow of drugs, weapons and young women continued unabated.

Ireland with its vast coastline and limited naval force was the ideal half-way house for any illegal shipments in and out of Europe.

Their new agreement stipulated that nine of Niall's men would remain to guard the drugs. Furthermore, they would fully cooperate with the Greeks in ensuring that the drugs were delivered as planned. This should guarantee neither double-crossing the other.

Niall was free to go.

'My friend, I wish you the best,' Dimitris said, bidding Niall farewell. 'And if the police stop you at the airfield, call me and I'll take care of them.'

'Thank you. I trust that won't be necessary,' Niall said as he waved goodbye, not believing a single word the Greek had uttered.

CHAPTER 17

Police Headquarters
Chania

The alleged traffickers had to be apprehended before they could flee Crete. By order of police head office, all available men were to report for duty. The island had to be sealed off.

This news depressed Vasilis immensely. There went his usual Friday night cavorting with his mistress away from his miserable overweight wife. His marriage was no different to so many others. Their once sweet childhood love had suffered a premature death a long time ago, suffocated by familiarity and boredom. Her overbearing character sickened him with her constant nagging, "We must paint the house, mow the lawn, wash the dishes, scrub the toilet. I'm not doing it, I'm not your bloody slave! No, not like that Vasilis! No, you shouldn't have said that … I need more money …"

The only highlight which remained for him was Friday evenings – his solution to a failed marriage. And on other nights, when he'd had as much as he could bear, he would sleep on his office couch – snowed under with work – not prepared to subject himself to her complaints.

All he ever saw of his once beautiful young bride was her shovelling baklavas, kataifi, or whatever else was at hand into her ever-gaping mouth. With relish, she would wipe the sticky syrup off her freshly grown moustache. And then to be subjected to her endless complaints about how old age was the reason for the loss of her once sensual figure. How their bed survived the traumatic events when she, dressed in tantalising lingerie representing a hippo in drag, jumped on him for her pleasure amazed him. Her oversized gold rings, bracelets and necklaces were an eternal nuisance. The accompanying racket was reminiscent of a herd of Swiss cattle stampeding down an Alpine slope.

What he would give to spend the evening with his beautiful, voluptuous young mistress. She was a real Greek beauty with sultry black olive eyes, shiny ebony hair and sensual Mediterranean curves. He could feel her firm young body move under and over him, pleasing him willingly ... his own little whore. And when she—

The persistent ringing of his mobile phone interrupted his lustful thoughts. He took one look at the number, answered, and said, '*Yassou*, my friend?'

'Can we meet? It's urgent. Forty minutes, same place as usual?' the familiar voice asked.

'Yes, can do,' Vasilis replied, wondering what new problem had surfaced. In any case, it did not really matter. He would gladly help Dimitris who had always been a very grateful man.

Dimitris had total confidence in Vasilis to find the diamonds. The investigation would be the perfect cover. Niall must have been dreaming to have thought that under these circumstances he would let him walk off the island with the stones.

Why not have it all? My reputation would be intact. Paul and the extremely efficient Greek police would be responsible for Niall's demise, Dimitris thought and smiled to himself.

74

CHAPTER 18

Chania, Crete

Niall, who trusted no one, least of all the smiling Greek with perfectly capped teeth, raced back to Chania. Certain no one had followed, they stopped opposite the main branch of the Bank of Crete.

'I assume everything has been arranged,' he said handing the briefcase to Michael with Vera by his side.

'Yes,' Vera said.

'Good. Michael, you know the drill.'

The thought of Vera seducing Michael and the two of them disappearing along with the stones, niggled. He knew only too well how fast new liaisons could be forged.

'I'll be back in an hour. That should be more than enough time to do what you must,' he said, impatient to fetch Irina and get her safely into the air.

Entering the hotel suite, Niall was welcomed by the suggestive overtures of *"Je t'aime … moi nonplus"* drifting out of his bedroom. Surprised, he paused. Not knowing what to expect he called out, 'Irina, are you ready?'

Pushing the bedroom door open he was confronted by an alluring temptress reclining on the bed. The transparent silk dress she had on revealed more than would be proper if she had any intention of travelling outside the confines of the room.

'Of course, I am …'

Her naked legs slid off the bed. Playfully she pulled the silk scarf through her fingers, across her slim neck and discarded the garment on to the floor. She took his hand in hers.

Niall hesitated; they had very little time. His jacket fell to the floor. She drew him closer, her lips warm and moist. Her hands moved nimbly, caressing him.

Niall's urgency to leave evaporated …

Recovering from the unexpected erotic interlude Niall looked at his watch. *Damn!* He had wanted to be off the island by now. 'We better hurry, time is ticking!'

Getting out of bed he dragged a giggling, naked Irina into the wet-room.

Lathering his chest, his stomach, she gently massaged the muscles which rippled to her touch. Her slender fingers played across his hips …

She was in no hurry to leave; whatever the rush, it could wait.

Inside the nondescript restaurant opposite the Bank of Crete, Michael and Vera sat in silence, patiently waiting. Storing the diamonds in her safe-deposit box had gone without a hitch. The manager had been as helpful as ever – obviously very fond of his client.

Vera stole a glance at the broad-shouldered, strong-jawed, rugged man with an eight-centimetre scar on his left temple as he slowly sipped his orange juice. It was one of the few opportunities she had to get to know him. She suppressed a sigh, frustrated, another man wasted.

Why do they all end up the same: crooks, hoods? And the scar? Most likely one too many pub fights.

He was a real dark horse. Despite trying to make light conversation since their return from the bank, he had remained distant. She assumed he had his reasons.

'Should we be concerned why they're taking so long? I hope they didn't run into any unexpected trouble?' he suddenly asked.

'Believe me, after what I've seen, I'd say any trouble would be self-inflicted,' Vera noted.

Michael did not reply and took another sip of his drink.

Behind him, in the back of the eatery, three men sat watching – Niall trusted no one, including Michael who was relatively new to the organisation.

A few minutes later the door of the restaurant crashed open as Niall and Irina burst inside. Michael looked at Vera, heaved his shoulders and winked, whispering, 'Yes, definitely self-inflicted.'

'Right, Vera, let's have it!' Niall snapped.

Dutifully she obeyed, handing over the key of the safe-deposit box.

'Michael, has she been any trouble?' Niall asked.

'No, no trouble whatsoever. All safely locked away, and nothing *fell* on the floor,' Michael said.

'Good. Then I'll see you and the lads back in Dublin. Come, Vera, the plane won't wait.' Clutching Irina's hand, he turned and left.

The nose of the jet crept out of the hangar, a tortoise tentatively sticking its head out of its shell, testing the air. Exposed to the sun's glare, Karl slipped his sunglasses on and commenced taxiing to the end of the runway. 'I've cleared our flight plan with Chania. We're set to go,' he confirmed.

'Thanks, then let's roll,' Niall said.

The next instant, a convoy of police cars with flashing lights, screeched to a halt in front of the plane, blocking its path.

'What the hell!' Niall shouted.

As dozens of police with sidearms at the ready spilled on to the hardstand, aiming at the wheels and cockpit, Karl cut the engines.

'Well, so much for my *friend's* promise,' Niall growled. 'Sit tight. I'll try and resolve this without too much hassle.'

Stepping on to the hot asphalt, Niall found himself face to face with a middle-aged, well-rounded police officer. The man was clearly not in the mood for a nice little chat to iron out any problems. Instead, he looked like he could be struck down by a fatal stroke at any moment.

'Good afternoon. I am Vasilis Kalivas, Chief Inspector, Chania police. I presume you are Niall McGuire. My apologies for delaying your departure. But I have orders to question you and your passengers, as well as search the plane.' Ending the official introduction, he rudely shoved a Greek search warrant under Niall's nose. Not waiting for a response his men rushed the plane and forced everyone outside.

Beneath the scorching sun, Irina nuzzled up against Niall, took his hand in hers, and whispered, 'What are they looking for?'

'I've no idea. Relax, there's nothing to worry about. We have not broken any laws. We'll be on our way soon,' Niall reassured her.

Vasilis was in a foul mood. Two hours of rummaging through the plane, nearly pulling it apart, had revealed nothing. There had been no trace of any drugs or diamonds. Furthermore, the body searches carried out on all the passengers had proved fruitless.

Maddened, he led the cavalcade of police vehicles back the way they had come. He pondered the mysterious disappearance of the diamonds. If they were not on the plane, then they must still be somewhere on the island. But where, was anyone's guess.

CHAPTER 19

Blackrock
Dublin

It was well past midnight by the time Vera unlocked the front door of the apartment. As she put her bag down a voice called out, 'Vera, is that you?'

'Yes, home at last!' she replied and rushed to greet her friend, hoping Sinead was well on her way to recovery.

'I'm so pleased to see you! I was really getting worried. I thought you said you'd be home by eight.'

'Be glad to see me at all. Thanks to that creep, Paul, we nearly got caught.'

'What?'

'He ratted Niall out to the Guards. For a moment I thought I wouldn't see you for a very long time.'

Sinead's eyes grew large. 'He did? He must be mad … Niall will kill him.'

Excited, Vera spoke non-stop, elaborating on the events in Crete. And more specifically about Niall's romance, seemingly, head over heels in love with Irina. 'I've never seen him like this, holding hands like a teenager!'

'Poor girl, what will become of her?' Sinead asked.

'I'm not so sure she's really such a *poor girl*. I wonder who'll need our sympathies more, him or her? I bet, if she can, she'll squeeze him for every cent he's worth. Anyway, enough about them. I need to freshen up. It's been a long day. And I have an idea of how we can get away.'

'How?'

'I'll tell you later.'

Sinead nearly dropped her mug of steaming hot chocolate as she listened to Vera's plan. It was madness. 'Tell me you're not serious?'

'Don't you see? It's our ticket out of here. In fact, it's our only one.'

'No. The only place this "ticket" will get us, is to the morgue. We'll be joining Paul. How nice.'

'So? Just look at you; next time he'll make sure you're dead. Please, listen, at least this way, you … we, have a chance … and it may be our last.'

For the next ten minutes, Sinead said nothing, allowing her friend to explain what she had in mind. And the more she spoke the less crazy it all sounded.

'OK, I'm in … I must be just as mad as you,' Sinead said, somewhat apprehensively. It was not quite what she had in mind. Securing work in Chile with the help of her brother would have been a far more sensible option. But Niall would eventually find her there, of that she was certain.

'Remember if we do somehow succeed you won't be able to return home for a very, very long time,' Vera reminded her. 'You think you can do that?'

'I know … it will be very hard. But the truth is, I don't care what happens. I'll do anything to be free,' Sinead said as her resolve grew stronger despite the prospect of never seeing her family, or her beloved Emerald Isle again, however inconceivable a prospect.

CHAPTER 20

Santiago Airspace
Saturday Evening

'Red or white wine, sir?' the air hostess asked with her robotic smile.

Sean returned the *friendly* gesture with an even more sincere one and replied, 'Red, thank you.'

The last thing he felt like was smiling. Appalled by the cramped *cattle class* seats, he regretted his own stinginess in not having opted for business class. He tried to figure out how on earth he was to move his arms while attempting to shove the *plastic* food down the hatch without elbowing his neighbour, yet again.

Oh, bugger!

Beside him the irate old man released a few animal grunts of protestation while chomping, trying to digest the tasteless concoction of chemicals served up as food. Sean returned the man's severe stare with a look which clearly implied, "I've apologised once, don't expect another. And I didn't design this sardine tin, so take your complaint up with customer services".

The old man shrugged his shoulders and carried on chewing.

It was going to be a very, very long night, Sean thought, wondering what happened to the joys of travelling.

From the moment he had arrived at the Santiago terminal

building, he had been confronted by an army of obnoxious ground staff – their attitude an affront to any civilised being. Then, he had to endure harassment by a bunch of utterly objectionable security staff, forcing him to half undress, exercising their seemingly unlimited powers, humiliating thousands of innocent travellers. He had been lucky to have retained his wallet with some staff hell-bent on relieving him of his valuables. The temptation to pose the question of whether he looked like a terrorist planning to blow the plane into eternity, including himself, had crossed his mind. Well aware that such a flippant remark would see him handcuffed and marched off to Guantanamo Bay, he had held his tongue.

By the time the lights came on for breakfast, Sean was in no mood for pleasantries. What a night it had been! And now to face the ghosts of the past. Well, so be it. He had wasted five years of his life on self-pity. No more.

The mere thought that he had fled Dublin like a wounded ferret, vowing never to return, made him sick.

By now he had kicked the whole sordid incident into obscurity. A life-lesson he had learned the hard way: never arrive home unannounced, no matter how eager to surprise your wife, or how much she said she loved and missed you.

With the construction of the hotel complex in Cyprus on target, and pining terribly for his dearly beloved, he had taken a few days off work and returned home. On the way from the airport he had stopped and bought some groceries: a bottle of red wine, a bunch of red roses and a box of her favourite pralines.

But all his good intentions had been crushed the moment he entered the house. Instead of giving her a surprise with a candlelit dinner, the surprise was on him. Dumbstruck he had witnessed Claire lovingly kissing a stranger. The realisation that he had never experienced such devotion, had crushed him. There was nothing to be done. No words, no amount of anger could have changed a thing. His lovely wife and university sweetheart had destroyed his faith in women.

And here he was back at last, his old, cocky confident self.

His renewed vigour was the result of an endless stream of Chilean beauties having frequented his chambers – their efforts having done wonders to his once bruised ego.

Sinead's midnight-call had been followed up by his youngest sister Laura paying her an unexpected visit. According to Laura, Sinead had suffered a severe beating at the hands of some drunk. A story she did not believe. She was positive Sinead was lying and in serious trouble.

Falling through the blanket of clouds on making their final approach into Dublin airport, Sean noticed the old terminal building strangulated by an octopus of glass and steel tentacles. Arriving inside the terminal the customary hospitable Irish faces were not to be found anywhere. Instead, he was welcomed by rude officials addressing him in broken English. He felt alienated, confused, wondering whether he had stepped on the wrong flight and landed in Islamabad. But on exiting the terminal his fears were allayed. He could smell home as the familiar grey mist embraced him like a well-worn damp coat.

Forewarned by Laura, he headed straight for Blackrock, having every intention to arrive unannounced – depriving Sinead of an opportunity to give him the slip. Or refuse to open the door as was the case with Laura's first attempt to see her – fortunately Laura had persevered. No, he had travelled too far for little games.

Reversing the rental into a parking space he was surprised by the number of expensive cars and modern apartment buildings surrounding him. Engaging the handbrake, he whistled loudly, wondering how she could afford such an address.

Lunchtime, good. Sinead can do the honours … if she's in. Tired and hungry, he squeezed out of the small car and dashed across the tree-lined street. *Well, let's see what really happened, Sis.*

Arriving on the fifth floor he was met by an ominous silence. But it was Sunday, people slept late.   .Undeterred, he rang the doorbell of apartment 502.

Nothing.

Again, he tried.

After his fifth attempt, his patience had run out. About to ring the neighbour's doorbell he heard someone fiddling with the lock. Slowly the door opened.

'Can I help you?' the young woman asked, her exceptional looks marred by her hostile expression.

Detecting a hint of an Eastern European accent, he said, somewhat unsure, 'Uhm … don't know if you can? I'm looking for my sister, Sinead.'

'You're Sean!? I should have guessed; you could be twins!' the woman replied as her face lit up with a warm smile.

'Yep, I'm afraid so. To her detriment.'

'Are you fishing for compliments?' she laughed. 'Anyway, you're a long way from home, are you not? Oh, please come in … forgive me, I'm Vera.'

'Thank you, don't mind if I do. How is she?'

'Could be better, but she'll be very happy to see you.'

Entering the spacious high-ceilinged lounge, he noted how the combination of comfortable modern settees, expensive antiques, plush rugs, original art pieces draping the walls, and tall indoor plants conveyed an undeniable sense of money. Sean frowned suspiciously. *At least someone in our family is making money. Or is some rich Russian oligarch-daddy paying for all of this? Most likely.*

'Have a seat. I'll call her,' Vera said and ran up the stairs.

Anxious, he ignored the offer and raced after her. As he reached the gallery Sinead stumbled out of her room. 'Sean!' she shouted and rushed into his arms. 'I can't believe you're here! What are you—' Her words faltered as she broke down in tears.

Shocked by the bruises on her face, neck and arms Sean blurted out, 'My God, what happened to you? I'll kill him! Who did this … where is he?'

Holding her in his arms, she answered his questions as best she could. Incensed, he wanted justice; he wanted the animal who did this locked up for life.

Not too distant from this emotional encounter, secure in his mansion in the Wicklow Mountains, the "animal" was unaffected by his handiwork, having just enjoyed an hour of intimate passion.

Since his return from Crete, Niall had not left Irina's side. The problems he had experienced in Greece for the moment faded into oblivion. How his men were faring in Crete was of little concern. He was rid of the drugs, he had his diamonds ... and Irina. And on top of that, Ciarán was hot on Paul's trail – it was only a matter of time before he would have his revenge.

Next to him, Irina stirred.

'My goodness, it's nearly two o'clock and look at us still in bed!' she exclaimed starting to get up.

'Where're you off to in such a hurry? You need to go to work?' Niall teased and pushed her back against the pillow.

'As it's Sunday, I think I need to go to mass. I have to confess my recent sins, Mr McGuire. Maybe you should too,' she said as she stretched her arms upwards, allowing the sheet to slip, exposing her naked breasts.

'Ah, but we have not sinned, Father. Are we not supposed to go forth and multiply?' he mocked.

CHAPTER 21

Mediterranean Sea
Sunday Afternoon

With the late afternoon swell and strong wind in their favour, the sails bulged, gliding the yacht along at an exhilarating six knots. Michael steadied himself against the tilt and wiped the salty spray from his brow, grateful to be out on the open seas, to be off the island.

For the moment, the past forty-eight hours' quarrelling between the Greeks and Irish had subsided. Throughout the preparations for the arduous journey, tempers had frayed. Disguised as tourists and dockworkers, they had managed – with the help of Chief Inspector Vasilis – to transfer the illegal substance of 750 kilograms on to the three moored yachts. With the cocaine concealed inside camera and grocery bags, boxes of equipment and tools, they had repeatedly passed through the net, undetected by sniffer dogs and undercover agents who had crawled all over the town.

Michael watched the flickering lights, demarcating the Crete coastline, recede in the distance. At their current speed, he estimated a full six hours remained to the drop-off point approximately 120 kilometres south of the Peloponnesian peninsula. Theirs was the second yacht to have sailed. Declan had left first having a three-hour head start. He was to rendezvous on the open seas somewhere between Santorini and Crete. And due to sail any minute now, was Stavros.

Escaping Chania, three sleek, grey Coast Guard vessels had sailed into the port, ships Michael expected to appear on the horizon at any moment – a confrontation he would rather avoid. Armed with small arms only, they stood no chance against such heavy artillery.

The last time he had found himself in a not too dissimilar situation was twenty-two years ago in Angola fighting alongside UNITA against the MPLA – David against Goliath. Soon after jumping into Angola's second civil war he had realised that the outcome was inevitable. Outmanned and outgunned, all the courage and self-belief Jonas Savimbi's eighty thousand strong UNITA force had mustered had made no difference. Deserted by America their fate had been sealed. Alone, they had faced the MPLA, whose ranks had been reinforced by a massive Cuban contingent of one hundred and sixty thousand men.

Michael could never forget those gruelling few years spent in the African bush. Initially, crawling in the dark through the scrublands infested by venomous snakes and dangerous wildlife had not come easily. Unlike so many young mercenaries who had exchanged their European comforts for the wild, only to scurry home spooked, he had doggedly carried on. He had been transformed into a lethal predator, a killing machine: hands as deadly as a sharp knife, a sense of smell which could define indistinguishable scents, hearing which perceived near inaudible sounds, and the eyesight of a hawk spotting dangers at distances previously conceived impossible. Blending into the veldt with the grace of a leopard, he had hunted his enemies down. The stench of blood oozing out of slit throats still tainted his nostrils.

Having had no reason to live, he had feared nothing. The will to continue had ceased the day Emily had died; a stray bullet would have been welcomed. But when confronted by the will to survive by those who had suffered a fate far worse than his –

families ripped apart, killed, maimed and victimised – a deep sense of shame and self-loathing had ended his pathetic death-wish.

Many nights while sitting on a small hillock, his mind numbed, Michael had tried to make sense of it all. Suckered by world rhetoric he would fume at his own naïvety, believing he was fighting a just cause! For hours he would glare into the deceivingly calm African sunset, at the golden sky pockmarked by the dark silhouettes of the grim reapers, the large African white-backed vultures perched on top of tall baobab trees. Like lethal loudmouth politicians, these dark shadows' piercing squawks would stir the hunters into action as they patiently waited to scavenge the slaughtered remains of the defenceless, scattered in the red dust and tall grass. With the deep shadows slithering like snakes towards him, threatening to constrict his motionless body, Michael had become one with the dry thorn trees whose roots were securely anchored in the dark soil. He had felt impervious to the ferocity of the night as the African sky and plains turned red, resounding with the death throes of the antelope and wildebeest. The melancholy of Africa.

Angola, South Africa, Afghanistan, Iraq, Libya, Sudan, Syria, Ukraine. Wonder who'll be next, ripped apart, destroyed through a manipulated conflict of civil unrest? Michael thought.

Being older and wiser his understanding of international affairs boiled down to one thing: if you have what these groups of very powerful people want, whether minerals, oil, land or gullible people to ensnare by a bank credit system, you either capitulate or you'll be in big, big trouble. These manipulators, under the banner of communism, democracy, freedom of speech, human rights, capitalism, globalism or whatever other suitable ideology they might invent on the day to justify their cause, would stop at nothing.

No matter which country, no matter how many deaths, they will not stop until they get what they—

'Calling Seagull One, come in! Calling Seagull One, come in! Over.'

The sudden blare of the radio interrupted Michael's reverie. Alarmed by the strain in Stavros' voice he jumped up and raced below deck.

'Seagull One, over,' Andreas responded.

'Current position, nine kilometres from Crete. Must abort, bogie approaching! Repeat, we have to abort, over!'

'Roger that, over.'

'Advise Albatross of imminent danger. Next contact will be exactly one hour if everything OK. If not assume mission compromised, over.'

'Will do. Good luck and out,' Andreas replied, signing off.

'Andreas, how much time to our rendezvous?' Michael asked.

'If we can maintain current speed, approximately three and a half hours.'

'Contact Albatross, establish their position. Keep an eye on the radar for any approaching vessels,' Michael instructed. 'Well lads, seems the fun is about to start. Let's get this stuff ready to scuttle.'

Soon a homing device was securely lodged inside each container, activated and checked. The beeping sounds confirmed the contraband was ready to be cast overboard – locating them later should be a formality. One by one the sealed containers were heaved out of the hold and wrapped in heavy chains. Secured to the rails they were ready to be shoved into the sea at the first sign of trouble.

As the hours dragged by the ceiling of rumbling clouds overhead started to light up. The air felt clammy, heavy. But despite the gathering storm, the men's spirits rose with the radar revealing no immediate danger. The only vessel encountered so far was a lonely yacht out on a night sail. The news of Declan being well on his way to Santorini, having rendezvoused successfully, further fuelled their optimism. But they could not relax. The fact was, Stavros had failed to make contact on the hour as promised; it was an ominous sign.

And still, the radio remained silent …

With approximately seventeen kilometres to their rendezvous, the men remained alert, conscious of their precarious position. The distance completed would be no match for a powerboat, or worse a helicopter gunship.

By the time the radio finally crackled alive tensions were running high. Straining to hear Stavros' voice their bickering fell silent. 'Calling Sparrow, come in … I repeat, calling Sparrow, come in … over.'

Michael immediately understood the message. An incorrect call-name meant only one thing: Stavros had been compromised. In a flash, he reached out and flicked the radio off. Whoever was with Stavros, was trying to locate them.

CHAPTER 22

Niall's Estate
Monday

Dimitris' gloomy voice reverberated in Niall's ear, 'Good morning, we need to talk.'

'It doesn't sound like a "Good morning". Just a sec,' Niall replied.

What now? Any call at three in the morning can only mean trouble.

Quietly he exchanged the comfort of the bed for the privacy of the adjoining study; a room which was out of bounds to all. Prior to Irina's arrival, he used to spend most nights here in solitude, ensuring his businesses ran smoothly, staying ahead of the pack. Sitting down in the large high-backed leather chair he braced himself for whatever news the Greek had to share.

'That's better. The line is secure. Please continue,' he said.

'Stavros and his crew have been arrested.'

'What? Where?'

'A few kilometres off the coast of Crete. Fortunately, they did manage to dump the contraband well before they got picked up. So, there's no evidence. But they're not in the clear as yet.'

'And the others?'

'Declan completed his run without a problem. Michael's boat is still out there. But we can't reach him. Radio's off and no cell reception it seems. Could also be in trouble? I suggest you prepare for the worst.' The damning words were delivered in a monotonous voice.

'Uhm … really?'

'You don't sound too worried. May I remind you it was your partner who created this mess, costing me a great deal of money. Even worse, irreparably damaging my reputation. When word gets out it will be very bad for business, for both of us. And for that, I hold you responsible. I'll need full re—'

'Are you accusing me? Get lost!' Niall cut him off.

The phone went dead, silence. Dimitris had hung up on him. Infuriated, he slammed the phone down on the desk. Nobody treated him this way and got away with it.

'What's wrong?' Irina's sleepy voice asked by his side, looking somewhat perplexed.

'Nothing. Only a slight hiccup with a business deal. It can wait till morning,' he said, trying to sound relaxed.

He got up, forced a yawn, and led Irina by the hand back to bed, despite sleep being furthest from his mind. If one of his men were to talk, he would have no choice but to lean on his friends in the Garda. Failing that, retiring to the Caribbean might happen sooner than he had planned. It was time to get his house in order.

CHAPTER 23

Malaga, Spain
Monday Morning

With the irate voice booming in Paul's ear from across the Atlantic, the nude painting opposite his bed was of no interest. 'Did you not promise, or how did you put it, "swear on your mother's grave" that by today we'd have him out of the way for good? Now tell me, is Niall behind bars or not?'

'No, Dermot, he's not. Someone must have tipped him off. Sorry,' Paul replied feebly.

'Damn it, man! Don't give me some lousy excuse. I risk exposure and the best you can do is mumble, "sorry".'

Dermot's reaction did not surprise Paul. The time and money spent on getting a foothold in Ireland – his potential gateway into Europe – had been massive. And if Dermot was having second thoughts about backing him, he would not be surprised.

'Come to think of it, he's umm … not quite in the clear just yet. His men are being questioned. They may talk. I believe the police won't give up until they find the shipment. As soon as I have more news, I'll contact you.'

Having ratted Niall out he needed Dermot's protection more than ever. He had to deliver Niall's head on a platter. Failing that the world would not be large enough for him to hide in. Niall would not rest until he was dead.

'Amen to that,' Dermot sneered unconvinced. 'You better pray they catch him.'

CHAPTER 24

Dublin
Monday Morning

'You did say Sinead O'Donovan. And this alleged incident happened on Friday the second of June?' the Garda on duty asked, looking rather perplexed.

'Yes, that's correct,' Sean replied.

'Then, I don't understand. I have checked and double checked with all the stations in the area. There is absolutely nothing on record anywhere. Sorry.'

Sean was dumbfounded, wondering what could have happened to this report of her alleged attack by some drunk. *Had the officer on duty been too lazy and never filed the report? Unlikely, not the way she looks. Is she lying? Why … what for? What's really going on?*

Exiting the building in a hurry, he shoved the revolving door hard, eliciting a stern rebuke from the officer on duty. Ignoring the reprimand, he did not alter his pace as he rushed to return to Sinead's apartment. He needed answers.

Sinead's face crumpled as she bit her lip, listening to the accusation levelled at her. Sean had not stopped ranting since his return from the Garda.

'You're lying! I'm waiting. Spit it out, now!'

She remained silent.

'Are you protecting someone … the guy who did this to

you?' he demanded, his patience at an end. 'Sis, I'm not angry with you, please understand. I came all the way to help. Laura thought you might be in trouble, and it seems she was right. The truth this time. What happened?'

For far too long she had lived a lie. If she could not confide in him, then who? He was her brother, he should understand. She started to speak, finding the first few words the hardest.

As the room filled with her sorrowful voice, Sean's complexion turned pale. Ignoring him she continued to vent her bitterness. Amidst tears she revealed her secret life, her struggle to come to terms with her chosen path. Her three years of hell.

Sean could not believe his ears. Agitated, he paced the room. He felt the walls close in on him. Shaking his head in disgust, he blurted out, 'How could you? What were you thinking, stooping so low? My own sister a slut, a filthy whore! Poor Mum and Dad; God rest their souls. And for what … a bit of money. You must have been mad!' He struggled to contain himself not to slap her. If it were not for the bruises he would have.

Cowering on the bed petrified, wanting absolution, Sinead said, 'But you don't understand …'

'"But you don't understand", what do I not understand? There's nothing you can say which can even begin to exonerate your actions. If you had been coerced or kidnapped into prostitution maybe then I could have empathised. But by your own free will … never!' Sean shouted. Tired, drained, he sat down on the edge of her bed and clasped his head. When he spoke again his voice was distant, 'Sinead, the fact is you sell yourself for money and that's the plain and simple truth.'

Sinead's rebellious nature had suffered as much chastising as she could endure, especially by him. Exasperated, she lashed out. 'What the hell do you know about my reasons, you who ran off crying like a baby. "Oh, she cheated on me", boo-hoo, poor little Seanie! Where the hell were you when we needed you? Leaving me with no money to help the others. No, you only thought of yourself, licking your wounds somewhere in Timbuktu … or wherever! You didn't care. Never even a word. Never any offer to help. And you dare to judge me?'

Riled with hurt, guilt, confusion, both brother and sister gave vent to their emotions and traded insults without restraint.

'Enough!' a voice shouted, cutting through their bickering.

The two siblings stopped and looked at Vera.

Embarrassed, Sean hung his head. He took a deep breath and said, 'Sis, I'm sorry … I have no right …'

'So am I. I don't know what I was thinking. I just wanted …'

'It's alright, forget it. You made a mistake. What's done is done,' Sean said pulling her close to him. 'Now what are we going to do about this guy?'

'Nothing. There's no need for you to get involved.'

'What do you mean? I can't leave you like this.'

'No. Please don't interfere. It's too dangerous. You have no idea who we're up against. You'll only get hurt.'

'If you insist, I won't,' he promised. It was a promise he had no intention of keeping. He would not return to Chile until his sister was free and out of harm's way.

'Sean, this Niall McGuire is a real piece of work. Your sister's situation is bad. As much as I'd like to help, I'm not sure I can. Are you positive you've never heard of him?' Ronan asked, seated behind his sleek desk. Behind him, across the river Liffey, the sloped curved façade of Dublin's Convention Centre glistened in the sun.

'Does ring a bell. Remember I spent most of the time in Cyprus and Chile, though.'

'Of course, of course. Then a quick update on the beast we're dealing with. During the boom, this guy became one of the biggest property moguls in Ireland and the UK. He is one of the very few developers who had somehow survived the crash. He's stinking rich. Rumour has it, he has *friends* – bought or blackmailed – in all the right places: businessmen, politicians, judges, and Guards. Therefore, without definitive proof of a criminal offence, no one will take him on. Nobody is that brave or stupid. No one will last a court hearing,' Ronan sighed wearily. 'What intrigues me is him running brothels, and who knows what else. That may explain how he had managed to survive the demise of the Celtic Tiger?'

'I hear what you're saying,' Sean replied frustrated, and asked, 'Anyone you may know who has a score to settle with him. Maybe I'll get lucky.'

'No, and don't try and find volunteers. If he gets wind of it, he'll kill you both. And sneaking her off to somewhere safe. Bad idea. I reckon she knows way too much to let her go. He'll hunt her down no matter where. Then, he'll come after you. Bottom line: you'll all die.'

Sean got up and stretched out his hand for Ronan to take. 'Thanks buddy. I get what you're saying. If I'd known who he was I wouldn't have bothered you. Just forget I was here.'

Rescuing his sister was not going to be easy.

'I didn't say I won't help, so sit your arse down and stop being a prat. I said: "I'm not sure I can." I do have some connections of my own in this town and scum like him we can do without. He's got to pay for his sins, for what he's done to her and God knows who else. But I need time. Tell Sinead to sit tight. We'll find a way out of this mess. How I'm not sure just yet, but we will.'

Traversing Dublin Sean felt guilty having taken advantage of an old friend's loyalty. Theirs was a friendship which over the years had nurtured mutual trust and respect. Many nights, together with their wives, they had wined and dined in the best restaurants Dublin had to offer. Quite memorable days … until the *love of his life* had acted the whore.

And who had stood by his side? Ronan. Supporting him in his decision to travel abroad, Ronan had used his extensive network of business connections to help him secure employment in Chile as an engineer.

It gave him a chance to lick his wounds, start a new life,

and forget the painful memories of the past.

CHAPTER 25

Niall's Estate
Monday Morning

The melodious singing of the blackbird outside Niall's study did nothing to ease his foul mood. Having been up for most of the night getting his things in order, he was not in good form. Even Irina had decided to give him a wide berth. Sensing trouble she had opted for the sanctuary of Dublin's National Gallery of Art.

Women! he huffed as he leaned out of the window, shooed away the annoying bird and slammed the sash shut.

Sitting down he plucked the phone off its stand and called Ciarán. 'Be here in two hours.' he ordered.

'Yes, boss,' Niall's henchman replied icily.

Niall ignored his tone. There was no point in chastising him – his usefulness was speedily coming to an end, and sooner than he could imagine.

Next, he rang Dimitris for an update on events in Crete. Since their last conversation, he had put his men on high alert, anticipating some unpleasant incident stirred up by the Greek – an unforgiving man at best.

'Good news; second exchange was completed. They're on their way home,' Dimitris informed him with not a trace of warmth in his voice.

'Right, right. Thanks,' Niall replied and hung up.

Phoning his contact at the Garda also delivered good news.

Without hard evidence, the Greek police had been unsuccessful in linking the three detained Irishmen to the shipment of drugs. So far, no one had caved in.

Niall smiled, the first of the day, although there was one more issue to deal with. Vera.

Without looking up from his papers, Niall hollered, 'Come in!'

Ciarán's head appeared around the door with the all too familiar lifeless grey eyes. Despite his promise of allegiance, he would never trust him.

Deceitful bastard!

'Morning. Any idea where my *friend* is?' Niall asked.

'No, but we're a hundred percent sure he's not in Ireland. He's gone missing since Wednesday.'

'Really? Wow, what a surprise!' Niall mocked. 'Three days and this is all you know. Anything else?'

'No.'

'Not good enough. What are you going to do about it, or must I do everything myself? His PA, Kevin, will know where he has buggered off to. Ask him *nicely*. He doesn't come across as someone who'll put up much of a fight.'

'We tried. He's nowhere to be found either. But we've traced Paul's plane. We'll have him soon.'

'Glad you're so positive, my boy. And when you do, I want the names of all those involved. I doubt he did this on his sweet little lonesome – he doesn't have the balls. Squeeze him, and then get rid of him,' Niall said.

'Will do.'

'Right. No loose ends. You know your way out.'

Arriving at Niall's door Vera's reception was not any warmer, greeted with a dry cough and a cursory, 'Sit down.'

He looked relaxed, a demeanour which gave her reason to be concerned, wondering what he was up to. 'Thanks. What?' she asked.

Stretching his hand across the desk, he said, 'Your phone.'

Vera's jaw dropped open, feigning surprise. Expecting

trouble, she had taken precautions before her arrival; her phone held no clues which could reveal anything, or implicate anyone related to their plan if he had somehow got wind of it.

'Of course … here.'

'Good, let's see what we have. Contacts,' Niall muttered as his fingers conducted the search, scrolling down the list, and raising an eyebrow every now and then.

'Ah-ha!' he exclaimed, not indicating whose name or what he was looking at. Expertly, he correlated all possible numbers under Paul Walsh or any likely aliases with the ones he had. Nothing else came up. Nothing of worth to help locate Paul. Before handing back the phone he made a quick scribble on his notepad.

'Is that it?' Vera asked.

'Do you know where Paul is?'

She nearly fell off her chair. 'Are you mad, why would I?'

'Do you, or don't you?'

'No, I do not,' she replied firmly, twisting her fingers nervously.

'OK, fair enough,' Niall said, showing no emotion. 'That's all for now. You're excused.' *Why so jumpy my dear, what are you up to?* he mused, tapping the note on the desk with his pen.

As she got up, he said in a conciliatory tone, 'We're heading to Crete this Sunday. A nice little trip. One I definitely don't want you to miss. Therefore, make sure you stay out of trouble until then. Understood, *partner*?'

'*Da … da*, of course.'

Once more he picked up the phone. After two rings a male answered, his voice unsure, 'Glen speaking.'

'Anything to report?' Niall asked.

'Nothing yet.'

'Good. Any change, you phone me.'

'Yes, Mr McGuire. Not to worry, they're being watched around the clock,' Glen said as he focused on Vera's taxi fifty metres ahead, speeding towards Dublin.

CHAPTER 26

Dublin
Monday Evening

'Wouldn't you love a piece of her?' Mark asked while his hands deftly fiddled with the dials, adjusting the camera's angles. He zoomed in on faces and genitalia. His experience in capturing the best possible footage was guaranteed to please his client.

'You bet!' Colim drooled, his attention fixed on the one metre HDTV showing a threesome engrossed in the throes of passion. The images relayed by the four hidden cameras in the adjacent room picked up every lustful act and sound.

Blissfully unaware of the recording, the middle-aged man flouted his strict Catholic values, enjoying the *willing* nubile bodies of the two prostitutes. Taking turns, they stimulated their unsuspecting client.

'It's live and better than the shite on sex-tube,' Colm quipped. Normally these sessions were quite boring, but not tonight. He was aroused to the point of distraction, impatient to lose himself in the arms of Muriel, or any slut to be found in a pub.

Two hours later Mark finished the recording's editing. 'That's it, wrapped up and ready to roll. By the way, any idea who this guy is?'

'Not a clue. But after this, I'm sure he's fucked. Where the hell is the prat?' Colm whined. 'I need some—'

A loud knock on the door interrupted his grumbling.

'Tell your boss it's all there, mate,' Mark said, exchanging envelopes with the courier – a thumb drive in lieu of their fee for services rendered.

Adding the *trophy* to his substantial collection of VIP clients, Niall smiled, pleased with the new recording. The damning footage of unsuspecting men, women, socialites, politicians and government officials would be used in the future as and when required.

Tonight's recording was of a father of five, a pillar of society, caught in some very compromising positions. The man just couldn't resist the temptation. The honey-trap was set two months ago and had finally paid off.

Niall placed the thumb drive in his library, referenced: Chief Superintendent/Garda Bureau of Fraud Investigation, Dublin, and duly dated.

Never know when I'll need your help, Superintendent, Niall chuckled as he poured himself a stiff Jameson. Rolling the clear amber liquid in the crystal cut glass, he wondered how events were panning out in Greece. Things have gone too quiet, far too quiet. Until his men were safely home, he remained vulnerable.

CHAPTER 27

Peloponnesian Peninsula
Mediterranean
Monday Midnight

Niall's concerns were not unfounded as at that very moment, Michael and his men were caught up in the midst of a fierce Mediterranean storm. The earlier gentle breeze, the harmless field of tiny white sails flitting across the dark sea had been replaced by a howling gale. Gushing in from the northeast the wind attacked the small yacht with vigour. Powerless against the three-metre-high waves they were tossed back and forth.

Michael held on and squinted into the driving rain, his vision severely curbed by the blackness of the night. On the port side, the rocky coastline of the Peloponnesian Peninsula threatened to demolish the yacht if they strayed any closer. Despite the heavy seas, he was confident in making landfall soon.

Ploughing north, the strong engine drove them forward; below deck, its monotonous purr gave some degree of comfort to the men sheltering in the confined space.

Once more the bow soared steeply into the dark and slammed down. A flash of light lit up the lethal, jagged rocks resembling the drooling teeth of Cerberus, the three-headed guard dog of the underworld. Loud thunder rolled across the water, adding to the unfolding drama.

Above the noise, Michael heard Andreas' anxious voice shout, 'Michael, quick, look at this. I think we have company.'

Crashing into the cabin Michael bent down to get a closer look. 'Where?'

As Andreas' trembling index finger stabbed at the monitor, he shouted, 'There. It's coming in fast and straight for us.'

'How far?' Michael asked, surrounded by the other men clamouring to see what was happening.

'Seven kilometres and closing.'

'We have ten minutes at the most. I suggest we get rid of the money,' Michael said, observing the unanimous nodding of heads.

'What about the guns?' Aiden asked.

'Everything goes, except the ones you're carrying. Or else we may have to explain why we're on a chartered cruise with enough weapons to start our own bloody holy war,' Michael cautioned.

Wanting to get a visual on the approaching ship he shoved past the men and scampered up the steps. But in the raging storm, it was impossible to see anything. He turned and shouted at the men who seemed to hesitate.

'What the hell are you waiting for?' Michael repeated, lifting the first container jammed with small bills.

Following suit, the men reluctantly shoved the few sealed containers with their homing devices into the wild sea.

With the evidence gone the three Irishmen went below deck and donned their survival kits brought along for such an emergency. Their weatherproof jackets contained enough rations, money and sealed travel documents to ensure a safe passage home.

As they re-emerged on deck the Coast Guard's spotlight hit their portside full-on, lighting them up like a proverbial Christmas tree. Feigning panic-stricken holidaymakers, the three men waved anxiously, desperate to reach the shelter of the nearest port. Above the storm, the dull clunks of the four grapplers hitting the deck were barely audible. Gripping securely the yacht was slowly reeled in. At two metres a gangway dropped on to the deck. Ignoring the pitch of the yacht, six armed marines and an officer raced on board. Without a word, they commenced their search.

Avoiding eye contact Michael glanced over his shoulder and watched Andreas confront the captain. The initial affable overtures were soon replaced by a fierce exchange of words, forcing Andreas to back down. Shunned, he turned and whispered to his fellow Greeks. The angry frown on Andreas' forehead did not bode well. As casually as possible, a challenging task under the circumstances, Michael edged his way up to the Greek. 'What's going on?' he asked.

'Nothing my friend, nothing,' Andreas replied. He looked nervous and was obviously lying.

'Rubbish!' Michael growled, tempted to grab and squeeze the truth out of him. But the only response he got was a nasty sneer and an apoplectic shrug of the shoulders. No further confirmation was needed; things were about to turn ugly. 'You try anything stupid and I'll kill you.'

It was time to get out of there.

Slowly he worked his way back to Aiden and Paddy, and whispered, 'If you want to survive follow me.'

Neither hesitated.

The three Irishmen moved further along the rail, away from the gunship. It was not much of a distance, but with the storm and total darkness, they might just have a chance. Behind them, Andreas was once more involved in a war of words with the officer. With arms waving, the Greeks' tempers were fraying fast. Shouts escalated. It was clear the rehearsed story of stricken tourists at sea did not convince anyone.

A loud clap exploded on deck as Alex fired his Smith & Wesson's .500 Magnum at point-blank range in the face of the captain, splitting his head wide open.

The next instant all hell broke loose as the 12.7mm machine gun mounted on the patrol boat's foredeck burst into action.

Alex was its first victim. Clothes and wads of shredded

money filled the space where he had stood a second before. As the bullets slammed into his body their impact somersaulted him into the air. For a fraction of a second, he hung suspended in mid-air as the bullets continued to rake his lifeless corpse, scattering body parts in all directions.

'Now, move it!' Michael shouted, ready to jump.

Behind him a battle erupted.

Firing wildly, the two remaining Greeks dived for cover, hunted by the spray of bullets raking the yacht. The sudden explosion blew Michael into the air as an orange ball of fire rose upwards, illuminating the blank faces of the marines standing on the patrol boat's foredeck.

Dazed and winded, Michael spluttered and coughed, fighting the water threatening to fill his lungs. Pulled under by the raging sea, he helplessly descended into the darkness.

CHAPTER 28

Niall's Estate,
Monday Night

'They have recovered seven bodies so far. At first light they'll continue their search. But there's little hope of survivors. It seems all of them died during the explosion. Even if some of them did manage to escape, no one would have reached land; the storm would have seen to that.' Dimitris' voice droned morosely over the phone. 'They will send in divers in the—'

'Um, right … just a sec,' Niall interrupted; he was on an unsecured line. 'I'll phone you back in a minute.' His foreboding had been correct; things had been too quiet.

A few minutes later his scrambled voice travelled through the airwaves, deep in discussion, arguing who was responsible for the disaster, with some of the bodies having had wads of cash-strapped to them.

Dimitris blamed the Irish and held Niall accountable for the loss of his twenty million euro. 'I want full compensation from you. Your men got greedy.'

'Really? Well, you can dream on. I won't pay you a bloody cent. By the way, what makes you so certain my men were responsible?' he asked, his voice even, unruffled, while silently cursing the deceased. Potentially, they could cost him a small fortune, and send the hounds after him. A full investigation was sure to follow. He felt no remorse for the loss of his men.

Woken by the drone of Niall's voice, Irina stirred in her sleep. She got up, and guided by the slip of light underneath the study door, approached without a sound.

Unable to catch much of what was being discussed, she turned away unperturbed. She would know soon enough what the row was about.

CHAPTER 29

Mediterranean Sea
Peloponnesian Peninsula

Emerging from the depths, coughing and spluttering for air, Michael was tossed about like a cork. Fighting the waves which crashed on to the Peloponnesian peninsula, his senses guided him towards safety. For nearly an hour, with muscles aching, he struggled on, trying to reach land.

Once more a wave lifted him up into the air and slammed him mercilessly against the rocks. Trying to hold on he was sucked back into the cauldron of foaming water. With his legs as useless as the tentacles of a jellyfish against the forceful pull of the tide, he thrashed the water, searching for a foothold. His lungs felt like bursting. At last, the tips of his shoes gripped on to something solid. He propelled himself upwards with all his strength. Breaking the surface, he hungrily gulped in mouthfuls of fresh air. Alarmed by the hovering searchlight a few metres to his left, he immediately disappeared into the depths again. Fighting to remain submerged with the bright light hanging threateningly above his head, he waited …

At last, darkness!

Exhausted, he broke the surface and pulled his battered body out of the sea. He looked up and stared in disbelief at the cliff face, a wall of solid rock blocking his way.

Crawling out of the sea a massive wave crashed down on

top of him and tossed him into the air yet again. He reached out and clawed at the slippery rock, further shredding his already torn fingers and nails. But he refused to let go; blocking out the pain, he held on. For a few seconds the sea relaxed its pull. He readied himself, and as it surged once more, he scrambled free.

Deftly, ignoring the driving rain and wind, his hands felt their way in the dark. Slowly he edged his way up. Having climbed a few metres he paused and waited for the giddiness to pass. With his pulse slowed down he continued his ascent, free-climbing hand over fist.

After what felt like an eternity, his burning fingers reached inside a crevice disgorging a timid stream of water. It was large enough to crawl through. He did not hesitate and slipped into the tunnel. A few seconds later he emerged inside a small cave of no more than three and a half metres deep with its roof narrowing steeply, ending in an opening of approximately fifty centimetres in diameter. It was a small cocoon, barely high enough to stand in, but more than adequate for the night. He sat down. With his back pressed against the hard rock surface, he breathed deeply and relaxed.

Fumbling in the dark he unzipped the pockets of his jacket and retrieved his survival kit. Ripping open a pouch he gulped down one of the energy drinks relishing the sweet taste of sugar his body craved.

Soaked to the bone he kicked off his Timberland combat boots, his socks, trousers, boxers, jacket and shirt. Having wrung out his clothes as best he could, he put his boxers and jacket back on with the rest spread out to dry. Thankfully the air was warm despite the storm. Next, he cleaned and dried his pistol and bullets. Sealed inside its protective pocket his phone was still in working order. But he had no reception.

Having disinfected his wounds – his torn hands, nails and fingers – he applied some waterproof plasters which lessened the discomfort to some degree. He sat back and fell into a fitful sleep, wondering whether Aiden and Paddy had survived.

Michael jolted awake, disorientated by the stillness and filtering dawn. The rain had stopped. A warm breeze filtered soothingly through the tunnel. The cave was dry, as were his clothes.

Lying in the mouth of the tunnel he found himself ten storeys above a mist-covered sea. It was as calm as a lake with not a sound to be heard. Looking down, he whistled out loud, amazed that he had succeeded in climbing the cliff in the thralls of a lashing storm. The Irish luck had been on his side.

Not someone to entertain such idle thoughts he planned his next move; his assignment had to be completed. Now was not the time to quit as too little intel had been gathered to date. He would have to persevere. But first, an alternative hiding place had to be found. Cooped up in this hole until nightfall wasn't a palatable thought. And any escape attempt to the top of the cliff in the moonlight would be madness. This time he might not be so lucky. On top of that, his hands hurt like hell.

Studying the little bit of shoreline visible through the breaking fog something in the seaweed caught his eye. He craned his neck for a better view.

A half-naked body!

It rolled over …

Aiden, his face mauled by the sea.

Michael sighed as the thought of Paddy having suffered the same fate troubled him.

A sudden distant rumble made him look up. Through the clearing fog a helicopter hovered above two patrol boats scouring the area. He cursed and disappeared back into the cave.

With the search in full swing he would not be going anywhere; sitting it out was his only option. Or he could try and worm his way through the opening in the cave's ceiling and escape to the top.

Standing upright he inspected the chute where a glimmer of light bounced temptingly down its throat. As he had thought, it was a possible way out.

Deftly his numbed fingers started to scrape at the brittle wet sandstone, searching for weak spots caused by years of decay. Soon small pieces came away in his hand. Using his hunter's knife, he raked at the soft stone. Bit by bit the opening grew in size.

A sudden loud thump-thump noise, accompanied by the ear-splitting whine of turbines, stopped his digging. As the light of the cave grew dark – the sun blocked by the helicopter – he forced himself into the throat of the chute and raised his feet out of sight. Half-seated he clamped his ears and waited for the noise to subside.

As silence returned to his lair he dropped on to the floor and hurriedly slithered to the mouth of the cave. He peered outside. Aiden's body was gone. There was no one to be seen anywhere. No one was searching the rocks below.

Ignoring the activities at sea, Michael returned to prising away the brittle stone in creating an opening large enough for him to escape through.

After a few hours he stopped; it would have to do.

Starting to climb, the thought of the chute narrowing and blocking his ascent, niggled. He disliked caving, always had and always would. While training as an insurgent in France, it was a weakness he had discovered on his first compulsory caving expedition. Fighting his claustrophobia, he laboured on and at about ten metres from the top, the chute widened.

He was free.

Two minutes later Michael popped his head out into the open. Feeling the comforting rays of the sun on his face he was tempted to continue. But with no fog as cover, he would be exposed, inviting unwanted attention. He could not rule out the possibility of several foot-patrols or some binoculars, combing the area for survivors.

He slid back down to the safety of the cave; it would have to do until nightfall.

CHAPTER 30

Blackrock, Dublin
Tuesday Afternoon

'Of course, I appreciate his help. But you must understand one thing: he'll kill him, his family and you,' Sinead said as an expression of dread spread across her face. 'Please, you have to stop him before it's too late. Actually, why am I asking? No, I insist,' she corrected herself. 'I will not live with your blood or theirs on my hands, no ways!'

'OK … I'll call him. But only if you promise to do as I've asked,' Sean replied.

'Yes, I shall. And believe me, I won't do anything foolish either. So, don't worry. When you are all, and I mean all, out of harm's way, I'll come to Chile,' she reiterated, smiling sweetly.

Sean was not convinced; her eagerness to comply was a dead giveaway. He knew she was lying. She was no longer the innocent girl he used to know. 'Sis, who're you kidding … why is it I don't believe you?'

She did not respond, except for feigning shock at the implied accusation.

'Right, sure, I'll see you later,' he said. Fed up with her game he gave her a quick kiss goodbye.

'Okay … until then … bye,' she said averting her eyes, hiding the welling tears as her hand fleetingly brushed his cheek.

On his way out, Sean rang Ronan. The news was not good. 'Sorry, buddy, I think it's too late. My contact would have phoned Niall by now.'

Sean stopped in his tracks, his hand resting on the doorknob. 'Please, for your own sake, stop him. Maybe he has not made the call?'

'I hear what you're saying, but this is the only way she'll go free. I don't blame her for being scared considering what he's done to her. Yeah, sure, Niall's dangerous. But he'd be deranged to try and touch me or my family,' Ronan said confidently. 'He is supposed to be an upstanding citizen and not some punk. It really is unimaginable that he would go that far.'

Swayed, Sean replied, 'Right, you've got a point. We'll do it your way. I won't tell her. And I'll speak to you later. Take care, you never—'

The chime of the doorbell stopped him short, and with a, 'Got to go, cheers,' Sean ended the call. Without a second thought, he opened the front door. 'Good afternoon, may I help you?' he asked.

Confronted by a pair of green eyes, twinkling inquisitively, he stood aside, welcoming the stranger in.

'Hello, Vera and Sinead live here?' the unassuming voice asked.

'Yes … um … yes,' he stammered, awkwardly. 'Yes … of course. And you are?'

'Irina Mironova.'

'Nice to meet you. I'm Sean, Sinead's brother. Just a sec. Sinead … Vera, someone's here for ye!'

The visitor's striking features not lost on him, he regretted leaving. 'Sorry, I've got to run. Hope to see you again soon. Cheers.'

On entering the lounge, Irina clasped her hand over her mouth, shocked.

'Who are you?' Sinead asked, puzzled.

'This is Irina,' Vera said, and turning to Irina, she

116

demanded, 'What are you doing here? How come you know where we live?'

'I bribed one of Niall's men, on the Q.T., to find your address – I was worried about Sinead. I saw her forced into the car at Niall's.'

'I'm just grand … thanks,' Sinead replied icily. 'If you were so concerned about my well-being, why didn't you try and stop them? Or were you too scared to upset your boyfriend? So please, spare me your sympathy and just go,' Sinead said, not interested in making further conversation.

'Manners, Sinead. Be nice,' Vera said, trying to ease the tension, wanting to know more about their visitor before she would leave. *Why this surprise visit, is this Niall's doing?* she wondered.

Ignoring Sinead's hostility, Irina persisted, 'I'm really sorry for what they've done. How do you feel?'

Sinead laughed sarcastically. 'I told you, just grand … I'll live.'

'That's good to hear. I hope the bruising will be gone in time for the big day.'

'What big day?!' Sinead asked.

'Your wedding with Ciarán, of course. Niall told me.'

Sinead's mouth dropped open in disbelief. 'Irina, I'll let you in on a little secret. Your boyfriend Niall is the reason I look like this.'

'And Ciarán, does he know he did this to you?'

'You don't get it. There's no wedding. Ciarán is Niall's butcher. He is not my fiancée. Never has … never will be. Niall's playing you,' Sinead corrected her.

'Oh … I see. But why beat you up like this?'

'You mean, "beat and rape you like this".'

'I don't quite follow …?'

'This is what one looks like after being tied up, raped, beaten and abused for six hours by a group of bastards.'

Irina's face turned pale. 'My God, who could do such a thing … Why?'

'Savages to whom this is normal. And why? Because I'm

117

sick and tired of whoring for him. Irina, truth is, I … we, are both escorts. I rebelled and this is the result. Wasn't the first time either. And next time I'll be dead, you can bet on that.'

'What are you going to do?'

'Nothing. There's nothing I … any of us can do. We'll just have to play the obedient little girls, keep our mouths shut and spread our legs,' Vera interjected, alarmed by the line of questioning. 'Tell me, what's this between you and Niall? How did you meet?' she asked, changing the topic.

'Right … okay. When I finished my law degree I—'

'You're not serious!' Vera exclaimed. As far as she was concerned only somebody ignorant would fall for one of Niall's scams, for a *better life* in the so-called *Free West*. And Irina was no ignorant young girl, of that she was certain.

'As I was saying, I came to Ireland to gain experience, improve my English, earn real money, return home and start my own business.'

'Fair enough. Makes sense. And are you also hoping to catch a husband while you're at it?' Vera scoffed sarcastically.

'No, no … Not yet, anyway,' she laughed.

'Did you ever do a background check on the company who arranged your work permit and documents?'

'Yes. Did I miss something?'

'Yes, you did,' Vera said.

'What?'

'Not everything that shines is gold; this can all just be an illusion … a scam. Just know this: he's extremely dangerous. So be very, very careful. Sorry, I didn't tell you this in Crete, but Niall had warned me to stay away from you, to mind my own business.'

'Oh … that explains your odd behaviour. Thanks anyway.'

'And make sure you don't end up in one of his brothels once he tires of you.'

'Don't worry, I won't. Thanks for the warning.'

'Another thing you can be sure of; you'll never see his office despite your glorious work permit. Best you get away from him as far as you can, and as soon as you can. And for

God's sake, don't get trapped ... don't fall for his charms. I'll let you in on a little secret. I fell for him when I was destitute, went through the same routine you're going through now and before I knew what was happening found myself back where I had started. I was not the first, and, believe me, neither will you be the last.'

Somewhat surprised by the news of Vera having shared her lover and still working for him, she asked, 'Then why are you still here, doing this?'

'Very simply put: he will not permit either Sinead or me to leave. We know far too much about his world, his businesses. If we talk, it will ruin him. So, we're trapped. The only way out for us will be with a bullet in the back of the head,' Vera said. Although a far deeper secret, one she intended to take to her grave, prevented her from ever returning to Russia. 'Irina, why don't you go home before it's too late?'

Irina nodded, contemplating Vera's words. Turning her attention to Sinead she said, 'Forgive me for asking, why did you choose this life?'

'What can I say? Look, I thought I knew what I was doing and walked into this with my eyes wide open. Depressed, feeling sorry for myself, the temptation of an easy life came along and I jumped for it. I was young, gullible and stupid. Very, very stupid. At first, the new *glamorous* world of an escort did earn me lots of money. But soon I became disillusioned, bitter. It was a world I had known nothing about, and it consumed me bit by bit. Life became a living hell, one I now know I can never survive. So here I am, stuck. Like Vera said, we know far too much about him. Best we accept our fate. As far as I'm concerned, I know he'll use me till I can't earn big bucks anymore and then he'll throw me into one of his brothels where I'll work on my back till I die.'

'Surely, you can get away … somewhere he can't find you?'

'No, Irina, there's nowhere to go. All we can do is stay on his good side and hope for the best. And my advice to you is the same as Vera's: run as far and fast from here while you still can.'

Having shut the apartment door behind Irina, Sinead asked, 'What do you make of her?'

'Don't know?' Vera replied. 'Something about her bugs me. I ask myself what is she really doing here … I mean, here in Ireland?'

'Do you think she was sent to spy on us? Maybe he suspects what we're up to? Maybe our flat's bugged?' Sinead asked, startled by her own words. In a panic, she anxiously looked around and started lifting pillows, portraits, lamps …

'What are you doing? Relax! If he was listening, we would already be dead,' Vera said, giggling. 'Look at you. One would swear you're in some spy movie!' Vera could not suppress her laughter as Sinead sheepishly replaced a reading lamp. 'If he had slipped in some bugs since we last checked, then Irina most definitely would not have been sent to spy on us. No, I think she was sincere enough and was only trying to make new friends. She really looked shocked and upset by your condition and what I told her. I do think she believes us. I just hope she doesn't now confront him. Although, somehow, I think she knows more than she pretends. Who can tell? Anyway, it won't really matter after tonight.'

'Yes, you're right. But to be honest, I'm very sad. I hate myself for having lied to Sean,' Sinead said, remembering the quick peck planted on his cheek as the blatant lie had seared her tongue. 'I'll miss them terribly.'

'You'll see them again, you will … one day. You're still young and Niall's threats may disappear with time. Or someone may take him out. With the number of enemies he's making, I won't be surprised. Okay, enough of this, we better get started. We only have four hours. And I still have to do my magic on you.'

CHAPTER 31

Niall's Estate
Tuesday Afternoon

Incensed, having dealt with uncooperative bankers for the past two hours, Niall wondered when the housing market would fully recover, chugging along in the aftermath of the most devastating building slump in Irish history. Nothing built for years, combined with uncontrolled immigration during this period, created a massive shortage in housing stock. And with skilled labour in short supply, many having fled with the demise of the Celtic Tiger, projects were slow to complete.

Thankfully, growth was evident everywhere, although still far from satisfactory. Potential house buyers were queuing up, but with no funds. Twelve years ago, the banks threw money at a gullible market and in the process wrecked the economy. Yet again, they're not helping, pulling in the reins too tight, stifling recovery.

At the first signs of an economic downturn with the bubble over-inflated to bursting, Niall had curtailed his investments in the Irish real estate market, thereby, surviving the economic implosion which had crippled the country, ruining most property developers.

For the past four years he had been buying repossessed vacant properties, sick building sites and buildable land. Reluctant to invest his own funds for construction he had turned to the banks but found negotiations frustrating at best, requiring a great deal of patience.

And, because of his cautious nature, he had insisted on diamonds as payment for the drug deal with Dimitris. The uncertainty of the euro, plus the increase of tensions between NATO and Russia, gave him good reason to be careful.

Diamonds, hard currency, was prime. Although it was of no value locked away inside Vera's safe-deposit box. He would sleep a lot better with these stones in his own vault. The sooner they were retrieved from Crete the better.

The shrill chirp of the phone interrupted his deliberations. 'Yes?' he answered.

'What the hell's going on, Niall?' a high pitch voice squealed in his ear.

'Who's this?

'Eoin.'

'Right, right. What do you want?' Niall asked, irate.

'A friend asked me to intervene on behalf of a certain young lady, Sinead O'Donovan. Apparently, she works for you. He claims she had been gang-raped and severely beaten at your behest. It's a very serious allegation. They want her released from your service without any vendetta, and if not, they intend to file charges.'

'Hang on, my boy. I've no idea what you're talking about. But, tell you what, I'll look into it. When was this supposed to have happened?'

'I'm not your "boy", and don't brush me off; I'm not an idiot!' Eoin shouted. 'You know exactly what I'm talking about. For God's sake, you don't need such exposure. Let her go. Believe me, they won't give up. She's not worth the headache. I'm warning you, this is no joke.'

'Do you hear me laughing? I said I'll look into it and do what I have to, if anything. Tell me, who made these wild allegations?' Niall asked, adding, 'By the way, a word of caution, never raise your voice at me again or you can kiss your illustrious career goodbye, Mr Minister of the bloody environment.'

The threat was all it took for Eoin to back down. Without further encouragement, he told Niall all he knew. Listening, Niall thought: *you may think you know me, but you have no idea what I'm capable of. You are so predictable you little prick! You've no stomach for a life without the fanfare, money and glamour!*

'You better contact your friends at the Garda to stop any investigation. Her brother Sean has already reported the incident,' Eoin cautioned.

'Right, right.'

'And what do I tell my friend?'

'Whatever the hell you want. You're the politician and bullshit comes naturally to you guys,' Niall mocked and ended the conversation.

Not complacent, he knew immediate action was required and jotted down a strategy to stop the rot from spreading – the situation could not be allowed to deteriorate. First there was Paul, then Ronan and Sean – some digging was needed to find out what made these two morons tick – and Eoin. Plus, the diamonds to be collected in Greece. He scratched his head as he looked at the names, somewhat surprised at how many candidates to eliminate had unexpectedly surfaced over the last few days.

His scribbles were interrupted by an update from Ciarán, confirming Paul to be hiding in Malaga. 'And I'm leaving in the hour to bring the rat home,' Ciarán said.

'No, forget that. Be here, six sharp,' Niall ordered.

With the next call, another meeting was arranged. Also, to be held in the privacy of his study.

Sipping coffee in the old farm-style kitchen, Irina asked, 'How long have you been working here?'

'About ten months,' Anne replied somewhat nervously, biting her already chewed fingernails, unsure of Irina's intentions.

'Relax, have a coffee ... please, sit down. I can do with some female company. Men can be so boring; if they're not saving the world, they are busy destroying it,' Irina said

123

conspiratorially.

'Thanks, but only for a minute. I have to finish the prepping for dinner or I'll be in trouble,' Anne said, smiling bashfully. Her highlighted brown hair was pulled tight into a bun behind her head.

'Mmm …' Irina responded and took another sip of her coffee while studying the spotless kitchen. No doubt Anne's handiwork, slaving away at all hours. The walnut units were polished to a healthy shine, as were the black granite worktops. Copper pots and kitchen utensils dangled neatly in rows from the suspended frame over the large island. 'Where are you from?' she asked.

'Castlepollard, West Meath.'

'Where's that?'

'Middle of nowhere. About eighty kilometres somewhere north-west of Dublin, I reckon. Small town, but it's home. All my siblings are still there, so.'

'How many are you?'

'Only seven.'

'Only seven! My goodness, that's a lot of mouths to feed!'

'Yeah, tell me about it. So, I help, so. My parents can't manage on their own. My dad was retrenched during the crash. He could never find another job since, except for the odd ones at minimum wage. He's too old. Mum helps at the local grocery store. So, as I said, I need this job.'

'Sorry to hear that. But between you and me, maybe it's a good idea to look for a better opportunity, one less stressful.'

'Is it that obvious?'

'Uhm,' Irina nodded. 'He hasn't offered you any other position by any chance?'

'No. Even if he does, I won't do it. I've heard rumours …'

'Such as?'

'Sorry, I've got to get back to work. And thanks for the chat so,' Anne said and got up just as the head chef made his entry.

'You're welcome,' Irina replied. Her voice warm, slightly relieved. *Well, at least she is still only a cook and nothing more.*

'Pardon me for not looking. How clumsy,' Ciarán apologised, bumping into Irina as he shut the study door behind him. He steadied her by the arm and looked her up and down, undressing her with his eyes.

'You mind!' Irina snapped, folding her arms over her breasts, blocking his gaze.

'Sorry, how rude of me,' he laughed, instantly disliking the cocky young woman who strutted about the house as if she owned it. *Enjoy it while it lasts miss. I'll get you to bend over when he throws you out.*

Pushing past him, she knocked on the study door.

'Come in,' Niall's voice boomed.

As she entered, Niall's dour face lit up, beckoning her closer. Ending his telephone conversation his voice trailed off like an old steam locomotive chugging out of a lonely village in the still of the night, 'Right, I've got to go. We'll talk later, bye-bye, bye … bye … bye.' Turning his attention to Irina, he asked, 'How was your day? Did you manage a bit of shopping while you were in town?'

'Yes, I did. Do you like it?' she said, pirouetting, letting the flowing floral dress swirl up, exposing her smooth firm legs. The dress which was bought on the way home without much ado, served as a cover story for her impromptu visit to Dublin. The item of clothing meant nothing to her, and it mattered even less whether he approved or not. Suppressing her welling anger, triggered by the disturbing visit to Vera and Sinead, she smiled feebly.

'What's wrong? You look upset.'

'Who was that?' she asked, pointing at the door.

'Ciarán. Why?'

'He seems a bit bold,' she laughed, playing down the annoying encounter.

'What do you mean, was he hitting on you?' he asked. 'If he did, I'll deal with him.'

'Yes … I think he was,' the words slipped out.

Infuriated, he started to rise, growling, 'Punk! I'll take care of him. Believe me, I won't—'

'Please, not now,' Irina cut him off. She could not risk Niall getting killed, not now. 'Just forget him. It was nothing, really.'

'You sure?'

'Yes.'

'If you say so. But, I'll have a chat with him later, guaranteed. It won't happen again,' Niall promised, simmering down. 'Right then, how about a smile? It's a beautiful evening, let's have a drink outside. Remember, in Ireland you'll learn to use every opportunity of sunshine as you never know when you'll be blessed with another spell of glorious weather. Trust me, these occasions are not to be wasted.'

He slipped out from behind the old mahogany desk, took her by the hand, and led her to the patio located to the rear of the mansion; it was a favourite spot to enjoy the late afternoon sun. She coyly played along despite his hand feeling like a burning ember in hers.

Surrounded by a huge expanse of wisteria in full bloom with clusters of violet clinging to the white wooden pergola, they made themselves comfortable on the cushioned wicker settee. Casually he stroked her hand. The mood was rather tranquil except for the scraping noise somewhere behind them where one of the gardeners, a well-built Pole in his early forties, feverishly weeded the flowerbeds.

'Jacek, you can attend to that tomorrow, thanks,' Niall ordered, somewhat riled. Without a word the man picked up his tools and scurried off. 'That's better, at last some peace and quiet.'

After a few minutes she withdrew her hand from his and said, 'Please excuse me. I have to phone my parents. It has been quite a while since I spoke to them.' Not waiting for his permission, she got up.

'Of course, my dear. Please, go ahead.'

'Thank you,' she replied, nearly blurting out, "The last thing I am is your dear!" Starting to punch in the number, she sauntered off to the solitude of her bedroom.

CHAPTER 32

Peloponnesian Peninsula
Greece
Tuesday Night

The moonlight bathed the plateau in deep shades of grey. For the second time in less than five hours, Michael's head appeared at the top of the chute, surveying the area. All seemed quiet. Careful not to dislodge any stones he climbed over the crumbling edge and started to leopard-crawl, letting his body merge with the near barren terrain. But with his skills rusty the fluid gliding motion of years ago did not come easily. Not wanting to crack a twig or frighten a small animal – alerting a possible nearby patrol – progress was slow.

At fifteen metres he paused and listened for signs of danger: a crunch of a boot, a cough, a whisper, the flight of a startled animal. But the only sounds he heard were the shrill courting rituals of tiny insects escaping from the fissures in the ground. Overhead the erratic flap of a bat made him look up. In the distance a dog barked. Nothing else. The night belonged to him.

He jumped up and ran crouched from shrub to shrub, swiftly moving towards the seclusion of the hills. The lights of a small settlement up ahead forced a detour. Reaching higher ground, he checked his location on his phone's GPS – still no signal!

Monemvasia was five kilometres to the south. Convinced the police would have the fortified coastal village under surveillance he headed in a south-westerly direction. With the coastline and the Greek Rock of Gibraltar on his left, he aimed to intersect the national road north-west of the small town.

Making steady progress the sudden sound of dogs yapping forced him to drop to the ground.

Trackers, damn!

The noise, coming from a small group of houses approximately four hundred metres east, was not getting any closer…

Is someone else out here?

Sheltering behind a bush, he waited.

A few minutes later a figure raced past: male, 1.8 metres tall, face darkened, cropped hair, young and lean. He looked familiar but it was hard to tell. Quietly Michael followed him. Suddenly the man tripped.

'Feckin' hell!' he cursed, grabbing his ankle.

Recognising the voice, Michael called, 'Psst, Paddy.'

'Jaysus, you're alive! I thought I'm the only one who made it!'

'Glad to see you too.'

'They won't get rid of me that easily,' Paddy chuckled. 'Just give me a sec, I sprained my ankle.' Gingerly, he got up. 'Okay, I'm good to go.'

'You realise Aiden didn't make it,' Michael said.

The young man's shoulders slumped. 'Poor Eileen and the kids,' he mumbled. 'Bad enough him being dead, but the news involving him in some drug deal will ruin her.'

'Yeah … well, no need for her to know the truth. We'll spin her some story. Right, let's go.' Not waiting for a reply, he turned and set off.

In less than thirty minutes they stepped on to the national road. Hitting tarmac, they fell into a rhythmic lope, their feet lapping up kilometre after kilometre towards Sykea. Occasionally their silence was interrupted by the recounting of their narrow escape, or when forced to dive for cover at an approaching car. After an hour of maintaining a punishing pace, they were dehydrated, tired, with the contents of their survival packs long since depleted.

'I can suck the sweat from a tinker's sock,' Paddy complained.

Thirsty, eager to replenish their sapped energies, the flickering neon light of an isolated country hotel lured them like moths to a flame. Casually, they strolled into the hotel's parking lot. There was still some activity at the pool and bar, a few late-night revellers.

Under the carpark lighting, Michael looked Paddy up and down and then at himself. 'I think you better do the honours. I most definitely can't,' he said.

'No problem. Yes, you're a right mess old man,' Paddy chuckled. Discarding his combat jacket, he cleaned himself as best he could.

'I'll get transport. See you back here in five,' Michael said.

Confidently, Paddy approached the bar. Spotting a vending machine his mind was made up.

Better deal with a mechanical contraption than an over-courteous barman.

Added to the cuts, bruises and filthy clothes which screamed for attention was his strong Irish accent to consider. For all he knew their photos might already have been broadcast on local TV as breaking news: "Irish Criminals Wanted!" Cherishing the thought, he raided the vending machine with gusto. With his arms piled and pockets stuffed with junk food, chocolate bars, crisps and soft drinks he strolled outside, trusting Michael had successfully hotwired a car.

The laid-back barman's eyes followed the dishevelled visitor leaving the building. The instant he was out of sight he dropped the tea towel; polishing the glasses could wait.

Slowly, not to draw attention, Michael swung their newly *acquired* Volkswagen Golf on to the national road.

Without a GPS – wanting to remain off-grid they had

129

removed their phones' batteries – Paddy searched the glove compartment for a roadmap. 'Got it.'

A quick glance confirmed only one major road leading to Athens, a destination where they planned to mingle with the large numbers of tourists. They had to reach Athens before their presence could be reported, therefore the slow side roads were ruled out.

As the hotel receded behind them, Michael accelerated towards Sparta, wanting to put as much distance between them and the steep cliffs they had miraculously escaped from.

But unknown to them, the news of a dubious-looking foreigner arriving at one in the morning at an isolated hotel in the Monemvasia region had already been shared with the local police, and in turn, referred to the commander-in-charge of the search operation.

CHAPTER 33

Blackrock, Dublin
Tuesday Midnight

The thought of Sinead and Vera lying spread-eagled on the floor crossed Sean's mind. Two hours ago, he had taken up surveillance in the quiet Blackrock street. But since then there had been no movement in the top floor apartment. The curtains had remained untouched, not a shadow had moved inside nor had a soul ventured outside on to the dark spacious terrace. There was no sign of life other than the lonely silhouette of a large crow perched on top of the balustrade – its short jerky hops towards an open window was not a good sign.

Unable to reach them by phone, he had made the journey to their apartment in the middle of the night, what by now seemed a wasted trip. Hammering on their door had delivered no results either. His initial thought that they might have stepped out for dinner, a drink and nothing more sinister started to evaporate.

Cooped up in the stuffy interior of the small rental his legs cramped. He needed a brisk walk to stretch his legs and get some fresh air. But something did not feel right. Ignoring the discomfort, he stayed put.

A few minutes later a black BMW 330i pulled into a parking space up ahead. Was it not for the occupants remaining seated, making no attempt to exit the vehicle, Sean would not have suspected anything odd. Nor did they seem to be lovers enjoying a moment in private.

With his attention focused on the black sedan, he failed to notice the Opel which pulled out of the parking bay five spaces back, followed by two pairs of curious eyes cast in his direction as the vehicle crawled past.

CHAPTER 34

Malahide, Dublin
Tuesday Midnight

The doorbell rang a second time. *Who could it be at such an ungodly hour?* Ronan wondered. Forcing himself out of bed, he put on his dressing gown and moccasins and went downstairs. Without a sound, he followed the line of recessed lights set in the polished marble floor. He yawned lazily.

Upstairs, his small family was sound asleep. He hoped it was not some bachelor friends desiring a nightcap after a night out, forgetting that he was now happily married and could not afford such interruptions any longer. His days of being free and single were something of the past.

He opened the door.

For an instant the sight of four hooded men made him freeze, unable to grasp what was about to happen. Barging inside, the biggest, a two-metre heavyset monster, grabbed him by the neck with one hand while the other covered his mouth. The large hand squeezed his throat. He could not breathe. Nor could he utter a sound to warn his wife.

'You, Ronan? If so, nod!' the man with grey lifeless eyes growled.

It was not a time for mind games. If he and his family were to survive, he better adhere to whatever they wanted. He nodded.

Without warning the first punch fell, its powerful force

lifting Ronan off the floor gasping for air. Hands pinned him against the wall as the punches rained down.

By the time the beating stopped, blood streamed freely from Ronan's nose, mouth and cuts. Semi-conscious, he had no idea what was happening. Neither did he feel the point of the knife which split the tender skin of his neck. He tried to scream, but no sound escaped his lips. As they released their grip he collapsed to the floor.

A voice hissed in his ear, 'Mind your own fuckin' business. Next time I'll kill you, your wife and your kid. Got it, mate!'

For an instant, Ronan focused on the soulless face, on the cold eyes. His body numbed; he did not feel the kicks which landed on his kidneys.

Ciarán closed the front door and tucked the A4 envelope inside his hooded windbreaker. With a sneer plastered on his face, he casually pulled the bloodstained gloves off and continued down the road, satisfied with a job well done.

CHAPTER 35

Heraklion International Airport
Crete
Wednesday

As Vera and Sinead's plane touched down in Crete, nearly six hours had lapsed since slipping out via the unguarded rear exit of the block of apartments, scaling the boundary wall, crossing the adjacent apartment's garden and climbing into the waiting taxi, their transport to International Departures, Dublin airport. With the music and lights left on inside their penthouse for the benefit of the men parked in the road below, they had fled undetected.

First, Vera had cleared security unhindered. And taking up a position inside the perfume shop opposite security, she had with some trepidation observed her friend's progress. Despite her best effort the make-up had failed to conceal all of Sinead's bruises. In fact, she had looked rather wretched as she had stepped through the scanner which luckily did not beep. Waved along, Sinead had reached the end of the counter and collected her few items: shoes, handbag and summer jacket.

It all was going just fine until a middle-aged security guard had moved closer, studied Sinead's face, and started asking questions. Calmly, she had obliged. Having managed to placate the man's curiosity she had finally collected all her belongings and proceeded through the glass, curved corridor towards their departure gate.

Having replaced the tester, Vera had thanked the saleslady, left and joined her friend in the dim-lit pub conveniently located near their departure gate. With a *Sláinte* and a, *Na Zdorovie*, they had drunk a vodka toast to their future on the run, ready for whatever life were to throw at them.

Although Vera's face had shone with excitement at the prospect of being free, as she had downed the clear liquid, her heart had felt like lead. The fact was, she was on the run yet again – the story of her life.

Disembarking at Heraklion International Airport, accompanied by their fellow passengers, they patiently filed through passport control. This time without incident.

Two hours later, at three thirty in the morning, they arrived by coach in the small seaside resort of Almyrida, twenty kilometres east of Chania. It was a typical tourist destination littered with an array of eateries, car rentals and bars.

'I hope for their sakes the place is livelier at night. If not, what will the poor lads do to keep themselves busy?' Sinead whispered to Vera, mocking the young men who crammed the coach.

Having hauled their luggage up to the second-floor apartment – a lift would have been too much to ask for – they understood why package holidays were so cheap. Escaping the interior of their *cosy* little abode as the brochure had proclaimed, they stepped out on to the balcony.

Facing a calm sea their trampled spirits lifted.

Vera rested her arms on the rails and gazed out over the water, wondering what the next few hours would bring. A strange sense of déjà vu washed over her. It all seemed so familiar, facing uncertainty which inevitably always ended in despair. After a life of disappointments and suffering, the conviction that she was cursed threatened to permeate her soul.

It was also during the summertime, nine years ago, when she had fled for the first time: young, frightened, insecure, longing to be safe, desperate to start a new life. But this time it would be different, there would be no place to hide. She knew that Niall's powers reached to every corner of the planet. And this time it would be personal, very personal.

She recalled only too well the rush of adrenalin on shutting the apartment's door in Moscow.

Armed with a small suitcase and a wad of roubles (eight hundred dollars) found inside a flour-tin in their kitchen, she ran, without looking back, to Moscow's Kievskey Vokzal (Central Station). Boarding the overnight train to Kiev in Ukraine, and with the third-class carriage filled to capacity, she squeezed herself in between two *babushkas* which turned out to be a big mistake. Soon the two strangers lapsed into incessant chattering, driving her nearly insane. And the tattered vinyl bunks, the graffiti-covered interior, the terrible body odours, and the passengers' pungent food was most distressing. But somehow, she persevered, her mind far away, wondering how it would all end.

At Kiev's Passenger Vokzal, she bought another third-class ticket for Odessa. And with a pie and coffee in hand, she boarded the next train. This time she was more fortunate, finding an empty corner seat opposite a Ukrainian girl named Olena, three years her senior, who worked in Kiev as a sales assistant and was on her way home for her mother's fiftieth birthday. Despite the ease of conversation, Vera struggled to pay attention, haunted by the previous day's terrible event replaying itself over and over in her head.

Snaking south across the vast moonlit landscape the train devoured the kilometres of never-ending steppe countryside. But at each stop, Vera wanted to flee, wanted to disappear into the wilderness, never to be found. Was it not for Olena, she would have.

Arriving in Odessa late the next day she was spared a night's sleep on the beach having been invited to join in Olena's mother's birthday celebration.

It was her first decent meal in a very long time, a

wonderful spread of tasty Ukrainian delicacies. Caviar canopies, salamis, smoked meats and vodka followed by salads, bread, roast pork and fish dishes. And finally, a selection of pastries. All evening the guests consumed litres of local wine, having no intention of calling it a night.

Despite her inner turmoil, Vera somehow managed to relax. To her surprise, she enjoyed the festivities, pleased to have found some sanity in a world gone mad.

The next morning while strolling on the beach, Vera recruited Olena's help to escape to Turkey. Immediately, Ivan, a family friend who worked for a shipping company with regular sailings to Turkey, was approached. The $800 Vera had – a small fortune with Ukrainians' average salary at $250 per month – was more than enough to convince Ivan to help.

Two nights later, concealed in the boot of Ivan's car, she was driven past port security. The $50 slipped into the official's hand was all it took to secure safe passage. Unknown to Vera, Ivan ignored the freshly printed photo of her as circulated by the Moscow police and now pinned-up on the notice board next to the security office window. She was a wanted criminal. But that what was none of his concern.

Once inside the restricted zone, Vera waited, cooped up in the boot of the car for the sniffer dogs to clear the area. Finally, she was sneaked into a container packed with electrical equipment. Sitting down on the hardwood floor, she wrapped herself inside a blanket. As the doors shut the container's damp, heavy darkness returned. Haunted by the thought of rats crawling all over her while asleep – biting chunks out of her nose and ears – she stared into oblivion. Without warning the container was heaved into the air and dumped on board the ship. She could not control herself anymore and broke down, weeping inconsolably, having no idea what was in store for her. Despite everything she had suffered in the past, she never felt so alone … so afraid.

By the time the container's doors opened, letting in a gush of welcoming fresh air, Vera was at her wit's end, unable to last a minute longer. Stepping on to Istanbul's concrete quay in the dark no one noticed the bedraggled girl. Assisted by her Ukrainian contact, Oleksiy, she obtained a two-month multi-entry visa, a simple formality with her Russian passport.

Remaining by her side, Oleksiy explained what she could expect in this mysterious ancient Christian city of exotic smells and sounds. From inside the taxi, she nervously observed the alien surroundings. The domed buildings, palaces, castles and minarets were a concoction of distinctive styles, evidence of the different rulers who had conquered the old citadel inside the walls of Constantinople. Traversing the bustling streets alive with a cacophony of blaring horns, and crossing the Bosphorus Sea to the Karakoy Beyoglu District in the western part of the city, progress was painfully slow.

During the drive she hung on to every word Oleksiy said, wanting to learn as much as possible before she would be left on her own.

Only twenty, Russian-speaking, with some broken English, and stuck in a foreign land she realised that life on the run was going to be a huge challenge.

Stopping in front of a building emblazoned in neon lights, displaying pictures of scantily clad girls, Vera's heart sank. Forced out of the taxi, Oleksiy said, 'Let's go. You can get job here. Money's very good. Don't worry about signs, not bad as it looks.'

In the near-dark foyer reeking of smoke and a strange sweetish scent, Oleksiy ignored her protestations and rapped on the glass screen.

Having listened to Oleksiy, the concierge disappeared for a moment before returning with a heavyset Turk. Showing great interest in her, he grunted a welcome. Quickly, Oleksiy explained what was required. Animatedly the man's face lit up, saying, 'Welcome, Vera. We have job for you.'

His Russian was broken, a limited knowledge acquired by socialising with the local Russian community of Bolshevik Revolution refugees' descendants. His eyes shone with glee at the thought of what money such a beautiful young woman blessed with a wonderful erotic body could make for him. His seedy establishment would see customers flood back, appreciative of her dancing … and more.

'I'm Hakan. You dance?' he asked, smilingly. 'Not worry, you safe here. You stay, I take care of you.'

'No, I don't dance,' Vera replied, unsure.

'No problem, I'll teach you. You only dance, okay? Nothing else,' Hakan promised.

Given the circumstances, it would be a start, a place to sleep and earn some money. She would find a way out. With no alternative, she agreed.

'Good, I'll show you room, come,' Hakan replied.

Shaking hands with Oleksiy, he slipped him a small wad of lira. And that was the last she would ever see of Oleksiy. With him gone she followed Hakan up the near-dark staircase to begin her life as an exotic dancer.

Soon enough she learned to accept that her body, which demanded regular feeding and warmth, was her biggest burden, and therefore it must earn its keep if it was to survive, even if the price grated against her beliefs.

Initially, the half-undressed dancing sessions and flirtations with customers drinking outrageously-priced drinks did not affect her too adversely. The dark interior and loud music offered her a sense of anonymity. Unable to see her eyes, customers were spared the venom which burned in them. The men reminded her of Yuri. The awful truth was, she realised, most men were like him, all womanising bastards!

Daytimes she roamed the streets, wandering aimlessly.

Three weeks later, passing by a travel agent, the colourful posters on display changed everything. The sceneries of cloudless blue skies, crystal-clear water with pearly white beaches below dramatic cliffs was all it took. Her mind was made up; she would leave.

The next day, without a word or a passport, she boarded a bus and headed south-west for the coast. It was a journey she never wanted to relive. The bus driver, guided by the will of Allah, and therefore indifferent to other road users, cut through bends, overtook cars on blind spots and drove like a bat out of hell. By some miracle, she arrived in Bodrum in one piece.

The whitewashed sprawling resort was packed with holidaymakers flooding the flea markets and harbourside cafes, stretching as far as the eye could see. Sleek yachts and beautifully crafted wooden gulets lined the huge marina which was guarded by Bodrum Castle, perched on a small hill at the edge of the breakwater. She had never seen anything so inviting ... so relaxing. It was a different world. No one seemed to be in a hurry ... or worried.

She did not hesitate and headed for the marina in search of work. By the time she reached the fourth yacht, with her mood dipping fast, her luck finally changed. The yacht's owner, an Englishman, welcomed her on board despite her poor English. Business was booming and he needed an assistant.

Grateful for this opportunity, Vera quickly settled in, tackling her training and work with youthful vigour.

And soon, she also learned the truth about her employer who continuously moved equipment from one yacht to the next, and so also their lodgings. But it did not bother her. His wit, sense of fair play and old-fashioned decency had earned him her loyalty. Happily, she condoned his minor business transgressions: living, unknown to his clients, for free on their yachts. But service was good. Customers never lacked for anything, delighted with the company and facilities offered. There were never any complaints. Therefore, money was plenty and the yachts' owners delighted.

For the first time since her mother's death, Vera enjoyed life, doing something worthwhile. Trained to cook and sail the open seas, she was soon left in charge during charter trips, allowing her employer, John Edgar-Jones, time to entertain the clients with droll stories of his world travels. The ambience of their surroundings accompanied by an endless supply of gin and tonics ensured total customer satisfaction.

Vera blossomed in the outdoors, becoming a radiantly beautiful woman. The male clientele who hustled for her attention were blissfully unaware that her beautiful smile was all they would ever be rewarded with.

As the season neared its end, it was time to move on. Determined to get to the West she sought her employer's help. Adoring her, he gladly obliged and sailed into Greek territory to rendezvous with a colleague. Transferred on to a thirty-metre yacht she headed for Cyprus, filled with renewed hope. And how that had—

'Penny for your thoughts,' Sinead whispered, startling Vera.

'Don't do that! You'll give me a heart attack,' Vera said laughingly.

'Sorry. Was just trying to make you smile. Anyway, here you go,' Sinead said, offering a cup of coffee and snacks brought from Ireland. 'Sorry it's black but you're lucky to get any at all. It's the only thing left behind by the previous big spenders.'

'Thanks.'

'Why are you so sad?'

'I was wandering *delightful* pastures, of Cyprus.'

'Oh, I see. Care to share them? Come to think of it you've never told me what really happened there.'

'You sure you want to know? It's boring.'

'The little I do know about your past is that nothing is ever boring. So, you won't get away that easily. Besides, I can't sleep and I don't feel like rehearsing our plan right now. It can wait,' Sinead said and sat down in a deckchair next to Vera.

As the sun skimmed over the horizon Vera took a sip of the scalding black liquid. 'Ouch! That's hot.'

'Quit stalling … and?'

'Okay. Arriving in Cyprus on this massive yacht the owner quickly introduced me to some local Russians. They welcomed me with open arms; I suppose the guy had some influence and his yacht and money must have impressed them no end. The only thing that matters to them is money, especially when you have lots of it. You know there's about fifty thousand Russians in Cyprus which is quite a lot for such a small island. Anyway, no one asked questions and everyone tried to help. I was like a kid, thrilled, dreaming of conquering the world. And soon enough I was offered a job by a guy called Boris, a real pig he turned out to be.'

'Aren't all men?'

'Uhm … maybe? But wait till you're free and Mister Right comes along, then we'll talk again. Suddenly, not all men will be pigs.'

'Will never happen, not after what they've done to me and what I've seen. No! And knowing what you do and what you've been through I'm amazed you're still dreaming of a hero in shining armour rescuing you.'

'No, I don't. You know I gave up on that a long time ago. But still, I cannot believe all men are evil. No.'

'Suit yourself, but I don't believe you. You are a romantic by heart and are still hoping love will find you,' Sinead said with a smile dancing in her eyes. 'So, back to your life, forget about mine. What about Boris?'

'I'll always remember the view over Paphos, driving through the steep hills towards my interview with him: the shimmering silver water in the distance, the pastel violet-pink sky, the sun a soft red, and the air filled with wonderful summer fragrances. It really was beautiful. I had felt on top of the world, young and free, dreaming of great things to come. This sentiment became even more profound when I entered his spacious home. And was that something! Simple clean lines, no clutter, high ceilings, walls of glass, polished marble floors … infinity pool. I was blown away. I wanted to live like that. And why not? Maybe this was to be my lucky day?'

'See, a romantic through and through! What will I do with you?'

'But as the sun plummeted below the horizon, so did my dreams. Sitting stone-faced, Boris bluntly rejected my offer to work on one of his yachts, not at all interested in my work experience in Turkey. Instead, he gave me two choices: dance in his club, or be deported at once – it would take only one call. Shocked, I did hesitate for a few seconds, and without another word, he picked up the phone and called the police. Begging him to stop, I agreed to dance; under no circumstances could I go back to Russia. The deal was simple. I'll dance and in return will get free board and lodging and two hundred and fifty euro a month. I could also keep all the tips customers gave me, and wait for it … a Cypriot passport. After six months, I'd be free to go.'

'And you believed him?' Sinead asked cynically.

'Of course not! I thought, if it's only dancing, I'll manage and find a way off the island before too long.'

'Only dancing, sure.'

'My handler took me to a small two-bedroom apartment which I had to share with five other dancers. My roommate was Ukrainian. She was my age. Fortunately, she was very nice, otherwise, we would have killed each other as the room was minute!'

'You mean, "cupboard was minute". I can only imagine …'

'I started work that very same evening. After a few hours of dancing the usual requests were made by customers, demanding sex. I refused, so Boris beat me to a pulp.'

'As expected, nothing ever changes. It's all they know. Oh my God, how I hate them! And you really think I want anything to do with them? No, never!' Sinead fumed. 'Did you try and get away?'

'I tried as often as I could, but always got caught. It's not easy to escape Cyprus stuck in the middle of the sea. Punished more than I care to remember, they sold me to all kinds of scum. How I had remained detached from this surreal sordid world, from the filth who violated me, I don't know. You won't believe how utterly repulsive some were with their horrible breaths, dirty teeth and slobbering kisses over me. I feel sick just thinking of it. Yuk! What we do for Niall is like a Sunday school picnic.'

'I take your word for it; this is bad enough, thanks!'

'And of my dreams … of having a life; there was nothing left. Was this it? No! I could never accept that. As you have wanted for so long, so did I – just to be free, to get away at all cost. But they watched me morning and night. In the end, being more trouble than I was worth, I was sold a few months later to some guy in Paris. With no money and a fake passport, I was trafficked there. And life in Pigalle lasted less than three months.'

'What happened?'

'One night while working a table with two German customers who slowly sipped their so-called *free beers*, waiting for the live sex show to start, one of the waitresses kept piling drinks on their table. Soon there were three rounds just sitting there untouched. Realising what was happening, they cursed, got up and left. But at the door, they were stopped and ordered to pay for all the drinks. They refused. Next thing, guns were pulled on them, forcing them to pay. Later that evening they returned, and having jammed the fire exit from the outside, they torched the place. Two of the crooks who had threatened them were found with their heads smashed in. During the chaos, I tried to flee but was grabbed and along with other trafficked girls sold on. The club's owners did not want to explain our illegal presence to the police.'

'In Brussels, in some fancy strip club, I was forced to perform night after night like a monkey, gyrating naked on customers' laps. By then I'd had more than enough of this humiliation. But strangely I somehow managed to act the idiot, feigning sheer ecstasy while despising … no, loathing, the fools in front of me. You know what I mean.'

Sinead said nothing and nodded understanding. Silently reliving her own experiences, she allowed Vera to continue.

'And the ceaseless dancing, twisting myself around the infamous pole with them leering and laughing was the most degrading. This strip club was nothing other than a glorified brothel. Having debased myself in front of these men and women I got dragged off every now and then for sex in some grimy back room. All I remember are those filthy couches and the sickening stench of used condoms. And after hours I was forced to accompany *special clients* to obscure hotels, to be used

145

as many times and in whichever way they wanted. Killing myself was all I could think of. But I couldn't.

'Tell you what, if I had a machine gun, I would have mowed them down, all those stupid, smug faces. What really infuriates me are the movies which always shows strippers as having the best time ever, misleading naïve, stupid young girls to fall for this rubbish! And once in, they start with the drugs to cope. Fortunately, back home, we were taught to stay away from the stuff. Also, I've seen too many girls die. Then the tattoos, oh dear! Why girls cover themselves in ink, beats me! Whenever I see a beautiful girl scarred by tattoos, I want to cry. Why do they do it? Why do they want to look like prostitutes?'

'Because we want to be naughty and think it looks sexy!' Sinead laughed. 'Don't worry I'll have my pretty butterfly removed once we're free and rolling in money!'

'Jeez, I forgot … sorry!' Vera said with a smile, not sorry at all. She had teased Sinead many times about her little butterfly, of just how *pretty* it would look when she hits fifty.

'Yeah, right!' Sinead replied and punched Vera playfully on the shoulder.

'Ouch! Okay, I asked for that.'

'Continue …'

'Well, that's about it. I had reached the end, had enough. I was twenty-one, and with nowhere to turn to for help, I gave up on my dreams …. on life. Well, that was until I was *rescued* by yours truly.'

'Yeah, and the rest is history, as they say.'

Vera sat up and swivelled around in her chair. 'Sinead, if anything is to happen to me, I want you to open this letter. It contains my will and solicitor's details,' she said handing over a sealed envelope.

'What are you on about, nothing will … so don't be so melodramatic.'

'We don't know, do we? Please take it.'

Toying with the envelope in her hands, Sinead prayed she would never have to open it.

'Looking back over the last nine years I'm amazed that I'm still somewhat sane. For this, I can only thank you. You know, you're the closest to family I have. I owe you so much,' Vera said.

Sinead reached out and patted her friend's hand, not wanting to hear any more.

CHAPTER 36

Greek Mainland
Wednesday Morning

Escaping the Peloponnesian peninsula had drained their reserves. Exhausted from being on the run for nearly thirty hours Michael and Paddy wanted nothing more than to put their heads down and sleep.

After their initial swift progress in the early hours, they had soon run into unexpected trouble. By the time they had reached Sparta, the police were busy setting up a roadblock opposite the Athletic Facility Complex. Forced to make an evasive manoeuvre they had swung into the nearest orchard and abandoned the stolen car. From there they had fled on foot. Dashing through the lines of orange trees they had passed undetected by the rows of houses and apartment blocks. Avoiding the roadblock, they had changed direction at Sparta Square and sprinted to the east side of the town. Having pilfered suitable clothing from a few washing lines along the way they had stolen another car for the next leg of the journey and fled along the E961 to Athens.

Guided by the early morning sun they continued to race eastwards, convinced that by now the owner of their car was running up and down the deserted street in Sparta looking for his precious Fiat Punto.

Paddy was first to express his concern. 'I suggest we

dump this Rolls and look for a Ferrari. Come to think of it, a Lear Jet would do nicely, thank you,' he quipped.

'Right, here goes,' Michael said.

Spotting the next exit, he swung off the nearly deserted motorway. But the small village offered no alternative means of transport with far too many people milling about. Two foreigners tampering with a car in the early hours was not a good idea.

'No luck here. Boy, these Greeks are up early! Most probably milking the goats,' Paddy mocked.

Slowly Michael cruised through the town to re-join the motorway three kilometres further along.

At that exact moment, the old tractor choked along the rows of orange trees in Sparta. The grey-haired farmer doing his customary morning drive cursed loudly, blaming the government and banks for his tribulations. The smoke escaping his pipe firmly clenched between yellow crooked teeth was no match for the clouds of diesel fumes belching out of the noisy machine. His swearing went up in tempo and quality when he saw the shape of an abandoned vehicle rammed in between some of his sacred trees, having broken the neatly installed irrigation pipes.

After much deliberation, he decided against acquiring the vehicle for himself by applying a new coat of paint and fitting some old registration plates. A rather reluctant call was made to the authorities reporting the abandoned car.

Michael took one look at the cloud of smog polluting the skyline: Athens, suffocating under a brown blanket of fumes.

Nearly there! he thought, wanting to get back to Ireland as soon as possible and get on with what had to be done.

Forty kilometres west of Athens at Kineta, Michael left the motorway and followed the coastal road. Reaching an isolated spot, he pulled up. Having changed into clean clothes they weighed down the two dirty bundles of rags and cast them into the blue waters of the Megara Gulf.

At Athens' main harbour they abandoned the Fiat. Considering the proximity of the ferry port, they hoped the authorities would conclude that they had sailed from there to one of the many destinations available – a decoy which should buy them some valuable time. Ignoring the departing ferries, however tempting, they boarded a bus to the city centre.

Shaken around for forty minutes, they disembarked in the bustling Plaka District, and parting company, they set off in different directions to buy food, clothing, some toiletries and newspapers.

Half an hour later, with a discreet nod, they rendezvoused in the sprawling gardens of the Acropolis. Seated in the shade of an old twisted tree, they tucked into their freshly bought rations and between mouthfuls studied the few international newspapers strewn over the boulders in front of them.

After a few articles, Paddy had seen enough. 'Not much to worry about, you say? No, Michael, just the whole bloody Greek army … police force looking for us! In case I haven't told you; your sense of humour sucks,' he complained bitterly, chomping on a souvlaki.

Unfazed, Michael shrugged his shoulders. 'With all the rioting and migrants flooding Athens we're the least of their problems. What you're reading is all a big show to placate the public. Relax, no one is going to find us,' he said confidently.

Having polished off the last crumbs, they headed for the public toilets to be transformed into clean-shaven tourists.

Twenty minutes later, unrecognisable, they reappeared. Smartly dressed, disguised in sunglasses and sunhats, they were ready to find suitable accommodation for the night.

In the meantime, the thorough search of the abandoned vehicle discovered in the orchard outside Sparta by the police had revealed that two fugitives and not just one had occupied the car. Convinced they had picked up on the trail of the missing men – originally thought to have drowned – they renewed their efforts to catch the perpetrators. Armed with this latest information, the Greek government had mobilised

150

some military units in support.

Soon the tracker dogs reached the end of the trail – a vacant parking space – where a very concerned man had reported the theft of his Fiat Punto a few hours earlier.

With the trail gone cold, orders were issued to find the missing car. In all probability, it would be in Athens by now. This theory was soon confirmed by the tollgates' surveillance cameras en route to Athens. Unfortunately, at every stop, the occupants' faces had remained concealed.

CHAPTER 37

Crete
Wednesday Morning

There was no cooling breeze, no rustle of leaves, no swaying of the tall brown grass. The heat was becoming unbearable.

'Surely a small canopy would not be too much to ask for, Governor, or have you spent the money on your mistress?' someone gibed, eliciting a murmur of accord from the group waiting in line for the bus to Chania.

As the sun scorched down on the bare shoulders of the two fair-skinned women, they braved the heat in silence. Vera and Sinead dressed in plain summer frocks, straw hats, flat sandals, and carrying large shoulder bags were just two more vacationers setting off to enjoy a day of shopping. The layers of make-up, some wide wrist and ankle bracelets, a silk scarf and a pair of sunglasses concealed most of Sinead's bruises. But for her exceptional beauty, no one would give her a second look …

Finally, they stepped into the cool interior of the bus. As the brakes hissed, releasing their grip on the drums, they travelled in the direction of town. Nervously the two friends took in the countryside and vista of the sea with its shimmering haze. They hardly said a word.

Sinead was first to disembark. Standing alone on the pavement she watched the bus continue its route.

'Vera, please, be careful,' she whispered. With her head hung low she followed. She felt alone despite the throng of people, doubting the validity of their plan. Would she ever see her friend again? Were they walking straight into the arms of Niall's men?

A few minutes later Vera also left the cool comfort of the bus. Glancing from side to side and seeing nothing out of the ordinary she hurried into the shade of the Municipal Market. With her phone held tight against her ear feigning conversation, she waited for a chance to mingle with the pedestrians passing by the Bank of Crete.

Where are they? she wondered, looking for Niall's men. Not for one moment did she think the bank was not being watched! *They must be here … somewhere …*

Fascinated, Vera the tourist, looked at the neoclassic building of light-coloured sandstone across the road, which, despite its imposing bulk, blended in well with its surrounding. Wanting to be one hundred percent certain no one was watching, she once more studied the cafes and pavements. This time, thirty metres to her right, she spotted the two suspicious looking men sipping coffee.

Tourists? I don't think so!

With their attention focused on the bank, they acted far too alert for holidaymakers. The thinner of the two removed his sunhat and dabbed a paper serviette to his forehead, wiping away the glistening beads of sweat. The cropped ginger hair was a dead giveaway. Phoning Sinead she warned, 'There are two men at Andreas' Taverna. You'll have to distract them … I haven't seen any others, but there could be more.'

'Okay, got them. Who said this was going to be easy? Please Vera, no risks. Stay where you are. I'll be back in thirty minutes, tops.'

At Andreas' Taverna, the bulky, young Greek teenager haggled with the two stern-faced Irishmen. 'And how about this genuine Knossos pottery dish, or this beautiful statue of Aphrodite?'

Ron looked up and down the busy street; all seemed normal. Grinning patiently, he returned his attention to the boy who unpacked some artefacts on the table. Skilfully the boy blocked the two men's view of the bank's entrance.

'Why do you want this rubbish?' Brian asked, not impressed. 'It's shite!' Lifting a white marble Aphrodite off the table, juggling it from one hand to the other, it nearly dropped on to the pavement, much to the boy's horror.

'Please sir, be careful! My boss will kill me. Just one piece for your missus, please, sir,' he begged.

From a safe distance, Sinead watched a group of pedestrians approach the bank. Amongst them Vera's hat bobbed along. No matter how much she tried to merge with the group, she stood out like a sore thumb. If anyone were looking, they would spot her immediately. Thankfully, her ploy was working; the boy was doing a great job in occupying the two watchers. Reaching the bank's entrance, the hat disappeared inside.

Being none the wiser of what had just transpired, Niall's men did not move, deep in conversation with the boy. With a sigh of relief, Sinead retreated to a side street and waited for Adonis to return with the remainder of the curios, and for the balance of his fee.

'Thanks, great job! And here ya go,' Sinead said, handing the boy thirty euro. 'You can keep the rest of the stuff. It should fetch you another couple of hundred. But before you go, do you have any older brothers … friends? The money will be worth it.'

'What's my share?' Adonis asked boldly, opening a new round of negotiations.

Inside the spacious banking hall, the cool air was a welcome respite. Familiar with the bank's layout, Vera by-passed the small queue at enquiries and headed straight for the manager's department situated on the mezzanine level.

Smiling brightly, she pushed the reception's door open. '*Kalimera,* Ianessa. How are you?' she greeted warmly as she

154

strode confidently inside.

'My goodness, back so soon! What a lovely surprise,' Ianessa replied.

'Could not stay away … the weather in Ireland got to me!'

'Careful what you wish for; you may regret it,' Ianessa laughed.

'I doubt that!'

'Do you want to see Mr Georgiou?'

'If possible, please. It will only be for a few minutes.'

'Let me see what I can do. And please, take a seat.'

'Don't mind if I do, thank you.'

Trying to make herself comfortable on the tubular Wassily chair, Vera prepared herself for a long wait, thinking: *fine looking chairs, but impossible to relax in!*

'Vera, can you wait twenty minutes? He's still in a meeting.'

'That's perfect, thanks.'

'Would you like a drink, sweet coffee, iced-tea?'

'Iced-tea, thank you.'

Inattentively she paged through the Greek newspaper depicting the financial crisis and the flood of economic migrants swamping the tranquil islands.

Dominating the front page was a detailed article about the tragedy at sea. The bold printed Greek letters reporting the government's anger and efforts in finding the culprits meant nothing to her. Neither did the photographs of the cadets who had died in the name of justice. Nevertheless, she did not put the paper down as it kept her hands busy, hiding the slight trembling. Silently she played out the conversation she was about to have, one which was key to their plan. If ever she needed to fulfill her role as an actress, then it was now.

'Vera, please follow me,' Ianessa's words startled her, deep in thought.

'Good morning, Alexander,' Vera said with a charming smile as she entered the manager's office. 'Thank you very much for seeing me without an appointment. I promise I won't be long.'

'No problem. You know you are always more than

welcome in my little office,' the manager replied, beaming from ear to ear.

Taking his outstretched hand, she held it just a fraction longer than protocol required. He was clean-shaven, his longish grey hair neatly combed and gelled firmly in place. The musky fragrance of his cologne hung heavy in the air. Her penetrating large blue eyes held his and lingered a few seconds before she coyly looked away.

'Please sit down. What can I help you with?' Alexander asked. Seated next to her, he turned his chair slightly askew, their knees almost touching.

Once more he was struck by her stunning features: 1.75 metres tall with sensual curves in all the right places. A tiny waist and flat stomach, slender arms, shapely legs and slim ankles. An exquisite heart-shaped face with high cheekbones. Her shiny blonde hair falling in layers below her shoulders. Without realising, his gaze drifted down to the exposed cleavage, to the roundness of her full breasts pressed against the light cotton fabric. He sincerely hoped she would not rush off. Maybe she would join him for lunch?

Thinking how basic men were, Vera allowed him a few more moments of self-indulgence before clearing her throat.

'Oh yes, sorry, as I was saying, how can I be of service?' he apologised, distracted.

'Alexander, I need two things. First, I must access my safe-deposit box, today. I'm selling and buying a property and the deed is in there, and I must be back in Ireland tomorrow to close the deal, or I'll lose this fantastic opportunity. Problem is, I cannot find my key anywhere … I'm sure it's somewhere safe though. But with all this travelling between here and Ireland, who knows where it is?' she said, pausing for a second, dismayed at her own negligence. 'Secondly, I need to withdraw forty thousand euro in cash.'

Hearing this the manager nearly fell off his chair.

Well, that got your attention! she chuckled to herself.

'I know it's none of my business but why the urgency? And why so much cash?'

'The deal involves some cash as well.'

'Yes, I understand. But why don't you give me the solicitor's details and I'll issue you with a bank draft? That would most definitely be a lot safer than walking around town with a bag full of money.'

'True, but it has to be cash,' Vera replied, not to be persuaded.

Accepting her words, he threw his hands up in the air. 'Fine, you win. As I said, it's none of my business. After all, it is your money.'

'Thank you, I knew I could count on you.'

'However, the key, well, that is rather more complicated. Not as simple as you may think. It involves other people and a lot of paperwork. And as you can see, I'm quite swamped. But maybe we can deal with the paperwork over lunch?' he suggested, his eyes conveying the unspoken word. Having seized the moment, he intended to exploit it to the full, to spend a few hours with this dazzling client … and who knows where it might lead?

Vera graciously accepted, having expected a trade-off. 'I would love that. Although, can't we deal with the key issue now and then go for lunch at our leisure?' she asked, her seductive eyes not straying from his.

'Come to think of it, yes, why not? It would be much better. Let me see what I can do.'

Thirty minutes later Vera had emptied her safe-deposit box. The diamonds and €40 000 in cash were safely placed inside her large holdall bag, covered by a few loose items.

Re-joining the manager, he said, 'All set, shall we—'

'Of course, and thank you again. Do you mind, I just have to make a quick call?' Vera interrupted.

Standing out of earshot, she spoke into her phone, 'It's all done but with a slight change of plan; I'm going for lunch with the manager.'

'Ooh … I love you,' Sinead purred.

'Is it safe to come out, now?'

'No, give me five minutes. Go and use the ladies or something. Five minutes, okay?'

On cue, a group of young men crossed the road in front of the bank. It was time to go. Sinead stood up and left enough money on the table to cover the cost of her coffee.

Behind her, a group of men walked into the taverna where the two Irishmen, Ron and Brian, dutifully sat watching the bank. A few seconds later a ruckus erupted behind them. Instinctively, they turned to see what was happening. At that exact moment, Vera and the bank manager stepped on to the pavement. With the fight ensuing across the road, the manager shielded Vera and led her away.

Five blocks further they entered a small restaurant.

Sinead, who had raced after them, followed inside. Without acknowledging Vera seated near the front, she found a vacant table at the back. As she sat down, she felt like screaming as the last thing they could afford was to waste precious time wining and dining. The race was on, one which they in all likelihood would never finish. Or, even start judging by the manager who seemed set on having things his way.

Sinead fretted. The instant Niall were to discover the empty apartment, the game would be over.

CHAPTER 38

St. James Hospital
Dublin
Wednesday Morning

Ronan watched her delicate hand brush a lock of blonde hair out of her face. The other hand clutched his, refusing to let go. He was guilt-ridden. He should have listened to Sean.

Thank God, she's not hurt.

'Marie, how's Tommy?'

His voice startled her. With bloodshot eyes, she looked up. 'Ronan, you're …' unable to express her feelings, she leaned forward and held him gently, careful not to add further injury to his battered body.

'How's Tom?' his scratchy voice repeated.

'His fine…we're fine. How are you, how are you feeling? Do you want me to call someone, or—'

'I'm okay, I guess. No need to call anyone, I'll live,' he said, stopping her despite being in agony. 'Where am I?'

'St James.'

'How long?'

'Since around two this morning.'

'Oh.' The relatively brief time spent in the hospital came as a relief. He may still have time to warn Sean.

'My God, you gave me a fright! What happened … do you know who did this to you?'

'Four punks. The bell rang. I went to check who it was,

159

opened the door, and bang, this! I've no idea who they were … why they attacked me.'

'I just don't understand—'

'Do you have my phone?' he interrupted her. 'I have a meeting today, a very important one … better cancel or I may lose the contract. You know what pain clients can be … how difficult it is to get contracts nowadays.'

'For goodness sake, can't that wait!? You must rest. The last thing you need is to make calls, or worry about work,' she replied firmly.

'No, I better. It should only take a sec.'

She sighed; there was no point in arguing. 'It's somewhere … got it! What's the number?' she asked, having retrieved the phone from her bag.

'It's okay, I'll do it. I may be hurt, but I'm not paralysed, I don't think—'

'What's going on?' she asked suspiciously.

'Marie, I don't know. As I've said, I've no idea who they were. They knew my name, so they must have been sent. But by whom, I have no idea. Last time I checked I had no enemies. Unless it's a competitor trying to get me out of the way. We're tendering on a few big contracts, so—'

'Please tell me,' she cut him off, sceptical.

'Sorry, I just don't know. Let's leave it at that. The Guards can find them,' he lied, something he was never good at. But tell her, he could not. 'Can you please get me some painkillers?' he asked, wanting privacy.

'Right, I get it. Fine, have it your way! Just don't blame me if, whatever it is, bites you in the backside,' she said and got up.

As soon as she stepped out of the room, Ronan rang Sean. With as cheerful a voice as he could muster, he said, 'Hi buddy, everything all right with ya?'

'Yep, right as rain. Why?'

'Good. Listen, I'm in the hospital, thanks to our friend. Some of his punks paid me a visit this morning – a warning to mind my own business.'

'What! You're serious?'

'Afraid so.'

'How're you doing?'

'Okay. Just don't tell anyone anything. No Guards, or he'll kill us.'

'I'm really sorry I dragged you into this.'

'Not to worry, don't beat yourself up. Remember it was my call. But I'll make him pay. If he thinks I'm just going to roll over and play dead, he's in for a surprise.' Hearing his wife's excited voice in the corridor, Ronan said, 'Have to go, keep your phone on and watch your back. Cheers.'

'How are you feeling, Mr O'Brien?' Dr Keane O'Dowd asked.

'So-so. What's the verdict?' Ronan asked, hopeful to be discharged within the hour.

'You're a very lucky man. According to the MRI, you have a slight concussion, nothing more severe. Some cuts to your face, which, I'm afraid, will leave you scarred. These and the neck wound we've stitched up. The broken jaw and nose we've reset. Then apart from three fractured ribs, everything else is intact. No punctured lung or spleen. But there is evidence of bleeding to your kidneys, which we're treating. With adequate rest, you'll be fine. Five days should do it. Therefore, you won't be going home just yet. You need to remain here for at least two more days. And, I reckon your body hurts a bit …'

'Yeah, just a little … that's putting it mildly,' Ronan said. Although pleased with the prognosis, he was not impressed at the prospect of being cooped up in bed for any length of time. He itched to make Niall pay as his lopsided grin hid his anger.

'By the way, I've given Detective Seamus Kelly permission to see you. Shall I send him in?' Dr Keane O'Dowd asked. 'I thought it better they finish their job and leave you to recuperate in peace. I trust it's okay with you?'

'I suppose so,' Ronan sighed, having wanted more time to prepare himself for this encounter.

If the consultant's observations are correct in that the perpetrators knew exactly what they were doing, it explains a lot, mused Detective Kelly. Attentively he listened to the victim's report of the incident. Not much was learned as he was unable to recall any specifics – the whole incident had transpired within a flash.

Detective Kelly frowned, scratching the back of his head with his pen, looking rather baffled. 'Let's see if I've got it right. You're saying the doorbell rang at about one in the morning. You went downstairs thinking it might be some friends. Instead, you were confronted by four thugs who barged inside, pushed you against the wall and beat you unconscious for no apparent reason. Correct?'

'As I recall, yes.'

'Well, something seems a bit odd. For starters, these four thugs who waltzed in off the street – purely by chance – were extremely tidy, leaving no clues to their visit. No fingerprints anywhere, stole nothing, touched nothing, and gave you no explanation why they had the urge to just about kill you. In fact, they beat you so badly that you are unable to give me any description whatsoever of any of them.'

The look of indifference on Ronan's face forced Detective Kelly, quite irate at this stage, to speak his mind in no uncertain terms. 'You honestly expect me to believe that you know absolutely nothing? Well, Mr O'Brien, things don't add up. Your beating was obviously a very serious warning. As you can appreciate, it would help a great deal in apprehending these thugs if you would cooperate more. You don't want to be charged with obstruction of justice ... do you now?'

'Sorry I can't be more helpful. There really is nothing to add. Their faces were covered. Don't you think I want them locked up? It may be competition trying to get me out of the way. But who, I don't know.'

'Possibly. We'll look into it. Hard to believe business is really that competitive.'

'Yeah ... right, believe what you want. If anything else comes to mind, be assured, you'll be the first to know,' Ronan replied. Through half-shut eyes he appraised the man in front

162

of him who seemed to be a live replica of Detective Colombo. All that was missing was the cigar. Ronan smiled.

'I don't see anything remotely funny. This is no joke, Mr O'Brien,' the detective retorted. 'Remember, if it wasn't for your dear wife who came looking for you, we might not be having this conversation. And, while you're wiping that smirk off your face, try to recollect events more accurately. Think of her and your son. You were lucky this morning. What will happen next time these guys pop-in for another *friendly* chat?'

Angered by the rebuff, Ronan said, 'If you don't mind, my head hurts like hell. I need to rest. When I remember anything else, I'll phone you. Goodbye Detective.' With that he closed his eyes, ending the conversation.

'Right, have it your way. But know this; I don't believe you, and I really hope you come to your senses before it's too late.' Turning towards Marie, he said, 'You better try and talk some sense into him. Maybe he's not thinking clearly right now because of the painkillers, who knows? If he says anything you think might help, please call me.'

'I shall,' Marie replied, baffled by her husband's odd behaviour.

'Now you better excuse me. Good day.' Furious at the young man's stubbornness, the detective left, eager to compile his report and start digging. He wanted the truth.

Ronan knew it would have been fatal, for him and his family, if he had revealed anything. Niall would act far more quickly than the Garda not on his *payroll*. His resolve to continue helping Sinead wavered. The best was to stay out of it. Although giving in that easily was not his nature; he never backed down.

An hour later – ignoring the hospital's visiting hours – Minister of the Environment, Eoin Murphy, blowing hot and cold, rushed into the ward, wanting to learn first-hand how his friend was doing, and what exactly had transpired.

The appalling sight of Ronan, his eyes reduced to two slits above the bandaged nose, made him hesitate. For a moment he considered going down to the canteen for a coffee and returning later. He was still contemplating whether to stay or go when a croaky voice made him look up. The usually amicable Ronan did not sound very pleased to see him.

'Hi, Eoin. What the hell did you tell Mr McGuire? And since when do you mix with his sort?' Ronan demanded.

Giving one of his politician's pretentious smiles, he replied, evading the question. 'Thank goodness you're alive! How are you feeling?'

'Cut the crap, Eoin. You're not on campaign. I asked you, what did you tell him?'

'Only what you told me. I asked him to release Sinead if he wants to avoid any further repercussions. I'm sorry I mentioned your name. But I never thought him to be a gangster. He must be mad thinking he'll get away with this. I promise, I'll see him locked up if it's the last thing I do!' the minister stated emphatically.

'Yeah, right, you do that,' Ronan said unimpressed by this false bravado. *Eoin, you're one cute hoor, and you'll only do what's best for you and no one else.* Although tempted to call a spade a spade he bit his tongue. Now was not the time. He needed the man's help. 'And how do you plan to "see him locked up"?' Not waiting for an answer, Ronan continued. 'No, Eoin, forget it. There's nothing you can do. All you'll get for your trouble will be a bed next to mine.' *Which will be well deserved*, he nearly added.

'You're wrong. How can I walk away as if nothing has happened? No, he must be held accountable.'

'Fine, I'm listening. Tell me how?'

'I'll contact colleagues who I think may have an axe to grind, people willing to testify against him.'

Discussing possible scenarios, plotting Niall's demise, they knew once the wheels were set in motion, failure would not be an option.

Deep in conversation, Eoin Murphy did not notice the traffic as he drove back to his office. 'You have a problem; you've crossed swords with the wrong guy. He's coming for you. He won't stop until you're dead and buried.'

'Let him try,' Niall laughed. 'Anyway, thanks for the warning. And as a sign of my deep gratitude, I'll organise a nice treat for you. Some company to massage away your worries. It sounds like you need it. What do you say?'

'Yes, I can do with a little relaxation.'

'Good, good. How about tonight, the O'Mara, 9:30? The girls will be the best, guaranteed.'

'Great, can't wait. I'll text you the room number as soon as I've checked in.'

'Right then. Enjoy yourself and remember to play nicely. No funny business; they're good kids.'

CHAPTER 39

Blackrock, Dublin
Wednesday Midday

'I don't like it. Lunchtime and nothing … No sign of the broads,' Dwaine said. 'If we still want our jobs, we better find out what they're up to.'

'Jaysus, give it a break! They're women. They sleep late in case ya don't know,' Cormac countered, happy to be paid for doing nothing, lounging lazily in his seat.

'I'm going to check. You can stay here!' Dwaine replied annoyed and jumped out of the car.

With his thick index finger, he impatiently pressed the insignificant white button, its desolate chime resonating in the hallway. Not easing the pressure he hammered on the door but to no avail. Placing his ear against the solid wood panel he heard music playing, nothing more.

After ten minutes he had no more doubts; they were not at home. It was time to update Glen. This information resulted in an emphatic, 'Kick the fucking door down, now!' shouted in his ear.

Glen was livid, left with the unenviable task of informing Niall, knowing perfectly well what to expect for his men's failure.

'Good afternoon, Mr McGuire, although I'm afraid it's not really such a good one. To cut to the chase; there's no sign of Vera and Sinead. The flat's empty. No one's home.

Anything you want us to do?' He knew as from that moment his life had become worthless, less than that of a flea on the back of a rabid dog.

'Oh boy,' Niall sighed. 'OK, I'll put it to you nicely. If you want to see Christmas, you better find them and quick, understood?' The words softly spoken, were filled with cold, controlled anger.

'Yes boss, we shall. Another thing, some bloke is also watching their apartment. What shall we do about him?'

'Really, any idea who it might be?'

'One of the chaps reckons he looks like Sinead, possibly some relation?'

'My guess, it's her older brother,' Niall said. Since Eoin's meddling, Niall had made some enquiries regarding Sinead's relatives' whereabouts. With the younger two brothers, Billy and Flynn, still at school in New Ross, they were ruled out. 'Must be Sean snooping around. Well, at least you're not totally useless. Do nothing for now. Just keep an eye on him, and whatever you do, don't lose him as he may lead us straight to her. He's our, no, let me rephrase that, he's *your* only hope.'

It did not take much imagination to grasp what had happened. They had either fled into hiding, or done the unthinkable, and gone to Crete to steal the diamonds!

Jumping up Niall raced upstairs. Inside his private study his fingers flew over the lock's touchpad. The door sprung open. With some measure of relief, he saw Vera's passport and safe-deposit box key exactly where he had put them. Was this proof that they have only gone into hiding? No. What would be the point of fleeing empty-handed? Nothing. To risk escape, they had to make it worth their while. Running to Crete and helping themselves to his stones was their only option … and, also true to their character. The small technicality of a passport and key would not deter Vera – for all he knew, she most probably owned several travel documents. Therefore, he must assume they were already in Crete. But they could not have been to the bank yet; his men

167

would have notified him. Or, were they also asleep like the lot watching the apartment?

Let's find out …

Careful not to raise any suspicions, Eileen's honey-sweet voice apologised most profusely to the Bank of Crete's manager for troubling him. She was urgently looking for Vera. There had been a death in her family. Despite having tried non-stop, it was impossible to reach her – her phone was switched off – and his number was the only one on file of any acquaintances she has in Crete. Therefore, any assistance in locating her would be very much appreciated.

Eileen's suggestion that Vera might visit the bank elicited an emphatic, 'No. Unfortunately, she has concluded her affairs with us. Pity, you just missed her. We parted company ten minutes ago.'

Listening attentively to his PA's report, Niall stopped her once she confirmed Vera's visit to the bank, 'Thanks, Eileen, that will be all.' He could not believe his ears.

But you'll be going nowhere, my dear!

The familiar smell of the well-oiled mahogany desk and wood panelling, the nurtured leather furniture, the neatly arranged rows of books, the thick amber carpet and the light cream velvet drapes – his usual place of solitude – he now found irritatingly stifling. Shunning this sense of near apoplexy, he phoned his men in Crete.

'Ron, what are you doing?' he asked, his words cold and measured.

'Watching the bank. Why, Mr McGuire?'

'For your information, Vera has just been to the bank and walked out of there fifteen minutes ago, under your fucking noses!'

'Can't be …' Ron stuttered, suddenly filled with uncertainty.

'Yes, she did. I suggest you and your buddy better find her, that's if you want to see Dublin again,' Niall warned. 'Any idea how you're going to do that?'

'Uhm, no, sir …'

'I suggest you get off your arses and start looking. Ask the café owner, maybe his brain isn't mush like yours!'

Having no confidence in his men, Niall phoned the only man in Crete who could help. 'Good afternoon, Dimitris, I trust you're well,' he greeted.

'*Yasou* …' Dimitris replied and paused, caught off-guard by Niall's conciliatory tone. 'To what do I owe this pleasure?'

'As we've both suffered a great setback, may I suggest we join our resources in beating the odds, and agree on a mutually beneficial arrangement for us both. But before we proceed with the details, I have another proposal you may be interested in.'

'*Parakalo,* please continue.'

Listening to Niall, Dimitris was at a loss for words.

'You're still there?' Niall asked.

'Yes, my friend. I must give them credit; they have guts,' Dimitris said and chuckled. 'And now, of course, you need my help.'

'What a perceptive man you are … and for a substantial reward.'

'Naturally. If I find them, I get fifty percent of the stones. If not, I'm not interested,' Dimitris proposed, and finally settling on a ten percent cut – nearly four-and-a-half million euro, plus half the cash lost at sea.

'You're a hard man to do business with. Just remember, this deal hinges on your success. Understood?'

'Understood. You did say she left the bank thirty minutes ago? Well, then I better start looking. They may still be in Chania,' Dimitris said. 'I can think of only one way they'll leave this island and that's by sea. Carrying a bag full of shiny stones through airport customs is inconceivable unless they have an accomplice. Any such chance?'

'No, I'm positive they're on their own.'

'Leave it with me. They won't get far,' Dimitris said, already thinking of the motor yacht upgrade he would get with

169

this nice little windfall.

'By the way, I have two men in Chania, Ron and Brian; they'll assist you,' Niall said, not that he had much faith in their abilities, but he needed someone on the ground. 'I'll email you photographs of the two girls. Oh yes, last part of our deal: when you find them, eliminate them both. Vera and Sinead are a danger not only to me but to you as well.'

'See it as done.'

Infuriated, Irina listened to the conversation. Despite the shut door, she had heard enough. He wanted Vera and Sinead dead. She had to reach them before it would be too late.

Unsure whether she would be able to hide her anger, she chose not to confront him. A note would have to do. Taking a pad from her bedside locker, she scribbled a short explanation why she must go to town. It may be a wasted trip, but she had to try. On her way out, she placed the note on top of the Davenport in the entrance hall. Without a sound she closed the front door and fell into a brisk walk, her shoes crunching loudly on the gravel drive.

At the main gate, the two Rottweilers chained outside the gatehouse strained on their tethers. The sight of these killers made her cringe as she gave them a wide berth.

'Good afternoon, miss. What can we do for you?' asked Mark, leaning out of the gatehouse window.

'Hello, can you please open the gate for me?'

'Can't do. The boss did not mention anything about you going anywhere,' he said, rather puzzled by her appearance.

Two more faces popped up beside him, saying nothing, suspiciously watching her. One reached for the phone.

'How could he if he doesn't know?' she replied. 'I'm arranging a surprise dinner for him. And please, not a word. I should be back in about two hours. If not, you can send the cavalry.'

Come on, just open the gate! she fretted.

'We have our orders, miss. No one is to leave without his permission,' the other guard, Diarmuid, commented, his hand resting on the phone.

'I know. I don't want to get you into any trouble, so you can blame me. But I did leave him a note. Please, just this once,' she asked, smiling conspiratorially.

'No problem then. OK, go,' Mark said.

The personnel gate clicked open.

'Can I get you anything in town?' she asked, sounding extremely grateful but having no intention of doing any such thing.

'No, we're fine. Thanks for asking,' Mark replied.

Behind him, Diarmuid remained unimpressed by Mark's lackadaisical attitude. There would be hell to pay, but not if he could help it.

CHAPTER 40

Blackrock, Dublin
Wednesday Afternoon

Sean did not need to be an expert to detect the forced lock. Cautiously he opened the door. The lights were still on with music humming monotonously in the background. Everything seemed to be in place, just as it was during his last visit, except for the distinct feeling of emptiness.

Venturing through the apartment it was as he had suspected – no one was home. Mercifully there were no bodies sprawled on the floor. Half an hour of rummaging through Sinead's personal items revealed nothing. Not a single note, sign, or clue of where they might be were to be found.

Dejected, he returned to the car.

What now?

He knew no one other than Ronan who could help. His siblings, Laura, Billy and Flynn were just as much in the dark as he was. Tired after a sleepless night – having dashed to the hotel several times – he decided to give it another few hours before paying Ronan a visit. He may have some idea what to do. Sitting back, he fretted: if this Niall character did not hesitate to just about kill Ronan, what would deter him from killing two prostitutes?

Arriving in Blackrock, Irina instructed the driver to drop her near Sinead and Vera's apartment. Spotting their building four hundred metres further along, she entered the first complex on her left. From its safety, she scouted the area for a better vantage point. Having picked one, she once more continued down the road, carefully observing the parked cars along the way. Slipping through the entrance gate she followed the cobbled path, opened the front door and stepped into the semi-dark foyer. She had a perfect view of the girls' apartment. The few people ambling about did not give her any reason for concern – none looked like Niall's men.

Five minutes later, intently focused on their apartment, the soft swish of the rear entrance door made her withdraw deeper into the shadows. To her surprise, the lonely, tall figure headed straight for her.

'Irina?'

'Sean?' she asked amazed and stepped out from behind the plants. 'Am I glad to see you. Quickly, please follow me.'

Climbing the stairs to the first floor, Sean asked, 'Who were you hiding from?'

'No need for Niall to know I'm here.'

'Of course.'

'To be honest, I was hoping to find you.'

'Why, what's happened?'

'Have you by any chance spoken to Sinead today?'

'No, I have not. Nor have I any idea where she is or whether she's even still alive. They're both gone.'

'Yes, I know. And they're still alive, but won't be for much longer unless we find them first.'

'What do you mean? What's going on?'

'Niall wants them dead. Sinead was lucky to have survived the last beating. This time she won't.'

'You know what happened to her? What she does for a living?' Sean asked flabbergasted.

'Yes, they told me everything. And, so be it. But believe me, I will not stand by and let him do what he wants. *Het*, no!'

'Thanks. But what makes you so sure they're still alive?'

'Less than an hour ago I overheard Niall telling some guy, named Dimitris, to kill them. He does not know where they

173

are. They may still be in Crete, or might have left by now, which I hope they have.'

'Good, then there's still hope. Let's go, no point hanging around here. I'll go and find them.'

'No, wait. I need to talk to you about all this, about what I think is going on. Niall mentioned something about them stealing his diamonds.'

'What diamonds … where?'

'The last day in Chania, collecting Vera opposite the Bank of Crete, she gave Niall a small key … most likely that of a safe-deposit box? Considering what I now know, I suspect she was asked to store his diamonds in this bank in case we might be searched at the airport – as we were. And now they've gone to Chania to fetch the diamonds for themselves, and disappear!'

'If what you're saying is true, then it's no wonder he wants them dead. What were they thinking?' Sean said annoyed, shaking his head, fed up. 'That explains her odd behaviour the last time I saw her … and lying through her teeth as well. If it wasn't so dangerous, I'd be rolling on the floor laughing! Damn, I told her not to do anything stupid. Well, so much for listening. The annoying thing is, I can't get hold of her; her phone is off.'

'You have to keep trying her number.'

'Right, here goes again. Maybe at some stage she'll read her messages.'

'Sean, best you go to this bank in Chania and start from there. They may have some idea where they are.'

'Yeah, exactly what I was thinking. It's a long shot, but seems the only realistic one.'

'I agree. And I'll do whatever I can from this side. I'm sure I can wheedle some information out of Niall to keep you abreast of progress. We have to find them before Niall's men do.'

Despite the dangers Sinead and Vera faced, Irina could not help smiling, knowing Niall stood to lose a fortune if they were to succeed.

And I'll gladly help them, she thought.

Parting company with her, Sean rushed to the nearest travel agent and bought a ticket for the first available flight to Greece – a late-night departure to Athens with a mid-morning connection to Crete. According to his estimation, the bank in Chania should be open by the time he got there.

A few minutes after Sean left the agency, two male customers walked in.

Glen spoke briefly, pleased with the breakthrough. 'Yes, I'm a hundred percent certain. He's taking the last flight, eleven tonight to Athens, and then to Crete. Two men will shadow him.'

'Good. Anything else?' Niall asked.

'I'm sending you a picture of this guy, now,' Glen said, and paused a few moments before asking, 'You got it?'

'Yes,' Niall said and chuckled to himself as he immediately recognised the face in the text: the spitting image of Sinead. 'As I suspected: Mr O'Donovan. Well, my boy, you'll be doing us a big favour and leading us straight to them. Right, Glen, you know what to do.'

CHAPTER 41

Chania, Crete
Wednesday Afternoon

Shoving a photograph of Vera in the restaurant owner's face, the bald stocky Irishman scowled, 'Have you seen her?'

Recognising the face, but having no idea who she was, the proprietor asked, 'Why, what's it to you?'

Without a word, the second foreigner pulled a knife and pressed it under the Greek's chin. Stunned, the three customers with whom he was enjoying an afternoon coffee on the pavement, gaped open-mouthed.

'OK! OK! She was here!'

'That's better. Now don't be shy, please continue. When did she leave?' Ron asked, pleased that it hadn't taken too long: the third eatery along and *voila*, success!

'About thirty minutes ago.'

'How … which direction? Where to?'

'On foot.' Having somewhat regained his composure, the proprietor blurted, 'How the hell would I know where to? *Vlákas!*'

'I hope you didn't insult me, you fuck!' Ron hissed. 'Time to teach him some manners! Will ya, buddy?'

'My pleasure,' Brian replied as the knife's point penetrated the soft skin of the Greek's throat.

Pointing a wavering finger to the south, leading out of town, the wounded owner blabbed, 'That way.'

'Ya sure?'

'Yes.'

'Was she alone?'

'No, she was with the bank manager from down the road. They looked like they were quite into each other. They might have gone to a hotel.'

'Got ya. Was she carrying any luggage?'

'No, only a large shoulder bag.'

'How large … what colour? Was it full or empty?'

'About seventy by seventy, light-brown leather, full, I think.'

'And this one, was she also here?' Ron asked, producing Sinead's photo.

'Yes, but she sat on her own. They did not seem to know each other.'

'Did they leave at the same time?'

'No, this one left ten minutes before the other two.'

'Which direction?'

'Same as the blonde, out of town, towards a hotel … who knows?'

'Ya sure?' Ron asked, confused. It didn't make any sense. Heading towards the ferry port would have been the logical thing to do if they wanted to get off the island. *Have they gone into hiding, or gone to fetch their luggage?* he pondered.

'Look, mister, I don't care if you believe me or not. They are nothing to me. Customers who have come and gone, that's all. Now please ask your friend to remove his knife from my throat,' the Greek asked through clenched teeth, barely controlling his Mediterranean temper.

Ron nodded for Brian to let go.

As soon as he did the Greek shouted, 'Get the hell off my property!' and without a second thought launched himself at a much younger and agile Brian.

Effortlessly, Brian stepped aside and jabbed the knife into the man's side, propelling him back on top of the few customers still remaining. Stooping down, he wiped the blade clean on the wounded proprietor's shirt, and hissed, 'Not a word to anyone or we'll be back!'

CHAPTER 42

Dimitris' Estate
Wednesday Afternoon

Leading the cavalcade of four cars the silver 7-series BMW's tyres screeched as it careened out of the tree-lined lane on to the main road. Stavros stared into the distance; his pensive mood did not encourage banter amongst his fellow passengers. His knuckles shone white through his dark skin with his hands clutching the steering wheel with brute force. Venting his anger on the groaning mechanical contraption, he kept the rev counter's needle locked in the red.

'If they think their uniforms will protect them, then they're mistaken,' he swore under his breath, still fuming at the harassment experienced in police custody.

The memory of being in captivity along with the three Irish and two Greeks did not sit well. He had never felt so powerless, left in the hands of fate, and Dimitris. If condemning evidence had been found, would his employer have helped, or just walked away, washing his hands of the whole incident? Who could tell? Honour amongst thieves only went so far. The fear of having to spend the rest of his life in prison had gnawed at his nerves like a hyena viciously devouring a carcass.

When a small fortune in euros had been discovered at the bottom of the ocean near Michael's destroyed yacht, he and the others had been released. Convinced they had caught up with the alleged drug traffickers, the authorities had concentrated their efforts in locating the culprits sailing somewhere on the open seas with the contraband on board.

He had hardly shaved and washed off the prison stench when he had been ordered on this assignment; one he wanted to get over with as quickly as possible. His instructions were clear: find the diamonds and kill the two girls.

The brown envelope containing colour prints of the two beautiful young women was tucked inside the door's pocket by his side. He deprived the other men the enjoyment of studying the images; he was in no mood for their juvenile sense of humour.

Vera, my dear Vera … what the hell have you got yourself into now, he sighed, regretting what had to be done.

CHAPTER 43

Vera was on edge. Clasped under her arm was the bag containing an unimaginable fortune, a fortune normally requiring an armed convoy. With small beads of nervous sweat forming on her forehead she was starting to attract unwanted attention. She looked and felt guilty.

Hailing a taxi, she jumped in, shut the door and slumped into the backseat. Searching the pavements for Sinead she fretted whether Niall's men might by now have caught up with her, or were merely following at a discreet distance. At last she saw her with her shoulders slumped and head down, looking rather dejected.

'Please pull over,' she instructed the driver. Throwing the door open she shouted, 'Sinead, quick, get in!'

'What took you so long? I was getting worried, thought he had dragged you off to a hotel.' Sinead exclaimed exasperatedly as she jumped in.

'He wishes,' Vera whispered. 'At least it's all done, just as we've planned.'

'Phew, that's a relief, because, I'm not going near that bank again. He must know by now … And why the lunch!?'

'It was the only way I could get it all done today. He was trying to get me to come back tomorrow. So, I had to humour him.'

'I gathered as much. But shame on you, playing him like that. Imagine, instead of being stuck here with me you could by now have been in his *strong muscular* arms, in some fancy room, experiencing heavenly bliss!'

'Ooh, the man of my dreams … yeah, right!' Vera laughed. The mere thought of the man's scrawny body gave her the creeps.

'Anyway, did you really manage to get it all?'

'You're not listening. Yes, my dear, I have,' Vera replied. Leaning forward, she gave the driver a fifty euro note to hurry – far too much time had been wasted.

Vera emptied the contents of her bag on the coffee table. In silence the two gawked at the pile of diamonds, neither having ever possessed, or dreamed of possessing so much wealth.

'Black-market price, forty-five million euro, give or take!' Vera exclaimed. 'Wow, I can't believe we've pulled this off! Whoever said, "Good fortune favours the brave", was absolutely right!'

'Can you imagine his face when he finds out?' Sinead laughed.

'Do you have to mention him? I was just starting to have fun,' Vera said. 'Anyway, I hate to end our little celebration, but we better get going. We don't want to be on this island come tomorrow.'

'You're right. Okay, half for you, half for me, so we don't lose the whole lot in case some moron makes a grab for our bags,' Sinead said, dividing the diamonds into two equal piles.

Lightheaded after their success, Sinead and Vera approached the ticket office of the Heraklion ferry port, itching to leave Crete. The queue ahead was short, consisting of seven travellers chatting excitedly.

Side by side the girls waited their turn.

'Finally,' Vera sighed, reaching the counter. 'Two singles to Athens with a stopover in Santorini, please,' she asked, not bothered about the cost.

'When?' came the curt reply.

'Sorry, next sailing,' Sinead chirped, smiling apologetically.

With tickets in hand, they hurried to board the ferry due to sail in thirty minutes. Sinead checked her watch. 'Just made it, but we're running out of time. By now Niall must know what we've done.'

'Yes, you're probably right. Relax, I'm sure it will take quite a while before they'll track us,' Vera replied. These words, expressed with little conviction, fooled neither Sinead nor herself.

'Sorry, I'm far too nervous to believe that … or, to relax. But I'll try.'

Seated in the ferry's lounge, Vera whispered in Sinead's ear, 'Are those men staring at us? Do you think they're somehow connected to Niall?'

Sinead glanced in their direction. 'No, definitely not. They're Greek, and they're leering. You really have no idea how pretty … stunning, you are, do you?' Sinead asked. 'Men will always gawk.'

'That goes for you too. So, I suppose we do make quite a pair. Two pretty girls, and with one beaten-up, will draw unwanted attention anywhere.'

'Just grand, we shouldn't have stuck together. Anyway, I'm sure they've no idea who we are. They're just being men.'

'So much for remaining inconspicuous,' Vera sighed, realising they had just made two major blunders – first at the ticket office, and now sitting side by side. Anyone asking questions will pick up their trail in an instant.

With the strong wind and waves buffeting the jetfoil out on the open sea, the crossing to Santorini soon turned into a rollercoaster ride. Thrown from side to side they strapped themselves in and held on. For the duration of the two-hour journey, they hardly said a word as each struggled with their own demons: past, present, and future.

At last, they disembarked, the solid ground feeling odd beneath their wobbly legs. Above them, awash in soft evening colours, clusters of small buildings clung precariously to the cliffs of the caldera. In the east the dark sky rolled in, filling them with eerie apprehension. Resisting the temptation to wander up to the top of the mountain to enjoy the views, which must be spectacular, they pressed on with their plan, albeit this time with greater caution. Taking turns, they purchased tickets for the next leg of the journey.

First Sinead booked an economy class, twin cabin to Athens via Mykonos. Vera followed a few minutes later and bought two tickets to Athens via Milo, due to sail in half an hour.

With reservations secured they joined the other travellers, hoping to blend in with the diverse groups of Greek families and young backpackers. This time, waiting for their departure under the darkening sky, they sat well apart, vigilant for any signs of danger.

CHAPTER 44

Crete
Wednesday Afternoon

Armed with what little information the two Irishmen in Chania had supplied, Stavros headed to the most likely place Sinead and Vera might have gone: Heraklion ferry port. The other three cars were dispatched to cover the small port in Chania, the marina in Heraklion and the airport.

Impatiently, Stavros listened to the smug official, a man in his mid-thirties, giving him the standard unhelpful answer. 'Sorry, my friend, can't tell you … it's the law. We're not allowed to divulge any information regarding passengers,' he smirked from behind the safety of the ticket desk, not in the least sorry.

The suntanned, arrogant official irked Stavros to the point where he wanted to jump over the counter and readjust his nose somewhat. An act which undoubtedly would deprive him of many a conquest over the young girls who pass through on their summer vacations, soaked in vodka, with their morals left at home.

'Listen, squirt, cut the crap or I'll—'

'I'd answer him if I were you.' Pedro interrupted, flashing his concealed weapon.

'Thank you,' Stavros said annoyed. 'Now that you know I mean business, please enlighten me and be quick.'

With the blood drained from the official's face, he did

not need any further encouragement, willingly confirming the girls' purchases, '… they left on the last ferry for Santorini approximately twenty minutes ago.'

'*Efharisto.* See how easy that was,' Stavros thanked the official and left.

Should not take long to catch them. An hour to the airport, wheels up and half an hour in the air, Stavros calculated as he raced back to the car. *This business should be over … max three hours.*

As estimated, Stavros and his team boarded the private jet an hour later. Another few minutes lapsed before, with the greatest ease, the plane's nose lifted off the ground and swooped towards Santorini.

The hunt was on.

The two girls' head start would soon be wiped out. All things considered, what chance did two alien women on foreign soil really have in evading them?

None.

CHAPTER 45

Santorini, Greece
Wednesday Evening

The threat was all it took to loosen the man's tongue. 'Yes, she was here,' the official confirmed, pointing at Vera's photograph while ignoring the other. 'She bought two tickets for the crossing to Athens. It left half an hour late. Sailed 21h00.'

'You sure? Which route?'

'Yes, positive, and via Milos … should be there in under an hour,' Stephanos confirmed, his expression compliant.

'Thank you,' Stavros replied and slapped a fifty euro note on the counter, in a hurry to return to the plane, wanting to reach Milos before the ferry would dock.

Turning the euro note in his hands Stephanos watched Stavros and his men pile into three cars and race up the steep mountain path. 'Good luck,' he muttered, incensed at having been threatened. He remembered only too well the badly beaten woman seated on the quay after the ferry for Milos had sailed.

Leaving the ferry port, Stavros had a hunch that the trip to Athens might be nothing more than a ruse with the girls hiding somewhere in Santorini. Therefore, two men were sent to search the passengers still waiting to embark. And if they struck out, they were to join the other five men who were on their way to the four villages perched along the top of the crescent-shaped cliff of the caldera.

Waiting for the ferry Sinead felt extremely vulnerable out in the open, not daring to let go of her bag containing so much wealth. Intuitively, she clutched it more tightly under her arm. The thought of what she could do with the money was mindboggling. She did not regard it as theft; it was the least he owed them for ruining their lives. With the money, she would buy something small and quaint, isolated, far away from everyone. And when strong enough she would rebuild her life and do everything in her power to help other women trapped in the sex industry. She would make good. And maybe someday, just maybe, she would find love, someone who would accept her for what she is … and possibly even have children. A beautiful dream, she thought as an inexplicable calm washed over her.

A sudden commotion made her look up. On her right, a small group of passengers were having an argument, ganging up against two men thrusting something in their faces. They looked Greek.

'Pssst, miss. Come with me!' someone whispered in her ear.

Alarmed, not knowing what or whom to expect, she turned around. Behind her stood a young official in a slightly crumpled uniform, smiling disarmingly.

'Don't worry, I'm Stephanos. I work for the ferry port. This way, you'll be safe with me.'

Seeing her hesitate, he pointed at the fracas which five harbour police were approaching, and warned, 'Those men are looking for you and your friend.'

Bewildered, Sinead looked at Vera in the distance and gesticulated with her head, unsure of what to do. Vera nodded, stood up and left.

With the brawl reaching fever pitch, the police did not waste any time in accosting Stavros' men and escorting them out of the passengers' waiting area. Their loud protestations had no effect on the officials.

As Sinead dithered, Stephanos urged once more, 'Come, hurry!'

Sinead stood up. 'Where are you taking me?'

'To our office. You can stay there until your sailing. Where's your friend?'

'Right here,' Vera's breathless voice sounded a few metres behind them. 'Why are you helping us, which we appreciate, but why?'

'I don't like Mafioso … scum, the whole lot! We can do without them – especially you two. Now please, come.'

Entering the walled yard reeking of stale urine and cluttered with discarded boxes, they fumbled their way through the dark. The scamper of a stray cat made Sinead jump. Once safely inside the staff canteen, empty at this hour, Stephanos updated them on what had transpired.

Their faces crumpled, unable to absorb the news of just how perilously close they had come to being caught. If it had not been for Stephanos their escape attempt would have been over by now.

'My God, how did they find us so soon, and so easily?' Sinead asked, petrified. She sat down, the strength drained from her body, her resolve obliterated. She felt like crying, having no energy to continue.

Noticing her friend falter, Vera said, 'I don't know … but we have to get away from here, right now!'

'No, best you stay. Your ferry should arrive in about twenty minutes. I'll make sure you get on board without anyone noticing. It is the only way. No one will know. You stay on this island, they'll find you,' Stephanos interrupted, trying to encourage them. 'Those two will not bother you tonight. Neither their friends. They're on their way to Milos. OK, you wait here. I'll be back in a second – you need uniforms.'

'Thank you, Stephanos,' Sinead whispered grateful, knowing full well that by helping them he had signed his own death warrant. 'You realise they will come for you, having

189

misled them.'

'Forget it. I'll be fine,' he replied, sounding more confident than he felt.

'Please, here's some money in case you need to get away,' Vera said and placed a bundle of notes in his hands.

'No, I cannot accept this.'

'Please, I insist. You'll need this, you must go away even if only for a short while.'

Taking the ten thousand euro he once more flinched at the bruises on Sinead's face. It reminded him of his late mother who had suffered many beatings at the hand of his father. Helping these two strangers was the least he could do. And they may be right, it would be best to take an unplanned vacation.

By the time their ferry arrived, an hour late, the howling wind had morphed into a gale. With Stephanos by their side, and dressed as crew members, they sneaked on to the ferry with their nerves in tatters, like linen scorched by the desert sun.

Shutting the cabin door behind her, Vera gave an almighty sigh and blurted, 'Thank God! And damn them … damn them all, may they rot in Hell.'

'Just grand … so what are we going to do? They know where we are. They'll find us.'

'No, they won't! We stick to our plan. Remember money talks … buys loyalties; that was at least one truth Niall had spoken. As long as we have these,' Vera said and shook her bag with the diamonds, 'we'll buy our way out of this mess. Now best we eat, shower and have a good night's sleep. You're okay with that?'

'Yes,' Sinead responded feebly, tired.

'Good, and no more negative talk. Dream of nice things … be positive, it's the only way to cope.'

'I'll try,' Sinead replied, wishing she had her friend's strength.

Having showered and eaten they collapsed on their bunk beds, exhausted. Ignoring the violent rolling of the ferry leaving port they soon succumbed to sleep.

Milos Island

As the wheels of the jet cleared the runway, returning to Santorini, Stavros growled into his phone, 'We have no idea where they are. They could be anywhere by now, or could still be hiding in Santorini. We'll continue there at daybreak. The trip to Milos was a decoy, a waste of time. I'll get the truth out of that little punk at the ticket office. Not to worry boss, I shall find them.'

'I know you will,' Dimitris replied, having the utmost confidence in his right-hand man.

CHAPTER 46

Niall's Estate
Wednesday Evening

Fed by melting wax the four flames idly consumed the braided cotton wicks. In the background, the hands of the decorative grandfather clock were about to meet on the Roman numeral ten.

'That was quite spectacular, thank you. I had no idea you were such a great cook,' Niall said and pushed his chair back, running his hands over his stomach. 'I may as well get rid of those useless chefs and leave you in charge.'

The rich creamy mushroom starter followed by succulent slow-cooked beef Stroganoff seasoned with a blend of hidden flavours and complemented by a splendid red Burgundy had been rounded off by sweet pastries.

'I'm delighted you enjoyed my effort,' she beamed, ostensibly appreciating his praise.

Having exchanged the large formal Georgian style dining room for the smallest of the mansion's three drawing rooms, they shared their events of the day.

He acknowledged her visit to Dublin as a logistical necessity in the preparation of the surprise dinner. But he would have to deal with the men. They knew the one rule which was not to be broken: access to and from his estate by anyone was only by his permission.

Seeing the slight frown on his forehead, Irina said, 'I don't think you enjoyed the meal …'

'Of course, I did!' he replied jovially, reassuring her.

Suppressing her anger, she allowed the farce to continue. 'Then what's wrong? You look upset,' she said, feigning concern.

'Remember Vera? Well, she has gone missing with some valuables of mine. I must admit it was quite unexpected as she is one of my most loyal employees. Comes to show – no one is to be trusted these days.'

'That is shocking! Must be very disappointing.'

'That's putting it mildly.'

'Do you know where she is?'

'Apparently in Santorini. Nice spot to hide; I must give her that. Anyway, she better enjoy it while it lasts as my Greek friends are onto her. It won't take long now. Real shame though; I always liked her … and, unfortunately, I can't let her go unpunished.'

'Of course not. Who are these—'

'Bloody hell, can't remember when we last had such a warm summer.' Niall said, cutting her short as he wiped his brow, changing topic, not wanting to spoil the evening by discussing Vera and Sinead. 'One upside of the so-called "climate change" I can get used to: no need to bugger off to the south of France to find some sunshine.' he said laughingly.

Continuing with idle talk, he was filled with desire, stirred by her sweet perfume next to him. He reached out and caressed her back. Undoing the small buttons of her dress he pulled the garment over her shoulders. Fleetingly, his lips brushed the nape of her neck …

Feeling his warm breath against her bare skin Irina steeled herself. Allowing him to have his way she fought the chills his touches evoked.

At the soft rap on the door, Niall paused and huffed, 'What now!'

'Excuse me, sir, I have an urgent call. A lady. She does not want to leave a message,' a voice said from behind the closed door.

'Right, right. Give me a second.'

As soon as Irina had composed herself, Niall opened the door and took the phone. 'Thanks.'

'Again, my apologies, but she insisted,' John the butler said and shut the door.

Attentively, Irina listened to the conversation which followed. It was a family matter, nothing to do with the two girls.

'Thanks for sharing the news of her death and suggesting I pay my respects. But I've no interest in attending Mum's funeral. As far as I'm concerned, she can rot in hell.'

'Niall, how can you say that? For God's sake, she was your mother. Don't you dare forget she carried, nursed and raised you with love. You once were a part of her! My God, what have you become?' his aunt asked, furious.

'You know full well what she did! She was no bloody saint.'

'If that is how you feel, then I truly hope you'll suffer a far worse fate than she ever had.' his aunt shouted, ending the call.

Infuriated, Niall threw the phone on the couch, no longer in the mood for romance, or anything else for that matter.

Unable to contain herself, Irina asked, 'Correct me if I'm wrong. Your mother died and you cursed her?'

His venomous dark eyes glared at her. But as he spoke his voice was surprisingly calm. 'Yes, that's correct. But before you condemn me to the Gulag – seeing I'm such a piece of lowlife – you may first want to learn the truth. I think that would only be fair, don't you?'

'Yes, please, do tell.'

'It's a long story. Let's have another drink, shall we?'

The formal drawing room decorated with huge paintings of dramatic Napoleonic battles depicting fallen horses and riders was cold, hostile and intimidating. It was the perfect venue for a stand-off Niall thought, for the moment forgetting the prospect of a life shared with Irina. His mind was like the endless tide, bound by no shore, rising and falling at will, controlled by some alien force. With drinks in hand they faced each other, the room shrouded in an uncomfortable silence.

Taking a sip, Niall commenced with the story of his life.

'My youth was spent in Sligo on the north-west coast of Ireland. We lived like most Irish back then, just happy to be alive: my father, mother, sister and me. With not much money to throw around, we attended mass regularly, visited families, played Gaelic football, went fishing, and so on. To have food on the table was all that mattered. But with the passing of time, my father became a well-respected property developer. He was a man I had idolised – my inspiration, my role model. As kids, we were both very fond of him; my sister even more so than me. And like a real doting father, there was nothing he wouldn't do for us. We completed his life.'

Niall's mood turned sombre as he continued, his mind filled with disturbing memories, 'I was sixteen, away on a camping trip with the scouts when I received news of my father's death.'

Irina did not interrupt, neither did she show any emotions.

'Apparently, after a vicious argument between my parents – which was quite common with my mother suffering regular black moods – she had chased him through the house, grabbed a knife in the kitchen and butchered him in my sister's room, stabbing him over thirty times.' It was an image seared into Niall's mind, haunting him for years, day and night, feeding his craving for revenge.

'That's terrible! But why?'

'Why? Because she was nuts, plain and simple. She never explained, except stating she hated him and would do it again. The little bit of sense they had managed to elicit from my sister confirmed my mother's story. Maura was outside playing and hearing the screaming, she had rushed inside and pleaded with my mother to stop. Ignoring her, she had killed him. Maura could never recover from the trauma. Refusing to speak or eat, she took her life eleven months later.'

'How awful, poor girl,' Irina said. 'And your mother, did she feel guilty … blamed herself?'

'Doubt it. Remember, she was crazy.'

'Sounds strange …'

'Look, as far as I'm concerned, she's responsible for their deaths. Therefore, I'll never forgive her. I've cut her out of my life. Another thing, just in case you do empathise with her out of some kind of female camaraderie, may I remind you she was nothing other than a cold-hearted bitch. Even during the trial, she had shown no remorse, callously admitting to the murder.'

'That is very sad to hear.' Irina said, lowering her gaze. *No wonder he's deranged, must be genetic!*

'At first, some thought she wasn't being honest, maybe he'd done something. But according to her, he never did. Psychiatric evaluations did not provide any evidence of mitigating circumstances either. The judge was left with no choice but to hand down a life sentence. The last time I saw her was when she was being escorted out of court.'

'Who took care of you and your sister?'

'*Dearest,* Aunt Cath, the one who just rang. I lived with her until Maura passed away at which stage, I'd had enough. So, I had packed my little bag, thanked and kissed her goodbye and left, wishing to never be subjected to her *lovely sweet* smile ever again. She had reminded me too much of my mother. Roaming the world for a few years, I finally ended up in London where I survived by working as cheap labour on building sites.'

'During all this time did you never try to contact your mother?' Irina probed.

'No, I didn't. But when she heard I was back in Dublin, she did write regularly, letters which I returned unopened, having no interest in her drivel.'

'Why not? I don't understand. Did you never consult a therapist? It sounds as if you were scared to discover the truth or something about yourself you might not have liked?'

Unhappy with her tone, he took a large swig of his whiskey and said, 'I have no time for shrinks, not then, not now. Look, it's water under the bridge and I prefer we leave it at that if you don't mind.'

196

Niall was in no mood to continue discussing his mother or himself. He hated her, period. There was nothing more to be said. Her actions were what drove him to abuse and kill women at will. Each one sent to an early grave was symbolic of a knife wound his father had received. He was fulfilling a vow taken when only sixteen: to avenge his father's brutal death.

'Sorry, Niall. I've no right to judge you. I might have reacted the same,' she apologised, realising he was becoming manic. 'As it clearly still haunts you, I hope you'll allow me to help you overcome those awful experiences.'

'Uhm …' he sighed, his amorous heart deflated to a point of indifference.

'What was it like in London?' she asked, hoping to lighten the solemn mood.

Given an opportunity to talk about his experiences, Niall relaxed somewhat and started relating his disappointments and successes as a young entrepreneur.

Images of sweating, tanned, half-naked bodies labouring in the midday sun covered in dirt and dust, pushing wheelbarrows for a pittance while transforming dilapidated old Victorian terrace houses to their former glory, were painted for Irina. Of tree-lined streets and flower boxes in full bloom. Of memorable summer evenings holding hands with pretty girls, strolling through Richmond Park watching herds of deer roam free.

And over time, how he had managed to save enough money to invest in property. Once on the ladder of success, nothing could stop him.

His next big venture was the opening of a nightclub in London's West End, raking in more money than he had ever imagined possible, ultimately selling the business for a fortune. The terrace houses initially bought, were soon replaced by mansions, till he was ready to return to Ireland. It was a fortunate time with the Celtic Tiger sprinting ahead of the rest of Europe.

Back in Ireland, Niall's empire had mushroomed. Housing

197

developments were snapped up, commercial properties were sold or let before they were completed. Money made in Ireland was prudently re-invested in commercial properties in England, China, the Middle East and the Americas.

He droned on, unable to stop himself from boasting, with Irina interrupting every so often.

But the real facts of how he had saved enough money to build his empire, commencing with the construction of a modest development project in London, Niall did not divulge. The reality was a very different picture from the flowery one painted for Irina.

If Irina knew the full extent of his crimes it would have destroyed the last tethers of faith she held in humanity. And it would most certainly have driven her to madness, knowing she had willingly given herself to such a demon – allowed his bloodstained hands to caress her.

The truth was the money earned on building sites had not been nearly enough to cover his basic living expenses, let alone generate a small fortune to launch his illustrious career as a developer.

Lonely at the time, he had frequented the bars and clubs in Soho. Especially one specific strip club had received his loyal support. Persevering, he had finally managed to introduce himself to a young girl named Cindy. She was from Wales, a pretty blonde with a very pleasant demeanour. Charmed by the handsome Irish brute she had soon fallen under his spell, permitting him to move into her apartment which she shared with two other dancers, Maggie and Tess. As he seemed a decent and likeable person the flatmates had happily consented; his looks and bulk had convinced them he could be an asset to have around.

The value of his presence had soon proved itself.

It was on a Friday night late when a drunken customer had followed Tess back to the apartment demanding sex. Niall had not hesitated in escorting the man into a back alley and when gentle persuasion did not work, had ripped his belly open with a knife, spilling its contents on to the pavement.

The young girls had been none the wiser of what had transpired in ridding them of that "most irritating fella". From then on, they had relied on Niall for protection.

At only nineteen years of age, it had been Niall's first kill.

Having tasted blood and suffering no remorse, he had been ready to take his first tentative steps in the shadows of the underworld. Soon the girls had trusted him with their lives, willingly sharing his bed as and when needed. His suggestion that they started to work for real money during the day was gleefully agreed to by all. He had assured them they would only sleep with men they approved of. No scumbags would be tolerated, guaranteed.

Their apartment had been cleaned up, a bar, and intercom installed while discreet advertising had taken place, aimed at suitable men with enough funds. Their little business venture had rapidly grown, forcing the acquisition of larger premises.

Within four years he had become the owner of a gentlemen's club, a secluded country home eight kilometres south of St Albans. It had been ideally located for commuters to stop over after a stressful day in London.

A cynical system had been employed in sidestepping the strict laws pertaining to prostitution: visitors became *temporary members* at a set price, having access to all services and facilities on offer. And as members, no negotiations or exchange of money between girls and clients were permitted. The girls working as full-time waitresses would serve the usual array of drinks, cigars and canapés to *gentlemen* ensconced in big comfortable leather chairs in the tastefully furnished drawing room and library, reading newspapers and journals, or while being pampered in the luxurious spa.

Due to the late hours the waitresses had to work the management had felt obliged, "purely out of concern for the well-being of the female staff", to offer them lodgings on the premises. For this purpose the two upper floors of the elegant, Georgian country house had been converted into luxurious double bedrooms with en-suite bathroom facilities. So, if it happened that during the evening a guest introduced himself to a waitress, charmed her so much that she wanted to show her gratitude in whichever way she felt inclined, then it was up to them what they did, even if it meant spending some time in the privacy of her quarters on the upper floors. After all, being consenting adults, they were not breaking any laws.

As was common at such venues, security cameras had been installed to all communal areas with some hidden inside the girls' rooms. These permitted the recording of hours of incriminating evidence; evidence that was used in blackmailing members, forcing generous financial contributions to Niall's rapidly swelling coffers.

However, there had been one golden rule: the possession or use of narcotics on the premises had been absolutely forbidden. If they did transgress, they were severely punished. It did not bother Niall if all the girls were heroin addicts. But as his business was still in its infancy, he did not want to give the police any reason to raid his establishment. In later years this rule was shunned as his nightclub in London had thrived on drug trafficking as an integral part of his operations. And the police on his payroll had cooperated fully, grateful for their share of the profits.

Maggie who still frequented Niall's bed had ignored this rule under the misguided notion that she had special privileges. When caught using cocaine the manager had dragged her into Niall's office and with tears streaking her cheeks, he had snapped her slender neck like a twig. Her body was never found. And as rumours had spread, the girls in Niall's service never again defied his wishes.

His third victim was an eighteen-year-old illegal Romanian – a beautiful brunette and gymnast. Ignorant about worldly matters – more specifically about her employer – the girl had miscalculated, thinking that if she played her cards right a great future awaited her as Mrs McGuire. Rushing to his chambers for her moment of glory she did succeed in pleasing Niall immensely. Encouraged by his smile she had expressed her dreams, offering to please his every desire. Amused by such

200

simple devotion he had continued to smile until the moment she proclaimed her undying love for him. The nonsensical blathering had flipped a switch in his head. Without realising he had reached over, grabbed the marble bedside lamp and cracked her head open like an overripe pumpkin. Not giving it a second thought, he had kicked her body off the bed, showered, dressed and called his henchmen to clean up the mess and discard the evidence.

A stunningly beautiful woman with silky black hair, crystal-clear blue eyes and an unblemished milky-white skin tightly stretched over an athletic body was the next to suffer the same fate. Her mistake had been simple: an assumption that beauty relieved her of any obligation to satisfy her partner. Remaining impassionate, she had offered an imbecilic sweet smile, fluttered her eyelids and feigned ecstatic pleasure – after all, he should be extremely honoured to share in such perfection. Incensed, Niall had jumped up, grabbed a blade and rearranged her features. Unfortunately, in his manic state severing the main artery.

After this incident, killing had its own satisfaction. His journey of revenge had taken on its own sordid form of pleasure as he unleashed himself on unsuspecting women. Overwhelmed by his handsome looks, the embodiment of what these women wanted in the man of their dreams – a combination of ruthless confidence, power and success – they had easily succumbed to the alpha male, to him.

But too many girls had disappeared, all somehow connected to Niall. With the police investigations into his life becoming a regular affair, he had been forced to sell his lucrative clubs and relocate to Ireland.

Back in the country of his birth, having set up his new headquarters in Blackrock, he had keenly watched how in record time his development company had grown into one of the biggest in Ireland.

Despite this achievement, he did not relinquish his vices: the brothels, escort agencies, and human, drugs and arms trafficking. These were continued under a cloak of secrecy, camouflaged by a myriad of insignificant pseudo companies and trust funds. This front made it near impossible to link him directly to any illegal operations, breaking of any international laws, or trade sanctions.

And being more cautious, he had delegated the murders to people such as Ciarán O'Reilly, leaving him free to quench his bloodthirst on the unsuspecting game roaming the forests of Poland.

By the time he finished the *courageous* and *honourable* story of his life, he was under the distinct impression she believed him. But to his surprise, Irina stood up and said, 'It's late. I'm tired and need some sleep. Please excuse me. Goodnight.'

She had stomached enough lies for one night. Without another word she walked out, leaving him to brood over his *fond* memories.

Agitated with her having gone to bed, Niall sauntered up to the private theatre. Flicking through the home cinema's memory bank he searched for a film which would help him unwind. Although the one he picked was a film which would make most sane people reach for a bottle of tranquilisers: The Boys from Brazil, starring Gregory Peck as the evil Joseph Mengele with Laurence Olivier in hot pursuit, determined to stop the Nazi Angel of Death from cloning little Hitlers, set to take over the world. And about to reach its finale – a few Dobermans ripping the old man apart – Niall's phone chirped. He paused the film and answered with a simple, 'Yes?'

'It's done. I trust my payment has been made through the usual channels.'

'Yes, of course. I'll be in touch. Thanks,' Niall said.

Switching his phone off, he returned his attention to the film once more.

CHAPTER 47

St. James Hospital
Dublin
Thursday Morning

The tasteless breakfast to some extent alleviated the rumbling noises, his appetite having returned despite his injuries. Much to Ronan's relief the throbbing headache of the previous day had ceased. Expecting Marie and little Tom to arrive at any moment, he shifted up against the pillow. Feeling much better he hoped to be discharged before the end of the day; enough time had been spent away from his family.

He looked up at the TV, catching the end of the RTE news broadcast involving the drowning of a young Irishman somewhere off the Greek coast. Apparently, the result of a disastrous raid carried out by the authorities. In the process a yacht had been destroyed, leaving ten dead: one Irishman, the rest Greek nationals. Two men were still at large, suspected to be Irish as well.

'What were these guys up to? Seems they booked with the wrong charter company,' he mumbled to himself.

The incident reminded him of a massive smuggling operation near Cork several years ago when a raging storm had scuppered the deal – the men, having barely survived the ordeal, had fled into the hills, leaving the mess to be cleaned up by the Coast Guard – cocaine worth millions of euro.

It was only on the fifth ring of his phone that he turned

his attention away from the news.

'Yeah,' he answered, distracted.

'Hi, buddy, how you're feeling?' Sean asked, concerned.

'Much better thanks.'

'Can you talk, or shall I call back later?'

'Now is fine. What's new?'

'Sinead and her flatmate have done a runner.'

'What! What do you mean?' Ronan asked alarmed.

'They've gone. Buggered off to Greece.'

'You're not serious?'

'I'm afraid so.'

'Bloody perfect! They'll ruin our plans just as I am getting people to collaborate. Sean, we need her as a state witness. You better find them before he does. And when you do … sorry, I've got to go. Marie's outside. Give me a call later.'

He hung up, none the wiser that Sean was in Athens.

CHAPTER 48

O'Mara Hotel, Dublin
Thursday Morning

'Calm down and get a hold of yourself!' the hotel manager admonished the hysterical chambermaid. What a mess, the manager sighed heavily, observing the marble tiles splattered with blood and brain tissue. The body was slumped over the edge of the bath, the revolver still clutched in its lifeless hand.

What happened? Rod Cullingham, the manager, wondered.

It was an unwanted incident at the best of times, but the timing could not have been worse. A fortune had been spent on upgrading and refurbishing the O'Mara Hotel in returning the struggling establishment to its former glory. The spate of bad publicity two years ago – a gangland execution of three men with the culprits never found – had not been forgotten.

'You sure you didn't touch anything?' Rod asked the young Polish girl, yet again.

'Yes, I'm sure,' she replied feebly.

'Good,' Rod huffed.

Not taking his eyes off the body, he spoke to his assistant, 'Jim, please contact the Garda and seal the room. No one enters.' He wanted the incident hushed up as quickly and quietly as possible.

Having glanced at the guest list on his way up, he was not impressed, realising who the man was: a regular client, a

205

politician. This spelled trouble.

Considering the colour photographs strewn across the bathroom floor, depicting the victim in some very compromising positions with several girls, it looked like a clear case of suicide, of someone overcome by shame and guilt. The wedding band on the man's left hand gave credence to this assumption. Although convinced it was suicide, he did not rule out the possibility of foul play which had pushed the chap over the edge. In his twenty-five years in the hotel industry, he had seen enough to know.

'Can't say I blame him. Imagine what this smut would do if it hits the tabloids? Poor wife and kids. No, won't be nice. Jim, we have to keep this quiet. No press. Let's spare his family the embarrassment,' he said as he locked the suite's door behind him.

'Yes, that's how he was discovered. The scene has not been disturbed or touched by anyone. The only people who did have access to the room were the chambermaid, my assistant manager and me,' Rod informed the inspector.

'Thank you,' Inspector O'Farrell replied.

'If you need anything else, I'll be in my office,' Rod said, excusing himself, but stopped and added as an afterthought, 'Oh yes, for what it's worth, he had a visitor last night. Didn't stay long; it's all on the video. But I doubt it has anything to do with this, which is clearly a suicide.'

'Aha, interesting, thank you. Also, for keeping this quiet,' Inspector O'Farrell said. *Can't recall how many times I've heard people solving crimes in a matter of minutes. Wish things were that simple,* he smiled to himself.

To the untrained eye it might be a case of suicide, but that the scene was staged, was evident. For one, the noise of the .45 revolver's two shots should have woken the whole floor. It did not. Nothing had been reported, no one heard a thing. But more importantly, he doubted very much that a minister would commit suicide over a few obscene photographs, however shocking.

206

And a visitor? Suicide … unlikely.

No, Mr Murphy, someone helped you meet your Maker. But rest assured, we'll find whoever is responsible, he promised the corpse with half a head clinging mockingly to its twisted body.

'What a mess! Right lads, stop gawking and get to work. I want every inch searched, full reports and no slip-ups. This is no suicide.'

He knew there would be hell to pay. Maybe these politicians can't stand each other in public, but never would they dream of hurting each other.

Having sifted through the room, their efforts were rewarded with very little: a few fingerprints lifted off the photographs – most likely that of the victim – the alleged murder weapon, and nothing more. The hastily scribbled suicide note left on the bedside table, begging his wife and children's forgiveness, seemed of no value either.

Proof of foul play soon became evident while reviewing the surveillance footage. The mysterious visitor – a tall, full-bearded man – had somehow come and gone, not once revealing his face to any of the cameras or hotel staff. His hand and hat had been effectively used to ensure anonymity. The locations of the security cameras seemed to have been first-hand knowledge; this, only a professional hitman would be privy to. Arriving fifteen minutes after Minister Murphy, and following a brief exchange of words in the doorway, he had entered the room without a scuffle. Eleven minutes later he had reappeared and vanished into the night.

But whether he was the murderer or only a blackmailer, having driven the man to suicide, remained to be seen. The Garda's hopes rested on the fingerprints and any forensic evidence found.

Waiting for the lab results they would diligently compile their report, listing all acquaintances, details of recent movements and telephone calls. As the pieces of the puzzle accumulated, they would be efficiently evaluated. Creating a skeleton profile, all possible suspects would systematically be eliminated in hunting down the real culprit.

Informing the family of the tragedy was left to the *Taoiseach* (Prime Minister); the suicide note and photographs were never mentioned. The official version stated that Minister Eoin Murphy had been callously murdered during an armed robbery.

CHAPTER 49

St. James Hospital
Dublin
Thursday Morning

With Tom playing on her lap, a much happier Marie recounted some gossip.

'Marie, hold that thought,' Ronan interrupted her. He turned pale as a photograph of Eoin Murphy was blasted across the TV, followed by flashing images of an ambulance. Grabbing the TV remote, he turned the volume up just in time to hear the Taoiseach make a statement.

Both Ronan and Marie sat glued to the TV screen.

'What! Unbelievable! He didn't …' Ronan shouted as the full impact of what had happened dawned on him.

'What are … who are you talking about?' Marie asked bewildered, staring at her husband's horror-stricken face. 'Oh no, Ronan! Don't tell me this has to do with you … with your assault?'

'I'm sorry, Marie, I never thought …'

She did not say a word. She moved closer and embraced him, filled with dread. For the first time in all their years together he looked scared. 'Tell me, please. What is going on?'

Ronan fretted; he dared not keep quiet any longer, compelled to tell her. 'It started on Monday when Sean came to visit me, asking for my help. I could not refuse him. After all, he's my friend. But I never thought this would happen, I never …'

Marie sat wide-eyed, stunned, refraining from criticising or chastising him as he spoke, revealing all. She fully understood why he had helped Sean. It was his nature; never would he turn his back on a friend. And not for one moment could he have known he was sending another to his death.

'You were right not to have told the detective. Although, I think this changes everything. You have to come clean before you end up in prison,' she said.

'Marie, please, there's nothing I would love to do more. But, don't you see, this is another warning for us to stop interfering in his affairs. We are powerless.'

Niall had made his point emphatically clear. Under no circumstances could Ronan continue, risking the lives of his family.

CHAPTER 50

Niall's Estate
Thursday Morning

'Thank you. That's a relief,' Niall said. Dimitris' call gave him reason to be upbeat. According to Dimitris' sources in the Greek police, Michael and Paddy had survived. Also, the girl's last confirmed location was Santorini. Even the massive penalty imposed by Dimitris for his cooperation – nearly ten million euro to make up for his losses at sea – was momentarily pushed aside. The prospect of retrieving his diamonds and eliminating the two girls outweighed all by far.

He spoke softly into the phone as he looked at Irina reclining on the settee, deeply engrossed in a Russian novel. 'You're positive they were last seen in Santorini and are now heading towards Athens?' he asked.

'Yes, one hundred percent.'

'Understood. A suggestion: as Michael's still alive, may be a good idea if he teams up with Stavros. What do you think?'

'Hmm, I have no problem with that. As long as it does not affect my fee. Do I have your word on that?'

'Yes, absolutely.'

'Good, we'll do that,' Dimitris agreed.

'As soon as I hear form Michael, I'll get him to contact Stavros,' Niall said. 'But it is imperative they …'

Irina had heard enough. Closing her book, she got up and mouthed to Niall, still deep in conversation, that she needed to

211

use the bathroom.

With her bedroom door firmly shut Irina lingered a few seconds, ensuring she was not being followed. Inside the bathroom she sat down on the edge of the bath with the door slightly ajar, permitting a clear view of the bedroom. Holding her phone to her ear she impatiently listened to the long beep tone. Finally, he answered.

'Hi, Sean speaking.'

'Can you talk?' she whispered.

'Yes, of course, what's up?'

'They were last seen in Santorini and apparently are on their way to Athens. A Greek named Stavros is leading the search. He'll soon be joined by Niall's chief of security, Michael. I'll try and get you some photographs so you'll know who you're up against. In the meantime, may be wise to only question women. It sounds as if none are involved in the hunt.' Absentmindedly Irina ruffled her hair. Distracted by the messy image in the mirror, she picked up a brush and started combing.

'Thanks, you just saved me a trip. I'll visit the ferry port in Athens; it seems the logical place to start looking. Maybe I'll get lucky and catch them as they disembark. Can't be too many arrivals from Santorini, I hope. Take care and no unnecessary risks, please.'

'I'm fine, trust me. I'll contact you as soon as I have more information—'

'Contact who and what information?' Niall's angry voice growled beside her as he gripped her arm. She nearly dropped the phone. 'Who the hell are you talking to?'

'Do you mind, you're hurting me! Please wait in my room. I'll be out when I'm done. And if you must know, it's Cynthia. She called me,' Irina replied icily.

He let go of her arm. 'Right, right,' he said suspiciously and retreated to the bedroom.

Remaining as calm as she could muster, she continued her conversation with Sean, 'Cynthia, sorry, where was I? Oh

212

yes … I tell you what, I'll call later. I promise. You heard Niall. *Dasvidanya.*'

'Got ya. Best you stop and immediately get away from him. He's on to you! Bye,' Sean said.

Having erased the call log on her phone, she took a deep breath and returned to her bedroom. 'Why do you treat me like this? I've done nothing wrong,' she said, deeply disappointed.

'Really?' Niall asked sceptically.

'Yes, really. I met Cynthia on a chat site. She's Canadian and is looking for work in Ireland. She does not stop pestering me, asking if I can help.' The hastily conceived lie was told with total conviction.

Niall remained silent. His piercing stare unnerved her. When he spoke, he was calm, too calm. 'Once this is over, I'll see what I can do for your *friend.*'

He doesn't believe me.

Resorting to old proven tactics, she asked, 'By the way, why did you follow me up here? Any particular reason, maybe some ulterior motive, hmm …' Not waiting for a reply, she took his hand in hers and started for the bed.

To her surprise, he pulled away and said, 'Not now. I have an associate waiting for my call. Maybe later I'll take you up on your offer.'

She stared at his back as he left the room, angry at herself for having offered to help Vera and Sinead; a deed which now threatened to derail her mission. As they say, "The road to hell is paved with good intentions." *So true*, she thought, *but how could I not help?*

CHAPTER 51

St. James Hospital
Thursday Afternoon

Not him again! Ronan sighed as the familiar, and by now unwelcome, face of Detective Kelly appeared in the doorway instead of his dinner.

'Ah, Mr O'Brien, you're awake. Well, I hope you don't mind me popping in unannounced? I need your help to clear up a few points. Something doesn't add up,' Detective Kelly greeted, his smile rather ambiguous.

'If I can help, by all means,' Ronan replied, wanting to get this over and done with.

'Thank you, most kind.'

The previous day's sympathetic tone was replaced by scathing sarcasm, a preamble to an unpleasant encounter.

'Don't you look chirpy today, nearly your handsome old self. Not that I would know, purely guessing of course. With the swelling to your brain nearly gone and after a good night's rest I don't suppose you can now recollect your thoughts sufficiently to explain what's going on,' he said and added a warning. 'And no more lies, Mr O'Brien. So please, think very carefully before you answer.'

'No, I'm afraid I've nothing new to add, sorry,' Ronan stated, shrugging his shoulders regretfully.

The detective looked at him with a sombre expression. 'Ronan, the situation is very serious and my advice to you is to

214

call your lawyer before I continue. I need an official statement.'

Alarmed, Ronan sat up and asked, 'Why?'

'Wouldn't you love to know?' came the cold reply.

For fifteen minutes Ronan tried in vain to reach Sean. Frustrated, he gave up and phoned Marie. 'Can you talk?' he asked as she answered. He felt and sounded miserable.

'Of course, why?'

'The Guards suspect me of being responsible for Eoin's murder. They have come up with a hypothesis built around circumstantial evidence. My fingerprints were found on a photograph, apparently used to blackmail Eoin. And added to that is the beating I got, the time of calls we had made, etc., etc. They claim I had him killed as a reprisal for the thrashing I received, supposedly a warning to stop my blackmailing!'

There was no response, only a prolonged silence.

'Marie, are you there?'

'Yes, I am,' she answered, crestfallen. 'Did you tell him the truth?'

'Yes, I did. He took down my statement and said his department would contact this mysterious Sinead. See if there is any truth to my story. Of course, Sean's word won't mean much without his sister's. Another thing, they suspect Sean of being my hired gun. He will most likely be charged with the murder. And as luck would have it, I have no idea where Sinead is. No number, nothing! They have me nailed until I can find her. And by then, she may be dead. The detective did not accept my claim of innocence and asked why I did not mention this before. He sees my confession as a cover-up, concocted out of desperation. My lawyer was not very positive either, as at this point the evidence is stacked heavily against me. I've been trying to reach Sean, but his phone's off.'

'Ronan, have faith; the truth will prevail. You've done nothing wrong. All you did was try and help an old friend.'

As much as he would love to believe her, he could not. Ignorant of the intricacies of the law, she had no idea how

215

twisted and corrupt the legal system was, strewn with loopholes and inconsistencies. No, he would not leave it to chance. He had to unmask the man responsible for this murder.

Another complication was the late hour of Sean's departure. He had unwittingly implicated himself as the likely murderer. Sean had to be warned as he was the prime suspect in a high-profile murder case.

Unable to fight back, Ronan resigned himself to the fact that Niall, being one step ahead, had won the first round with lethal precision. In a matter of only two days, Niall had neutralised him and his friends!

Although it was not over, he could still turn the tables, but that depended on one person and one person alone. Sinead. Finding her was imperative.

CHAPTER 52

Niall's Estate
Thursday Afternoon

Irina ventured deeper into the old Georgian manor, calling, 'Niall, here's a parcel for you.'

From somewhere in the rear of the house an irate voice echoed, 'I'm in the kitchen!'

Making a ciabatta sandwich, layered with smoked Black Forest ham, matured Tomme de Savoie cheese, sundried tomatoes, crispy fresh lettuce, and drizzled with olive oil, Niall looked up as she entered. Without a smile, she handed him the neatly wrapped shoebox-sized package and said, 'Here.'

He took the article and gave it a light shake, curious as to what it might be. Having read the sender's name on the label, he said, 'Boys-o-boys, she just won't give up! Most likely some of my mother's paraphernalia.' Without further ado he walked over to the bin, ready to discard the box.

'Don't you think you should at least open it,' Irina suggested, her words stopping his arm in mid-air.

'Why?'

'For heaven's sake, why not?'

His shoulders jerked upwards.

Instinctively she tensed. Without warning he flung the parcel at her head. But in time her hands shot up, catching the flying object with the greatest of ease. She looked at him defiantly.

'Have I not warned you to stay out of my affairs, especially where my mother is concerned!' he roared as the vein in his temple throbbed.

She placed her feet slightly apart and shifted her weight on to the balls of her feet. If it came to a fight, she was ready for him.

'I know what you've said,' she replied unafraid. 'For once, please listen. Don't you think you owe it to yourself … to see if there was any more to what happened?' Her words struck home. His shoulders sagged for an instant. *There it was again: a hint of uncertainty, hidden somewhere in the fathomless depths of his psychotic mind.*

Straightening up, he did not respond. Nothing stirred in the room with the staff having faded into the shadows. Without another word he turned and walked out of the kitchen, leaving the sandwich untouched and Irina holding the package.

The situation was unravelling fast, too fast! She needed more time; she must complete her assignment. But the truth was, she was not any closer to success than the day she had arrived. Knowing what he did, and tired of him, of playing this charade, of his moods, she realised there would be no stopping him if he decided to strike. The psychopath had revealed his colours, brazenly parading them out in the open.

CHAPTER 53

Mykonos, Greece
Thursday Evening

Watching Vera attempting to shoo away the screeching seagulls swirling overhead, Sinead smiled. The loud racket was ruining the tranquillity of the early evening. Unaffected by the noise, her gaze drifted across the town below and beyond the windmills etched in translucent warm gold colours, standing idle on the water's edge. Lazing on the recliner her trampled spirit lifted with her thoughts on everything and nothing, permitting exhaustion to spread through her body. The exploration of the old town, the tension, the constant fear of being caught was taking its toll.

During the day they had visited the congested town. Guided by a detailed map each had wandered for hours through the myriad of narrow streets, marking possible escape routes, dead-ends, and scouting for the most suitable locale for the planned rendezvous. Famished, they had fought the temptation of the delicious aromas hanging in the alleyways, tantalising their taste buds. The nagging fear of Niall's men lurking somewhere in the shadows had kept them focused.

All they desired was to get this over and done with as soon as possible, to rid themselves of the stones, and vanish.

As the daylight's rumpus subsided Vera reappeared on the patio with two cocktails in hand. 'Here you are. Enjoy, we don't know when we'll have another chance. To our future!'

Vera said, handing Sinead a drink. '*Na Zdorovie!*'

'*Sláinte!*'

Sitting down, Vera spread the two maps covered with scribbles on the coffee table.

After an hour's discussion, Vera arched her back, stretched her arms and stifled a yawn. 'Okay, that'll do. It's time to see if he's in.'

Having tapped his private number into her phone – a number secretly obtained during one of their previous drug-runs to Crete while he was asleep – she anxiously listened to the continuous ringing in her ear. About to hang up, a familiar voice answered with a simple, 'Hello,' and no more.

'Paul, is that you?'

'Yes, and you are?'

'Vera. Please don't hang up. I need a second of your time, please,' she implored. 'I have a proposal which I'm sure you'll like – a chance to get even with Niall.'

There was no reply, only silence. Sixty seconds … one hundred seconds … Unable to control herself, Vera asked, 'Paul, are you still there?'

'Still here. Okay, you've got my attention. What do you have in mind?'

It took Vera less than five minutes to explain her plan.

'You're joking! You actually robbed him? My dear, you've signed your own death warrant and now you want to drag me in as well? Did you fall on your head or something?'

It was not the reply she was hoping for, but it was neither unexpected. Undeterred, she continued, 'Come to think of it, you signed your own the minute you ratted him out. I was there when he received the news. All I can say: he will not rest till you're dead!'

Mulling her words over, Paul did not know whether to laugh or cry. He had never expected such a turn of events, to be thrown a lifeline which could remedy his earlier mistakes. A chance to regain Dermot's trust.

'Paul, you've gone quiet again … are you still there?' Vera asked, trying to hide the nervousness in her voice.

'Yes, yes, of course. And for God's sake stop asking whether I'm still here. I need a moment … you've caught me a bit off-guard.'

'Uhm … all I want to know is, are you in or not?'

'Vera, relax, you thought right. I'll do anything to see him go down. But I first have to consult my partner. What's your number … where are you?'

'In Siros, Greece,' Vera lied. And having given him her new phone number, she warned, 'You have one hour. If I hear nothing by then, it will be bye-bye to a fortune you could have had.'

'Hang on, Vera, slow down. One hour. Bye.'

'*Paka.*'

'So?' Sinead asked excitedly as soon as Vera put her phone down.

'I think he's on the hook.' Vera blurted.

'Time to celebrate.'

'Slow down. Remember we still must reel him in. Wonder what scheme the little worm and his so-called *partner* will dream up? Doubt he has one.'

CHAPTER 54

Alicante, Spain
Thursday Evening

Paul did not hesitate in exploiting this windfall to the full. It was too good an opportunity to let slip by. He listened intently to his American backer, Dermot Mullane.

'Right, this is how we'll play it. Offer her a tenth of what they're worth, but only on one condition: she turns state witness. Otherwise, there's no deal. Having been in Crete when things started going south for Niall, she'll be able to point the Garda in the right direction. With her on our side, we'll get him locked up for life. The knowledge she has of his chicanery should ensure that. You can explain my involvement – but no names; it's too soon – guarantee her my protection. We'll look after her.'

'What if she says no?'

'Then, my friend, you agree to her terms, we meet her, relieve her of the stones, and dump her body somewhere. That way we'll save ourselves a few million.'

'Fair enough. What's my cut?' Paul asked.

'Forty percent and the balance to me. Sounds fair, agreed?' Dermot's voice boomed in Paul's ear, leaving him under no illusion that the topic was closed.

'Agreed,' Paul said. 'Problem is I only have my forty percent in cash. You'll need to transfer the rest.'

'Can't do. Best I meet you there. We'll be wheels up in a

few hours. When you have more information, you can update me.'

'Sounds like you don't trust me.'

'Maybe, maybe not. After your recent display of loyalty towards your good old ex-partner, what do you expect? Go figure,' Dermot said and laughed. 'Tell Vera we can meet Saturday afternoon late. That should give us—'

'Hold that thought. Something's happened. I'll call you back in a minute,' Paul interrupted as a crash of breaking glass outside made him jump up.

Pocketing his phone, he walked to the open patio doors and flicked the lights off, leaving the terrace bathed in the soft moonlight. Sliding the door shut he heard feet shuffle nearby. Withdrawing his pistol from its holster he released the safety catch and took aim. He was ready. Detecting a slight movement in the shadows he fired without hesitating. Unhindered the bullet sliced through the double-layered laminated glass, leaving a perfect round cobwebbed hole, as it raced towards its target.

'Aargh!' a voice cried out.

Good. That'll teach you, whoever the fuck you are! Paul grinned, indifferent as to whether the shot was fatal or not.

The next moment lights flooded the neighbour's rear garden, spilling on to Paul's property – the loud bang and groan of pain had attracted unwanted attention.

Paul took one look at the injured man crouched on the ground before he raced to his bedroom. In the dark, he grabbed his jacket and checked the pockets for his wallet and passport. Some more fumbling. *Briefcase. Got it!*

Exiting through the bedroom's patio doors he heard the wounded man pant to his right. He turned in the opposite direction. From the corner of his eye, he saw two figures storm the house, waving their firearms from side to side. Neither of them bothered to remain inconspicuous. He ducked into the shadows and froze.

'Where're ya?' a voice shouted.

'Over here … hurry! The gobshite got me!'

223

'Serves you right, ya feckin' eejit. Next time blow a trumpet just to be sure,' an unsympathetic voice growled. 'Do ya know where he is?'

'I think inside … he got me in the thigh. Jaysus!'

'Niall won't be impressed, another royal cock-up,' the man who seemed to be the leader, grumbled. 'Where's Thomas?'

'The front …'

'Larry, go and get him. We'll meet back at the car. Hurry!' the man in charge barked at the small stocky man by his side – a man in his mid-thirties with a crewcut and a skull tattoo in the green of his country and its fair share of shamrocks emblazoned on his neck. 'And you, let's get you to a doctor. Give me your arm.'

At less than ten metres, shielded by some plants, Paul tried his best to remain invisible. Watching the two men retreat towards the rear fence and open field beyond, his cowardly temperament ridiculed him, urging him to shoot the assailants in their backs. Taking aim his finger started to squeeze the trigger, but the sound of approaching sirens stopped him. He lowered his firearm. There was no time to waste; he had to conjure a plausible explanation for the gunshot.

By the time the doorbell rang he was ready for them, his confidence bolstered by a large triple whiskey.

The scene of the reported gunfire turned out to be nothing more than a two-litre glass cola bottle having exploded on the kitchen floor next to the open patio doors. The sticky syrup still dripped off the walls and kitchen units. Satisfied by Paul's version of events, the police did not bother to investigate the matter any further. They apologised for the intrusion and left.

Paul, who had remained remarkably calm during the short visit, snapped out of his near lethargic state, grabbed his briefcase, locked the house and pulled his car out of the driveway. He had very little time to beat Niall's men to the airport.

With screeching tyres he accelerated and ignored the

speed restrictions and cameras, covering the distance to the airport and boarding his Lear Jet 40XR in under an hour. And by the time he remembered Vera's one-hour ultimatum he was already thirty-five minutes late. Well, she could wait.

First, he had to report to Dermot.

'Ask yourself how difficult it is to trace someone's location when a mobile call lasts more than a few minutes? Can't you see what the hell just happened? You've been set up by the little hussy. My boy, there's no deal. You've been had. I'm afraid the bugger is smarter than we thought,' Dermot spelled out the obvious.

'No, I disagree. Not where Vera's concerned. I know her. She hates him more than any other living soul on this planet.'

'You're so gullible. Don't you think she might have been forced to make the call?'

'No,' Paul said, fed up. 'I'll double check and let you know. And whether you're in is your call. As for me, I'll follow this through on my own if I have to.'

'You do that. I'm not putting a foot outside the US of A until you can convince me otherwise,' Dermot said.

CHAPTER 55

Mykonos, Greece
Thursday Evening

A slight frown creased Vera's forehead. She shifted her gaze from Sinead back to the silent phone on the coffee table, an action repeated countless times during the last sixty minutes. Did they miscalculate? What was Paul up to? Did he contact Niall? Her worrying ended when her phone sprung to life with a shrill chirp. Before the phone could buzz a second time, she held it tight against her ear and said, 'What kept you? Next time you do as I tell you or I walk.'

'Yes, my dear, of course,' Paul replied scathingly. 'And next time you try and set me up I'll kill you! Did you and Niall think you could trap me that easily? Well nice try, missy. Tell your friend one of his thugs is crippled. If he wants a war, I'll give him one!'

'What! Set you up, how!?' Vera asked, confused. 'Paul, just listen to yourself. You sound like a lunatic. Niall and me working together? You're crazy. You know I hate him and want nothing to do with him, not now, not ever! After what I've done, I can never return to Ireland. Does that explain enough?'

'Keep talking.'

'Nor do I care about your little war. I told you the truth. You have fifteen minutes to think it over. Phone me if you're still interested,' she said and hung up. Her whole body shook.

So close … and now this!

'Niall has found him and he thinks I helped! Oh dear, how stupid … what shall we do?'

'Nothing,' Sinead remarked. 'We wait. I'm sure he'll call back.'

'You're right,' Vera agreed half-heartedly, seeing their plan going up in flames. *What were we thinking!*

Flustered, the two barely spoke. For the first time, they entertained the very real possibility of failure and the subsequent consequences. If forced to find another buyer or buyers, word would spread like wildfire and Niall would swoop down on them with a vengeance.

The chirping of Vera's phone broke the mood of doom and gloom permeating the room. 'You're back,' Vera said, struggling to contain her deflated emotions. 'Please, before we continue, tell me what happened?'

Having listened to Paul, the incident in Spain gave her real reason for concern. 'You sure you're not being followed?'

'Positive.'

'And you ask how he found you? Surely, you must realise he knows everything about you: your plane's details, every property you own, places you visit, your phone records. The fact is, you cannot hide from him; he'll find you no matter where!'

'Ooh, I'm petrified. But maybe an alternative form of transport will be sensible … therefore I'll need more time.'

'How long?'

'Day or two.'

'I can live with that. Back to our deal. What's your offer?'

'My partner—'

'Oh, you really have a partner. I had my doubts,' Vera smirked. 'What's his name?'

'Yes, I do. Though I can't tell you his name just yet.'

'Why not?'

'His call.'

'Okay.'

'Right, as I was trying to say, he has agreed to go along on one condition: he wants you to turn state witness. We all, including you, will sleep a lot safer with Niall securely locked away.'

'Hmm … state witness. Well, I reckon I know a thing or two about him. But question is, can you protect me?'

'Of course! My partner is American and far more powerful than the *honourable* Mr McGuire. He guarantees your safety. What do you say?'

'Yeah, sure, you'll protect me,' Vera replied sceptically. 'Okay, I'll do it. How much?'

'Ten percent in cash, a solid four-and-a-half million euro.'

'You're kidding, right? I may be a *dumb whore*, but I'm not that desperate,' she mocked. The offer was nothing less than what she had expected. 'The least I'll settle for is forty percent and not a cent less. That's eighteen million euro. And if you are not prepared to pay, then there'll be no meeting. You have one hour to reconsider.'

'My dear, you're nuts. Nobody will pay what you're asking. The best you'll get anywhere is twenty percent,' Paul insisted.

'One hour. *Paka*,' Vera said and hung up. 'Men! It's not going to be easy. He'll squeeze us for every cent … and why do you look so chuffed with yourself?'

'I can't help enjoying the moment … getting back at them both. If Paul knows I'm involved he'll phone Niall, never mind the risk!'

'Don't get too excited just yet; there's still a long way to go,' Vera cautioned.

'You're right. Anyway, I guess even if we get a third, we'll be doing extremely well, seven and a half million each. That will do me just fine, thanks. How about you?'

Vera nodded. It was unimaginable … impossible to have such wealth!

The call came on the hour. 'Right, we agree. One-third and not a cent more,' Paul stated as if it was of no real concern.

His casual tone stirred the butterflies in Vera's stomach,

not trusting him one bit. 'Good. I'll see you in Siros, Saturday, four p.m. sharp. I'll phone around ten in the morning and give you directions,' Vera replied and hung up, not wanting to listen to another word he had to say. 'Done!' she exclaimed nervously. 'I feel like celebrating … maybe a bit premature, but so what?'

'No, no celebration. I think you're just looking for an excuse to have a drink. My dear, you don't need an excuse, you deserve a drink … and I don't mind joining you. God, my nerves are shot.'

Refilling their glasses, they did not care whether they were about to jinx the deal or not.

'Here's to our life as free women,' Sinead said and raised her glass.

'And to me turning *state witness*,' Vera quipped, nearly choking on her champagne from laughter. 'Can you imagine even proposing such lunacy? Do they honestly think I'm that naïve, me, state witness!'

CHAPTER 56

Mediterranean
Thursday Night

Cruising at an altitude of twelve thousand metres above the Mediterranean, Paul was deep in conversation with Dermot, bringing him up to speed regarding the final terms of the agreement. Ending the call, he said, 'I think I might have been compromised in Spain. I suggest we meet in Athens and I accompany you to Siros.'

'Fine, Athens it is. Just make sure no one follows you to the hotel. I will not tolerate any more mistakes,' Dermot warned. His tone left Paul under no illusion what to expect if he failed again. Most probably the same as planned for Vera: a .45 calibre bullet to the back of the head.

Trailing Paul by seventy kilometres in the night sky over Sicily, Ciarán felt confident playing the hunter, guided by the powerful homing device attached to Paul's jet. 'Any idea where he's heading?' he asked, popping his head into the cockpit.

'Dead east … definitely not Rome. Best guess, Athens or beyond … could be any of the islands?'

'Thanks, I'll let the boss know,' Ciarán replied.

Elated – a hundred percent certain of success – he was unaware that a few thousand kilometres further west another far more powerful jet crammed with armed men was soaring through the dark skies towards Greece.

'Athens!' Niall exploded, instantly grasping the situation as explained by Ciarán. 'Paul in Athens. Vera and Sinead on their way … or, already there. Explains it all. They're in this together, have been all along. Wonder what else they've been up to? Stick to him like a limpet and when they're enjoying their short-lived victory, do what you have to.' In his mind's eye, Niall could see the bullet-riddled bodies of Paul, Vera and Sinead squirm on the ground. He smiled contentedly.

'My pleasure,' Ciarán replied as his plane touched down in Athens and his eyes followed the round figure scuttle across the asphalt in the direction of the customs office. Preoccupied, the man was not the least bit interested in the Lear Jet taxiing a hundred metres to his right.

Before Ciarán's plane could roll to a stop the door opened. As the steps unfolded, Thomas and Larry jumped out, sprinted for cover, straightened up, and followed close on Paul's heels. At customs, the two Irishmen flashed their passports and were waved through. Reaching the front of the terminal building they stopped the first available taxi, shoved a fistful of fifty-euro notes under the driver's nose, and ordered him to accede to their every demand. Sniffing an opportunity to make easy money he did not need any further encouragement. Maintaining a safe distance, they followed Paul's taxi. Smiling broadly the driver weaved through the traffic and finally pulled up near the five-star Aegean Sun Hotel on Attica Avenue, Athens.

In a flash, Larry was out of the car and raced after Paul. Having a clear view of all movement in and out of the hotel, Thomas remained in the taxi.

At three in the morning Larry entered the hotel's plush foyer. A sudden chill ran down his spine; Paul was nowhere to be seen. The only sign of life was the two bored staff members behind the reception desk. He frowned confused. It was inconceivable that Paul could have registered in under a minute. Had he spotted them and vanished out the back?

Noticing the receptionists' curious stares, he approached the counter and made the usual enquiries regarding costs and availability for the night, all the time keeping an eye on the area beyond the kiosks and foyer. There was no movement. Fretting, he thanked the staff and left.

'We need more men to find him or Niall will have our guts for garters,' he muttered to himself, in a hurry to contact Ciarán. Pausing outside the entrance he took another look at the empty foyer. Much to his relief he saw Paul walk towards reception. Larry turned slightly and lit a cigarette. Lingering, he puffed on the tasteless tobacco and watched Paul fill out what seemed to be a registration card. Next, a credit card was presented. With the transaction completed, Paul picked up his briefcase and headed for the elevators. Larry threw the cigarette on the pavement and raced back inside, just in time to catch sight of Paul stepping into an elevator.

Waiting for another, Larry kept an eye on Paul's ascent, anxious to establish his floor number.

Fourth floor!

A minute later, stepping out of the elevator on the fourth floor, Larry caught sight of Paul struggling to unlock his bedroom door located at the end of the corridor. Quickly, before Paul looked his way, he withdrew into the elevator and pressed the ground floor button; it was time to take up surveillance for the night.

CHAPTER 57

Athens
Friday Morning

Paul's uncouth insistence on being served a full breakfast despite having arrived fifteen minutes late finally succeeded. Reluctantly the maître d' conceded defeat, thereby ending the unpleasant squabble.

The buffet, although badly depleted by 10:15 a.m., still displayed a great enough selection for Paul to choose from. Not in a mood to be ushered about, he pushed past the staff – his tray piled with enough rations for two – and sat down in the far corner of the breakfast room. Noisily he slurped down his juice, scoffed the porridge and then attacked the assortment of warm dishes with relish. With his attention focused on the morning newspaper's cover story, describing the activities surrounding the search for two Irish men in Athens, the taste of his breakfast whether good or bad was immaterial.

Studying the pictures illustrating the result of his handiwork, his finger traced the debris floating in the blue waters, all that remained of the obliterated yacht.

Yes, old buddy, and tomorrow I'll drive home the final stake, he grinned to himself.

The irritating vibration in his pocket stopped his fantasising. 'Are you here, yet?' he answered rudely.

'No "good morning"? Well, my boy, let me set things

straight. If you have any hope of us remaining partners, you'll never take that tone with me again. Is that clear?' Dermot warned.

The icy words were like a butcher's knife cleaving Paul's sizeable gut open, letting the hot air hiss out of his over-inflated ego. He nearly choked on his egg benedict and spluttered a reply which bordered on something like an apology as he blamed the breakfast staff for his foul mood. Having marginally smoothed things over, they scheduled a rendezvous in the hotel foyer's bar for five in the afternoon.

Dermot had some other *pressing matters* to attend to, leaving Paul with ample time to visit the bank, buy some clothes and avail himself of some sightseeing.

Paul gulped down the remainder of his coffee, got up, wiped his moustache with the neatly rolled white linen serviette and threw it on top of the leftovers on his plate. With a grunt he carelessly pushed back his chair, blocking the aisle. Stomping out of the breakfast room he remained oblivious to the waitress' look of disgust at the mess he left behind.

He was also unaware of another pair of eyes which followed him, equally unimpressed by his behaviour: Thomas, seated at the next table. A phone message was sent to Larry waiting in the hotel's foyer, informing him of Paul's departure, as well as the five o'clock meeting.

Forty-five minutes later, Larry trailed a puffing Paul up the incline leading to the Parthenon built on top of the Acropolis. Progress was painfully slow. *Here's a man sorely in need of a diet and some exercise if he has any hope of reaching sixty,* Larry grimaced to himself, realising that at this pace it was going to be a very long day. He wiped his brow. The stifling heat was more suited for a day at the beach or an erotic Nuru massage, rather than playing this ludicrous game of follow the leader. *Why the hell did I sign up for this crap!* he mused, looking forward to his break.

By now, Thomas, who had slipped past them a few minutes earlier, was waiting inside the museum, ready to keep an eye on Paul.

CHAPTER 58

Athens
Friday

The young man's sweat-drenched, white cotton shirt stuck to his back, a result of the unrelenting midday heat. Deep in thought, he bumped into the two tourists blocking his path. With a mumbled, 'Sorry,' he continued on his way without pause.

'Bugger, watch where you're going, buddy!' Michael growled annoyed. 'Under different circumstances I would have taught him a lesson or two.' Focusing his attention on the young man racing towards the tourist office he rubbed his chin pensively. 'Wonder what's eating him? Seems a bit stressed.'

'Yeah, okay, you're right. We'll, forget him. We have enough problems of our own. Let's just get the hell out of here before someone starts asking questions,' a very nervous Paddy huffed.

Michael, with frappe in hand, faced the street watching activities outside as Paddy kept an eye on the few customers inside the near-empty café. Consulting the timetables of all eastbound ferries in front of them, they planned their next move: escaping from Greece. Parting company Michael would sail to Samos and Paddy to Kos, then by private charter slip into Turkey, and from there board flights home.

'There's our friend again, still in a hurry,' Michael said as the young man came rushing out of the tourist office.

'Good for him. Now may I suggest we contact Declan and get the hell out of here,' Paddy responded with indifference. Not waiting for Michael to reply he stood up, glanced at the TV relaying a lame football match and left.

Making their way to the port, they were still in the dark with regards to the Greek authority's progress in apprehending the criminals involved in the fatal explosion at sea.

By now the authorities had obtained adequate descriptions of two of the suspects from the yacht charter company. One matched that of the body airlifted out of the sea at Monemvasia. The other was that of a foreigner recorded by CCTV in the middle of the night at a hotel en route to Sykea.

Michael's identity had not yet been established. As if by some fluke he had never been present at any dealings, always remaining in the background. However, Paddy was not so lucky. His photo had been circulated to all departments involved in the search. The same photo flashed over the café's TV twenty minutes after the two Irishmen had left.

Recognising the wanted man, the ever-attentive owner did not hesitate in dialling the contact number displayed, already spending the ransom offered for information which would lead to his capture. He regretted not having had invested in surveillance for his small establishment. If so, both men would have been recorded, valuable information the authorities would have paid handsomely for.

Before continuing, they needed intel. Again Michael tried Declan's phone; the only man he considered somewhat trustworthy.

'Michael, thank God you're okay! Where are you?' Declan asked excitedly.

'Can't tell. And please, no names.'

'Sorry, got a bit carried away. How did you—'

'That can wait,' Michael interrupted. 'We need to know what odds we're facing here and at home.'

'We? Is he with you?'

'Affirmative. An update, if you don't mind.'

'Right. Locally, things are not great. Suffice to say your companion's picture was flashed on national TV a few minutes ago. You'll have to get him out of sight,' Declan warned.

'Ouch, that ends his travel plans.'

'The boss is looking for you. There have been some new developments which need immediate attention.'

'Such as?'

'Vera and her friend Sinead stole his booty and are hiding somewhere in Greece, possibly Santorini. We suspect they may be on their way to Athens.'

'Wow! Are you for real?' Michael asked.

'I am. Our instructions are very explicit: find and eliminate them. I'll let the boss fill you in on the details.'

'Now I wish I hadn't called. Slight problem. Vera, I know, but not so Sinead. Can you send an ID?'

'Yes, coming up right away.'

'OK, I'll report in and get back to you in a couple of hours. I'll be on the next ferry to Santorini.'

Facing Paddy, he pocketed his phone and said, 'I better get you to a *safe house*. You've become very popular, an overnight TV celebrity.'

'What!'

'Your face is all over the news. Do I need to say more? Not to worry; I'll make sure someone will come and get you. In the meantime, you'll be going nowhere.'

Two hours later, standing on the stern with his back to the breeze, Michael looked at the jumble of insipid white buildings piled on top of one another with the odd splash of red breaking the monotony. Athens. On his right, the headland of the Athens peninsula jutted out into the blue sea, releasing the ferry from the grip of the concrete urban mass. Settlements straddled the hills as far as the eye could see.

With Paddy gone, nothing linked him to the exploded yacht, allowing him the freedom to move around at will without having to look over his shoulder. Needing some refreshment, he turned around to find a vending machine. To his surprise, strolling towards him was the same young man he had spotted outside the tourist office. Dropping on to one knee he fidgeted with his shoelace and watched the man stride past.

Face looks somewhat familiar.

Straightening up he casually scanned the small group of travellers milling about. Immediately he spotted them: two men watching the young man.

Well, well, what do we have here?

Keeping them in his peripheral, Michael extracted the orange soda from the narrow slot in the vending machine. With a soft fizz he cracked the can open and let the refreshing cool liquid spill soothingly down his parched throat. He took out his phone and looked at the photo of Sinead. The resemblance was uncanny – they must be related! The situation was becoming more intriguing by the minute.

Best hear what Mr McGuire has on his mind.

Retreating further in amongst the passengers, he greeted Niall with a cool, 'Good afternoon.'

'That took you long enough! I heard via the grapevine that you've made it. Although, I was starting to have my doubts. You're in good form, fit to travel some more, I trust?'

'Yes, why?'

'Your specific skills are needed in Athens,' Niall said and briefed Michael fully.

'Sorry, can't do right now. I'm on my way to Santorini.'

'Then I suggest you disembark at the next stop. The information I have leads me to believe they are definitely heading for Athens.'

'Maybe so. But if not, we'll all be studying the Parthenon while they slip away. You have Ciarán in Athens. He and his merry men can cover that arena. May I suggest I pick up the trail where they were last seen,' Michael said. He had his reasons: the young man. If related to Sinead, he was most probably on his way to her. This he kept to himself. 'I have a possible lead. Give me till tomorrow morning to follow it through. If it's a dead end, I'll head back to Athens.'

'Makes sense. Do it,' Niall consented.

CHAPTER 59

Mykonos
Friday

A hundred and fifty kilometres east of Athens on the small island of Mykonos, Vera and Sinead frittered the time away in hiding, oblivious to the clouds of doom rolling in from the West. Taking turns, they spent a few hours in the sun next to the communal pool trying to relax.

Despite the warm weather and few glasses of cold Chablis, Sinead could not help fretting. The fear of something terrible befalling her siblings: Sean, Laura, Flynn and Billy gnawed at her nerves. Filled with guilt, having subjected them to a witch-hunt they had no part in, she was desperate for news. It took all her willpower to resist the temptation of phoning them; an action which could give Niall an opportunity to extricate her whereabouts. Undoubtedly, he was waiting for just such a mistake.

The thought of finding a new identity, undergoing reconstructive surgery, returning to the unspoiled Wild Atlantic Coast of Ireland and living out her life in peace elicited a dreamy smile. She sighed. What she would give for anonymity, for a small stone cottage with a warm crackling fire, heavy wooden beams, rich timber floors, and walls of glass facing the stormy waves breaking on unspoiled beaches. It all might just be possible if they could leave the island alive. And the only chance of that was if they could successfully conclude the deal with Paul … and for that a miracle was needed.

Looking at her fellow sunbathers lazing like lizards in the sun, she imagined herself being just like them. To be able to enjoy without fear the simple pleasures life offered, and never again succumb to others' demands. No longer to be used as a piece of meat! Determined to fulfill her dreams she took another sip of her wine, savouring the moment, shutting out the world around her.

CHAPTER 60

Athens
Friday

Exhausted after a day wandering through the ancient ruins, Paul arrived back at his hotel soaked in sweat. He regretted not having returned sooner for a little siesta. Entering the cool air-conditioned suite he headed straight for the minibar.

The crackling of ice cubes in his glass could be heard loud and clear in the cabin of the jet parked at Athens International; the sound being relayed via the bedroom one floor above Paul's. During his excursion, suitable micro-electronic listening devices had been installed in his room and attached to his clothing.

'Perfect. It's working just fine, lads,' Ciarán commented. 'Right, you take up position in ten minutes.'

'Will do, boss,' Larry replied.

By 16h30 four of Niall's men were strategically positioned in the hotel's foyer, armed with hidden digital cameras and surveillance equipment trained on Paul who was seated at the bar. Patiently they waited.

At precisely 17h00, five stone-faced men entered the hotel with not a hint of warmth amongst them. Without breaking their stride, they scanned the foyer. Leading the way was a dour-looking man in his late sixties, tall and erect. Spotting Paul, he acknowledged him with a subtle nod of the head. Brushing the sleeves of his dark Armani suit he whispered to the four well-built men by his side – their crewcuts, muscular build and postures smacked of ex-military. None of them seemed older than mid-forties, nor younger than thirty.

Reaching Paul, the older man shook his hand. The rest of the party showed no interest in him as they formed a protective ring around the two men. Despite this manoeuvre, Niall's men had sufficient time to record their features and relay the imagery upstairs for identification.

With ears pricked, Ciarán listened to the conversation. Nothing of note was being discussed, that was until Paul asked, 'Did you manage the cash for tomorrow's meeting with Vera? Doubt the bank in Siros will let you withdraw so much in one go, or that they even have that kind of money on the island?'

'Yes, of course! What do you think I'm here for?' the older man snapped. 'And no more talk. You never know who's listening. Let's go!'

'I think you're unnecessarily paranoid. No one followed me here and no one's listening. Do you see anyone staring?' Paul asked irritated.

'Yes, of course, you're right,' the man replied cynically as he made his way to the bank of elevators.

Elated by the news of the meeting in Siros, Niall's men did not move, concentrating on the rest of the conversation being transmitted.

Neither did the two Americans seated opposite them. Within earshot, they peered from behind the magazines at Niall's men. Five minutes later the taller of the two Americans stood up and left.

'Positive?' a startled Dermot asked.

Not waiting for a reply, he scribbled a few words on a piece of paper and shoved it under Paul's nose who instantly turned pale.

Dermot shook his head, furious. Without a word he

walked into the en-suite bathroom, opened the shower, and flushed the toilet. Only then did he speak. 'Geoff, they're not ours. Sweep Paul's room. If you find any bugs, leave them in place and confirm your findings.'

Returning to the suite's lounge he scribbled another note, telling Paul to strip and not ask why. Meekly he obliged, listening to Dermot narrating business as usual.

The subtle change of topic was not picked up by Ciarán.

Meticulously, Dermot's men searched the pile of discarded clothes and found two listening devices. Satisfied, Dermot indicated for Paul to get dressed. Another note instructed him to carry on as normal.

They would lure whoever it was out into the open.

CHAPTER 61

Niall's Estate
Friday Afternoon

'Right, right … tomorrow. You're a hundred percent positive it's Siros, and with Vera?' Niall asked.

'Based on what Paul said, yes. They don't know we're here, so no ways he said that to mislead us. He did seem very anxious for confirmation from this Dermot Mullane character regarding the funds needed.'

'Presuming you're right, then let's prepare a welcoming party for them. How I'd love to be there!' Niall exclaimed.

Despite his upbeat mood, he was very surprised that Paul had succeeded in teaming up with someone as powerful as Dermot, a worthy adversary. *But if you think you can replace me, then you better think again!*

'What's happening in Siros?' a curious voice asked behind him.

Irina! Damn, when did she sneak in?

If he didn't know better, he could swear she was spying on him. 'They've found the girls in Siros and the police are ready to act,' he said, hiding his suspicions.

'That's good. Then by tomorrow evening you'll be able to put all this behind you. Maybe, even go on a long vacation?'

'Good idea! As soon as this is wrapped up, I'll take you to my little hideout for a nice break. Nothing will distract us there. You'll love it!' he offered, encouraged by her conciliatory tone. It would be an opportunity to rescue their faltering relationship.

'That sounds wonderful,' she replied. 'I'm going to mix myself a cocktail. You want one?'

'No thanks, I'm fine.'

On the way to the kitchen, Irina sent a text to Sean: "Sinead in Siros, tomorrow".

CHAPTER 62

Ferry, Athens to Santorini
Friday

For goodness sake, why can't life be easier! Sean agonised, having read Irina's message. He would need a miracle to get there on time. And even if he did somehow manage to beat the odds, he still had no idea where in Siros. *Well, at least it's a lead.* He needed to get to Siros and fast!

Making his way to the customer service desk he could not help mulling over the news received from Ronan, distracting information he could have done without. *Me, prime suspect! What rubbish! I've never even met this guy, let alone killed him, or anyone else for that matter!*

Despite the truth, he realised all too well that it was a very real problem; he lacked a credible alibi for the night of the murder. Therefore, he could not return to Ireland without Sinead. She was the only person who could verify his and Ronan's story and confirm Niall's hand in all of this. Unless of course the real murderer could be found. And the chances of that seemed to be nil! Not while Niall was pulling the strings.

Michael followed the young man to the customer service desk. Standing within earshot he idly paged through a holiday brochure. Hearing the name Sean O'Donovan spelled out as a ticket was purchased for Paros with an onward connection to Siros, his fingers paused for a second.

Bingo! Sean must have heard from Sinead. How else could he know about Siros? Time to update Niall.

'Jaysus, Michael, why was your phone off? It seems you don't appreciate the seriousness of the situation.' Niall shouted, answering the call. 'I'm not going to repeat myself again. You stay contactable at all times, got it!?'

'Right,' Michael replied unfazed. *"Seriousness of the situation", what is the man on? If the world is about to implode, or a terrorist attack is imminent, that would be serious. Catching ... killing the women and getting his diamonds back may be serious to him, but to no one else.*

'We have new information which suggests the meeting is to be tomorrow, somewhere in Siros,' Niall said before Michael could speak. 'Best you forget about—'

Michael did not let him finish, and asked, 'Who is your source, and when did you receive this information?'

'Ciarán ... about half past four. Why?'

'Are you aware Sinead's brother is in Greece?'

'Yes, I am. And?'

'Really. Well, you could have told me,' Michael said. *So that's who the two spooks are.*

'I didn't see any point in distracting you. I have a few men following him.'

'Yes, I know. And did they report Sean's sudden change of itinerary?'

'No, they did not. How do you know about Sean ... and what change of plan?' Niall asked, taken aback.

'That's what I thought. Well, right now I'm watching the three of them – as I've been doing since Athens – and at exactly 16h45 your time Sean had received a text message. Immediately after reading the message, and without making another call, or chatting with anyone else, he headed for customer services and bought a ticket to Siros. He's due to jump ship at the next port.'

'What! How the hell does he know about Siros?'

'Good question. Maybe he has been in contact with his sister or considering the time of the message, someone tipped him off. The latter seems more likely.'

'You're saying someone here, or Ciarán could have told him?'

'Probably. Who besides Ciarán & Co. knows about the new venue?'

'No one I can think of. I don't see how Ciarán's lot would be acquainted with Sean. What baffles me is how this information was leaked so fast.'

'My point exactly. I suggest you sweep your house for bugs, and I get off the phone right now. I'll be in touch, cheers,' Michael said and switched his phone off.

Fifteen minutes later he was in possession of a new ticket: Paros to Siros, ETA, Saturday, 08h00.

Next, he updated Declan and Stavros, requesting a rendezvous at 10h00 on the island of Siros.

CHAPTER 63

Niall's Estate
Friday Afternoon

Niall swore violent retribution if Michael's suspicions proved to be correct. In the background, the sweepers dashed through the house while he scribbled down the names of all possible suspects, including Irina's. Hers was the one name which rankled the loudest. She was the only person present when he had received the information regarding Siros. Not forgetting her seemingly innocent question, "What's happening in Siros?"

Why? But then again, she does not know Sean. No, can't be her.

The presence of some listening device in the house would exonerate her to some extent. But who else then? Planting them could only have taken place during the past five days – since the last sweep. As much as he tried, he could not find a reason why Irina would or could be involved.

And his house staff were all loyal, or were they? Quiet, nervous little Annie … always busy here and there. Did someone pay her, maybe?

Ciarán and his men could not be ruled out either. Niall was not ignorant of their sentiments with the inherent jealous nature of employees always lurking below the surface. Betrayal was a very real possibility. But helping Sean held no benefits, nothing he could think of … or were there? Did someone hope to gain Sean's trust, thereby winning Sinead over and

250

structuring a deal … share the diamonds and help her get away? He never trusted anyone, and now even less.

Shuffling the printed images of Dermot, Paul and the five bodyguards taken in Athens in his hands he decided it had to be them. There were far greater forces at play than the interference of some Russian peasant girl. And none of his men had the guts to take him on. He realised full well the incident in Crete had marked the beginning of a turf war. They were coming for him!

'Excuse me, Mr McGuire,' a voice interrupted his thoughts. 'May I come in?'

'Right, right, what have you got … I trust the house is sterile?'

'I'm afraid not. Someone has been very busy since our last sweep,' Liam replied.

Niall jolted upright, 'Continue. How many, and where?'

'Three bugs in your office, three in the main lounge and dining room and a further three in your upstairs study. Your phones are also tapped.'

For an instant, Niall's body sagged: if some of the week's conversations were to be leaked to the authorities, he would be ruined! He straightened up, his face filled with anger. Smelling Dermot's hand in this, he vowed revenge. Not a man to submit to defeat without a fight, he grinned stoically. In his mind's eye he saw Dermot and Paul spread out in the dust under the hot Greek sun, blood spewing from their wounds. He could smell the stench of death, attracting clouds of flies to feast on their lifeless bodies.

Any precious recordings you may have will never see the light of day; it will perish along with you, that I guarantee! So, enjoy your last day under our beautiful blue heavens, you bastard!

He was in charge in Ireland, a status he intended to hold until the day he died.

As he simmered down, the question remained: who was helping Sean, and why? Given the circumstances, Sean was nothing more than an annoying flea to be clipped between one's nails. His foolhardy involvement meant nothing, except

251

that he may lead his men to Sinead and Vera. And if he were in cahoots with Paul and Vera, he would not now be *lost* at sea. No, it didn't add up.

But the more pressing question was: who installed the bugs? Whoever it was had to be found, and fast – he could not allow any evidence to land in the wrong hands – and the bastard would pay the ultimate price.

Better start digging!

Leaving his study, he caught sight of Irina sprinting up the sweeping stairs. 'What's your hurry? Is there a fire somewhere?' his voice thundered in the hallway, tempted to run after her. *What in the hell is she up to?*

'Back in a sec,' she replied without breaking her stride.

'Fine. And while you're up there put on an evening dress or something appropriate, we're going out for dinner. Hurry!' His fingers twitched, praying she was not somehow involved in all of this. He would hate to hurt her.

Retreating into his study he realised it was time for them to have a nice long chat, time to smooth out the bumps in their relationship. But whether he really wanted to, he was not so sure anymore.

Irina closed her bedroom door and quickly sent a final message to Sean, severing all communications for now: "… I'll contact you once it's safe. Until then, take care. *Paka*."

Selecting a revealing grey silk dress, she draped it over the edge of the four-poster bed and took her time to undress. He could wait. Entering the bathroom, she paused in front of the full-length mirror and studied her reflection. Her heart sank, thinking of the years of strenuous exercise and endless training she had endured in achieving and maintaining a toned, near perfect body. Especially the hours put in after the birth of her baby girl two years ago, having had to shake off the too many extra kilos. And having juggled motherhood and work on her own after that useless man had run off the minute she got pregnant. And, for what? When tested, she seemed to be failing. She had gained Niall's trust through painful personal sacrifice and now it was slowly slipping out of her grasp.

No, I refuse to accept that!

Infuriated by this self-doubt, she stepped into the wet-room, opened the tap and released a torrent of icy water to cascade down on her. With jaws clenched tight she blocked out the stinging needles striking her bare skin. After thirty seconds she adjusted the setting, releasing a nearly unbearable spray of hot water. As her body recoiled, she resisted the temptation to reduce the heat and waited for the burning sensation to ease. Several times she repeated the same routine until she could not differentiate between hot and cold.

Relaxed, vowing to return to Russia a success, she stepped out of the shower, her skin aglow, and her uncertainties washed away. Even when fraught with danger trapped inside the house of a madman, she would persevere; it was a path chosen a long time ago.

While applying the final touches to her make-up, his voice boomed from downstairs, 'I'm waiting! What's keeping you?'

'Nearly done,' she replied calmly, not raising her voice. Whether he heard her or not did not matter. She hated shouting and being shouted at.

Picking up her handbag with its usual contents, she placed her passport, phone and all her cash inside, however minimal. Items which might be needed if he were to discover the truth.

Who am I kidding? If he does, there'll be no need for any of this!

Descending the stairs Irina's long, toned legs were revealed by the flowing, split maxi dress. Amused, she watched the transformation on Niall's face with the severe scowl replaced by a boyish grin. But she was not fooled by this seemingly innocent charm, knowing he could explode at the slightest provocation. He was the living epitome of Dr Jekyll and Mr Hyde.

Seated next to Niall in the chauffeur-driven car, Irina stared across the mansion's perfectly manicured lawn at the tall oak trees, their girth heavy with years of growth. Briefly, she caught sight of Jacek standing in the deep shadows – too distant for her to notice the concern in his eyes.

She hardly spoke during the thirty-minute drive despite Niall's attempts at light conversation. Neither did the space between them diminish. As a result, Niall reverted to his phone for company, checking the latest events and gossip on Twitter.

'Well, we're here … let's go,' Niall announced as the car came to a stop outside his restaurant opposite Stephen's Green in Dublin. He struggled to sound somewhat pleasant, to remain civil. His hopes of their relationship improving were fading fast. *I suppose she wants a formal apology. Oh boy, women and their juvenile games of manipulation!*

Entering the restaurant side by side, he made the usual small talk with his staff who clamoured for his attention. Irina followed him up the walnut hardwood staircase to his favourite table located on the mezzanine level. Overlooking the main dining room, it granted him an opportunity to inconspicuously keep an eye on the customers and staff.

Sitting down, he thought, *If you're just playing hard to get, there's hope … or maybe, you're nothing other than a cold, calculating little bitch. Well, let's see. Here goes.* 'Irina, I owe you an apology,' he said with just the right amount of sincerity and warmth.

'Why?' she replied, her voice soft, filled with concern.

'My behaviour last night is inexcusable, but I hope you will forgive me,' he stated with deep-felt regret. But the truth was he nearly choked as the words spilled from his lips. Never in his wildest dreams had he ever imagined apologising to anyone, least of all to a woman. Irina said nothing and stared past him at the picturesque old park across the road.

That did not go down well! So much for trying. 'Anything special you prefer?' he asked, glumly.

'A salad. I'm not hungry, *spasibo*.'

'Are you sure? Come on, let's forget our differences. What do you say?'

'Thank you. A salad is really all I want,' she insisted,

struggling to maintain her composure.

That's it. I've had enough! Niall fumed. 'Suit yourself. I'm starving, so trust you don't mind,' he grumbled and placed their orders with the ever-attentive young waitress. His six fresh oysters, a medium rare 450-gram ribeye steak and a bottle of vintage red wine was to be followed by dessert.

Broaching the subject of the previous night's incident, Niall broke the silence. 'It seems things between us have taken a turn for the worse, or am I wrong? As I recall, not that long ago we were thinking of a holiday in the sun, and now we're barely talking. Please, try to understand; over the last few days too many things have gone wrong and I overreacted.'

'Yes … I do.'

'Good. Oh yes, and regarding my mother, I have thought about what you've said and agree that there's no harm in reading her letters. They may even help bring closure to a messed up … difficult part of my life.'

'I'm very pleased to hear that, and I hope for your sake you'll find some answers. To be frank, your moods scare me. Under no circumstance do I wish to live in fear, not knowing when you'll explode next. My parents never fought, at least not that I know of. So, I expect nothing less from my relationship.'

He took her hand in his and stroked it gently. Her vulnerable eyes held his. 'Thank you for caring … please, forgive me,' he whispered.

She squeezed his hand lightly. 'I do. Just promise me, no more outbursts.'

As they spoke the tension between them receded and Irina's warm smile returned. But Niall was not deceived; she was not paying attention. He let slip, 'Someone hacked my house. We discovered these little bugs all over the place. How, and when this was done, I'll know soon enough. And God help the man … or woman, who did this.'

Irina sat up, alert, giving him her full and undivided attention. 'That's terrible! Who would've done such a thing?'

'Why? Well, that's obvious, and whom … it seems one can never tell,' he replied icily. The flicker in her eyes at the mention of the bugs struck a raw nerve; he could not ignore the nagging feeling that he was being played.

'Please excuse me, I need to powder my nose,' Irina said and stood up.

'Sure … of course.'

As she made her way through the rows of tables, Niall remained seated and nodded at the two men standing behind the tall broadleaved plants near the entrance.

With the cubicle door locked inside the ladies' restroom, Irina touched in the number she knew off by heart. After a few rings the familiar deep baritone voice answered, 'Hi, anything the matter?'

'Yes, I think I've been compromised. I need backup. The Lorelei, opposite Stephen's Green, north side,' she said, her voice barely audible.

'I'm sending five men. They'll be there ten minutes tops. Once they're in place and you still feel you need help, with your right hand wipe your brow and leave. We'll take it from there. But remember, we rely on you, so try and see this through.'

'Thank you. I shall. *Paka.*'

She pocketed her phone and waited for a few seconds.

Overhead the dimmed recessed lights cast a soft reflection on the polished marble tiles. The romantic guitar music piped over the restaurant's music system veiled any movement outside the cubicle. Straining her ears, she was positive she was alone. Nevertheless, she flushed the toilet. Unlocking the cubicle, she opened the door. The next instant a meaty fist hit her under the chin, sending her small frame flying backwards. As her head slammed into the ceramic wall tiles, she was knocked unconscious.

Without remorse Niall watched her limp body flop down on top of the toilet bowl. One of his men pushed inside and pulled her upright, presenting a defenceless target. The other readied himself to deliver a few more punches. Niall stopped him – with her unconscious, there was no point in further punishment.

Opening her eyes, and flanked by two big men, Irina was unable to move. Lifting her aching head, she stared with unadulterated hatred at the back of Niall seated in the front of the racing car. Outside, the darkening sky was murky, threatening to release a deluge of water over the streets of Dublin's suburbs. Her head throbbed. Her mouth tasted of blood. Running the tip of her tongue over her teeth, none seemed chipped or broken, but she felt the cut inside her mouth. She moved her aching jaw – thankfully, it was not broken. With her hands tied there was nothing she could do for now except play along with whatever he had in mind.

'Where are you taking me?' she asked.

'Aha, the little princess is awake! Patience, my dear, you'll see soon enough,' Niall scoffed, turning to face her. 'Just tell me something: what makes you think you can take me on? I must admit somewhat admirable, but very stupid. And, like your friends, you'll also learn just how stupid. In your case even more so. You do understand you have spoiled our chance of a *wonderful* future together. Now, that thought, really grates me, especially as I was willing to give you everything. A new life of splendour. But no, you could not leave well alone, you had to play the Good Samaritan.'

Without warning, his hand shot out and grabbed her left ear firmly, tugging it as if admonishing a young child. 'Some part of me says, "Give her a break; she's still a kid". But then you're not, are you? So, what am I to do? As far as your friends are concerned it's easy; now I have even more reason to kill them.' He laughed. 'And what to do with you, well, that's a real problem,' he said and fell silent.

'I don't care what you think. I did nothing. You're assuming things and—'

'Shh … not another word. You'll have a chance to explain yourself. For now, just shut up!'

Irina did not respond; there was no point in agitating him any further. She needed to stay alive and talk her way out of this mess. She must see this through …

257

Reaching the south-western outskirts an isolated building surrounded by a four-metre-high steel-palisade fence with stone pillars came into view. Behind it, the austere plain brick structure was lit by a few amber lights. By now the rain was lashing down, pouring over the three-storey structure with its steep slate roofs, small dormer windows and its scattering of tall brick chimneys. The eerie gloom emanating from the building made the fine hairs tingle on the nape of her neck. The closed shutters on the upstairs windows added to this haunting feeling. Amidst the sprawling gardens, security personnel patrolled the grounds with their drooling guard dogs straining on short leashes. The premises unmistakably spelled "NO ENTRY". Anyone venturing inside without an invitation would have to be very brave, or mad.

Behind her the entrance gates swung shut with a dull clunk. A few seconds later the car doors flung open. Someone grabbed her arm and pulled her outside. She did not hesitate and kicked the offender in the face, breaking his nose. But he just sneered, oblivious to the blood and pain, he tightened his grip. Assisted by another man, they threw her out of the car. Landing on her feet, two burly men in black jeans and white T-shirts seized her; brown leather holster straps crisscrossed their broad chests.

'Good evening, Mr McGuire. You've got yourself a real feisty one here,' the one man huffed, concentrating on not letting go of the offending elbow which had dealt him a painful blow to the temple, nearly knocking him senseless.

With her hands tied and outnumbered four to one, Irina gave up her struggle before she could sustain a serious injury. She would get another chance.

'It's ready as you've asked for,' one of the men said.

'Fine. I'll teach her to behave,' Niall replied from under the cover of the entrance porch canopy.

Furious, Niall led the small party through a large smoke-filled salon. The mostly foreign male clientele lounging in the dim-lit room ignored them. No one looked in their direction, they knew the rules of the house – and, the less they saw, the better.

Flanked by Niall and four men, Irina traipsed into an office approximately seven by five metres in size, located at the end of a long, stone corridor.

Quickly, she made mental notes of the semi-dark, oak-panelled room, looking for an alternative way out. A small door and two sets of heavy curtains offered possible escape routes. The narrow door was instantly ignored as an option – its size, location, and absence of a guard suggested it most likely led to either a store or bathroom. And behind the curtains? Probably metal-barred, bulletproof glazed windows. Her only escape option was the main door guarded by an intimidating bulk of one hundred and ten kilograms of muscle, standing nearly door height. However, this monster did not deter her, having dealt effectively with far bigger opponents during training.

And, as for a weapon, there were a black wrought iron poker and a glass vase. The rest of the furnishings comprised of two comfortable couches, a large coffee table, a few magazines, a solid wooden desk, three leather chairs, a well-stocked glass drinks cabinet, two floor lamps and five erotic paintings. If forced to fight her way out, the fire poker would do as a weapon, but only if she could free her hands and reach it in time. Also, the vase was within grasp; only one lethal shard would be needed.

But heavily outnumbered, the only realistic choice was to remain calm and talk her way out of the room. Charming him was no longer an option.

'Thinking of making a run for it, really?' Niall asked amused, having watched her take in the details of the office. He found her stoic defiance in the face of overwhelming odds quite entertaining. 'Forget whatever you're thinking. You're not going anywhere. I've arranged some entertainment for you. Now sit down!'

Shoved into a chair, they untied her hands and immediately wrapped leather straps around her wrists. With her hands and feet clasped securely to the chair's frame, unable to move, she lowered her head, not interested in what he had to say. But a soft hiss made her look up. The wood panelling on the wall facing her slid open, revealing a bank of TV screens.

Once more, she dropped her head, refusing to give in to him.

'No, you don't,' Niall said, and grabbed her by the hair, forcing her to face the monitors. 'Whether you like to or not, you shall watch!'

Irina remained silent. Seeing the tray of canisters, elastics, and syringes on the desk, she realised what was in store for her – if they don't find her soon, she may never see the outside world again.

'You've really disappointed me, snooping around, conspiring with the bastards who're trying to bring me down. Whatever your reasons, you know I cannot allow such disloyalty. But seeing, I *love you so much*, I'm prepared to forgive and forget,' he said, his voice dripping honey-sweet sarcasm. 'You either tell me what you're up to or you'll experience a living hell. I suggest you pay close attention to our little show before you say anything.'

As the monitors jumped to life, Irina's heart sank. A screen displayed a girl of no more than eighteen years slumped over a low bench, handcuffed to its legs. Two men were raping her. A third man with a drink in hand gazed lustfully at the girl, his eyes set deep in his dark, pockmarked skin. Ignoring her suffering, he emptied his drink in her face, threw the glass on the floor and forced her mouth open.

'Are you mad? Let me go!' Irina screamed, struggling against the manacles.

'Shut up and watch!' Niall shouted, slapping her across the face.

The other monitors showed different rooms hidden in the dark interior of the old house. A communal area filled with scantily dressed girls of different nationalities, drinking and smoking in an atmosphere of resigned desolation – their grief intolerable. Red-lit, semi-dark rooms where girls lay indifferent

260

to their circumstances – their brains anaesthetised by a cocktail of drugs – being used by the men hovering over them. A chamber of horrors, the walls covered in hooks, winches, chains and leather whips. A beautiful young girl was dragged inside by two men, their naked bodies covered in tattoos. She tried to resist. They flung her against a metal rack, chained her spread-eagled to the frame and hoisted her a few feet off the ground. Her golden blonde hair draped on to the floor. With a leather whip they flayed her naked white skin. The soundless suffering of the poor girl made Irina repulse in horror.

'How can you do this? How?!' she shouted. She had heard about it all. She had been warned. She thought she knew. But the debauched reality was far beyond anything she could ever have imagined or was prepared for. Looking at Niall, she spoke, her voice soft, unnervingly calm, 'As God is my witness you shall pay for this. That, I promise you.'

'Now, now, temper, temper, my dear, or do you really want to join your little friends?' Niall mocked.

'Let them go, please, I beg you.'

'Stop whining and let's get on with it. Answer me truthfully and you'll be fine. If not, you'll end up in one of those lovely suites,' he hissed. 'Right then, let's start at the beginning. Who are you helping? No lies, you've tried my patience long enough.' Picking up a syringe, he inserted the point of the needle into a small canister.

Watching the liquid fill the cylinder, Irina blurted, 'Sean … I'm, helping Sean!'

'Really … Sean? Wow, that was quick! Maybe a bit too quick, don't you think? No, my dear, you can do better than that. And, don't take me for a fool.'

'I promise it's him.'

'Okay, let's pretend you're being honest. Then, why him of all people?'

'He was desperate and asked for my help after Sinead had disappeared. I had no idea what they'd done …'

'Continue. What are you waiting for?'

'So, whenever you had information, I told Sean.'

261

'Well, that's obvious. And, how do you know Sean?'

'By chance. A few days ago, I bumped into the three of them in Dublin while I was shopping.'

'Rubbish!'

'Whether you believe me or not doesn't matter, it's the truth.'

'Okay, let's leave this fairy tale of yours for the moment which I may or may not believe. But more importantly, did you also help them plant the bugs in my house? To me, you're the only person who could have. And, while you're confessing, you may just as well tell me who you phoned? Come on, I want the truth; it might just save you from becoming a TV star in this establishment,' he said, pointing at the monitors with the needle.

'I knew nothing about any bugs until you mentioned them in the restaurant, I swear. And I phoned Sean's friend for help. I was afraid for my life,' she said, defensively.

'And what's this *mysterious* friend's name, Irish by any chance?'

'I don't know who he is … and he sounded Irish. I only have his number. For his protection they did not want to tell me more. If you think I'm lying, then so be it; do what you must,' she said with a sigh.

'His number, now!'

'Uhm … 087 … 4610 … 317, I think.'

Without another word Niall tapped the number into Irina's phone. After a few rings a deeply concerned Irish voice asked, 'Irina, are you all right?'

Niall did not respond and cut the connection.

After a prolonged silence, he ordered, 'Let's go.'

He dropped the needle on the tray with a clatter, released her and led the group back to the waiting car. He was doubtful whether she was telling the truth, but he would let it slide, for now, and see what she would get up to next, give her enough rope …

Irina did not speak. She knew she was not in the clear just yet. He might have accepted her story, but one wrong word or act may see her back at the brothel within a flash … and in chains. And this time there would be no reprieve. She avoided eye contact, fearing he might see the small victory-flames dancing in her eyes. Instead, she focused her attention on the now much lighter handbag in her lap with her passport, phone and money confiscated.

'From now on you'll do exactly as told. You will remain in the house. There'll be no liberties. I'm warning you, if you displease me in any way, or give me the slightest reason to suspect any disloyalty, you know where you'll end up,' Niall said, snapping his head in the direction of the old house behind them swallowed by the downpour.

But overruling all was the fact that he wanted her at home for his pleasure; visiting the brothel whenever the need arose would be far too laborious. Nor was he prepared to share her with the dubious clientele who frequented his establishment, or anyone else for that matter.

Irina looked at the digital clock, 3:00 a.m. With all the lights on in her bedroom she waited for daybreak. What happened earlier could not be repeated; she would not fail, not after all this.

The last she had seen of Niall was when he had shoved her into her room. His few parting words, "See you later," still rankled. Since then her bedroom door had remained firmly shut.

Propped up in bed fully dressed in a sweater, jeans, runners, and her auburn hair tied back in a tight ponytail, she continued to page through a gossip magazine with sleep furthest from her mind. The tablets she had taken somewhat reduced her throbbing headache. But the disturbing images of the trapped girls haunted her. It must end!

She battled to stay awake, anticipating the turn of the key at any moment. If he came for her, her condition would not deter him; proof of that she had seen enough. If he persisted, he would experience no pleasure, he would be raping her. Her initial thought of killing him if he dared touched her seemed

263

pointless, as then, even in death, he would be the victor.

'She's back. Bad bruise on her face. Is extraction required?' Jacek asked.

'Negative. You cannot risk exposure.'

'Understood,' Jacek replied and ended the call.

The operation to install Jacek on Niall's estate six months ago had taken more than a year of careful planning, paperwork, and calling in favours. If Jacek's identity were to be discovered it could derail the FSB's ongoing investigation into Niall's network of international criminals trading in stolen and illegal weapons. His involvement in the drug and human trafficking industry was not their concern.

CHAPTER 64

Mykonos, Greece
Saturday Morning

Vera fretted, craving absolution. *Could she even begin to understand*, she wondered? Clearing her throat and with a slight tremor in her voice, she said, 'Sinead, many times you've asked me why I left Russia, why I never wanted to go back. Well … maybe now is a good time to tell you. We don't know what will happen today. But only if you promise not to ever repeat a word of what I'm about to say. Nor judge me.'

'Oh boy, that sounds serious!' Sinead replied light-heartedly, not wanting another *final farewell.*

'I'm serious. Very serious. Promise.'

The smile on Sinead's face froze, replaced by a look of deep concern. Void of any joviality, she said, 'But of course, I do. Forgive me, I just hate your assumption that things will always go wrong.'

'Sorry, my past has ingrained this constant pessimism, despite always trying to sound upbeat.'

'That, I do understand.'

'Uhm … sure,' Vera said, unconvinced.

'So …'

'Nine years ago, with only one month left to the birth of my baby girl–'

'What! You have a child somewhere in Russia and you never told me?' Sinead interrupted, amazed.

'Please, let me finish.'

'Sorry,' Sinead said and moved to the edge of her seat, paying close attention, ignoring her half-eaten breakfast.

'I was married to a man called Yuri Egorov.'

'Grand! And, married as well!' Sinead blurted. 'So, what happened to them?'

'Please.'

'I promise, not another word.'

'Where was I? Oh, yes … the nursery. With what little money I could scrape together I had prepared our bedroom to welcome my baby into the world: a soft yellow teddy, a cot, and very little else. Despite the lack of things, I had vowed she would receive all the love a child deserves. To never feel unwanted or unloved. Her birth was to be a turning point in my life. At last, I was to have a real family. My own.'

Sinead knew the teddy only too well. It was the one article Vera had refused to leave behind in Ireland.

'Nineteen and very healthy, I had suffered no morning sickness, nothing, but I had one big problem, Yuri. He drank too much. And when drunk, he would punch me at the slightest provocation.'

'That's terrible. Why would he do such a thing?' Sinead asked, dumbfounded, unable to comprehend why any man could hit his pregnant wife.

'Why? You tell me. But one thing is certain: Russian men do not like to be told what to do, especially when it comes to alcohol.'

'Not only Russian … sounds like a lot of men I know. Did no one stop him?'

'Oh, sure. His parents gave him some half-hearted talk not to hurt me again. Their concern was purely for the well-being of their future grandchild. They had never approved of me, some trash rescued from the state orphanage by their *loving and caring* son. My threats to leave were also ignored,' Vera said. 'How I came to meet him is another story …'

Vera's stomach turned at the memory, still loathing Yuri after so many years.

'My mother and I were abandoned by my father when I was three years old – I've never heard or seen him since. When I was ten my mother died of breast cancer. With no grandparents alive, or any other family willing to take me in, I was sent to the Alexandrov Orphanage #31 on Ulitsa Petrovka in the Chekhovskaya district in Moscow. It was an awful place. Heavy metal gates, dark grey building, real institutional. I still remember the welcoming words on the gate, promising a normal family life filled with love and care. But the cold walls of the orphanage were as I had feared – heartless, void of love or care. I was bundled into a room with fourteen other girls – that took some getting used to! You know how bitchy we *lovely* girls can be. Now, imagine fifteen in one room. On the bright side; at least I had a roof over my head and a bed to sleep in. And to keep us out of the carers' hair, we were forced to make sure the place stayed spotless, top to bottom. The last thing our *loving* carers wanted was to be lumbered with a bunch of idle brats and their endless teenage insecurities.'

'Sounds a bit like the Magdalena laundries we had here.'

'I guess so. Anyway, I managed to survive just fine. Well, that was till my sixteenth birthday when I was gang-raped by four male and female staff. According to them, they were doing me the biggest favour, preparing me for my life as a whore, shouting obscenities, and saying, 'What else do you think you're good for, you little slut!" And how true those words turned out to be.'

'No, don't you say that! Life has been terribly cruel … unfair to you, from the very beginning. That's over now. You're still young and will never have to go through such humiliation again. We're out, free, in case you haven't noticed,' Sinead said, surprised by her own candour.

'Thank you. But until we're rid of these stones, I'll reserve judgement, if you don't mind,' Vera said with a smile.

'Did you report them?'

'To whom? They were all covering for each other. I just had to learn to live with the regular raping, the same as many of the other girls had to. About a year after the first incident, I met Yuri. He was young, strong and handsome with the most incredible blue, piercing eyes. The leader of the pack. We fell for each other and started dating. I told him what was going on at the orphanage. Incensed, he and a group of friends intervened. The bodies of the one couple were found next to the Moskva Reka with their genitalia badly mutilated. Apparently, the other two rapists had fled, so we were told. To me, Yuri was my knight in shining armour, the man of my dreams. And as usual, the reality was to be quite something else. The murder of those carers should have been a warning. But hey, love is blind.'

'Once married, we moved into his parents' apartment. Soon I fell pregnant. It was also then that his alcohol abuse surfaced, becoming unbearable. Weekends, whenever his parents were in the country, life became hell. No amount of crying, begging him to stop, helped. It only incensed him, forcing me to stay out of his way. One Saturday night, he and his friends once again drank themselves into a stupor. Despite the noise, I had fallen asleep in our room. Much later I was woken by some annoying giggling. All was quiet except for this persistent noise. I got up to see what was going on and found him having sex with two girls. As any wife would, I exploded and grabbed the girls by their hair, pulling them off him. Big mistake. Yuri jumped up and punched me in the stomach. They then joined him in beating me to a pulp. Ignoring the pain, I did my best to protect my baby. But Yuri just wrung my arms free, and with my stomach exposed, told the girls to kick the "bitch" I was carrying. I'll never forget their wicked laughter, their cruelty …' Vera said as her voice broke, overcome by the dreadful memory. 'Begging them to stop only made it worse. As I was bleeding … almost comatose, they finally stopped, fell on to the couch, and continued their sex. I passed out.'

Shocked, unable to believe her ears, Sinead stammered, 'How … how could they …' She reached out and wiped the tears from Vera's porcelain skin. 'How did you survive such …

such madness? And what happened to your child?'

'Somehow, I did survive … but, not my baby …' Vera whispered and closed her eyes, biting her lip. After a few moments of silence, she cleared her throat and continued. 'If it was not for the police arriving, neither would I have. How many times I've wished I didn't survive …'

'Stop saying that … please.'

'I know, but it's the truth.'

'What happened to Yuri and his friends?'

'Nothing. The police handling the case told him to apologise, and in future take his girlfriends somewhere else; it was dumb to bring them home. To these men, giving one's wife a hiding is part of life.'

'And for killing your child?'

'He had friends in the right places. The official report stated I had fallen down the stairs, and that was that.'

'Incredible!' Sinead exclaimed, horrified. 'And what happened to you?'

'I spent three weeks in hospital, consumed by anger … hate. The only people who showed some compassion were other would-be-mothers who had suffered miscarriages. Believe me, I hated life. And him. I hated him more than anything in the world. All I wanted was to run away so he could never find me,' Vera said, heaving a ragged sigh.

'Sinead, you have no idea how cruel some of my people can be. While in hospital the girl in the bed next to mine returned from the bathroom in tears. Asking her why she was so upset, she told me between sobs. On her way back to bed she had accidentally looked inside the small utility room. On the floor next to a pile of dirty swabs, medical instruments and bloodied bandages – wastage to be burned – was a premature baby. Horrified, she had asked the nurse why the tiny body was there. Continuing to move more waste into the room the nurse had replied bluntly, "Oh, that … the same as the rest of the stuff in here. There are no incubators to spare. Anyway, it won't survive the day." And, as the nurse spoke, the baby had stirred and raised a tiny arm as if to block the glare of the sun

269

pouring in through the small window.'

'Excuse me … I need some water … I'll only be a moment,' Sinead said and stood up. Shutting the bathroom door behind her, she slipped on to the floor. Overcome by despair, she wept inconsolably.

Returning to the lounge blurry-eyed, bravely trying to compose herself, Sinead sat down.

'Sinead, I'm sorry. If you prefer, I'll stop …'

'No, please, ignore me.'

Vera continued, but refrained from revealing too much: her loneliness, her struggle walking the few kilometres back to that dreadful apartment, filled with a deep sense of loss.

'After three weeks I was strong enough to leave. I never wanted to see my husband, or his family again. The little love I still felt for Yuri had died the day he had killed our child. But leaving was not to be easy. While packing, eager to slip away without anyone noticing, he had arrived home unusually early: drunk, reeking of vodka. Realising what I was doing, he attacked me: punching, kicking, swearing. Having vowed he would never lay another finger on me again, I was ready for him, armed with a sharp knife … I'll never forget the sound of the blade slicing open his stomach—'

'My God. You killed him.' Sinead exclaimed, shocked.

'Yes, I did. I watched him die …'

Having recovered from the initial shock, Sinead blurted, 'Good for you! One less pig in this world, so much the better.'

'Maybe so, but believe me, it was terrible … something I have to live with for the rest of my life. I never wanted to kill him. All I wanted was my freedom, to start a new life in St. Petersburg, or somewhere. True, many times I had wished him dead, though actually killing him, no. But I could not allow him to hurt me again.'

'No, Vera, he deserved it! And it was self-defence, not murder. You must remember that. Well, that explains why you can never go back to Russia,' Sinead said, wishing she had the courage of her friend, thinking of all the men who were like

Yuri, treating women like meat, sex objects to be abused and beaten at will. No, her friend did herself and the world a big favour. 'What happened then?'

'Traumatised, I had wrapped his body in a blanket and hid it under the bed. While showering, scrubbing the blood off my hands … my body, trying to erase the smell … trying to calm myself, all I could think of was to get away. But to where? Europe? I knew the police would not believe I killed him in self-defence. So, I had to flee to where they could never find me. And the only place I could think of was the West.'

CHAPTER 65

Dublin
Saturday Morning

'"Ciarán, get some fingerprints. And I don't want him dead, not just yet.'

'Right boss, see it as done.'

'Good. Then off with you.'"

Inspector Clinton Maher was the senior officer on duty. Barely one hour at work and he locked himself inside his small office and listened to the recording once more. What started as a normal Saturday, faced with the usual routine, morphed into a nightmare.

As the last words hung in the air, he let out a loud whistle. There was no doubt; the CD was an untampered recording. Neither was there any doubt whose deep baritone voice instructed Ciarán to carry out an attack on a certain individual whose name was a mystery – the alleged victim's details were inside a folder handed to Ciarán.

Nervously, Inspector Maher fidgeted with the envelope. Feeling lightheaded his eyes drifted aimlessly over the few words written on the outside, "Item One – Urgent!"

Who could have sent this? he wondered.

Thirty minutes had elapsed since the ominous parcel had landed on the Incidents Desk of the National Bureau of Criminal Investigation's branch in Harcourt Street. Duly

272

documented, opened and listened to by Sergeant O'Leary on duty, the parcel had been raced upstairs for immediate action. The sergeant's sudden spurt of energy was obviously not the only reason for him being out of breath when placing the CD on Inspector Maher's desk; its contents having had a far more profound impact.

Again, Inspector Maher pressed play, letting the second dialogue bounce off the four walls. The temperature in the room felt as if an arctic wind had wrapped its freezing tentacles around the small cocoon.

'"Please, have a seat.'
'Good evening, Mr McGuire.'
'Glad you're here. It seems you're the only man I can rely on, not having failed me once.'
'It's my pleasure. You know I always aim to please. That you can count on.'
'Good, then I'll be brief. In the first envelope are the details of the target. I will make sure the individual will be at the O'Mara Hotel by 21h30 tomorrow evening. I'll confirm the room number later. In the second envelope are several photographs you must leave at the scene. Be careful how you handle those, they have someone's fingerprints on them; I don't want it smudged. There's a suicide note as well, spelling out Mr Murphy's regrets for his past sins, etc., etc. That you can leave anywhere suitable.'"

Inspector Clinton Maher's finger shut the CD player off. He had heard enough. 'Just perfect, you, smug jerk! Niall, my friend, you're fucked and I doubt if there's anything I can or even want to do,' he cursed under his breath.

The full implications if caught collaborating with Niall were unthinkable. And what was the alternative; to permit Niall to disclose to his superiors their five-year-long relationship, of his personal involvement in Niall's illegal operations while in office?

'You must be bloody bonkers! I knew you were trouble

273

the day I met you,' he muttered, knowing it was far too late for regrets.

At the time of their introduction, Clinton Maher had freshly arrived in Dublin, having relocated from Tralee. It was to be a promotion, regarded as a fantastic opportunity, the first step on the ladder to chief superintendent. But the adjustment to city life for him and his family of five did not come easily. They had missed with great sentiment the beauty of Kerry and the long hikes along the lakes and mountains. But the biggest difficulty they had faced was the huge increase in living costs, expenses which had exceeded their expectations by far. They were forced to juggle daily with an inadequate budget, trying to make ends meet. This continuous struggle had resulted in many nights of fierce arguments at home. And so, the rift between him and his wife had steadily grown, verging on the brink of no return.

To rescue his marriage, he had been forced to spend more hours at work, away from home. Introduced to local businessmen, he had dined out more than required. Ignorant that he was being groomed, he had never refused an invitation. By this stage, his financial predicament was common knowledge amongst his close circle of friends. Judged to be trustworthy, these friends had offered to help, initially only involving him in some legitimate opportunities to make additional money, except for a friendship with one businessman, in particular, a certain Mr Niall McGuire. Soon he was sucked into the world of deceit; a world he was entirely unprepared for.

Witnessing the transformation by his wife – recapturing her old vibrant self mainly due to these financial rewards – any feelings of guilt had evaporated. His marriage had entered a new phase of fulfillment; sacrificing longstanding principles was a small price to pay.

Inspector Maher considered the previous week's allegations of drug trafficking in Greece levelled against Niall. And now this!

Niall's untouchable empire was about to come tumbling down, taking the whole lot of them with him. He knew he was not the only one on Niall's payroll. But who the other colleagues were, he had no idea. If this recording had been heard by any member outside Niall's circle, then his hands were tied.

He looked at the note scribbled on the envelope. It was a clear warning that more evidence was to follow. He could hear alarm bells ringing as far afield as Galway. Whoever the anonymous donor was, they had every intention of removing Mr McGuire from civilian life ... for good. There was no time to waste.

He picked up the phone. 'Sergeant O'Leary, my office, right away!' Inspector Maher growled.

'Right away, sir,' the sergeant echoed.

Grilling the sergeant confirmed he was not affiliated to Niall in any way; ruling out an opportunity to lose, swap, or edit the evidence. Even worse, the sergeant stated he had contacted the detective chief superintendent, who was on his way as they spoke. Apparently, he was a man on a mission, wanting to evaluate the information first hand, eager to learn the truth behind the death of Mr Eoin Murphy.

Having dismissed the sergeant, Clinton Maher left his office without delay. He needed privacy where the walls had no ears. Niall had to be warned.

Just about to push open the front door, the familiar voice of his superior boomed behind him, stopping him in his tracks, 'Good morning, Inspector!' Reluctantly he turned and faced his boss. What he would give to be an insignificant piece of crumpled paper on the pavement, blown freely about amongst the few ramblers. His freedom was something which may soon only be a distant memory!

'Going anywhere in a hurry? I trust not. It seems we have some work to do. To my office, if you please,' he ordered, not to be disobeyed.

A deeply worried Inspector Maher dolefully obliged and followed on his superior's heels, contemplating how to turn this situation to his advantage. Maybe he should come clean

275

before it all blew up in his face?

Behind him, Sergeant O'Leary happily brought up the rear, carrying the condemning evidence, grinning from ear to ear.

Detective Chief Superintendent Griffin sat dumbstruck, listening to the recording for the second time. It was blatantly obvious to those present that Niall McGuire had instructed the murder of the minister of the environment, Eoin Murphy … and the brutal assault on an unidentified male.

This new evidence was added to the drug smuggling allegations already on file, a document which was growing in stature by the minute.

The ongoing investigation at the Garda National Drugs Unit at Dublin Castle in liaison with other departments had so far unearthed a conglomerate of phony companies and trust funds. It was a network built on a string of dubious business deals with less than reputable organisations. Also surfacing were reports of some rather suspicious relationships with several government officials.

At first glance, the recording seemed to be condemning enough to drag Niall McGuire into court. But after some deliberation, Chief Superintendent Griffin concluded a court hearing, if challenged by an astute lawyer, would be blown out of the water. The recording would not be permissible in court. He needed hard evidence if they were to have any hope of success.

Facing his colleagues, Chief Superintendent Griffin dropped his gold-rimmed glasses on the table and folded his hands. 'Contact Interpol and see what their investigation has come up with regarding Niall McGuire. As from this moment he is our prime suspect in the murder of our esteemed Minister Murphy. Sean O'Donovan may or may not be the killer. His height and build seems to fit that of the mysterious visitor at the hotel. Therefore, his status remains unchanged. The second voice on the recording could be that of Sean's boss … if not his. But Niall gave the order. Therefore, I don't care what you do and how you do it, even if you must break every liberty or right the prick may claim he has! If necessary, you dig up the foundations of his house. I want the truth. And as far as this Ronan, Ronan … what's it again?

'O'Brien.'

'Thank you – O'Brien is concerned, he's still a suspect until we find evidence to the contrary. My gut tells me they are all in cahoots. Well, get on with it. I expect your reports on my desk before sunset. Thank you, gentlemen. That will be all.'

CHAPTER 66

Athens, Greece
Saturday Morning

'Got them. One's about five-foot-seven, stocky, ginger hair, skull tattoo on neck, white T-shirt, blue jeans. The other, six-foot, lean, black hair, wearing light blue–'

'Affirmative,' Dermot cut him short. 'Keep your distance and let's see who else is about to join our little shindig.'

Having covered another two hundred metres, Dermot had seen enough. The delay caused by the game of cat and mouse with Ciarán's men had been worth it: they now knew exactly who was trailing them. He stuck his arm out, nearly stepping in front of the speeding taxi. 'Athens International, Terminal Two. And step on it.'

With the usual Saturday morning traffic congesting the roads, the journey to the airport did not go as smoothly as anticipated. But once clear of the city centre, the hooting, breaking and swerving stopped. The taxi accelerated, trying to make up lost time. Dermot sat back and turned his head; Ciarán's men were not far behind. Content, he lit a cigar, happy to lure the mouse into the trap.

In a few days' time, he would control operations in Ireland; an ambition long sought. Based inside the EU, he would operate with ease across the territory with no borders, and with the millions of lawless streaming in, prospects looked more promising by the day. His future drug market would be limitless.

With a flight cleared for Siros, Paul taxied to their holding station. Dermot chuckled and pocketed his phone having received Ciarán's plane's details from his backup team. *Only one planeload of overeager chumps to contend with. This guy can surely pick them!* Dermot looked at Paul next to him, fondly stroking the yoke of his plane, and grimaced annoyed. *And I'm stuck with the biggest schmuck of them all!*

Fifty-five minutes later, Ciarán frowned as Paul's plane flitted through the skies up ahead. 'Jaysus, don't tell me our information is shite. Niall will have a cadenza!' he cursed and looked at his watch; twenty minutes had elapsed since they had flown right over Siros Island.

Suddenly, Paul's plane banked sharply left and veered around, heading back in the direction of Siros.

'What the …?!' Ciarán shouted confused and sat back, pummelling his brain, frustrated. 'Just follow them wherever the hell they're going!'

As Siros Island reappeared far below, they followed Paul's descent. Anxiously, Ciarán peered out of the small window not wanting to lose sight of Paul's plane coming to a stop near the small terminal building. Only three other planes sat on the asphalt.

'What! You want us to be at the windmills in Mykonos Town by four! Stop fucking with us you little slut!' Paul shouted into his phone and flopped back into his seat, infuriated by Vera's words.

Yes. And don't ever speak to me like that again. See you at four,' Vera replied calmly.

With the line dead, Paul chucked his phone into the seat's pocket, rolled his plane back on to the runway, and lodged a new flight plan for Mykonos via Samos.

'Pull up! Pull up! The bastard is taking off again!' Ciarán

shouted, baffled, just as they made their final approach into Siros airport.

'We have to clear a new route or we'll be forced down by these edgy Greeks!' the pilot warned, having no idea where to head to.

'Which direction are they going?' Ciarán asked, focusing on the small dot up ahead.

'East ... meaning any one of a hundred islands. Take your pick. Here's a map.'

Ignoring the sarcasm, Ciarán did as the pilot suggested. After a minute he looked up. 'Ikaria looks as good a bet as any.'

'Ikaria ... you sure?'

'Yeah. Just do it!' Ciarán ordered. Returning to the cabin, he updated Michael waiting in Siros.

'Great, and here we are, armed and ready!' Michael said, not impressed.

'Best ye lot stay put until we know where the fucker's heading,' Ciarán ordered.

'Right, Einstein, brilliant plan, cheers,' Michael mocked and cut the call. Not having slept much in the last twenty-four hours he was already in a foul mood, and now this. Exactly how many hours remained until the proposed meeting, he had no idea. The only chance of staying with the pack rested with Stavros. And if not him, then he may have to get help – forget orders, there were innocent lives at stake.

Ringing Stavros, his request for assistance was met with a friendly, 'No problem. After all, we're on the same team.' Stavros, seated in Dimitris' Gulfstream G450 parked at Siros airport, had expected such a request after witnessing the arrival of two private jets shortly before Paul's, followed by his quick departure, nearly crashing into Ciarán who was about to land!

'Thanks, Stavros. Declan and the lads will be with you shortly,' Michael replied, refraining from correcting the Greek's assumption that they were on the same team.

Five minutes later with all his men gone including Sean's two *shadows*, Michael once more turned his attention to the befuddled *rescuer*. At the soft buzz of his phone, he answered.

'*Yassou*, Michael,' Stavros said. 'You better warn your men we have more company than we have bargained for. American mercenaries … I think?' While waiting for Declan's party, Stavros had spotted three groups of well-built males arrive at the airport, board a large Falcon 2000 private jet, and race after Paul and Ciarán. He had no doubts.

Michael cursed, fully aware where this fracas was leading. 'Thanks, Stavros, I'll warn Ciarán. Please get Declan and my men there, pronto. And try to avoid a bloodbath.'

The odd request left Stavros somewhat bemused. It was not what he had expected from the chief of security of one of the biggest criminal outfits in the underworld this side of the Atlantic. An order to permit the men to kill everyone and anyone who got in their way would have been more in tune.

CHAPTER 67

Niall's Estate
Saturday Morning

The quick rap on the door was repeated twice before Irina stirred. She sat up, warily. Slowly, she slid across the bed and faced the door.

'Irina, may I come in?' a male voice asked.

The butler?

'*Da*, please do.'

John was in his late sixties. His thinning grey hair revealed the soft skin of his scalp. He cast a look in her direction and immediately averted his eyes, not wanting to stare. He had seen enough. He shook his head in dismay; the bruised jaw will be with her for a while. Thankfully, she was still alive.

'Good morning, Irina. I thought you may want some breakfast,' he said, silently simmering with rage. Having been in Niall's employment for two years, he had witnessed many unpleasant incidents within the confines of the sprawling old walls. And the way things were going, the poor soul on the bed had very little chance of surviving the madman much longer.

'Thank you very much. That's very thoughtful of you.'

'When ready, you may want to avail of the lounge instead of remaining here in your room. It would be for the best. Mr McGuire has been up for a while, and as is customary on Saturday mornings, is working in his study,' he cautioned, believing the presence of the staff would deter his employer from overstepping the boundaries. Although that was no guarantee.

'I will … thank you,' Irina replied, grateful to have found an ally.

As she ate, showered and dressed she did not lower her guard for a moment. And when finished, she partly heeded the butler's advice and went to the kitchen to make herself some more coffee.

With the aroma of freshly ground beans drifting up, she patiently waited for the black liquid to trickle into her cup. Ignoring the concerned expression on Anne's young face, she looked outside, taking in the peaceful ambience of the colourful flowerbeds where a robin redbreast foraged for food. Her apparent calmness cloaked her dark thoughts of young girls raped, abused … images of immense sorrow. Last night she was powerless to do anything, but end their suffering, she would.

The dark piercing eyes stared unblinkingly at her, or was it her imagination? She turned around to find only one other person in the kitchen, Anne, preoccupied with her head down. Confused, she returned Jacek's stare. For a second his eyes held hers. He winked and with a subtle tilt of the head indicated for her to meet him outside. She did not respond and poured a drop of milk into her coffee.

Sauntering on to the patio, the mid-morning sun felt remarkably warm on her skin. Seeming bored, she sat down on the chaise-longue close to where Jacek was dutifully pottering, tugging at some unwanted weeds. She remained silent, waiting for him to speak.

'*Dobroe utro, kak vi?*' (Good morning, how are you?)

The words spoken in accent-free Russian took her by surprise. About to face him, Jacek warned, 'No, don't. And don't look so surprised, not all *Poles* are averse to the Big Bear. Some of us have even mastered Russian to a fair degree.' The perfect Russian rolled off his tongue, touched with a hint of humour.

Polish, of course you are! No, you're as Russian as I am. She

283

smiled to herself.

Turning more sombre, he prompted, 'How are you?'

'I'm fine, thank you.'

'Uhm … you sure? It doesn't look like that.'

'Really, I am. Positive.'

'Do you need help?'

'No.'

'Understood. However, if you experience any more trouble, day or night, then remove the vase of flowers in your window. I'll be watching. Remember, you're not alone.'

'Thank you,' she replied without looking at him. She had no doubt he was Russian FSB. It all added up, explaining the efficiency of the bugs placed inside the house. She had wondered where the messages were being transmitted to. It had to be somewhere close by. What better place than the gardener's flat?

Reclining on the padded chaise-longue, the combined effect of the sun, fresh air and the knowledge that someone was watching over her soon lulled her to sleep.

'Get up, hurry!' Maurice's voice thundered in her ears.

'Why?' Irina asked, immediately wide awake.

'Boss's orders. Pack your bag; we're leaving. Hurry! What ya waiting for!' Gerry, the one nearest to her scowled as he reached out to grab her arm.

Swift as a cat she dodged him. 'I wouldn't do that if I were you!' she warned as a snide sneer spread across her face, ready to pounce on the stout man.

For a brief second, Gerry froze, baffled by her defiance. 'What the fuck! Jaysus, who do you think you are, slut!' Infuriated, he closed in on her.

'Everything all right, miss?' Jacek asked, blocking Gerry's way.

'Stay out of it, Pollack!' Gerry shouted and pulled a pistol on the gardener.

Undeterred, Jacek inched forward.

'I'll be fine, Jacek, thanks,' Irina said.

'Are you sure?' he asked, standing his ground.

'Yes. Shame, little puppies can't really hurt anyone,' she said disdainfully and brushed past Niall's two men.

Back in her room the two men checked every item she packed. Satisfied, they slammed her suitcase shut and ordered her to follow.

How quickly things have changed, Irina thought as she picked up her suitcase.

Beneath the dull grey sky, Jacek calmly strolled around the big Georgian mansion observing all windows to be shut and doors locked. This was his second recce through the vast estate. He had seen enough. Quickly he tapped in the number of the office in Dublin, based inside the Russian Embassy.

'Our prime suspect fled fifty minutes ago. I doubt he'll be back. The house is locked, five guards on duty. He took Irina. I believe he'll kill her if he discovers the truth,' Jacek warned, troubled.

'We know. We're tracking him. Your concern regarding her is noted. Don't worry, she'll be fine. She's trained for this and can look after herself,' replied his handler.

'I hope you're right.'

'Let's stay positive. She knows what to expect. We have the utmost faith in her,' came the curt reply. 'But time's running out. Search the house; see what you can salvage. Maybe he did not cover all his tracks.'

'Yes, I'll do it tonight. There are too—'

'No, do it right away. The Garda could be there any minute,' his handler interrupted.

'Copy that. *Dosvidaniya.*'

Having ended the call, he sprinted the two hundred metres to his apartment, collected the tools required for the task ahead and raced back to the empty house. Unlocking the kitchen door and deactivating the house alarm was done in record time. Checking the alarm control panel, he re-activated all external openings' sensors, permitting him the run of the house.

Standing in front of the empty safe in Niall's upstairs study, his suspicions were confirmed – their suspect wouldn't be back for quite a while. Not discouraged he raced downstairs and searched the sumptuous office, the safe, the computer, the desk. He shook his head, disillusioned.

Nothing here, upstairs, go!

Sprinting to the top, his heart didn't skip a beat taking the steps three at a time. Once more he sat down in front of the desktop computer and commenced downloading its entire contents. Checking the monitor's display there was nothing of any value nor a hint of where Niall had fled to. With all files downloaded Jacek removed the hard drive for analysis by experts in the FSB – it might contain valuable information – and placed it inside his small haversack.

Suddenly, a loud crash echoed through the house, followed by incessant banging on the front door.

Time to clear out!

Expertly he replaced the cover of the now useless computer, grabbed his bag of tools and scanned the room for tell-tale signs of his visit. Starting towards the door an almighty thunder echoed downstairs, the front door having splintered under a barrage of sledgehammers, simultaneously triggering the alarm.

Ignoring the ear-piercing blare of the siren, he ran into the main en-suite and opened the window. Behind him the house filled with loud shouting and running footsteps. Peering outside the way was clear. He stepped on to the windowsill, slid the sash window shut behind him and effortlessly sailed down the drainpipe. Two metres above the ground he let go, and landing on both feet, dashed towards the garden shed.

With his bag stowed away behind some garden tools, he closed the shed's door. Straightening his clothes, he jogged to the front of the house, appearing the concerned employee investigating the racket. He had taken no more than five paces when he bumped into three armed Gardaí. They did not hesitate in handcuffing and marching him off to the waiting vans.

Turning the front corner, Jacek was amazed to discover the presence of what must be the total sum of all the Garda units of Greater Dublin. Submissively he followed his escort to one of the waiting vans, knowing he would soon be free, able to collect the hidden bag.

But he knew his mission as an undercover agent in Niall's employment had run its course. He would soon be on his way back to Moscow to be reassigned.

CHAPTER 68

Mykonos Airport
Saturday Afternoon

Stavros' plane was the fourth to touch down at Mykonos, all within the space of half an hour. With raised eyebrows, the customs officers of the small airport pondered what the furore was about with hordes of dubious-looking men arriving unannounced in the middle of the day on their precious island. The threatening looks cast in their direction were enough to deter them from taking any action.

As one group after the other bullied their way through security, the senior customs officer, Tassos Vandrakis – seated behind the one-way glass screen – jumped into action and contacted his head office in Athens. Maybe, they or Interpol had some inkling of what was underfoot? If not, then he'd better bring them up to speed. What was a bunch of Mafioso doing in Mykonos? Their body language spelled trouble. Considering the number of arrivals, the small local police force would be heavily outgunned if a gang war were to erupt!

Maddened, Tassos Vandrakis followed Stavros outside. Keeping a discreet distance, he watched Stavros and his men pile into the five hired cars and speed off in the direction of Mykonos Town. With a subtle nod of his head he gave the go-ahead for the two unmarked cars to shadow the newly arrived visitors. Their instructions were clear. Keep your distance. Act only if necessary. Wait for reinforcements from Athens.

Leading the cavalcade into Mykonos Town, Dermot and his men were blissfully unaware of Stavros tailing them, bringing up the rear. Seeing the lead car cut recklessly on to the main road, Stavros chuckled to himself, 'Wonder what's their hurry? Must have discovered a pot of diamonds at the end of the rainbow!'

The number of men racing to trap the two girls in Mykonos Town had reached a total of thirty-seven with more on the way.

CHAPTER 69

Siros Island, Greece

Michael rushed forward, tired of the endless wandering through the streets of Siros Town since the early hours. He had about as much as he could take of Sean dashing from one establishment to the next, waving with great hopes the photograph of Sinead under the noses of the hotel staff. He was getting nowhere and time had run out.

'Let me buy you a drink, my boy. I think you need one?' the deep, pleasant Irish voice boomed in Sean's ear.

Damn, the last thing I need is some drinking buddy, Sean sighed and turned to politely decline the offer.

Confronted by an intimidating bulk of a man with no sign of pleasantries on his face despite the friendly overtures, Sean stammered, 'Thanks ... not now ... I don't have time. Maybe later.'

'Sean, I suggest you take the drink.'

'What! How ... how do you ... do I know you?'

'No, you don't.'

'Then, who are you?'

'A friend. I'm here to help. Name's Michael, Niall's head of security. Any more questions?'

'Right, "A friend". Get lost, I've got nothing to say to you!'

'Fair enough. In that case, you better listen.'

'Why?' Sean asked as a slight panic crept into his voice.

Any thought of fighting his way past this monster vanished into thin air as the lean muscles rippled in the huge forearms and scarred hands gripping his shoulder. He was not to be tested.

'Relax … hear me out. And you're right; time is something we don't have. What will it be … pint?'

Steering Sean with a drink in hand to a corner table in the bar, Michael pulled out a chair and sat down. It was the moment Sean was waiting for. Tensing to make a run for it, Michael's voice stopped him. 'If you want to save your sister you'll stay put and listen to what I have to say.'

'Why should I? So, thanks, but no thanks, buddy!' Sean said defiantly.

'Calm yourself, lad. Let me fill you in on what's going on. By the way, if I wanted to kill you, I would've done that last night on the ferry – it would've been days before someone would've discovered your body, that's if.'

'Okay … right,' Sean mumbled – this was way out of his league. He sat down.

Within a few sentences, Michael summarised events which had led him to Siros. 'And that's how I've found you. Pure Irish luck. By the way, in case you haven't noticed, you've been tailed all the way from Dublin by two of Niall's hoods,' Michael said. He could not resist a smile as a look of horror spread across the young man's face. 'And you thought you could do this all by yourself. They would've been waiting, ready to pounce the instant you found your sister.'

At a loss for words, Sean sipped his beer, mulling over this information, unsure of what to do next. After a few minutes he spoke, 'Then you must also know that I've no clue where Sinead is. And, even if I did, what makes you think I'd tell you?'

'Listen, Sean, I'm not here to test your resilience. I'm here to find your sister and Vera before it's too late. They're in grave danger. If we can't reach them before the others, they'll be dead this time tomorrow.'

'Like I don't know that? What the hell do you think I'm

trying to do?'

'Cut it out!' Michael barked, angrily. 'Look, I need your help to get close to them if they're not to get hurt.'

'Yeah, of course. Why should I believe you? The way I see it; you want to use me, and kill them yourself.'

'Wrong, I don't,' Michael said, fighting not to lose his temper. 'Sean, the situation is far too serious to waste time bickering. Every second we sit here while you consider whether I'm to be trusted or not could be another second closer to their deaths. I'm catching the next ferry to Mykonos with or without you. Do you understand?'

'Mykonos!' Sean said surprised. 'Why do you think they're there? If so, then why are you here?'

'Because, we know they are. And, it was my decision to stay and help you and the girls. Let me explain a bit more. Currently, three teams of men are in Mykonos with instructions to kill them. The only way they can be spared is if we find them first and you convince them to hand over the diamonds. If they do, I'll make sure nothing happens to them. That's it. Believe me, I do not want their blood on my hands.'

Sean's head dropped. It was far worse than he had imagined. Up to a moment ago he was under the impression they were still safe, in hiding. 'How do I know this is not some ploy? Why would you want to help them anyway?'

'You won't know, except that you have to trust me. I'm going. The ferry is leaving in forty-five minutes,' Michael said. With one gulp he finished his juice, stood up, and gave Sean a stern look.

Slowly Sean got to his feet, his face distraught, uncertain.

'Good, right choice. Let's go!' Michael said as he led the way out of the small bar and into the bright sunlight.

CHAPTER 70

Mykonos
Saturday Afternoon

The attractive redhead sat three rows in from the front, idly paging through a fashion magazine. With the cheap sunglasses, wig, and straw-hat Vera was guaranteed anonymity. The frappe on the small coffee table was sipped with great care. She seemed relaxed. Casually she looked at her watch; ten to four, the fun was about to start …

On cue, Paul, overweight and sweating, huffed past in the direction of the windmills; the physical demands in the afternoon heat was not appreciated by his overburdened heart. No one followed him.

Good! Vera smiled to herself, satisfied.

But the next instant she nearly choked on her drink. The sight of Ciarán with five men in support appearing out of nowhere, turned her body into jelly.

My God, not him! Where did he come from? Oh, Paul, you are so stupid … what have you done?!

When another group of men sprinted around the corner in pursuit of Ciarán, her heart nearly stopped, leaving her in a near state of apoplexy.

Who are they? she fretted, strung like an over-stretched bow ready to snap.

There were too many … and how many more were hiding in the shadows? Her courage waned. With the passing

293

of each second, getting the money became less and less important. Their brilliant plan now seemed wholly flawed. If anyone spotted her it would be game over. Suppressing her fears, she thought, *who cares, it must end somehow. But you won't get me that easily.*

A brisk ten minutes crisscrossing the town centre's winding alleys delivered her to the old harbour. She briefly glanced at the row of restaurants along the quay and entered the one picked as a venue for the meeting.

It was not overly busy. She headed for a vacant table near the window offering a clear view of the waterfront. Waiting for her coffee she studied the crowds promenading along the quayside. There were no familiar faces. She switched her phone on and called Paul.

After only one ring an irate voice snapped. 'Where the hell are you?'

'Before you jump on your little high horse, did I not tell you to come alone?' Vera asked, calmly. 'So far, I've counted at least eighteen men, including Ciarán. Therefore, if you still want to make this deal you better lose them on your way to the old harbour … the old church. I'll call in fifteen minutes.'

'She's somewhere near the old harbour,' Paul said. *How could they have missed her? One of Ciarán's men, or ours, must have seen her …*

'She's one cute hoor, you must give her that,' Dermot said, rather amused. 'Just stick to the plan and stay calm. If she picks up you're nervous, she'll run. Give the men five minutes to get into position before you make your move. If she thinks it's going to be easy, she's in for a surprise.'

Exhausted, Paul arrived at the quayside. Catching his breath, he shuffled his feet impatiently, waiting for Vera's call. When it came, she directed him to Zorba's taverna, forty metres to his right.

'… and don't forget, I'm watching. One wrong move and I'm gone. No phone calls,' Vera cautioned.

Entering the semi-dark taverna, Paul spotted a redhead

beckoning him. *Who's this?*

Approaching the woman, he scowled, 'Where's the bi—' but he stopped himself. 'Oh, it's you.' Flopping into the empty chair next to Vera, not remotely interested in making polite conversation, he asked, 'Let's get it over with. Where are the stones?'

'Not so fast. I told you to come alone. And did you? Oh no, instead, you brought half of Ireland. Tell me, what guarantee do I have that you'll let me walk out of here once we're done?'

'My word.'

'Your word, sure. I'm not Niall. No, Paul, your word means nothing. Most likely, once we've finished our business I'm done for. Is that not the plan?'

'Think what you want, but please let's not waste any more of each other's time than necessary.' Noticing the oversized shoulder bag held guardingly on her lap, he smacked his lips, his snake eyes glistening.

Watching him carefully, Vera's right hand slipped inside the bag which contained just over a million-euro worth of diamonds. As her fingers clasped around the cold stones, she extracted a few for him to examine.

Making sure no one was paying any attention to what they were doing, Paul turned the diamonds in his hands and mumbled his approval, 'Good … very good. And the rest?'

'Hang on; before you get too carried away, where's my money? Your briefcase is not nearly big enough to contain fifteen million euro.'

'It's one million. The rest is at the airport. If all the stones are as good as I suspect they are, then you can join me for a celebratory drink before I leave. We can complete the transaction in private,' he said, fiddling with the briefcase's tiny locks. A few muted clicks and they sprung open. Paul raised the lid sufficiently for Vera to peek inside. She nodded and sat back in her chair, unimpressed. Ignoring her frown, Paul returned his attention to the samples.

Her hand dipped into the bag and after some rummaging

reappeared. She stretched her hand out and said, 'Here, take these.'

'What's this?' he asked, somewhat bewildered.

'The balance. What you now hold is about one million's worth, give or take. Your briefcase, please. The rest you'll get when I have my money. No point calling for help. I'm not that stupid to have walked in here with the whole lot – a friend is guarding them, waiting for my safe return. If I don't show, the stones will be sold to someone else.'

Paul did not flinch. Unfazed by her demand he handed over the briefcase and said, 'Sure, take it.'

As she stood up, he touched her arm and cautioned, 'Vera, you're playing a very dangerous game. Remember, I'm not the one you should be afraid of. If Niall gets hold of you, you're dead. And the chances of that are very real with Ciarán in the neighbourhood.'

'Thanks for the warning. But maybe that's why I'm reckless; it's either all or nothing. I'll meet you in the morning. Same routine … I'll phone the time and place. Please, let's not waste any more of each other's time than necessary now that you know I have the diamonds. Bring the balance or else this will drag on forever. *Dosvidanya*,' she said. Picking up her hat, bag and newly acquired briefcase she turned towards the rear of the restaurant where the aromas laden heavy with slow cooking meat, garlic and oregano drifted in from the kitchen, filling her nostrils. She felt giddy, having had enough of the place, smells, and of Paul.

Rushing through the confined kitchen, she apologised to the surprised cooks before bursting into the bright sunlight. Ignoring their shouts, she side-stepped the clutter of bins, stacked wooden tables and chairs, and raced towards the flight of stairs located in the far corner of the courtyard. She did not break her stride as she sprinted up the stairs, taking them two at a time. Reaching the flat roof, she dashed across the warm asphalt and up the next flight of stairs leading on to the adjacent roof. Pausing for a moment she looked back. To her surprise, no one was following her.

Maybe they're just slow? she thought as she continued up the remaining few steps.

Hiding behind a screen she ripped off her jumper and wig in one fluid motion. Digging in her bag she pulled out her next disguise, to be transformed into a brunette within seconds.

Three storeys above the alley the brunette in a white summer dress and black cardigan effortlessly cleared the three-metre gap to the adjoining building – not a soul had noticed her short flight.

From behind a solar panel, Vera peeked out; she was still alone. Crouching, ready to run at the first sound of approaching feet, she took a few moments to catch her breath. With her nerves on edge, she emptied the contents of Paul's suitcase into her own bag. When done, she got up, walked to the edge of the building and flung the suitcase on to the next roof. Sliding in underneath a water tank it stopped with a loud clunk against one of the tank's steel supports.

Descending three flights of stairs she reached an enclosed courtyard. Quietly, she ran across the grey pavers, her eyes darting from side to side; luckily the owners were not at home. Looking up, the stairs remained empty. She smiled to herself, knowing they must have planted a tracking device inside the briefcase.

Well, good luck with that!

But there was still Ciarán to contend with.

Cautiously she slid back the bolt of the blue painted wooden gate. Opening it a fraction, and with the coast clear, stepped into the alley.

As Dermot and his men entered Zorba's taverna the mood was calm with the few patrons having returned their attention to their meals. The slight commotion caused by Vera storming out through the kitchen had been forgotten; no one had bothered to chase after her.

Dermot pulled out a chair, wiped the seat with a clean napkin and sat down. 'What's the score?' he asked.

'It went precisely as we thought it would. She did not

bring all the stones; she has a collaborator.'

'As expected, and the quality of the merchandise, any good?'

'Absolutely!'

'Good! No need to panic, my boy; the homing device is working just fine,' Dermot said. 'We'll track her, do what we have to so I can return home and finish the bugger off for good.'

Irked at being called "my boy", Paul shrugged his shoulders and continued to describe Vera's attire to Dermot's men. 'You'll be looking for a blonde. By now she would have dumped the red wig and gone natural.'

Fifteen minutes later Paul's assumption proved correct as two of Dermot's men returned to the restaurant with the empty briefcase, a red wig and a squashed sun hat.

'Very sneaky, I must give her that,' Dermot said. The more he got to know Vera, the more he liked her.

Agitated, Ciarán sat in the shade of Christos' extensive awning. He was running blind. He had no audio surveillance. Eight hours ago, this advantage had mysteriously ended. In all probability, Paul had discovered the bugs and discarded them. What was even more frustrating, he could not say with any degree of certainty that Paul was meeting either or both Vera and Sinead. Up to now, the hunt was based on one snippet of information garnered in the hotel's foyer in Athens. Maybe he was meeting someone wholly unrelated to Vera and Sinead.

All he had witnessed so far was Paul's round figure panting about in the old town and disappearing into Zorba's taverna. That was an hour ago, and still, there was no sign of him or the girls. With the arrival of Dermot and his men, his confidence had been somewhat restored. Although, for all he knew, the lot of them could be having a nice lunch and nothing more sinister.

As for the two spotters covering the rear exit, they had nothing to report. No one had tried to slip away through the back alley.

All he could do was wait for Paul to reappear and follow him.

Vera's heart raced as the boutique hotel came into view. So far, she had been very lucky. She could not help feeling elated; their plan might just work. They may leave this island as very wealthy, free women.

The room with its stunning sea views had been booked the day before, five nights paid for in advance and in cash. The name of the hotel she had kept from Sinead. After checking in, Vera spent a few minutes hanging up some newly bought clothes, and placing a few toiletries on the marble vanity top in the bathroom and some expensive make-up on the dressing table.

Entering the hotel, she avoided reception, crossed the pool deck – ignoring the leers of a few male sunbathers – and slipped into her room. Twenty minutes later she re-emerged with no wig, a new attire and a briefcase in hand containing the one million euro.

Facing the amicable hotel manager in his office she explained her predicament. 'I'm planning to travel around Mykonos … maybe do some island hopping as well, and was wondering if you could do me a small favour?'

'How can I help?' he asked, her charms having elicited the response she had hoped for.

'In this briefcase, I have a few very valuable documents which I don't want to drag around with me,' she said, placing the briefcase on top of his desk. 'Could you by any chance store this in your safe?'

'Of course, of course, it will be my pleasure. You don't look like a terrorist or smuggler, so definitely no bomb or drugs inside?' he jested good-heartedly.

'You have my word, most definitely not!' Vera reassured him, remembering the saying, "behind every joke, there is some truth".

'In that case, you have nothing to worry about. The documents could not be in a safer place. You go and enjoy yourself and I guarantee your case will be here for whenever you need it.'

'What happened?' Sinead asked excitedly, answering her phone.

'Paul's so predictable; it went just as we thought it would! And we'll complete the deal tomorrow.'

'Did he at least pay a deposit?'

'*Da!* One million euro which I have stored in the hotel's safe.'

'How much?'

'One million euro!' she repeated.

'Wow! Then why don't we just disappear and sell the rest when we need to? Why risk another meeting? Come on, what do you say?'

'Hmm … not a bad idea. But we have a slight problem. Ciarán and his men are here, and in numbers. So, we may need Paul's help to get off the island.'

'No … you're joking, right? Ciarán! No! How did he find us?'

'Beats me. But don't worry, we'll do the deal and pay Paul enough to help us escape. After all, he has a plane.'

When Sinead spoke again her voice was barely a whisper, 'We were so close … now, we'll never get away …'

'Of course, we shall. We'll just have to be very careful. Come on, cheer up. At least we're still free, and millionaires, even if only for one night. Who cares what happens tomorrow,' Vera laughed, fighting to remain resilient. But with her friend so distraught it was difficult. 'First thing in the morning I'll meet Paul and convince him to fly us out of here. So, snap out of it!' Despite these words, Vera shared Sinead's despair. Maybe she was right; maybe they would never leave Mykonos.

'I wish I could, but I can't,' Sinead replied. 'Paul will not help me, not after what I've done to him. You, yes, but me, never. He'll gladly watch Ciarán put a bullet in my head. No, Vera, I won't be going anywhere.'

It was twenty-five minutes past five by the time Michael and Sean disembarked in Mykonos. Kept abreast of events by Declan, knowing that the hunt was still on, they hurried to find a hotel for the night. For now, Michael chose to keep Sean's presence on the island a secret.

An hour later Michael, Declan and Stavros rendezvoused at the five windmills where a plan to trap the girls was soon devised.

At 22h00 all the men were deployed in pairs a few hundred metres apart at the periphery of the town. This ring of men effectively sealed off all escape routes out of town. It was not one hundred percent fail-proof, but the chances of anyone slipping through the net were very slim. And trapping them would only succeed if – and it was a big if – Vera and Sinead were actually in Mykonos Town.

With all men in position by 23h00, they converged as one on the old harbour, visiting each hotel, holiday apartment and restaurant along the way. At every stop, the same question was asked: "Has anyone seen these girls? Their families are extremely worried; no one has heard from them for three weeks. This was very unlike them: no selfies, tweets, nothing …"

By 23h45 confirmation was received that Vera and Sinead had been seen in Mykonos the previous day. This news stirred the hounds on. Having smelled blood they scratched harder, growled louder, already savouring the tender limbs of their prey.

But it was not all plain sailing.

A few establishments refused to divulge any information regarding their guests, forcing the posting of men in the immediate vicinity, compromising the hunt. But as the net tightened, fewer men were required with every metre gained. Their confidence grew, aware that soon the doomed girls would be flushed out.

CHAPTER 71

Marrakech, Morocco
Saturday Afternoon

Irina paced the spacious suite, having no interest in the views or splendours on offer at the Atlas Haven Palace, ten kilometres north-west of Marrakech. Since their arrival, she had been isolated inside one of the five, three-hundred-square-metre presidential villas. Outside, Niall's men stood guard on the suite's patio and her bedroom door. Her phone had been confiscated in Ireland. For all intents and purposes, she was now his prisoner, unable to contact anyone or go anywhere.

But this did not bother her.

At least, I'm still alive and still his "partner", his "plaything", or so he thinks!

Her patience was wearing thin, not only with Niall but also with her mission. So far, her endeavours had delivered no concrete results except for the sacrilege of her body and mind. Hanging her clothes in the wardrobe she wondered how long the stay in Morocco would last before she once more would have to throw her small collection of dresses into the suitcase, to be carted off to some undisclosed destination.

Maybe, just maybe, it all will be worth it. Who knows? He's on the run and every step he takes the noose is tightening.

The faint drone of Niall's excited voice, deep in conversation in the adjacent room, caught her attention. She quickly unscrewed the cap of her lipstick and applied a fresh layer of soft natural pink to her dry lips. Satisfied, she gave the uncapped canister another two twists and placed it upright against the dividing wall. Holding the small mirror in her hand, she inspected her bruised face; it looked as bad as it felt.

Well, it will heal …

In silence, she listened to Niall's amplified voice resonating in the small earpiece's minute speaker, transmitted by the uncapped lipstick canister. This signal was further enhanced and relayed by the handheld mirror with its concealed satellite antenna.

'Damn sure! Look, I've no time for games. You phone me as soon as you have done what I've sent you to do!' Niall growled.

A few minutes later her ears perked up once more, intrigued by Niall's words. The news he was receiving was not good, and as usual, bad tidings were not accepted with grace. But despite the cursing he came out fighting, spelling out his demands in no uncertain terms, warning those who would fail in their loyalty, to be ruined along with him. That, he guaranteed.

The next conversation explained the rushed departure from Wicklow.

'What do you mean you have no more control over what's going on than you have over the bloody weather? Your seniors may have taken charge, but you, Clinton, will take it back! I fully understand the complexities. So, to help you, I'll email some condemning photographs which you can print and personally deliver to the head of the Garda Bureau of Fraud Investigation, the honourable Chief Superintendent McNamara. I'm sure, seeing himself fucking some young ladies, he'll manage to lose the incriminating evidence very quickly. Include the note I'll attach, explaining what is expected of him if he values his life. How he'll foil this investigation, I leave up to him.'

The reply was too muted to hear.

'Don't act the prick! You know how this works. Put it in

a nice brown envelope and say it was hand-delivered to you by courier. Trust me, you'll be fine. It shows good will on my side not having mailed it to his house where his wife, or children, could have opened it. He'll appreciate my *thoughtful* gesture,' Niall scoffed.

Again, Irina was denied the response – her office's attempts to hack into his mobile's live conversations had failed because of his phone's anti-hacking apps.

'Yes. Now be a good boy and do as you're told or a letter implicating you in some illegal business dealings may just drift into the general office's *info@* mail box. I'll contact you soon to get an update. Goodbye, Inspector Maher.'

Her boss had been right. Forwarding the recordings to the Garda had worked, sending Niall running for the hills, into hiding, and thankfully taking her along with him.

But to succeed, she must stay alive.

The large wooden ceiling-fan whirled idly overhead, stirring the air, keeping the mosquitos at bay. The two waiters assigned to look after the guests' dinner stood patiently by. The atmosphere between the young woman and her older companion was tense. In silence, they admired the man's good fortune in having such treasured company, especially as he seemed a vile obnoxious man; the bruised jaw must be his doing. What did she see in him, they wondered? Must be money; it always was.

Accompanying the couple were five men lounging on deck chairs out of earshot.

'Have you decided what you want?' Niall asked, shutting his menu.

'Yes,' Irina replied, icily.

She turned towards the waiter, politely placed her order, and looked at the mountains in the distance, ignoring Niall.

Their starters were eaten in an uncomfortable silence; the only sound was the intermittent clink of cutlery on porcelain. Niall, unable to come to terms with his reprobate mind was at a loss for words. As he glared at her, a sudden gust of warm air ruffled her hair. With delicate fingers she brushed back a few locks, looking alluringly sexual, much to his annoyance. Her defiant posture, her confident manner, her beauty, all traits he used to admire, suddenly annoyed him immensely.

He gulped down his third glass of wine and took a bite of his starter, not appreciative of the delicate flavours. His temples throbbed. He was reaching the end of his tether. For a fleeting moment, he contemplated taking her to his room to teach her a lesson or two. But now was not the time, nor the place.

Patience, she'll get over this once she understands how lucky she is, his delusional mind reasoned.

As the main course was being served, the head waiter cleared his throat, 'Pardon, sir, there is a call for you, a Mr Petrov.'

'Thank you, I'll take it in my room.'

With his bedroom door shut, and away from inquisitive ears, Niall asked, 'Tarik?'

His precautionary measures served no purpose: every word spoken was transmitted by the receiver in Irina's room to a very receptive audience in Moscow.

'Welcome to my beautiful country,' the deep voice rumbled pleasantly.

'So, it is you! How did you find out that I'm here?'

'I have many ears on the ground. Your name will always be on my desk within seconds once you've registered in any establishment in my country,' the Moroccan said and let out a loud guffaw.

'Uh-huh,' Niall huffed – he would have to be more careful in the future. 'How can I help you?'

'No, no, don't worry, no business tonight, only social. I would like to invite you to my humble abode for some light entertainment if it's not too much of an inconvenience?' Tarik offered.

'When?'

'Tonight.'

'Sounds great. The atmosphere here is quite stifling,' Niall said, accepting without hesitating.

Tarik's stretch limousine glided ghostlike across the hotel grounds, not a bump could be felt. Irina stared into the dark, her thoughts far away, wondering what had happened to Vera, Sinead and Sean. *They must still be okay or he would have told me,* she reasoned, but for how much longer could they evade him? Her deceptive calm belied her anger, her frustration, having to continue her role as a seductress. Seated next to him she struggled to remain focused; the urge to kill him was unbearable.

As if reading her mind, he said, 'Forgot to tell you, your friends have been spotted in Mykonos. Maybe you want to phone Sean and tell him?'

'Really. How kind.'

'Anyway, there's absolutely nothing you can do for them anymore. You may just as well enjoy the evening. From experience, it promises to be quite spectacular.'

'If you say so … I might just do that.'

'Right, you do,' he replied with a slight frown, not sure what to make of her words as a bout of jealousy clouded his mind.

Racing through the outskirts of Marrakech, heading towards the north-eastern hills, the driver ignored the speed restrictions with the car devouring the kilometres like a hungry serpent. As the limousine made a sharp left turn on to a private lane, Irina looked at her watch, estimating the distance covered to be about fifty kilometres. None of her fellow passengers were aware of the high-frequency signal being emitted by the plain-looking accessory, activated when leaving her room. Continuing along the winding path, she looked at the moon-washed mountains, safe in the knowledge that her every move was being watched.

Clearing a small rise, they were confronted by a spectacular world of lights. Perched on top of a hill was a modern temple consisting of white marble, massive columns and vast sheets of glass. The classic lines were floodlit as if heralding the Second Coming of Christ. At the main entrance a small party waited. As the car glided to a halt, a stout, bald man in his mid-fifties, stepped forward with outstretched arms in a welcoming gesture. The rays of the bright overhead lights shimmered in the small beads of sweat on the man's hairless scalp.

'Welcome, Niall! It has been quite a while since we—' he bellowed but stopped mid-sentence when he saw Irina. 'Who is your most gorgeous companion?' he asked, smiling even more broadly, shifting his attention to her. Noticing the bruise, he flinched. *Ouch, that must have hurt. Wonder who did that?*

He was the archetypal host: warm, friendly and charming. But his flattering overtures concealed the dark eyes which pierced deep into the hearts of his guests with the canny ability to judge man or beast in seconds, differentiating between friend or foe.

'Irina, and she's out of bounds, my friend,' Niall replied, putting his arm possessively over her shoulder. The slight recoil of her body was not missed by the Moroccan.

I belong to no one, least of all you! Irina smiled to herself.

Ignoring Niall's comment the host offered her his hand and introduced himself. 'I'm Tarik. Will you be my guest of honour?'

'You are most kind. I gladly accept. Thank you,' Irina responded, her voice filled with delight. Behind her, Niall's face turned a shade darker as Tarik whisked her up the stairs.

The mansion's three-storey-high, sumptuous hall was reminiscent of a luxurious hotel foyer, large enough to accommodate a row of terraced houses. Crossing the vast hall, they ascended another wide flight of stairs and proceeded through a row of ornate arches opening on to a grandiose courtyard. Entering the mysterious world of seductive, musky fragrances, colourful fountains, and rippling ponds, the air bristled with the hypnotic rhythm of Andalusian music. Irina felt an unexpected calm wash over her.

Secluded alcoves, filled with oversized satin pillows, lined the courtyard. Centre stage to this seductive setting was a

307

banquet set for a king. To one side, the elevated dance floor was occupied by a band of Moroccan musicians. Beneath the blinking star-filled sky, she momentarily succumbed to the powers of this mystical world, a galaxy removed from the previous night's sickening scenes. But taking her seat next to Niall, these disturbing images returned in all their horror.

From out of the shadows white-uniformed waiters appeared and offered her champagne. Politely she took a glass but remained vigilant.

While feasting on the delicious Moroccan spicy dishes and wines, Irina caught Tarik leering. She smiled pleasantly while hiding her disgust.

In the background, the music increased in volume with the rhythm moving up in tempo, hardly noticeable above the cheerful babble. Surreptitiously a sweet-voice mingled with the noise, slowly bringing the raucous to an end. Fascinated, the guests' heads followed the sound, towards the curvaceous brunette whose hips gyrated provocatively. With her voluptuous body visible through her thin satin attire, she elicited a chorus of approval. Effortlessly she slid to the floor and rolled on to her back. With her legs splayed she swayed her hips and arched her back erotically, much to the delight of her audience.

Distracted by the exotic dancer, Irina became aware of the slight pressure of a hand on her arm. To her surprise, Tarik had swopped seats with her bodyguard. As she courteously removed his hand, the Moroccan apologised and moved even closer. She found herself trapped between two men she loathed; one she knew only too well, and the other, she could only imagine.

'Would you like to switch seats? I don't mind. That way you and Niall can chat more easily,' she offered.

'No, no, there's no need. Rather let me make more room for you,' he said bullishly. But instead of moving away, he leaned over her as if she did not exist and started some nonsensical conversation with Niall.

Clearly, he did not care what she thought. His boldness

tested Niall's resolve; was she truly spoken for? Sensing the man's bravado, Irina shrivelled back in her seat; this she had to see …

'Tarik, do you mind,' Niall snapped. 'You're squashing Irina.'

Raising both hands, Tarik sat back. 'Pardon me, how inconsiderate. My most sincere apologies, Irina. I did not mean to offend,' he said, not averting his gaze.

Bolstered by too much alcohol and the fact that she clearly did not belong to Niall, he knew he would have her, whether she would agree or not. *Surely, she was no different to all European women: just another slut!*

Abruptly Tarik turned his back to her and fell into light banter with some of the other guests, sharing an anecdote which elicited spontaneous laughter.

Niall, who had not been tricked by his shenanigans, knew perfectly well what was to happen. 'I think we have overstayed our welcome. Let's go,' he whispered to Irina.

Much to his surprise, she replied, 'No, not yet. I'm having fun.'

'No, we go now!' Niall insisted.

Ignoring him, she tapped Tarik on the shoulder, and said, 'Excuse me, I was wondering where your star is from? She's superb!'

Irina's words were all the encouragement Tarik needed. Forgotten were the other guests as he recounted Leila Khalifa's rise to stardom, a remarkable story. Listening attentively, she played her own game, seducing Tarik into a lustful world spawned by pure fantasy.

By the time the evening drew to a close, Tarik was convinced Irina was his for the taking. It was much more than he could have hoped for, she willingly giving herself to him. Crossing swords with Niall would have been extremely dangerous, and worse, it could have ended a very lucrative partnership. Content, and with his ego inflated far beyond the realms of reality, he would wait for her to come to him. But as for tonight, he was quite happy to spend it in the arms of

Leila.

With no sign of Niall anywhere, he took Irina's hand in his and gave her his phone number, adding, 'I would be most honoured if I could see you tomorrow?'

'I would love that. I'll call you as soon as I know what Niall's plans are,' she replied alluringly and gently squeezed his hand.

The delighted host raised her hand to his lips. The sweet scent of her porcelain skin drove Tarik to a state of unrestrained passion. Aroused, he pardoned himself and walked off in search of the singer, to find release in her arms.

Irina looked at her watch. *It's time to leave before he returns.*

'Find Niall, and hurry,' she ordered the two henchmen by her side. 'Or we may not leave here at all!'

Having poked their heads into nearly every nook and cranny without success, they once more looked inside a secluded red-lit alcove. Swamped by a slithering bevy of lusting young women, half naked with their exotic costumes discarded, Niall's bare chest and head popped up from amongst the cushions. His eyes were vacant, captured by the carnal sensation surging through his loins, evoked by the girl astride him, her slowly moving pelvis locked to his. The girls were doing exactly what Tarik had instructed, occupying Niall for the night.

'Niall, if you don't mind, I suggest you finish up,' Irina said, interrupting his erotic world.

Glaring at her, he said, 'My dear, you might not have noticed, but I'm extremely busy. I suggest you run along and don't bother waiting up. Nighty-night!'

'Well, I'm glad to hear that as I have a date with Tarik. Take your time; I'm in no hurry either.'

Turning away, she did not miss the childish grin wiped off his smug face. Without another word, she walked to the waiting limousine.

CHAPTER 72

Mykonos Town
Saturday Night

As the moonlight washed over the sleepy town the four men in black combat fatigues blended into the deep shadows of the thick hedgerow. The few hours spent traversing the paved alleyways and streets had paid off. Listening to the beep emitted by the monitor, it was strongest with the antenna pointed at the Bay Mykonos Hotel. There was no doubt; what they were looking for was across the road.

Methodically they scrutinised the area for security cameras and found only one tucked in underneath the entrance canopy straddling the main gate. With no time to waste Greg sprinted the fifteen metres across the road, scaled the low wall and took up a position near the locked front door outside the field of the camera lens. He peered inside. At three in the morning the dim-lit main foyer was empty. Deftly his hands unlocked the front door. Slipping inside his eye caught sight of the small security camera in the far corner. Immediately he dived for cover in behind an overstuffed leather couch – if someone were watching, it would be game over. He craned his neck from behind the bulky piece of furniture and took aim with the silenced pistol at the open door to his right, ready to fire.

Ten, fifteen … thirty seconds he waited as soft music spilled out from behind the door.

One minute, still nothing, no one. Convinced his presence had not been detected, he swiftly covered the few metres to the open door and peered through the crack. One person only; a security guard engrossed in a film on TV, was seated with his back to the door. Greg stepped inside and struck the unsuspecting man against his neck, rendering him unconscious.

A quick look at the bank of security monitors relaying footage from different parts of the hotel confirmed all to be quiet.

Having taped and gagged the unconscious guard, he returned to reception and flicked the lights once. Under a minute he was joined by the rest of his team.

'Well, let's see where it is,' Joe carrying the homing device said and switched it on.

Following its signal, Greg gave a soft whistle as he came face to face with the hotel's formidable safe. Without the right tools, they were stumped – fiddling with the lock might trigger some silent alarm. 'Bugger! Right, change of plan. Time to pay the young lady a visit.'

Opening the hotel's registration book, Greg's search ended at Room 107. 'Any plan of the hotel anywhere?' he asked.

'Here you go,' Manfred said, having found a pile of visitor's leaflets on a stand. 'No wonder they have these; anyone will get lost in this jumble of a building.'

The master key lifted at reception allowed them easy access to Vera's room. Without a sound they surrounded the bed and took aim with their silenced pistols.

Greg switched the light on …

Baffled, they stared at the empty bed.

'The sheets are cold; she definitely didn't sleep here. Search the place!' Greg snapped.

Having combed the room, Joe announced unimpressed, 'No diamonds here, and no money either!'

'Agreed. Let's go.'

Backing out they left the suite untouched, none to be the

wiser of their visit.

With his team gone, Greg returned to reception and forced the cash drawer open, emptied it, then proceeded to delete the last twenty minutes of recorded security footage, untied the unconscious guard, and finally retraced his steps to the hedgerow across the road.

Convinced Vera would return to collect the million euro, the team settled in, ready to strike.

While transferring the money into her briefcase, Vera had missed the homing device hidden amongst the wads of notes.

Having patiently listened to the police's grilling of the security guard, the hotel manager was quick to conclude that it was nothing other than a break-in by someone in need of quick cash. Turning on the security guard, he fired him on the spot for incompetence. The disgruntled man's protestations, pointing to the red marks on his wrists, were to no avail. The manager had made up his mind. End of discussion.

On the other hand, the police, on high alert after the tip-off by their airport colleagues, were not convinced. Nothing was to be treated lightly. With concern they noted the guard's comments claiming the break-in to be far more sinister.

But the manager remained unmoved. He wanted the police gone, fearing their presence would cause unnecessary distress amongst his guests. Skilfully, he slipped a few fifty-euro notes to the officers for their cooperation. After all, the small amount of cash in the drawer was nothing to fuss about.

Despite the bribe, the police had every intention to report the incident to their superiors for their action.

Dimitris' two minions who had followed Dermot's men to the Bay Mykonos Hotel had a perfect view of the building and surrounding area. Lying flat on his stomach, not daring to move a muscle, Titan whispered into his phone to Stavros the events he had witnessed: Greg's break-in, his retreat to the hedgerow, the police's arrival, their departure thirty-five minutes later, the hapless security guard leaving, furious.

'Good … maybe this doesn't concern us. But one can't help wondering why Dermot's men are still there. Find the security guard and see what he has to say, *amésos!*' Stavros ordered.

'Yes, boss.'

'So why are you still on the phone?!'

Half an hour later Stavros grinned broadly as he again listened to Titan's voice. The security guard's story confirmed his suspicion. Dermot's men hiding in the bushes were most definitely waiting for someone staying at the hotel. And this could only be Vera or Sinead. They finally had a lead!

Phoning Michael, he greeted him, his voice tense, '*Yassou,* Michael, I think they've been found.'

'Where … who found them?'

'The Bay Mykonos Hotel. Dermot's men are staking out the place. I think they're waiting for them to get up and nab them as soon as they set foot outside the hotel.'

'What makes you think that?'

Stavros' explanation made sense, but it was still only a guess, although a good one. 'Sounds good, best we—'

'No, not good, not good at all. They'll beat us to them,' Stavros interrupted, his voice strained, leaving Michael somewhat puzzled. Did he detect a hint of concern for the girls, or was it because of the possibility that he might lose the diamonds?

Steady my boy. Only thing he's worried about are the bloody diamonds!

Fully briefed by Stavros, Michael jumped out of bed and grabbed his clothes off the chair. Slipping his trousers on, he looked up at the yellow ball rising above the horizon, its soft rays gently caressing the still waters, peeling back the light blanket of blue-grey morning mist. The salty sea air drifting in through the window rekindled old memories, fond memories of Emily, of their honeymoon in Leros …

They had been very young, deeply in love, looking forward to a wonderful life together. But unknown to them cancer had spread with vile anger through her young body.

And by the time her stomach had resembled that of a woman in her third term, she had finally succumbed. Alone, disillusioned and filled with resentment he had lost his sense of purpose. Driven by a death-wish he had joined the war in Angola as a mercenary. Despite living on the edge for years, despite his reckless endeavours he had by some miracle survived the madness of the African bush.

And now, yet again, he faced the possibility of powerlessly watching the death of someone special. He barely knew her, but he had seen enough. Since spending the few minutes alone with her in the coffee shop in Chania, he could not stop thinking about her. Vera – resilient, warm and kind.

No, it won't happen again!

'Sean!' Michael shouted and banged on his bedroom door. 'Get up. We've got to go! Hurry.'

CHAPTER 73

Bay Mykonos Hotel
Sunday

At twenty minutes past five in the morning, Sean, armed with photographs of Sinead and Vera, strolled up to the Bay Mykonos Hotel. He ignored the men hiding in the shadows watching him, having no idea who he was. And, he had every intention to be gone before they could discover his identity.

'Good morning,' he greeted the small Greek at reception, someone obviously not in the mood for idle talk. 'Can I please speak to the manager?'

'A bit early for the manager to be up and about, don't you think?'

'Yes, I realise, but it is very important. Please.'

'And you are?' the man asked, his bushy black eyebrows raised, arms folded across his chest, his feet planted firmly apart.

'Sean O'Donovan. Please, I really need to speak to him. It's urgent.'

'About what?'

'If you don't mind, I'd rather speak to the manager,' Sean persisted.

Andreas Pappas looked Sean up and down, contemplating whether to call the police or spare the young man a few minutes of his time. During the past twelve hours, too many dubious-looking men had asked questions. But he was different, seemed decent enough … and rather desperate.

To Sean's surprise the man said, 'Yes, you may. Please, this way Mr O'Donovan.'

'Oh … right,' Sean replied, surprised, and traipsed after the manager.

Shutting the door to his office, Andreas asked, 'OK, what's so urgent?'

'Thank you for asking …'

'*Parakalo* … please, continue.'

'I'm looking for my sister and her friend and wondered if you have seen them. I have photographs,' he said, placing two on the desk. 'And here's my passport in case you doubt who I am.'

The manager took one look at the familiar face of Vera, wondering what the hell was going on; she seemed to be very *popular*. He picked up Sinead's photograph. The resemblance was uncanny, leaving him in no doubt about Sean and her relationship. 'I'm afraid I have not seen this girl,' Andreas said, pointing at Sinead's photo.

'Are you sure?'

'Yes, I am. Her friend, that's another matter. She's staying here … should be in her room. I'll call her.'

'Thank God!' Sean blurted out, relieved. At last, he had found them … and just in time.

Holding the phone in his hand a puzzled look spread across the manager's face. 'Strange, wonder why she's not … Oh yes, how forgetful of me. Of course, she must still be out, had a date last night. Or tired and does not want to be disturbed. Well, best to make sure. Follow me.'

In less than ten minutes they once more found themselves seated in the office. Andreas did not seem too worried. 'She'll be back sooner or later. She left some valuable documents in the safe.'

'Right … you sure?'

'Yes, I am. And I'm positive they're both fine. Give me your number and I'll tell Vera to contact you as soon as she returns.'

'Thank you. But please, it's imperative she calls me immediately. I can't stress that enough.'

'Of course, I'll tell her,' Andreas said, trying to ease Sean's concern.

It was quarter to six by the time Sean reappeared from under the Bay Mykonos Hotel's portico. Also, at which time Andreas reconsidered the security guard's words. What were these girls involved in? Best to contact the police again; the last thing he wanted was a gangland shootout at his hotel. As liberal and accommodating as he was, he would not tolerate criminals running riot in his establishment.

At this stage, Stavros and Declan's men had surrounded the hotel in a half-kilometre radius: the trap was set.

Across town, Ciarán kept Dermot, Paul and the rest of their men under surveillance.

But unknown to the men watching the hotel, a few plainclothes police had them in their sights.

'Sean, you realise, as soon as Vera or Sinead show up it will be game over,' Michael said, unimpressed by the positive news of having found them.

'I do, believe me, I do. On my way back here, I must have rung Sinead at least ten times. Her phone's off. We have no way of warning them other than the messages I've sent. Maybe I should go and wait at reception. Surely, they won't kill us in front of a bunch of witnesses.'

'They won't hesitate to kill anyone who gets in their way. You, Vera and Sinead will die. Dermot may be more careful and only act once Niall's men have left the island. Or, he may just walk away. Who knows? No, the risks are too great. Best we reduce the odds, divert some of the men elsewhere,' Michael said.

Spreading a map of Mykonos Town on the coffee table his heavy fingers traced the alleyways and roads leading towards the south-east side of the old town to a point approximately two kilometres from the Bay Mykonos Hotel. He stabbed at a large apartment complex and said, 'Right, this should do.'

Immediately, he rang Declan. 'Got them. They're staying at the Windmill Holiday apartments. Send the men there, right away. We'll catch them in their beds. Tell Stavros to join us. And just in case they've already left – although that's unlikely as it's far too early – I suggest you leave two men at the Bay Mykonos Hotel. Do nothing till I get there.'

'You sure?' Declan asked, somewhat confused.

'Absolutely. Call it a fluke or plain old Irish luck. While sipping my espresso, I got tipped off by a waiter when I showed him photos of the two. He didn't hesitate to tell all. Apparently, he does a double-shift in the evenings at Androniki's eatery opposite to where they stay. He waited on them last night and couldn't stop crooning over their looks – an unforgettable couple. He had eyed them till they entered their apartment on the first floor.'

'Sounds too good to be true … but a break's a break,' Declan replied, pleased. 'Yeah, best to catch them in bed instead of having an ugly scene with Dermot's men at the Bay Mykonos. I'll let you know when we're in position.'

'Good, see you shortly,' Michael confirmed. The situation looked rather grim; it was going to be close, very close. And as for Sean fidgeting by his side, he would be of little use if a fight were to erupt. Michael was under no illusion that he was on his own. 'Let's go!' he said, having checked his weapon and secured it in its holster.

Twenty-five minutes later, Michael and Sean were lying on top of a roof north-west of the Bay Mykonos Hotel. They had a perfect view of their surroundings: the access roads, Dermot's men and the two men Stavros and Declan had left behind.

As Michael scrutinised the area, he noticed a sudden reflection in a first floor window approximately fifty metres to his right. From behind the solar panel, he focused on the open window. 'Yep, we've got some more company. Looks like cops,' Michael whispered, the binoculars having given away the two plain-clothed policemen's position. 'Well, well, the

Greeks are not asleep after all. Good, that may just even the odds a bit!'

He returned his attention to the hotel and made himself comfortable, waiting, ready to jump into action when needed.

CHAPTER 74

Mykonos
Sunday Morning

Vera, donned in a dark wig, dithered on the threshold. 'I'll be back in an hour. Switch your phone on in forty minutes. And if not … or you hear nothing by then, run.'

She gave Sinead a quick peck on the cheek, turned and dashed along the terrace, down the flight of steps. Falling into a brisk walk she headed for the Bay Mykonos Hotel. Despite the streets being near-empty, she dodged in and out of whatever shadows there were, a necessary precaution which prolonged her journey across town considerably. The threat posed by the many pursuers prowling the alleyways was all too real. Maybe she should have waited until the streets were abuzz with tourists, but postponing her return to the hotel would have increased the risk of walking into a trap tenfold. No, she was doing the right thing: get the money, face the next hurdle.

'We've got company,' Michael said – tensing, ready to act – spotting a woman enter the narrow street, hug the whitewashed walls of the terraced houses and sneak into an alcove one hundred twenty metres to his left.

The woman did not move, remaining out of sight.

'I think it may be one of the girls,' Michael said. 'Did you see her?'

'No.'

'Give her a few minutes … aha, there she is!' Michael said as the figure reappeared and aimed for the next recess.

'Yeah, got her. Doesn't look like Sinead, same colour hair, but not her.'

'Looks like Vera, same height, size, shape …'

'You seem to know her pretty well. Right, now I get it … no wonder you're helping,' Sean said and winked.

'What are you on about? Never crossed my mind,' Michael replied, playing dumb. 'There she goes again. Yes, that's Vera alright.' At thirty metres he had no doubt despite the wig and sunglasses.

In silence they watched her pass through the hotel's gate.

At the same time, Dermot's and Dimitris' men stirred, ready to strike.

'Thank God … made it!' Vera sighed as she entered the hotel. But her upbeat mood was immediately stifled. Much to her surprise, the manager was at reception, not looking happy, paging through the guestbook.

She paused, unsure …

Snap out of it; whatever is eating him has nothing to do with me.

'Good morning, Andreas,' she greeted, chirpily.

He looked up with the scowl still firmly in place. 'Ah! And a good morning to you too, Ms Petrova. Seems to have been a very long night … and believe me if I tell you, for me as well,' he stated with not a trace of humour in his voice.

'Hope no one misbehaved after too many ouzos!' Vera jested in an attempt to lighten the gloomy atmosphere. But the manager just sneered. 'Well, I had a great time. No complaints, except for my boss waking me up, insisting I return home immediately, as he needs me back at work. Imagine that, having to cut my holiday short!' as the words slipped out, she realised only a fool would have believed her quickly concocted story.

'Glad I don't work for him,' Andreas replied sarcastically, not impressed with her lie. He could not imagine any employer phoning an employee early on a Sunday morning while on holiday, making demands. 'You don't mind if I call you Vera?'

The manager's tone left her under no illusion that there was a problem.

'Of course not.'

'Good. Please follow me so we can talk in private.'

Seated in his office, she asked, 'Is anything wrong?'

'Hmmm … anything wrong? Well, good of you to ask. To be frank, I was wondering what kind of trouble you're in?'

'Why? What do you mean?'

'Please, stop playing games,' he said in a stern voice as if admonishing a child. 'Vera, you look like a nice person, so I'll let things slide, but only if you come clean. Understood?'

'Yes … of course.'

'*Efcharistó* … okay. Since your arrival, I've had several unexpected visitors, all flashing your picture, asking questions – of course not a brunette version of you. Must admit, none of them seemed very nice, not the kind you should be hanging out with, except for one.'

Vera paled. 'Who were they … how did they find me?' she stammered, bewildered.

Have they been watching me all this time? No, can't be. There's no one outside the hotel … or is there?

'Greek, Irish, American. I think that's about it?' the manager said, watching her panic-stricken face. 'Don't worry, I told them nothing. They were fishing. I guess they don't know where you are. But there was this one very concerned young man who I did tell, your friend, Sinead's brother.'

'Sinead … Sean!' Vera said alarmed. *It can't be!* 'I never told you about either of them. How do you know he's her brother?'

Andreas was becoming rather impatient with his young guest, wondering who she was and what she was involved in. At least there were no drugs or other contraband in the briefcase as ascertained by the police sniffer dogs.

'Please, give me some credit. He showed me his passport and his sister's photograph. He wants you to contact him immediately as you are both in grave danger. That was all; he didn't elaborate. However, he gave me his number,' he said, handing Vera a folded piece of paper.

With the blood drained from her cheeks and a limp hand, she took the note. 'I'm sorry for doubting you. It's only that I can't believe Sean is here. For my peace of mind, can you please tell me who this is?' she asked, proffering a picture of Sinead displayed on her phone.

'Sinead.'

'Thank you. And, I apologise again for any stress I might have caused you. I think it will be best if I leave right away. So, if you could please hand me my briefcase, I'll be out of your hair as soon as I've packed.'

'No need to; I have saved you the trouble,' he said, leaned back and, much to her surprise, retrieved her packed suitcase from behind his desk.

Clutching a small suitcase, handbag and briefcase under her arms, Vera raced out of the hotel, yanked the taxi door open and jumped inside. The next instant the taxi leapt forward and careened down the road.

Watching her speed off, Michael cursed. Ahead of the taxi, the vapour trail of the parked Toyota 4x4 was just about visible. As soon as the taxi gunned past, the Toyota swung into the lane and raced after it.

'She's going to lead them straight to Sinead,' Michael hissed. 'Let's go!'

Not waiting for Sean to reply, he jumped on to the roof below, landed with a thud, ran and leapt from roof to roof across narrow alleyways below, his eyes fixed on the two vehicles racing up ahead. Reaching street level, the Toyota was two hundred metres ahead of him. A car was needed if they had any hope of keeping up with Vera!

Slowly walking towards the white delivery van with its doors open, he cautioned Sean rushing to his side, 'Wow, easy does it! Try to relax or you'll spook the driver.'

Offloading baskets of vegetables, the unsuspecting

324

driver's legs folded under his weight as a swift chop to the neck knocked him senseless. With one arm, Michael dragged the hapless driver out of the road and dumped him on to the footpath, shouting, 'Get in!'

Mindful of the few pedestrians and cars around this early in the morning, Vera's driver raced through the narrow streets, motivated by the five hundred euro, to lose the 4x4. Crisscrossing the town at a reckless speed, the gap between the two vehicles steadily grew. Reaching the outskirts, and hugging the coastline, they continued south-easterly towards Aghios Ioannis. On entering the next village, the 4x4 with its two male occupants were nowhere to be seen. The nondescript small blue car driving at a hundred metres behind them was of no concern.

'Thank goodness!' Vera exclaimed, relieved. 'Now, can you please find another way back to town?'

'My pleasure,' the driver replied and immediately doubled back to Mykonos.

Vera slumped into her seat and massaged her hands. Her knuckles were white from clutching the briefcase on her lap as if her life depended on it. She had underestimated Paul and his partner. If she was going to succeed, survive the day, she needed help. But whom? The only person who came to mind was Sean.

But what can he do? Nothing!

Who else is there? No one!

As her slender fingers fished out the piece of paper tucked inside her jean's pocket, another question niggled.

How did he find us? Someone must be helping him. Wonder who?

Despite these misgivings, she tapped his number into her phone, hoping it really was him.

'Hello, who's this?' an Irish voice asked, unsure.

'Sean, is that you?'

'Vera, thank God! I need to—'

'How did you find me?' she blurted out, stopping him short.

'It's not important how. Just believe me when I say you're not alone. You have friends, people who want to help. I'll explain later. But, are you aware that you're being followed? A light blue Fiat.'

Vera turned and looked through the rear window and swallowed hard. 'Yes, is that you?'

'No, it's not. We're tagging along further back. The Fiat started tailing you after the 4x4 disappeared. Listen, there's a horde of men after you with instructions to kill you both!'

She did not respond.

'Are you still there?' Sean asked.

'Yes … I am.'

'Did you hear me? We have to meet; there's a way out of this.'

'What do you suggest? Hang on,' she said nervously as the taxi slowed down.

Damn, what now … an accident?

Blocking the road was a white Hyundai and a cream Lexus 4x4. Pulling up beside them the taxi driver popped his head out of the window, and asked, 'Everything OK? Need help?'

The three men involved in a fierce argument in the middle of the road ignored the Greek. Offended, he joined the shouting, demanding to pass.

Distracted by the raucous, Vera did not notice the Fiat sneak up behind them, nor did she see the two men exit the vehicle. Sean's warning shouts over the phone were in vain, drowned by the loud racket the men were making. Suddenly the taxi's rear doors were flung open, and before she knew what was happening, she was pulled out of the car and bundled into the Lexus.

One of the abductors returned to the taxi and scooped the briefcase off the backseat. Another gave the driver two hundred euro, and warned him with an intimidating growl in his American accent, 'You've seen nothing. She never existed. Is that clear?'

Petrified, the driver nodded his head.

'Good, then, get lost!'

Michael swerved off the main road and pulled in behind a dilapidated barn. Slamming the brakes, he cursed, furious with himself for not having intervened at the hotel!

What was I thinking?! Damn … man!

Well, it was too late for regrets. He had to save her. He was the only one who could.

'What shall we do?' Sean asked, his voice filled with dread, hoping Michael had an answer.

'Nothing, my boy, nothing,' Michael muttered, frustrated. 'That is, for now. Whether we like it or not, we need backup or else we'll both be playing a harp in the heavenly blue skies above,' he warned cynically. Pulling his phone out of his shirt pocket he called Declan and gave him a quick update. 'And when you do catch up, keep your distance. We'll move in only when I say so. Dermot and his men will be expecting us. It's going to get messy.'

'Right you are. I'll contact Stavros, and once we've regrouped, we'll prepare a plan of attack,' Declan confirmed. 'In case I don't make it on time, you'll have Ciarán to back you up. He's still trailing Dermot.'

'I haven't forgotten, thanks.' Michael said, not happy with that prospect. Ciarán, a lowlife, a born and bred killer – someone who enjoyed his trade too much – was the last person he wanted in support. He was not ignorant of the hostility in Ciarán's eyes the few times they'd met. With him in the vicinity, a stray bullet in the back could not be ruled out.

Returning his attention to Vera, he watched the three vehicles speed away. Slowly, the taxi followed, keeping its distance.

'Sean, check your phone,' Michael said. 'Do you hear anything?'

'Yes, some guy shouting. Don't understand a word he's saying. Sounds like Greek. Listen,' Sean said and handed the phone to Michael.

'Yeah, you're right. She must have dropped her phone

when they grabbed her. Ok, hang on! This could be our only chance to turn the tables … to contact Sinead!'

With tyres screeching, he backed the small van on to the main road, jammed the gearstick into first and slammed his foot on the accelerator.

A minute later he overtook the white-faced taxi driver clutching a bundle of notes in one hand, his mouth moving animatedly. Hitting the brakes, Michael jerked the steering wheel hard right, and as the rear of the van started to sideswipe, he spun the steering hard left, locking the front wheels in the direction they were going. The van skidded to a stop, blocking the road. Michael jumped out and pointed his gun at the taxi which screeched to a halt a metre from his feet. Immediately, Michael lurched forward and jerked the back door open, shouting, 'Sorry my friend, I'll only be a second! I think the lady dropped her phone.'

Ignoring the Greek's protestations, he bent down and searched underneath the front seats. As his fingers closed around the small device, he shouted, 'Got it, thanks!'

Backing out of the car, he shut the door and banged on the roof for the driver to get out of there.

Vera scrutinised the bulky men by her side, must be Paul's! She had had enough. Undeterred by their size, she lurched for the door. But her escape attempt was futile. The instant she moved a vicious punch to her temple knocked her out.

CHAPTER 75

Mykonos Town
Sunday Morning

Sinead grabbed the buzzing phone off the coffee table and sighed with relief. At last! 'Vera, where are you? What's keeping you?' she asked, exasperated.

'Hello, Sis, it's me! We need to talk. Please don't hang up!'

'Sean?! What … where's Vera?'

'Paul's friends took her.'

'No! No … impossible!'

'Yes, it's true. Listen. Wherever you are, you have to get out of there right now!' Sean pressed. 'They have orders to kill you. Find a place to hide and as soon as we have Vera, we'll fetch you. Did you hear me?'

'No, it can't be! No …'

'Sorry, Sis. But we're following them and—'

'What do you mean … who's with you? Tell me, now!' she interrupted.

'It's not important—'

'Who … how did you find us … how did you get Vera's phone? How?!' Sinead demanded as the reality of what was happening started to kick in.

'I had help. Michael, Niall's head of sec—'

'You're joking, right?! Bye!' she exploded and shut her phone off.

Sean's face turned scarlet with rage. 'She hung up! Can

you believe it?'

'Just what I thought she'd do. Don't worry; she got the message. Now we have to save Vera.' Michael said unfazed as they entered Ano Mera, a small village located in the centre of the island.

He must be mad, insane! Michael! Why? The thought of one of her siblings having been used to manipulate Sean sprang to mind. It was the only plausible explanation. Why else would he conspire with men who wanted her dead?

So be it ... but best I heed his advice and get out of here!

Sinead's hands shook as she grabbed the overstuffed shoulder bag containing their documents, a few personal items, the cash and the diamonds hidden at the bottom. The key to their *safe house* she tucked into her jeans pocket. Vera had insisted not to be told the location of the apartment which was arranged the day before. It was an added precaution, one they had hoped would never be needed.

A three-hundred-metre brisk walk through the alleyways delivered her to the small apartment, her temporary safe house. By the time she locked the door behind her, she was convinced Vera would not survive much longer – a few hours at the most. They would torture her, get what information they needed and then kill her. And it would all be for nothing. She crossed her heart as the tears started to well in her eyes.

'Sorry, Vera. I'm so sorry,' she whispered.

With the bag on the floor beside her, she looked at the bare soulless room, confused, frightened, unsure what to do next. But whatever she did had to be good enough to save Vera. And how? She had no idea.

A trade-off? Yes, that may just work ... or would it? Sounds simple enough, but may also be the surest way of getting us both killed. Nothing will stop them once they have the diamonds. Come on, think! she scowled, angry at her innate weakness of always taking the easy way out.

As she considered her options, she knew they were very limited.

She could phone the police. But a crook on someone's payroll could not be ruled out. They would both end up dead! And if not dead, then charged with theft, drug smuggling, who knows what else? Bottom line, they'll end up either dead or in prison. No, it was most definitely a last resort.

Or hand over the diamonds to Paul? Yes, but only if Vera was with him. Penniless, they would have to run from Niall who won't stop until they were both dead. But together they may have a chance. Yes, a definite option!

And lastly, dear Sean. But why was Michael helping him? He was someone she knew nothing about, except for Vera having mentioned him … giving a distinct impression that she liked him.

Sean, I know you're not stupid, so, I'll have to trust your judgement.

CHAPTER 76

Ano Mera, Mykonos
Sunday Morning

Michael left the main road the moment Dermot's men turned into a yard a hundred metres up ahead, stocked with cars. Without delay, he manoeuvred the small van in between two parked cars and jumped out.

'You see that tree? I suggest you go and make yourself scarce in its shadow. Stay out of sight ... and mind the snakes,' he said, pointing to an old crooked olive tree leaning against a ruined limestone wall.

'Are you sure you won't need help?'

'No, I'll manage. If not, so be it. Listen, there's no point in us both getting killed. Your concern is Sinead. Who'll save her if you're also dead?'

'Yeah, got you ...' Sean agreed, half convinced.

'OK, if I'm not back in thirty minutes you get the hell out of here and find your sister. Go to our hotel; you'll be safe there. I'll contact you latest twelve midday. If you hear nothing by then, open this; it's your way out of here. But under no other circumstance do you open it or you'll be in serious trouble. Is that clear? And whatever you do don't come looking for me. This place will soon be swarming with armed men. You get the picture?' Michael said, handing Sean a sealed envelope.

'Yes, understood.'

'Good, I'm out of here! See you later.' With a wink and a friendly pat on the back, Michael turned and disappeared behind some derelict buildings.

Reaching the two-metre-high, chain-linked perimeter fence, he ducked in behind three oil drums and phoned Declan. 'I'm at a Yiannis's garage, Ano Mera. They have Vera inside the workshop. Park near the village church and head north on foot, about five hundred metres. You can't miss it. I have two bogeys in the yard and no idea how many inside.'

Peering out from behind the drums he readied himself. 'Right, buddy, I'm going in. Good luck, and drive that car like you stole it.'

He switched his phone off, pocketed the device and sprinted towards the small timber shed located two metres inside the perimeter fence. Crouching low he tested the bindings; it felt secure, no rattling, and thankfully there were no coils of razor wire on top. It would do. Biding his time, he waited for a car or some other noise to break the morning's silence. Finally, he grabbed hold of the top bar and propelled his hundred and twenty kilograms frame up and over, landing on the tarmac, the crunch of his boots muffled by the drone of a car's engine.

Shielded by the shed, he peered out. The nearest guard was no more than fifteen metres in front of him with his back turned.

Michael dropped flat on his stomach and slithered towards the parked car, bringing him within a few metres of the steroid-fed American. As the man busied himself lighting a cigarette, Michael took up a crouching position, and when ready to launch, whispered, 'Psst!'

Surprised, the guard spun around. Seeing Michael, he sneered derisively. But his overconfidence was his first, and also, last mistake. Slowed by the huge muscles, every action and twitch of a nerve was telegraphed long before it could manifest itself. As his arms swung uselessly through mid-air, Michael moved in with the speed of a leopard and with lethal force his knuckles crushed the tender cartilage of the man's

Adam's apple, cutting the flow of oxygen. Incapacitated, a look of horror spread across his victim's face. With his lungs burning, gasping for air, his big hands grappled in vain at his throat trying to clear the blockage. Going down on one knee he started to keel over, staring vacantly into space.

Michael crouched down, shoved the corpse in underneath a truck and waited a few seconds to be sure no one had seen or heard the commotion.

Nothing stirred.

Preparing to move in on the next guard, the noise of a fast-approaching car stopped him in his tracks. Dropping to the tarmac he rolled in under the truck, next to the corpse, and watched the charcoal coloured BMW career into the yard with tyres screeching. Five men jumped out.

'I trust she's ready!' a voice bellowed at the remaining guard.

'Yes, sir!'

'Good. Paul, you better hope she sings, and quick. We have to be gone before the owner turns up!' the man who clearly was in charge – *has to be Dermot* – ordered. 'Greg, once we have the information, you and the boys torch the place. Make sure no one will be able to identify her body.'

Michael fumed. Despite the insurmountable odds, there was no way he could wait for backup; he was on his own.

Dazed, Vera barely flinched as the bucket of freezing water hit her face, stinging her eyes; with her hands tied she could do nothing to ease the discomfort. Her head throbbed, she felt queasy, the room started to spin. Through tears she tried to focus, to stop the creeping lethargy.

She was inside a workshop reeking of oil. To her left, stained drums cluttered the floor with car tyres stacked high. A few metres in front of her was a car with its bonnet open. Someone had been working on the engine with tools piled on top of a dust cloth covering the front wing. The briefcase containing the million euro was perched on top of the car's boot. Further to her right weak sunlight filtered through the dirty, high-level windows, barely visible behind the ceiling-high storage racks loaded with spare parts and more car tyres.

She shook her head, trying to stay awake.

How long have I been here? she wondered.

Filled with disdain, she watched the seven men leer at her, at her heaving bosom, visible through the thin, wet blouse. With alarm she noticed the fresh syringe mark in the crook of her arm. *What did they pump into me?* she groaned, dreading a lethal concoction which would slowly drain the life out of her.

'Cut it out! You're not on bloody holiday! Go and make yourselves useful. On guard, outside, now! We're expecting company, move it!' a loud voice boomed. Immediately, the men scampered out of the workshop.

'Good morning, my dear … aha, my money!' Paul gibed and grabbed the briefcase off the car's boot. 'Where was I? Right, introductions. My partner, Dermot, and this, of course, is our lovely, elusive, Vera.'

Filled with loathing, she did not respond.

'Well, finally, I have the honour of meeting the young lady who had us running around like puppies looking for their mummy's titties. Not bad, not bad at all. Pity, such a waste,' Dermot said and lifted her chin, studying her sensual features. Vera cringed at his touch. 'She could have been very useful,' he said with a sordid cackle.

'What do you want?' Vera asked, spatting the words out.

'Simply put my dear: the diamonds. Let me explain myself some more in case you don't understand. As I see it, you have two choices. One, you cooperate with us and you live. Two, you don't and you die. How does that sound?'

Michael started to roll from underneath the truck but froze at the loud bang of the workshop's door.

Seven men stormed outside and split up. Three took up positions in the front yard while the rest ran off in different directions. He had to move fast, before someone found the corpse.

First, he aimed for the guard who took up a position near the front right-hand corner, beneath a lean-to roof. Above the roof was a row of clerestory windows, and judging by their size, he should be able to squeeze through. It was his way in.

Like a flash, he closed in on the man blocking his path. Not anticipating someone sneaking up from inside the yard, he was caught by surprise. With incredible force, Michael fell him to the ground; his limp body missed the stacked corrugated roof sheets by millimetres.

Having concealed the unconscious man behind three oil drums, Michael reached up and grabbed the overhead, diagonal roof brace. Placing his right foot on top of a drum, he hoisted himself up and over the lip of the roof and warily crossed the flimsy contraption. In broad daylight, anyone looking up from inside the yard would immediately see him. He dared not linger.

Pressing his body firmly against the workshop's wall, he looked inside but found his view partially blocked by a shelving unit. He moved a little sideways. There she was, strapped to a chair in the middle of the room, surrounded by six men.

Contorting himself, he squeezed through the small window-opening and expertly slid down the steel frame of the shelving unit. Dermot and Paul's shouting – trying to coerce an almost comatose Vera to talk – masked the slight rustling noises he made. As his feet touched the concrete floor he crouched down, withdrew his gun and moved towards the huddle of men. He needed to get as close as possible. In case of a shootout, he could not afford to miss. Each shot had to count.

Hiding behind a pile of tyres, he found an opening and took aim at Dermot's head. Running through possible conflict scenarios he knew that even with surprise on his side the odds were stacked heavily against him. If forced to act he would kill two, maybe three at the most, by which time the others would have retaliated. Using Vera as a shield, and supported by the men from outside, he and Vera would die under a hail of gunfire.

Biding his time, he studied the men surrounding her, deciding who to take down first in case anyone tried to kill her. In all probability, they would only kill her once they had the information they were looking for. He doubted if all of them, especially Paul and Dermot, would stay and watch Vera murdered – it was a case of the less one knew the better. But that was no guarantee.

Three of the men were partially shielded with no clear line of fire. If he did fire, chances were extremely high that Vera would be hit in the crossfire. Therefore, the others would have to go down first. Next, he would have to reach Dermot before any men stormed inside. Dermot was their only hope of leaving alive.

Just as he settled his aim on his first target, shouting erupted outside. Immediately, the men surrounding Vera drew their firearms, turned around and took aim at the door.

Except for Paul. Instead, he grabbed Vera's hair, and ignoring her squeals, pressed the barrel of his pistol against her neck, using her as a shield.

The other men spread out. Some slipped in behind oil drums, tyres and the car, with two taking up position on either side of the personnel door.

Michael aimed his pistol at Paul's head. He had no doubt his bullet would kill him but it was also a certainty that Paul's hand would contract and send a bullet to split open Vera's head. He had to get the threatening weapon to point in another direction, if only for a fraction of a second. He needed a distraction.

'Let me go!' Vera hissed, trying to move her head clear of the pistol.

'Shut your trap Russian whore, or I'll splatter your brains all over this dump!' Paul snapped, pulling her head back, pressing the menacing weapon even harder against her pale skin.

Vera said nothing. Her shoulders slumped as she succumbed to the pressure of the cold metal cylinder. She felt the slight tremble in Paul's hand.

His trigger finger started to squeeze…

Thank God, after so many years I'll be free …

'Get it over with, please. I beg you,' she said, her voice barely a whisper. With her head tilted upwards, she closed her eyes and surrendered herself to her fate.

At last …

CHAPTER 77

Marrakesh
Sunday Morning

Announcing his return with a loud bark as the sun's first rays flooded the hotel's grounds, Niall demanded breakfast. He was ravenous. He needed to regenerate his lethargic body after an all-night session with the three nubile young girls.

As expected, his staff jumped to attend to his every need, except for one who was conspicuous by his absence.

And where's Irina? he wondered.

'Oision, what time did Irina get in?' he asked somewhat indifferent.

'About one. We headed straight back after she spoke to you.'

'Good.'

'No worries, Boss.'

'And where the hell is that lazy-arse Brendan?'

'Was outside last time I checked,' Oision replied.

'Get him!'

In less than thirty seconds Oision crashed into the lounge, barely coherent.

'What the hell's wrong? Get a grip, man!'

'He's dead! His throat's cut!'

'What, where, show me!' Niall asked, jumping up.

Propped upright against the wall Brendan's corpse was not a pretty sight.

'Jaysus, who the hell did this!?' Niall shouted and looked up, furious.

Above the corpse bloodstains streaked the terracotta coloured wall as the assailant had wiped his hands leaving the scene. Bewildered, he followed the smears and realising where it was leading, his stomach turned. Reaching Irina's open patio doors, he barged inside.

Empty!

There was no sign of her…

The room seemed untouched except for the bed linen strewn across the floor.

He checked the bathroom. Not there either!

'She's been abducted!' he shouted, hoping that was the least of it, hoping she was still alive. Fearing for her life, his earlier buoyant mood vanished. The thought of her spending the remainder of her days in a harem in the mountains of Morocco, belonging to some Arab, was unthinkable. A string of obscenities cascaded from his mouth as he fretted, wondering when exactly she was taken.

Best start at the one person who may be responsible. Did he not make his intentions very clear last night!

Without a second thought, he rang Tarik with the image of the Moroccan lusting over Irina, taunting him. 'Tarik, you have fifteen minutes to return her, and for your sake, I hope she's unharmed or I'll—'

'Hold on, Niall, what are you saying?' Tarik asked, stunned.

'Don't play games with me! Where is she?' Niall shouted. 'And why the hell did they kill one of my men? I thought we were—'

'Whoa, hang on … calm down! You've got the wrong man,' Tarik said. 'As Allah's my witness, I have nothing to do with what you're saying. Why would I want to ruin our friendship? Please, you're making no sense. What happened?'

'Someone kidnapped Irina and killed one of my guards,' Niall replied, and described the scene which had awaited him on his return.

'I'll be right over. Don't touch anything and don't phone the police. I'll deal with them. I'll bring some men and a good friend who can help find her. Believe me, once she is safe, I'll kill the bastards who did this,' he cursed and spat on the ground.

For a big man, Tarik moved surprisingly fast as a diatribe of instructions echoed through the halls of his mansion. His large body resembled that of a charging bull, and the subsequent commotion was as if a whirlwind had struck. Instantly, staff armed themselves, piled into the waiting cars and rushed to the scene of the abduction.

From inside his limousine, Tarik continued his enquiries, discussing the abduction with some close friends who were at the banquet. Amongst them was the best detective in Marrakech, a man Tarik trusted with his life. Without hesitating, he summoned the detective to the hotel.

It was obvious, one of his guests must be involved. A very stupid man if he thought he could get away with this. He was also a dead man!

By 8:30 a.m. a ring of men had sealed off the villa, keeping any staff or curious bystanders at bay.

The detective, a wiry man in his mid-sixties with greying temples, combed the room and patio for clues, an exercise Niall considered a waste of time. What was needed was to confront the hotel staff, period! Someone on the inside had a hand in this. It would take Niall and his men less than five minutes to find the bastards. Not this playing Hercule Poirot nonsense!

Tarik, having similar thoughts, stormed into the hotel manager's office and demanded to view the security camera footage.

Estimating the time of the abduction to be between two and five in the morning, he started running the tapes, searching for any vehicles entering or leaving. To his surprise, there was a far greater number than he had anticipated. Most drivers had stopped for a brief chat with the security personnel at the gate, compelling him to regard them all as possible suspects. Scratching his bald head, he stomped his feet – there had to be some evidence!

On the villa's patio, Niall watched the detective examine the gaping wound to Brendan's neck. With his handkerchief, he chased away the flies which were becoming a real nuisance. Disgusted, Niall wanted his employee's body covered and removed.

After a few more minutes the detective straightened up and told the coroner, 'You may continue. I've seen enough.'

His search for clues at an end he called Tarik to join him and waved at Niall to follow.

'There is not much to go on as the police will verify once they've completed their investigation. The odd fingerprint or possible hair. Then, of course, any fingerprint found may be useless without the apprehension of the perpetrators – which is unlikely – unless they have a criminal record.'

Niall had enough of this laborious explanation and asked annoyed, 'Are you saying there is nothing which could help find her? Then why the hell are we wasting time here?'

The detective patiently raised his hand. 'Not quite. If you permit me to finish, I'll explain. She was rendered unconscious by smothering her face with chloroform – the distinct odour on the linen is unmistakeable – then carried to the waiting car and driven out of the hotel grounds.'

Really, like they would have walked her out of here! Is this man for real? Niall simmered but remained quiet, allowing the detective to finish.

'The security cameras might have recorded some unusual activity in one of the cars. We shall see. But the most telling clue we have is the wound which was made by a special dagger. At the end of the cut, there are two swollen puncture marks in the skin. These were made by two needle-sharp projections fixed to the hilt of the dagger of which the tips were covered in lethal venom, ensuring no victim would ever see the light of day again. In this case, an unnecessary precaution. I have seen this wound once before. I'm convinced it must be the work of the self-proclaimed…how do you say in English … I think … Twin-tailed Scorpions. This is their trademark. They are a new band of smugglers numbering anything between thirty and fifty. It's rumoured they're based in the Atlas Mountains directly south of Marrakech. Tarik, can you please check the hotel security footage again. Look for a small golden twin-tailed scorpion embroidered on a dark blue Saharan turban worn by the guests.'

'Allah, help the child,' Tarik sighed. 'We better hurry. They'll gangrape her – break her in so to speak – and sell her to the next group of pigs by the end of the week. Or slit her throat and feed her to the vultures.' His head swayed, distressed by his own words. 'Before I go, do you have any idea where we can start looking?'

'I suggest you follow Highway 203 south and look for a remote house somewhere in the mountains. Won't be easy but it's all I can offer for now. Best you get there immediately while I' make some enquiries.'

'Thank you. Hope you find something more tangible,' Tarik said, and shook hands with his friend.

Crammed with armed men the cavalcade of off-road vehicles raced towards the Atlas Mountains. Leading the way was Tarik with Niall by his side. En route an urgent call was made to another close friend, Colonel Mohamed Bendriss of the Marrakech Special Services Response Unit, the SSRU. Colonel Bendriss immediately agreed to mobilise more than a hundred men and join the group of vigilantes sweeping up the mountain road.

Colonel Bendriss also shared some positive news, having a fair idea of the suspected abductors' location. After a second victim was discovered ten days ago, displaying two prick marks on the neck, they had only made marginal progress with their investigation. Nevertheless, the police informants had indicated a likely base approximately twenty-five kilometres

343

west of Highway 203.

CHAPTER 78

Mykonos
Sunday Morning

Vera did not move. With her face tilted upwards, she waited for Paul to pull the trigger. She showed no fear, no anger, no hatred, only a calm serenity.

Michael swallowed hard as he looked on helplessly. Never had he seen such beauty. He fought the urge to jump up and pluck her from under Paul's nose. He wanted him dead, killed in so many ways imaginable, along with anyone else who had ever caused her pain.

Forced to maintain his position, he did not move a muscle.

And neither did anyone else.

Michael noticed Paul's index finger slide off the trigger and on to the trigger guard.

At last, a clear shot!

Taking aim, he gently applied pressure on the trigger, waiting for the right moment, wanting to be sure Vera would not be harmed.

Paul looked at Dermot, took a step back and half stumbled over the briefcase lying at his feet, slightly increasing the gap between him and Vera.

Just another metre ... move punk, move! Michael coaxed Paul in silence. If he fired, the bullet would travel the eight metres and split Paul's head open. *He'll never know what hit him.* But the others remained a serious threat with two of them pointing their guns at Paul and Vera. Spooked, they may release a volley.

Too risky.

The silence hung like a putrid, deadly stench in the workshop with everyone on edge.

A phone rang, cutting through the stillness.

'What do you mean we're surrounded, outgunned? Ridiculous!' Dermot's voice roared, filling the emptiness.

Vera's eyes opened wide as if waking from a trance. Bewildered, she looked at Dermot, not knowing what to expect.

'They have us at gunpoint. They want the girl and Paul, or we'll face a further bloodbath – we already have five men down!' the grave words echoed in Dermot's ear.

'Understood, put him on,' Dermot said, visibly stunned by the news.

'Ciarán, speaking. I presume you must be Dermot Mullane.'

'Yes.'

'Mr McGuire has no beef with you,' Ciarán lied, ignoring Niall's instruction to kill Dermot as well. 'All he wants is what belongs to him, and of course the whore and that fat rat you call a partner.'

Dermot knew he had lost, for now, although the war was far from over. 'Right, we'll come out, but only if you allow my men to fetch the wounded. Do I have your word?'

'Of course, mate. By the way, great to meet a boss who cares about his men. A bit late though; they're all beyond help,' Ciarán sneered. 'OK, enough bullshit! And no funny business or none of you will leave here alive!'

Dermot walked over to Paul and said, 'Well partner, I have to go. When you're free, you know where to find me.'

'Dermot, please don't leave me here, they'll kill me!'

Ignoring him, Dermot turned away and shrugged his shoulders indifferently. Paul started to follow.

'Take one more step and I'll kill you!' Dermot warned his

gun trained firmly on the squirming head which immediately disappeared in behind Vera. 'She won't save you. She'll die first and then you. Stay right where you are!'

Paul's pathetic cowardice, hiding behind the young woman, disgusted Dermot. He knew neither Paul nor Vera would leave the workshop alive. Looking at Vera he crossed his heart, turned, and stepped through the door.

Thirty-five minutes and still no sign of Michael or Vera. From his position the workshop was obscured. But Sean did see the men arrive in numbers and stalk the yard. Having heard the panicked shouts he was under no illusion as to what had transpired. He had no more time to waste – Sinead was all that mattered now.

With the way clear he left the shade of the tree, raced to the van, jumped in, and sped towards Mykonos.

He rang Sinead, and, despite her phone being on, she did not answer. He held on, listening to the never-ending beep sound. About to give up, a rude voice answered, 'What do you want?'

'Sis, please, don't cut me off! We must get off the island. I think Michael and Vera are either dead or captured. I'm not sure.'

'What?' she shouted. 'Where … when?'

'Michael went to rescue her and has not returned. I'm not sure what happened.'

'Maybe he just played you; he may still be helping Niall?'

'No, you're wrong, so please stop doubting me! What's your address? I have a way out of here, but we have very little time. And if you don't want to tell me, it will be a big mistake. They shall find you.'

This time, she did not argue and mumbled, 'Number 18, Studios Dimitra, Aghias Paraskevis 27.'

With utter contempt, Vera stared at Ciarán who could not hide his pleasure. 'Lads, look what we've got here: two in one! The fat pig and my dearest Vera. Vera, Vera, at last, we meet again,'

347

he chimed, looking her up and down, still soaked to the bone. 'Nice, very nice indeed! Maybe you can do us all one last favour before we waste you. Not a bad idea, what do ye say lads?' he said and fondled her breasts, ignoring the round figure which squirmed behind her.

'Ciarán, let's be reasonable. Surely, we can make a deal?' Paul piped up, his mouth twitching nervously.

'Oh, it speaks! My goodness, for a moment I thought it was a big, ugly, fat rat!' Ciarán sneered.

'Ciarán, let me explain. She does not have the diamonds. Someone is keeping them safe. She was just about to give us the name and address of her friend. I suggest we find this person and we share the diamonds. You'll be a rich man! I'll *wash* them, and you'll be rewarded handsomely, I promise. I have a million-euro cash in this briefcase and more in my plane. There's no need for you to be Niall's dog for the rest of your life. What do you say?' he pleaded. 'And then we get rid of the two witnesses!'

This was what Ciarán had in mind all along; it would be a solution to all his problems. Nodding perceptively, he winked at the two men by his side. 'You agree?'

'We're with you,' Larry and Thomas said in unison, delighted at the prospect. 'What about the lads outside?'

'We'll pay them off. Leave it to me.'

'Right, Boss, no worries then,' Larry said cheerfully, grinning from ear to ear.

'OK, mate, it seems you have yourself a deal. But remember, if you try to fuck with us, we'll kill you. Agreed, *partner*?'

'Of course,' Paul said relieved and stepped out from behind Vera.

'Good, then let's get to work,' Ciarán said, not daring to lower his guard with his pistol aimed at Paul. He would never trust a squealer.

'Right, Vera, you've heard what we want, so out with it. Where's Sinead?' Ciarán demanded.

'Who? The bitch who did this to me!' Paul shouted,

pointing at the fresh scars on his face.

'Are you deaf? Then let me spell it out for you: S I N E A D. Who else did you think it was, the fucking tooth-fairy?' Ciarán mocked.

'When we find her, give her to me. I need to teach her a lesson!'

'Yeah, right!' Ciarán snorted.

Aided by the drug, they managed to wheedle Sinead's address out of Vera. Focusing on the task in hand, neither Ciarán, Paul nor the other men noticed the tall man step soundlessly out from behind a pile of tyres.

Taking aim at Ciarán's head, Michael spoke, his voice calm. 'Right, lads, you have what you came for. So, I advise you to back away from her. I'm sure Niall will be delighted with your success.'

In disbelief the four men spun round.

'Now go and get Sinead. I'll take care of Vera. Move it. What are you waiting for? Go!'

The group of bewildered men did not budge, waiting for Ciarán to take the lead, unsure of how much Michael had heard or how many they were up against.

'Right, as you say. But don't you think it's better to check whether she's actually telling the truth before you waste her?' Ciarán cautioned.

'Yeah, you have a point,' Michael agreed with his weapon still aimed at Ciarán. 'Larry, untie her … easy does it.'

As soon as Vera was free, Michael pulled her out of the chair towards him. Drugged and mentally drained, she offered no resistance. 'Okay, Ciarán, lead the way.'

'And what about him? I have my orders,' Ciarán said, pointing at Paul.

'Forget him. Your orders have just been cancelled. Nobody's going to die,' Michael said and shifted his gaze to Paul. 'So much for your little alliance. Didn't last very long now, did it? Teach you not to cheat.'

Suddenly, Paul's head exploded with the impact of the bullet sending him reeling backwards, knocking over the

349

vacant chair and collapsing on to the floor.

'Idjit! What the hell? You really are deranged!' Michael shouted, turning on Ciarán. 'You've quite finished, or is there anyone else you would like to kill before we go?'

Ciarán looked at him defiantly, tempted to shoot.

'Yes, buddy, I dare you,' Michael said with a sneer, ready to shoot.

CHAPTER 79

Mykonos
Sunday Morning

Inside apartment number eighteen at Studios Dimitra, Aghias Paraskevis 27, Mykonos Town, Sean wrapped his arms around Sinead. Unable to control her emotions, she broke down. Calmly, he stroked her hair, waiting for the heaving shoulders to cease.

'I can't believe Vera is dead … and all because of me …'

'Sis, for all we know, she … both of them may still be alive. Try to be positive.'

'I know … I'll try.'

'Good. Now we better get the hell out of here before they come looking for you.'

'Yes. Just give me a minute to pull myself together. I can't go out looking like this. Any idea where we can go?'

'We'll hide at my hotel. Michael is to contact us there by twelve, latest. If not, we must get off this island immediately. He gave me instructions on what to do. Have you got anything you can use as a disguise?'

'Yes.'

While she fitted a blonde wig, Sean told her how he had found her, from the initial assistance by Irina, and when all had seemed lost, by Michael. But he refrained from mentioning the possibility that Irina might also have been compromised. Neither did he tell her about the murder of the politician who tried to help; a murder which he was to be charged with.

She kissed her brother on the cheek.

'What's that for?' he asked, surprised.

'For being stubborn, for not giving up on me. OK, I'm ready. Once we're out of here, I'll return these damn stones to Niall, otherwise, we'll never be free.'

The Road to Mykonos Town

Vera clung to Michael, not knowing who to trust. On the other side of her, Thomas, lost in thought, stared out of the window. In front, Ciarán was counting the money in the briefcase. And behind the wheel was Larry, concentrating on keeping the car on the road. Racing to find Sinead, the car skidded on the gravelled hard shoulder as the narrow road got the better of Larry, yet again.

If Michael had things his way, he would end it now. First, he would eliminate Thomas, then Ciarán and when Larry pulled over, he would let him walk away. Well, that would have been possible if it was not for the two cars following, carrying ten of Niall's men. Men he didn't trust. He was outnumbered and needed help. Stavros, a man he suspected not loyal to Niall's cause, was his only hope.

'Stavros, it's Michael. We're on our way to pick up Sinead. Maybe you want to join us?'

'Of course. I got your message … what happened?'

'Paul's dead, as are quite a few of Dermot's men.'

'*Gamó ton Día*!' Stavros swore. 'And Vera?'

'She's with me.'

'Is she OK?'

'Yes.'

'Good! Tell me where I can meet you?' Stavros asked.

Stavros' expressed concern regarding Vera's well-being confirmed Michael's suspicion. He smiled to himself as he replied, 'The holiday apartments Athena in Mykonos. We should be there within a few minutes. Any idea where Declan is?'

352

'Last I heard, he was tailing Dermot. Apparently, he caught up with them as they were racing out of the village.'

'Can you please tell him to join us and forget the Americans, they're out of the picture … for now.'

'*Nai, nai*, my friend, will do.'

Five minutes later, the three cars came to a screeching halt opposite the Athena apartments in the old town. Immediately, Ciarán and his men jumped out.

'Back in a sec!' Thomas shouted.

Unperturbed by the curious onlookers, he led the entourage of thugs up the steps and raced to Vera's apartment. Dashing over the open terrace they callously shoved a young girl out of the way, sending her flying across the tiled floor. Ignoring her enraged parents' protestations, they raced on.

Facing the apartment, Thomas tried the door; it was locked. He nodded for the others to stand back and with a well-aimed kick splintered the flimsy door. They barged inside.

Vera did not let go of Michael's arm, fighting her welling emotions. She had failed to warn her friend; this was not how she had imagined it to end.

Waiting for Thomas and his men to return, Michael did not dare take his eyes off Ciarán, not wanting to suffer the same fate as Paul.

It did not take long before Thomas came racing down the steps, shouting, 'She's gone, nothing here! Only some feckin' note about her heading back to Ireland to return the stones to Niall!'

Ciarán turned on Vera, 'Where is she? And no more bullshit!' he snarled, his fist hovering in her face, ready to land a punch.

Michael blocked his path and hissed, 'No, you don't! Get it through your thick skull, she doesn't know, she was strapped to a chair not that long ago, remember!'

'Yeah, yeah, maybe,' Ciarán mumbled. 'OK, lads, I think the whore can't be far. Spread out, find her!'

Leaving the apartment Sinead was confronted by a jumble of whitewashed walls and flat roofs dashed with splashes of bright-red bougainvillea. The atmosphere was tranquil, deceivingly calm with the sun's warm rays radiating lazily up from the flagstones. A few holidaymakers meandered through the alleyways, enjoying the shops' displays.

Preoccupied, she hurried to keep up with Sean striding a few paces up ahead. The next instant she crashed to the ground, knocked off her feet by a man who charged into the alley.

'Sorry, miss!' Thomas apologised, bending over to help her up. For a second his eyes held hers, sitting on the ground with her wig askew. Slowly, a nasty sneer spread across his face as he said, 'Hi, Sinead, we meet again!'

As she jumped to her feet a silenced gun appeared in his hand, pointing at her stomach. 'Not another step, stay right where you are!' he hissed, digging his phone out of his pocket. 'Ciarán, I have her! I'm on—'

But he never finished his sentence.

From behind two arms encircled his body, heaved him into the air, and threw him over the low terrace-wall. As his foot snagged on the coping stone, he hurtled headfirst on to the paving nine metres below. The dull thud of his body hitting the ground was followed by a terrifying scream, shattering the still of the morning.

Sean peered over the wall.

Thomas lay motionless – his neck having snapped on impact. Next to him lay his smashed phone and smoking gun. Alarmed, Sean turned and looked at his sister, her face drained of blood. She reeled backwards, tripped over the wall, and started to fall as her bloodstained fingers clutched helplessly at thin air. Sean dived forward with outstretched arms and grabbed her by the ankles. With a dull clunk, her body came to a stop. Weightlessly the blonde wig continued to float down and landed on top of Thomas' body.

Assisted by two bystanders, Sean pulled Sinead up and

laid her down. Cradling her bleeding head in his lap he remained unaware of the crimson, cobweb-stain on the far side of the whitewashed wall.

'Please help! Somebody, call an ambulance!' he cried out. Desperate to save his sister, he covered the wound in her side as the blood continued to seep through his fingers.

'Thomas, speak up! Have you got Sinead? What!' Ciarán shouted, confused by the background noise and Thomas' failure to respond. The phone went dead. He did not hesitate. With pistol in hand, he was first to move in the direction of the scream.

Michael and Vera looked at each other, nodded understanding and raced after him.

Arriving on the terrace a small crowd blocked their way. Unable to see what was happening Ciarán waved his pistol at the astonished bystanders, clearing a path. Reaching Sean and Sinead, he bent down and snatched Sinead's bag off the ground, having no interest in the tragic scene confronting him.

Well, she looks dead alright ... saves me the trouble, he thought without any remorse despite having known her for more than three years.

'Gotcha!' he sneered, feeling the hard stones through the bag's soft fabric. 'I have what I came for. Right, I'm out of here. Michael, are you coming?'

Not waiting for a reply, he turned away. But after four paces he paused, swung round, and facing a distraught Vera clinging onto Michael's arm, said with a broad grin, 'Oh yes, I nearly forgot. Sorry, dearie, I have my orders. See ya!' He raised his arm, aimed at Vera's stomach, and fired.

A fraction of a second before the bullet exploded from the barrel, Michael threw his full weight against Vera and fired two shots in rapid succession. The first bullet exploded Ciarán's head and the second ripped his chest open. Michael watched him collapse in a heap, knowing he was dead before he hit the ground.

He turned and looked at Vera. Her face was contorted in

anguish, filled with dread.

'Vera, no!' he groaned, realising he had acted too late.
Please God, not her as well!

He blinked, trying to clear his vision, desperate to know how badly she was injured.

She started to fall … her mouth open … she screamed.

But no sound escaped her lips.

The bystanders rushing forward were also silent.

He tried to focus …

Vera seemed to hang motionless in mid-air …

Keeling over, he did not feel the bump as his head hit the flagstones.

In the distance, sirens wailed … loud chatter, shouting. *What happened, why am I on the ground?* Michael wondered, confused. Nothing made sense.

'Michael … Michael, can you hear me?' Vera's voice cut through the haze clouding his mind, her eyes brimming with tears.

He tried to speak … coughed.

Damn, the pain!

He grabbed his chest, wanting to dig out the burning sensation with the bullet lodged somewhere deep inside. As his head started to clear, he understood what had happened. 'Vera, are you all right?' he asked, relieved.

'Of course, I am,' she replied, her voice tender, warm. For Vera her world had been transformed. The belief that no one cared whether she lived or died, least of all risk a life for her, had been obliterated. 'Thank you,' she said and kissed him gently on his forehead. Holding him tightly, she applied light pressure on the wound to try and stop the bleeding. 'How do you feel? Can you move?'

'I'll live. Don't worry. Please, check on Sinead, and hurry; we have to get out of here.'

'No, Michael, you need help.'

'I'll be fine. I just have to get up,' he groaned, trying to lever himself upright against the wall.

'Let me,' she said and placed her arm underneath his shoulder. Struggling with his massive bulk a few bystanders stepped forward and helped him back on his feet.

'Thank you,' Michael grunted. The pain was unbearable. 'Now … Sinead, please!'

Michael shuffled over to where Ciarán was lying on the ground – nobody had dared venture near the lifeless body. Ignoring a wave of dizziness, he bent down and picked up Sinead's bag. Looking up he searched the small crowd. There he was, hiding in a doorway, looking petrified: Larry. As Michael's eyes locked on his, he turned and scampered away – the threat in Michael's eyes was all it took: if he or anyone else came any closer, they would die.

Michael staggered back towards Sean and Sinead.

Grief-stricken, Sean looked up. The first impression Michael got was that Sinead was beyond help. But to make sure, he kneeled beside her.

Inspecting her wound, he knew the bullet had missed the vital organs and arteries. He moved his hand round her waist, searching. Having located the small exit wound, he pulled his hand free, covered in blood. Thankfully, no hollow-point bullet had been fired – a lethal round which would have ripped her body apart, killing her instantly. Without saying a word, he felt her pulse. Parting the bloodstained hair, he exposed the fracture at the back of the skull: it looked grim.

'Sean, she should be OK, but must get to a hospital, and fast!'

'How can you tell?' a distraught Sean asked, wanting to believe Michael.

'She's badly concussed. The bullet wound looks worse than it is. The problem's the head injury; only a scan can tell just how bad. And how I know she's okay, believe me, I've dealt with my share of gunshot wounds.' Moving closer to Sean's ear, he whispered, 'We have to go. We can't get caught or all of this would have been for nothing. Vera will take care of the bag. We'll contact you within a few days. This is far from over; I must still deal with Niall. Oh yes, the envelope.'

Sean nodded, not fully understanding what Michael meant as he fumbled in his pocket and retrieved the unread letter.

'Thanks,' Michael said and shook him by the shoulder. 'Snap out of it! Remember, Sinead is now in your hands. When questioned by the police, tell them Niall has a contract out on her. Apparently, she knows too much about his business and has threatened to report him to the authorities. That's all. Don't mention the stones … not a word. Now we must go. Good luck.'

Shaking Sean's hand, Michael gave him Sinead's passport, having retrieved it from her bag.

The two ambulances' sirens fell silent as they skidded to a halt. Four paramedics jumped out and rushed to attend to the injured. But the silence was short-lived, replaced by the wailing of police sirens descending on the area from all directions.

Michael, lightheaded, unsteady on his feet, took Vera by the hand, but nearly doubled-over in pain as they side-stepped the paramedics. Vera did not hesitate and slipped in under his arm, supporting him. Struggling under his weight, she turned one last time and looked at Sinead, surrounded by the paramedics, and whispered, 'Til later, *moy kotenok.*'

Silently, people parted, letting them pass.

Having reached Vera and Sinead's apartment it took all Michael's willpower to barricade the broken door. Sweating, out of breath, he lay down on the settee and phoned Stavros. 'Where are you?' he asked.

'With Sinead and her brother. And you?'

'Close by, their apartment, Athena Apartments, no 314. Do you kn … know any surgeons here? I need pat … patching up,' Michael stammered.

'Yes, I do. We'll be there shortly. Take it easy, you don't sound well, my friend. How's Vera?'

'Fine, she's un … untouched.'

The news elicited a string of praises to Zeus.

I know how you feel. You're not the only one who is pleased,

Michael thought.

Struggling to concentrate, he phoned Declan and briefed him on what to tell Niall. 'Declan, you're a good man. Some advice: quit … disappear. Don't ask why, just do it, or you … you'll go to prison. Hope … see you again. Good … luck.' Michael coughed, his chest burning with each breath.

'Michael, please rest,' Vera said, pressing a towel against his wound. Her eyes met his. She did not know what to say. Never had she experienced such warmth, such a feeling of endearment for someone else. She could not stop herself and leaned forward and kissed him tenderly.

Tasting the salt on her soft, full lips, Michael felt a deep sense of calm wash over him. After so many years of being alone, of being lost, he had found someone to love. Despite his elation, he felt drained, tired.

'Vera, please … don't let m … me fall asleep. I must stay awake … must not drift…' His lips stopped moving, his words fell silent, consumed by the stillness of the apartment. His arms dropped to his side.

As his eyes closed, Vera's heart broke. Her barely audible cries were consumed by a fathomless abyss of despair.

'No, please God. No … no … no…'

CHAPTER 80

Atlas Mountains, Morocco
Sunday Morning

The drone of Tarik's convoy left the national road fifty-five kilometres south of Marrakech. Twenty minutes later their numbers were boosted by three SSRU helicopters carrying thirty-two heavily armed men, followed by Colonel Bendriss and one hundred commandos. Immediately, the colonel took command and deputised Tarik and his men. Being a Moroccan affair, Niall and his men were excluded. Frustrated, Niall stomped in the dust, cursing, making veiled threats at the colonel.

'Tell your friend to calm down or I'll have him incarcerated!' Colonel Mohamed Bendriss warned Tarik.

'Niall, show some faith, some respect. If she's here, they'll find her,' Tarik said, trying to placate his business partner.

Concealed in the shade, a temporary command post was established. The civilian force, divided into three smaller groups, were positioned at intervals along the two-kilometre dirt road leading back to the main road.

Underneath the camouflage netting, Colonel Bendriss watched the relayed images on the monitor, captured by the eye in the sky – the size and shape of an eagle; the drone circled at high altitude gathering much-needed intel: the terrain, target and numbers.

'There!' the colonel snapped, ending the silence, pointing

at the small square on the monitor. 'Zoom in,' he ordered.

Magnifying the image, a stone farmhouse with an enclosed yard was visible. And, in whatever little shade there were, men loitered unperturbed.

'Zoom in on them.'

An instant later their facial features were clearly discernible, as were the small gold embroidered twin-tailed scorpions on their dark blue turbans. 'Excellent, got them!' Colonel Bendriss said. 'Lieutenant, carry out one more flyover and sweep back; make it count.'

'Yes, Colonel,' the operator replied as his fingers danced over the keys, compiling a detailed report for analysis by his commander.

Three helicopters popped over the small rise, their muffled rotors sending frightened animals scurrying into their burrows. Tilted forward, and at an altitude of fifteen metres, they raced to the drop zone situated sixteen kilometres west. Each helicopter carried eight men.

By the time the helicopters lifted off for their third and final sortie, Captain Omar Gaouar and his men had covered the last four kilometres to the farmhouse and taken up an elevated position fifty metres south of the yard.

The camouflaged digital camera, placed on top of the boulder above Captain Gaouar's head, combed the base. Intrigued, ignoring the flies buzzing around, he watched the bandits, oblivious of the threat facing them.

Twenty minutes later, the second and third force were also in position, deployed west and north of the farmyard.

They were ready.

The captain frowned: things did not add up. The behaviour of the bandits puzzled him. They looked bored, relaxed, too calm.

'Colonel, it's too quiet,' the captain's voice crackled over the commander's radio.

Colonel Bendriss puckered his lips, and said, 'I concur. Let's wait. See what happens. Any luck with the high-tech kit?

If she's there, you should be able to locate her. We must be a hundred percent certain. I'll not permit a slaughter based on incorrect information.'

'Roger that, Colonel. May I suggest—'

'Hold the thought. I have a report just in,' Colonel Bendriss interrupted the captain. 'We have a limousine approaching fast. Number of occupants unknown – damn blackened windows! Two vehicles in support with four civilians each. This changes things. What would bring money to this forlorn place? Either an abducted girl or drugs.'

'Makes sense.'

'Any update on the numbers in the yard, still only eighteen?'

'Affirmative. And the infrared imagery gun indicates we also have thirteen bandits inside, could be more. Two rooms are impenetrable.'

'What's their mood like?'

'Idle chatter, relaxed … just a sec', Colonel,' the captain stopped himself and perked his ears. The tone of the voices relayed by the high-frequency directional microphone changed. Inside the farmhouse men jabbered excitedly. And then, there it was again, a woman's faint cry! 'Colonel we have them. There's definitely one distressed female present. Hold on …'

As the captain watched the small monitor, three hunched-over, flickering red images shuffled into the room – they were no longer concealed by the walls of the secured room where they had been held captive. 'Correction. We have three, repeat, three captives, not only one.' Five more images became visible on the screen, but taller, erect, pushing the smaller images forward. More bandits! The total force opposing the SSRU consisted of thirty-six men.

'Colonel, we can't risk moving in; the hostages may not survive a full-frontal attack. I suggest we wait for the deal to be completed and ambush the buyer somewhere along the mountain road. We can clean this place up once the girls are safe. Unless, of course, you have an alternative in mind.'

'Fine, we'll go with your plan. But wait for my signal

before you start your clean-up operation; we don't want the girls neutralised by an untimely phone call. Roger that.'

'Roger that, Colonel, and out.'

The news of the three girls' presence confirmed they were facing human traffickers. Colonel Brendiss was delighted by the prospect of ending this group's existence.

Above the farmyard, Captain Gaouar instructed his snipers to select their targets, ready to fire if need be.

The tyres crunched over the pea gravel as the limousine came to a halt. The heavy doors swung open. Climbing out was a man of small stature with slicked-back grey hair and dressed in an immaculate cream tailored suit. In direct contrast was his host: a gangster who did not waste a second on self-prettification. Someone whose sole existence evolved around power, money and satisfying his perverse sexual needs.

Inside the sparsely furnished lounge, three European girls stood squirming, trying to hide their nakedness from the men surrounding them. Ignoring their plight, the little man in his tailored suit walked up to them and scrutinised each with a critical eye. Rudely, he pummelled their legs and buttocks.

'Good. Open their mouths!' he snapped. The last thing he wanted was damaged goods; a mistake he did not want to repeat, forced to spend money on an orthodontist.

Satisfied, he again ordered, 'Spread their legs.'

Rough hands grabbed the girls and forced them to oblige, pinning them to the floor. Having completed his examination of the girls, he stood up and wiped his hands on his silk handkerchief.

'Happy?' the bandit asked.

'Yes. And, I have your guarantee they're clean?'

'Of course!' the bandit replied, not caring whether they were or not.

'Good. Get them dressed and take them to my car.'

'Yes, but first the money.'

'Is this the lot?' the little man asked nervously.

'That's it. Now the money.'

'But … there's supposed to be more. I cannot leave without—' the buyer started to object.

'These are the only ones. Now, the money. I won't repeat myself,' the bandit warned as a dark storm brewed in his eyes.

'Fine, my misunderstanding.' Having removed the excess fee, he handed over the suitcase. There was nothing he could do but leave.

From his vantage point, Captain Gaouar witnessed the deeply distressed girls ushered into the waiting limousine.

The image of his sixteen-year-old daughter, a beautiful child, flashed in his mind's eye. 'Allah, please, may she never fall into the hands of such vermin,' he prayed. He loathed these cowards. To him, they were not men. They were a disgrace to mankind, to their own people, a breed of mongrels who should be strung up in the mountains for the vultures to rip apart!

'We have three European girls in the limousine – one auburn, two blondes – plus four men and the driver. Other two bogeys are riding shotgun front and back. They've left the yard. Colonel, we're good to go whenever you are, over.'

'Roger that, Captain, standby.'

Faced with a highly improbable extraction, Colonel Bendriss had to think fast. The thought of letting them drive-by and track them to the next destination crossed his mind. But what guarantees were there? Would the girls even survive such a journey? No, the risks were too great. Surprise them when they least expected it, and that would be right now.

A few minutes later a car was manhandled on to its side beyond a sharp bend in the winding mountain road. Completing the scene of the *accident*, two *injured passengers* slumped inside the car with a third sprawled in the road next to an open door. Their weapons remained concealed. Snipers were brought into position.

Evaluating the staged accident scene, Colonel Bendriss was satisfied. The road was blocked, leaving no space for anyone to drive past.

Patiently, he and his men waited for the convoy's arrival.

The lead car slammed on its brakes and came to a stop near the overturned car. Cursing, the driver got out to investigate the accident. Behind them, the other vehicles were forced to stop with only the bonnet of the limousine visible.

From behind the rocks and shrubs eight commandos emerged, and within a flash the lead car's doors were flung open and the occupants forced out at gunpoint. At that exact moment the *injured* of the *accident* overpowered the befuddled driver and catapulted him on to the ground next to his friends, their hands and feet cuffed behind their backs.

Beyond the bend, the other two cars were simultaneously surrounded by Colonel Bendriss' men. Taken by surprise the occupants filed out on to the road. Two tried to flee, but a lethal volley of rifle fire brought an abrupt end to their futile escape attempt.

Without a word, the three petrified girls were helped out of the car. Frightened by the many armed men surrounding them, they were not sure whether they were being rescued, or kidnapped once more.

With the girls safe, Colonel Bendriss radioed Captain Gaouar and instructed, 'All clear. Carry on, over.'

'Roger that, and out.'

Niall frowned as the three traumatised girls slowly walked towards him. 'She's not with them!' he shouted.

'What do you mean she's not here?' Colonel Bendriss asked, taken aback.

'No!' Niall retorted and turned on the girls. 'Was there another girl with you? She should have arrived this morning.'

'I no English, please. Uhm … I … Tanya … Belarus. Help, please,' the one blonde responded nervously, pointing to herself and the two girls by her side.

'None of you speak English?' Niall asked, exasperated.

The three girls shook their heads.

'OK. Don't worry. They'll take care of you,' Niall replied.

'Tarik, anyone here speak Russian?'

It did not take long to establish that no one did.

'No luck. But maybe that scum can tell us where she is?' the colonel said, glowering at the small man who was having a tantrum about the blatant violation of his rights.

Without warning the colonel punched the trafficker in the stomach, collapsing him on to the ground. The next fist landed before the disgruntled man could get back on his feet. With the greatest of ease the colonel grabbed him by his jacket and threw him on top of the car's bonnet. His large hands encircled his neck, pinning him down; it would require very little pressure to squeeze the life out of him. The colonel fired what sounded to Niall like incomprehensible gibberish at the distraught man.

One minute later he straightened up and shoved the trafficker into the arms of his men. 'Cuff him! Get him out of my sight!' he ordered. 'Mr McGuire, there was supposed to be a fourth girl. But he has no idea what happened to her. I doubt he's lying,' the colonel said pensively. 'In my opinion, they most probably got a better offer somewhere else, or wanted to keep her for themselves.'

'Then she may still be alive. She might be locked up in the farmhouse or in an outbuilding.' Niall blurted, hopeful.

'Damn.' the colonel cursed, grabbed the radio and shouted into the microphone, 'Captain, come in, over!'

'What's going on, Colonel?' Niall asked alarmed.

'Come!' Colonel Bendriss shouted, grabbed the radio and ran towards the nearest helicopter.

'Colonel, receiving you, over,' the radio crackled.

'Stop the assault, she's still there!'

'Colonel, it's too late, we're moving in to clean up.'

As the wheels lifted off the ground, the colonel conveyed the news to Niall. 'They've finished the assault and don't know whether she survived. They are looking for her.'

Straightening up from under the rotor blades spinning overhead, Colonel Bendriss lifted his chin and approached the shackled bandit.

'Where is she? What have you done to her?' he hissed at the gutless creature kneeling in front of him and pressed his service revolver against the man's turban. 'You have five seconds to tell me what happened to her!'

The man spat on the ground. 'Fuck you!'

The next instant a bullet ripped through the bandit's knee, splintering the bone. Above his screams the colonel kept count, 'Four … three …'

The bandit glanced at the twenty-seven corpses on the ground next to him, fully aware that a refusal to cooperate would have only one result: death. 'Yes, yes, okay, we took her, but she escaped! She's gone. I don't know where she is …'

'Bullshit! What have you done with her? Last chance.'

To the colonel, Tarik, and the other men the story sounded like a cover-up.

'No, no! Please stop, no more! As Allah … my witness … it's truth! Stop!' the man pleaded, stammering, barely coherent as the colonel shoved the barrel of his revolver into the open wound, crushing the splintered kneecap into raw flesh.

Colonel Bendriss turned to Niall. 'He claims she escaped. But I think he's lying. They must have killed her. We'll search the farm and area for her body. I'll also send the choppers on a recce just in case she did get away. If so, they'll spot her easily enough. But don't get your hopes up. Fact is, we got here too late. Sorry.'

367

CHAPTER 81

Atlas Mountains, Morocco
Sunday Morning

Four hours had expired since Irina had regained
consciousness, retching on a vile rag in her mouth, struggling
to breathe.

As lucidity returned, she realised where she was. Above the
noise of humming tyres and the drone of an engine, men's
excited chatter could be heard.

*Who are they … Tarik's men? No, he has no reason; I did
promise to call, or did he see through me? No. One of the guests wanting
to trade me? Most likely …*

With her wrists tied behind her back, she felt her arms to
be bare. Annoyed, she remembered placing the watch on the
bedside table before turning out the light. So much for the
tracking device; she was on her own.

Wriggling her hands, she managed to slip the bindings
down, enabling her fingers to tug at the soft fabric and untie
the knot. Next, she pulled the rag out of her mouth and
greedily gulped down the stale air. Her head cleared. Fumbling
in the dark, she managed to unlock the boot, careful not to let
it pop open. Holding the boot slightly ajar, she peered outside.
Not a settlement was to be seen, and towering over her were
the Atlas Mountains.

At their current speed, she suppressed the urge to jump;

it would be suicide. Waiting for the right opportunity she bided her time, appalled by the prospect of being gang-raped in preparation of becoming a sex slave, sold from one band to the next, trapped in a never-ending cycle of misery in some godforsaken hellhole. She remained confident such a scenario would never unfold as she would kill herself first if left no choice. But she would not die alone; they would pay dearly!

Using the bindings, she tied the lid down, leaving enough space for her to wriggle through. First her right arm, then a leg, and finally her head and body slipped out of the boot of the car. Holding on for dear life, she crouched on the bumper of the speeding car as it swerved through the bends, up the steep incline of the mountain.

Finally, the driver applied the brakes, slowing the car to a crawl in making a sharp right-hand turn on to a dirt side road. Confident no one was about, she softly pushed the lid shut and jumped clear of the car. Dropping flat on to the tarmac, she watched the car's rear lights being swallowed by a cloud of dust as it accelerated into the night.

With the car gone, she shot up, and ignoring the sting of the unyielding tarmac under her feet, raced down the mountain, putting as much distance between herself and the kidnappers. The option of seeking help at any one of the few isolated farmhouses along the way was summarily shunned; it was far too risky. A half-naked white woman banging on someone's door for help in the middle of nowhere was not a clever idea.

After four kilometres she came to a stone bridge spanning a stream twenty metres below. With her mouth dry, she lowered herself on to the stone plinth and slid down the embankment to the bottom of the ravine in search of a drink. Standing next to the stream, surrounded by scant vegetation too barren for a rabbit to hide in, she contemplated her next move. While eagerly scooping handfuls of pure, cool mountain water – tasting like the sweetest honey – the distant drone of an approaching car abruptly ended her deliberations. Guided by the bright moon, she scampered up the embankment on to a stone ledge and vanished into the deep shadows of the bridge.

Above her, the car geared down and stopped. Doors opened, people jumped out, running feet, shouting. Trapped, she flattened her body against the substructure's hard stonewall as two silhouettes peered into the dark. After a minute they shouted angrily, looked down the embankment and shouted some more. Finally, they climbed back to the road.

Doors slammed, an engine roared and raced off.

For ten minutes she did not move in case it was a trap.

In the semi-darkness, the scorpion's movements were barely visible. Its oversized curved tail, in stark contrast to its small pinchers, looked rather farcical. But she knew if stung it would be anything but funny. Calmly, she watched the seven-centimetre creature crawl over her hand towards her legs. Lifting her arm out of harm's way she did not hesitate to bolt off the ledge and skid down the embankment, hoping not to bump into a snake on her way down.

Having crossed the stream, she wearily climbed the opposite bank. Reaching the road she started jogging towards Marrakech. Drained after a punishing fifteen-kilometre run, and with the city's skyline in the distance, she once more left the road to rest and regain her strength.

With her feet dangling in the cold stream, Irina leisurely chewed on an apple. Two hours of rest had done wonders; she was glad to be alive and free.

She looked up at the pale blue sky, and relishing the smells and sounds of the mountain, fond memories of hikes at Lac Baikal were rekindled: of camping next to the vast freshwater lake surrounded by unspoiled countryside and forests teeming with wildlife, stretching as far as the eye could see, across never-ending rolling hills.

Time to go, enough daydreaming.

She stood up, stretched her tired muscles and followed the river. But progress was slow as the sharp stones and driftwood played havoc with her feet, forcing her to boulder hop. After a short distance, she considered returning to the road which would be a much easier option. But clad only in a torn nightdress it would not be wise. She had to find some fresh clothes.

With the increasing presence of goats and sheep grazing on fresh green leaves, the possibility of herders lazing about, curiously watching her, could not be ruled out.

At the fourth farmhouse, its wooden shutters still shut, she found what she was hoping for. Hanging on the washing line was a full-length black burka, a costume which would guarantee her anonymity.

With no one in the yard, she quietly pulled the dress off the line and slipped it over her head.

At the sound of a deep rumbling noise, she looked up just in time. With fangs bared, the ferocious animal rushed at her. Instinctively, her right hand shot up, gripped the overhead washing line, and with a powerful jerk snapped the cord free from its rusted fixings. As the dog jumped, she was ready. Waiting until the last moment, she ducked sideways, narrowly avoiding the exposed teeth, and in one fluid motion looped the cord around its head, and yanked downwards with all her strength. The speed and force felled the dog like a stuffed animal. Hitting the ground, the cord once more encircled its thick neck, forming a perfect garrotte. Pinned down by one knee, she pulled tight, cutting its air supply. Ignoring the pathetic squeals, whimpers and jerking legs, she held on.

Releasing her grip, she dropped the line on top of the heaving beast and sprinted into the open countryside. Behind her the incapacitated dog slowly recovered, having no desire to chase after the running figure clad in black.

In her haste, Irina did not notice the two shadows who had watched with lustful glee her transformation from half-naked white woman to an indigenous Moroccan. With daggers drawn, their sandaled feet flitted over the stony ground, pursuing her, their blood stirred by the prospect of satisfying an age-old lust for fair-skinned women.

Chewing on some long grass the three boys herding the bleating goats and sheep along the riverbank ignored the woman who loped past. Neither did they take any notice of the two dark-clad figures following at a short distance.

The sheer agony of putting weight on her cut and bruised feet reduced Irina's progress to a sluggish stride. What she would give for a pair of shoes. Tired of having to stop every few metres to extract tiny thorns from her soles, she tore two long strips of cloth off the dress and wrapped them tightly around her feet with the ends tied above her ankles. It would have to do. She got up and once more set off towards Marrakech.

Following her, they kept their distance. They knew the terrain, they knew where they would strike, and they had plenty of time.

A sudden movement on her left caught her eye. Irina's senses went on high alert, shaking off the creeping lethargy. There it was again. She paused and studied the row of young orange trees where a small piece of black cloth protruded amongst the green foliage.

Someone was watching …

She veered across an open field back to the main road, remaining close to a stone wall on her right. She increased her pace and peered over her shoulder.

A dark figure followed, the dagger's blade glistening in the morning sun.

Irina started to run.

The man took up the challenge and raced after her.

She stretched her legs, trying to outrun him.

Without warning a straight forearm shot out from behind a tree, catching her in the throat and felling her flat on to her back, the air knocked out of her lungs.

In a flash the two men jumped on top of her, their steel blades pressed hard against her neck, leaving her gasping for air. Pinned down, they ripped the cloth off her face. Next, they tore away the full-length burka and nightdress, exposing her breasts, stomach, hips, thighs and her virgin white skin.

Driven by uncontrollable lust, they jabbered incessantly. With their free hands they violated her modesty. The tallest got up, eager to ravage the young woman.

Prepared to wait his turn the other man removed the torn rags and parted her legs. She did not resist. She seemed to be in a state of shock … or, was she as they have heard, the same as all white women: a slut? He grinned. 'You want this, white whore?' he mocked in his native tongue as he exposed himself. 'Not to worry, we'll take our time. And tonight, we'll share you with some friends!' As his hand grabbed her breast, he let the point of the dagger trail across her stomach and down the length of her arm.

When Irina moved it was with lightning speed. Grabbing the intrusive hand, she snapped his fingers sharply back and twisted his wrist. A paralysing pain shot up into the attacker's shoulder. He dropped the knife and tried to free his arm. But Irina held on. He had reacted just as she had calculated. Finding enough leverage, she catapulted herself off the ground, seized the knife and in one fluid motion plunged the blade into the man's exposed groin, severing a main artery.

Ignoring his screams, she jumped to her feet, ready to face the second attacker.

Seeing his friend curled up in a heap, the man launched himself at her.

Undeterred, she stood her ground.

With teeth drawn, the man swung his dagger, slicing through her torn rags. His hand caught in the cloth. With brute force, he jerked Irina off her feet towards him, towards the hidden blade.

An excruciating pain shot through her side as the knife parted the soft tissue below her ribs. Ignoring the pain, she pushed him away with all her strength.

Having recovered her balance, she circled him and ripped the hampering clothing off her arms, not to be caught off-guard again. She felt the warm liquid run down her side, her leg … Feeling giddy, her vision blurred. She knew the signs, what it meant. If she were to fall, she would never rise again.

Remembering the instructor's words, she drew on her inner strength, preventing the body from giving up, fighting the self-doubt, knowing her next move could also be her last.

Block the pain. Breathe deep, slow … focus, breathe … wait, breathe … wait … show no emotion … wait …

Seeing her hesitate, her attacker sneered, and smelling victory, he moved in for the kill.

But duped by her silence, he had missed the deep-gold, hazel-green eyes' determination: the deceivingly calm, vacant look of a predator before it struck.

When he swung his blade, he knew he had walked into a trap. His courage failed him. His aim was wild, feeble, his muscles had lost their purpose.

With agility and speed, he never expected, least of all from a wounded woman, she crouched in under his arm and lunged forward. The point of the dagger speared his neck as the blade sank up to its hilt. Flitting past him, she pulled sideways with both hands, ripping the blade free.

She turned, ready to strike again.

There was no need.

Disgusted, Irina threw the dagger on to the ground next to the nearly severed head. Wiping her bloodstained hands on her rags, she pulled the torn cloth tightly around her body to stem the flow of blood. Retracing her steps to the river, she did not look back at the two bodies sprawled in the sun next to the old stone wall. Attracted by the metallic smell, a cloud of flies buzzed over the corpses.

Tired and drained, she staggered forward, wanting to clean the wound and wash away the stench of death which clung to her skin. She struggled to remain conscious.

The first helicopter sped down the valley and followed the national road. Ten minutes into its flight the pilot spotted a few wild dogs scavenging something on the ground two hundred metres east off the main road. He circled and took a closer look. Horrified, he watched two corpses being torn apart by the pack. Reporting the incident, Colonel Bendriss ordered him to land and investigate.

With guns ready, they approached the dogs.

As the beasts turned with their hackles raised, the lieutenant and his co-pilot crouched down. The bloodstained fangs snarled menacingly, guarding their food. Taking aim, they commenced firing on the raging animals, killing them one by one. It took five kills before the last two scampered aside, growling.

Sighting the savaged remains of the mutilated bodies, the pilots retched. Having composed themselves, they covered their mouths and crept closer. Next to the corpses were two discarded bloodstained knives. It did not make any sense. Neither did the trail of blood leading towards the river. Had they been murdered before being scavenged? Was someone else responsible for this slaughter? Was there a survivor?

The young lieutenant followed the path of blood while the co-pilot remained at the scene, keeping the two dogs at bay. Reaching the river, he discovered more blood, a substantial amount … and fresh. Sweeping his pistol from side to side, he radioed for backup.

Watching the pilot, Irina remained hidden behind a bush. Swaying on her feet, she fought the dizzy spells which washed over her. Taking a deep breath, she stepped out into the open with her hands on top of her head. Her legs felt weak as she struggled to cover the thirty metres.

Confused, the pilot looked at the dishevelled European girl in a torn and bloodstained burka. Was this petite woman responsible for the two corpses lying in the dirt? Or, did they fight over her, killing each other?

'I need help … I've been kidnapped … attacked, but I—' she slurred. Unable to finish her sentence, she collapsed on to the ground.

CHAPTER 82

Marrakesh, Morocco
Sunday

Fortunately, the wound inflicted by Irina's assailant was a deep cut and not a stab wound. The blood loss, although substantial, did not warrant a blood transfusion.

Crowding her hospital bed in the Clinique Internationale Marrakech, the group of men listened intently to her story. The facts surrounding her escape left Tarik and Colonel Bendriss speechless, especially the fate which had befallen her two assailants. This drove Tarik into a state of absolute adoration. And ignoring Niall by his side, he asked her for her hand in marriage, a life of endless splendour, guaranteed.

Smiling sweetly, Irina graciously declined this offer due to longstanding commitments in Russia.

Despite Niall's pleasant smile at this frivolous banter, he could not stop himself from tripping into a dark mood, tortured by one question: who was Irina really?

And as for Colonel Bendriss and his men, they were delighted at having eliminated the group of bandits who no longer roamed the dark folds of the mountains. Neither did it take the police long to establish the identity of the man who had masterminded the operation. The cocky buyer, still in his tailored suit, had squealed like a pig when given two choices: to walk away as a free man, or face death by firing squad if he refused to cooperate. Having acknowledged his involvement, he, in the end, would find himself behind two centimetres of steel for his trouble awaiting execution – the police having found condemning evidence at his home linking him to the deaths of several girls.

The remainder of the day Irina was left alone to rest, guarded by three men stationed outside her door.

At six thirty in the evening, Niall returned to the hospital and convinced the medical personnel and police that she may just as well recuperate at the hotel under his protection. This was agreed to. But on their return, much to his disappointment, Irina ignored him and locked herself in her room, not to be disturbed.

Alone in his suite, Niall listened to Declan's report on the day's events in Mykonos.

'Are you saying that Michael, five men, the two whores and Paul are all dead? Bloody hell!' Niall cursed, realising full well the repercussions these killings would have. The only comforting thought was that the rest of his men had escaped unharmed.

'What happened to my diamonds?' Niall asked.

'They're gone. The police confiscated the lot. I'm sure some will turn up in court as evidence. But knowing these Greeks, I reckon most of it won't.'

Next door Irina held the minute speaker to her ear. Her shoulders sagged at the terrible news.

All dead! No, it can't be!

Niall went quiet, with not another word spoken. All she heard was someone moving around, groaning … angry … Suddenly a door banged open, followed by racing footsteps.

'Pack your things, we're leaving. Now!' Niall shouted as he hammered on her door.

'Where are we going?' she asked.

'None of your business!'

High above the Atlantic, Irina was in the dark as to their destination, and even more so about what was unfolding at

377

that precise moment in Morocco.

With Colonel Bendriss' blessing, Tarik had been let loose on the mastermind responsible for Irina's abduction. Therefore, escorted at gunpoint in the middle of the night, the abductor found himself stumbling barefoot across an unforgiving mountainous terrain of thorns, shrubs and sharp stones. Having endured a kilometre of sheer agony, his journey abruptly ended when Tarik tripped him up and sent him sprawling headlong into a three-metre deep pit, his fall cushioned by a mass of unsuspecting writhing cobras.

With glee, Tarik and his men watched the squealing figure engulfed by the slithering coils. Immobilised by the neurotoxic venom his lungs soon stopped expanding as his muscles failed to respond to the excruciating pain of the fangs which sank into his lifeless body.

Peering out at the night sky, Irina distinguished the shape of a small island far below. Studying the stars, she calculated that they were somewhere over the Caribbean.

Sitting back, she felt the soft bump of the jet's wheels touching down on the runway. On her left trees blurred past, and on her right the ocean. Nearing the end of the runway the plane braked hard, swerved through a breach in the bank of foliage and on to a confined levelled field. Slowing down the plane rolled towards a granite cliff where a vertical strip of light appeared with the large camouflaged hangar doors sliding open.

Entering the brightly lit cave the engines throttled down. Carefully, Karl manoeuvred the plane, avoided the parked helicopter, and with the nose pointing towards the runway the drone of the powerful engines fell silent.

Having sensed their employer's foul mood, the Latin-American ground crew greeted him politely and proceeded to offload the luggage. Reciprocating their subdued welcome, Niall responded with a nod of the head and led his small party up on to a raised platform. Next, to a nondescript door, he pressed his hand against a wall-mounted square, glass panel, unlocking the heavy, armour-plated door. Inside the secured foyer was an elevator, and to its right a flight of steel stairs spiralled upwards.

As the spacious elevator ascended, a rush of exhilaration tingled under Irina's skin. At last, she had found his lair! Her resilience had paid off.

Stepping into the main foyer fifty storeys up, the full-height, glass wall offered her a splendid view of the never-ending ceiling of shimmering stars and of the luminous moon's glow which danced like shoals of fish in the phosphorescent waves below.

The house itself was extraordinary. A vast structure of five floors nestled against the cliff face, a design far removed from the old period house in Ireland: ultra-modern and brimming with high-tech equipment.

The nearest corner of the building was shaped by walls of angled glass and steel floating in mid-air, anchored by horizontal lines of natural stone and glass, following the gentle curve of the mountain. The lower three levels blended discreetly into a landscaped garden of lush tropical plants. On the bottom terrace below the main foyer the twenty-five-metre heated pool, chiselled into the mountain, sparkled invitingly.

Irina's face remained expressionless as she wondered what security measures were in place. Where was the second entrance? It was inconceivable that everyone arrived by plane. Her deduction was correct.

Concealed from view was a sixty-degree angled monorail with an adjoining winding stairway, connecting the T-shaped jetty to the tropical gardens above. Moored in this confined port was Niall's forty-five-metre motor yacht, carrying a price tag of thirty-two million euro. It was his pride and joy, and therefore guarded day and night.

Built in Holland, she was alleged to be the largest and most powerful yacht to have left the Dutch shipping yards the previous year. The interior consisted of Canaletto walnut veneers complemented by Loro Piana fabrics. Five cabins provided sumptuous accommodation for ten guests, all with en-suite bathrooms. The aft deck was one of several areas designed for outdoor entertaining with its ten-seater island table. The top deck offered an eighteen-metre sunning area with cinema, additional dining space, a square pool and an infinity terrace. The three Sea Keeper gyroscopic stabilisers ensured minimal roll at sea when engaging the massive diesel engines, travelling at twenty-two kilometres per hour.

One thing was certain, the location and design of the house guaranteed absolute privacy. Isolated from the rest of the world in the middle of the Caribbean, it was the ideal retreat where Niall could run his illegal operations in human trafficking, and drug and weapon smuggling.

CHAPTER 83

Caribbean
Monday Morning

Irina stirred and rubbed her eyes, woken by the peaceful sound of distant rolling waves drifting in through the patio doors. The bright morning light filtering through the satin curtains made her blink. She felt tired, reluctant to get out of bed just yet. But she had to act, and act quickly; time was ticking.

The superb setting, the twenty-four-hour room service, the well-appointed suite of four rooms and private patio she would have welcomed, if there by choice, but she was not. She was a prisoner on Niall's island, at the mercy of the psychopath.

Ignoring the burning pain in her side, she showered, dried herself and slipped into a pair of faded jeans, a T-shirt, comfortable runners, and a light summer jacket. Having applied some make-up, she strolled through the house making mental notes.

Traversing the vast open living areas, defined by a few columns, natural boulders and tall plants, she hardly noticed changing levels via a few discreetly placed ramps and steps. In contrast to the ultra-modern structure, the furniture was a combination of Persian rugs, warm-coloured, marble floor slabs, aged-brown leather chairs, comfortable upholstered couches and richly-polished antique tables. Carefully placed sculptures by Rodin, Thornycroft, Bernini, and other famous artists created an ambivalent mood of peace and harmony, challenged by a ubiquitous air of excitement.

After twenty minutes of wandering through the house, Irina understood why house rules were superfluous – except for the fifth floor being out of bounds. The sprawling premises were littered with surveillance cameras, backed-up by twenty-four-hour armed security.

Not deterred, Irina acted like any nosy visitor would when overwhelmed by new surroundings. With a look of *sheer amazement,* she continued to poke her nose into every conceivable and inconceivable nook and cranny.

Ignoring the one and only rule, she meandered up to the top floor where an impregnable door blocked her way; a door constructed of titanium sheeting sandwiched between two twenty-millimetre thick Cherrywood panels polished to a glossy sheen. Gripping its satin steel handle, she tried to open the door. It refused to budge.

Having triggered the silent alarm the instant her skin had touched the sensors embedded in the door handle, a tiny red light started to blink next to the eye-scanner. She turned away, an alternative route had to be found.

Trying the internal elevator linking the sleeping quarters, the living and dining rooms, home theatre, squash court, gym and indoor pool was to no avail either. The elevator stopped on the fourth level and would go no further. The fleeting thought of fiddling with the electronics was ruled out by the tiny security camera installed in the ceiling of the cubicle.

There must be another way; there always is. Maybe from the outside, at night? she reasoned.

Having decided this to be her only option, the next few hours were spent in the shade of a tall palm in the garden. From behind her sunglasses she studied the rock-face above the house.

One crevice, hardly noticeable from her vantage point, had potential. *Yes, it's possible. Dangerous, but possible*, she thought.

Twice during her time in the garden, Niall had confronted her under the misguided notion that she would lovingly forgive and forget who he was and what he had done. His audacity did not surprise her. And her response offered the same amount of warmth as the ice sheet covering Antarctica. But on the second occasion, her obstinacy had clearly touched a raw nerve. She knew she had pushed his patience to the limit and had felt the proverbial noose tightening around her neck.

Reclining on her bed in the dark, she had serious reservations about her plan. The more sensible option would be to rest one more day to give her body time to heal. But the expression on Niall's face had left her under no illusion. She couldn't wait as this may be the only chance she'd ever get.

Time had run out.

Crouched below the patio wall, Irina edged towards the garden located at the far end of the terrace. She looked at her watch, exactly half past two.

Confident there were no guards in the vicinity, she darted across the twenty metres of open space and merged into the shadows at the base of the cliff. In the grey light of the moon, she located the fissure visually tagged during the day. A quick glance over her shoulder confirmed the coast to be clear. Standing on her toes she reached up and ran her fingers along the ledge, seeking a suitable grip. As her hands tightened over the edge, she pulled herself up. But an excruciating pain tore through her side. Immediately she let go and dropped to the ground, doubling over in pain. The freshly stitched knife wound felt as if it had been torn wide open.

Unsure whether she had uttered a sound, she did not dare move. Her head spun. Pearls of cold sweat formed on her skin. Placing her head between her legs, she waited for the dizziness to pass, for the pain to ease. As she regained her composure, she raised her eyes up at the vertical cliff, doubting whether she could continue. In her condition the climb seemed impossible.

Mustering all her courage, she once more reached up, and with the toes of her runners firmly secured, she catapulted herself upwards. Remaining inside the shade of the fissure, and gritting her teeth, she inched her way towards the ledge seven storeys up: a natural shelf extending half the length of the house.

After thirty minutes of climbing – double the time she had envisaged – she reached for the ledge, her body pushed to the limit. Far below, the house and gardens were shrouded in darkness with no guards or sweeping beams of light anywhere.

So far, so good, she thought, relieved at having avoided the security cameras. Although that was no guarantee. For all she knew he could be watching, waiting for her …

But there was no turning back.

She stood up and sidled along the remaining thirty metres of the narrow shelf. Twice she lost her grip, nearly plummeting to her death.

Reaching the point of descent, she turned, faced the cliff and slowly crouched down until the full weight of her body rested on her arms and hands. Carefully, she lowered herself over the edge, her toes searching the rocky outcrop.

Where is it?

With her body suspended at full stretch and her side burning like fire, she frantically looked to her right and left – she had miscalculated by two metres. Her toes scraped the smooth rock surface, trying to find some leverage. With aching fingers, she moved sideways.

The pain was unbearable, her head swam …

Her right hand slipped …

Her left hand started to lose its grip …

With the little bit of strength she had left, she swung her leg sideways. Contact … and just in time! With her foot firmly secured and gripping the shelf with her left hand, she clung to the vertical wall like an insect.

Having recovered her balance and calmed her breathing, she continued her descent. At one metre above the house, she readied herself and jumped, comfortably clearing the two-and-a-half metre gap. Landing soundlessly on top of the flat roof she quietly crept to the front of the house. Sweeping the area, and seeing no one, she lowered herself over the eaves and dropped on to the terrace below.

She had made it undetected to the fifth floor.

Peering through the dark patio glass doors, no motion sensors or infrared beams were detectable.

Strange, she thought. *Niall not taking precautions in safeguarding the centre of his universe? Unlikely!*

Wasting no time, she sprang the lock and slid the large door open. The room was uncluttered and sparsely furnished with a comfortable settee, two leather high-backed armchairs, coffee table, minimalistic modern desk and a chair. The smooth panelled wall behind the desk most likely contained his filing archives. But that could wait. Determined, she walked over to the desk and sat down on the leather chair. Testing the drawers of the rolling cabinet underneath the desk, she found only one to be locked. That could also wait.

Moving the electronic mouse next to the PC's keyboard, its monitor jumped to life. Thankfully, the computer was on standby with no screen-lock, saving her valuable time in trying to find a password.

Scanning the desktop for folders that might be of interest, she clicked the cursor on one named, IAS. *Possibly an acronym for International Arms Sales?* But access to the document was restricted. Undeterred, she set about cracking the code. After a few minutes, she typed ARUAM: the name spelled backwards of the only person who seemed to matter to Niall. His sister, Maura.

Spasibo! she sighed gratefully as the document opened.

Scrolling down the monitor all the information she wanted appeared. Her previous attempts in Ireland had failed, but this … this was like discovering the Holy Grail!

Amazed, she watched dates, references of arms shipments from Russia, names of the Russian traitors and their contacts, name places and routes of each shipment – including Tarik's involvement – flash on the screen.

It seemed Tarik was someone who had earned a great deal of money for them both in illegal weapon sales: Niall sourced and shipped supplies from the Ukraine and Russia, while Tarik Beyomar distributed the merchandise to countries blacklisted by the UN and the USA. General Petrov, an alias for General Andreyev based in Russia, was a key player in this peculiar syndicate, willingly complying with the extensive demands for weapons.

Then another list of names and contact details appeared: the hackers her government wanted, those who had accessed some of the most secretive files of the Armed Forces of Russia.

Success, at last! She had found what she had been looking for. It was time to go home!

But she had not quite finished.

Searching his other subversive activities involving his drug network, sex trafficking and slavery, she found the names of those involved, places, dates, as well as details of his financial empire shrouded by a horde of bogus companies and trust funds. She sat spellbound faced by the full extent of his sordid world.

Before closing each folder, its full contents were saved on to the minute 250GB memory stick. She also copied all evidence of Niall's illegal activities stored on the hard drive.

Satisfied she had it all, she retrieved the memory stick, sealed the device inside the waterproof lipstick casing, and placed it inside her windbreaker. Having erased any sign of her visit, she stepped out on to the terrace and shut the door. Climbing over the glass balustrade, she dropped on to the level below, and then on to the next.

Dashing into the garden, she stopped at the slim trunk of a Royal Poinciana and glanced back at the house. Only a few dimmed lights were on in Niall's suite on the fourth floor. The office was still masked in darkness.

Confident there had been no silent alarm, she relaxed a little and turned towards the steps accessing the pier. Avoiding the surveillance cameras covering the path, she detoured through the lush gardens.

Inside the security operations room, Niall watched in silence, how, with athletic skill, Irina had landed on top of the roof, pounced catlike on to the patio below, broken in, accessed his computer and finally disappeared over the balcony into the night. A mission carried out to perfection. A mission which was the domain of trained men from the Special Forces – experienced insurgents – and most definitely not for some snip of a young girl!

Who the hell are you? And where do you think you're going, surely not my yacht? You're not going to try and steal that as well? he mused.

Alerting the guards at the pier, he instructed four heavily armed men to intercept her. Another four were sent from the house, covering any possible retreat.

She was trapped.

Who are you spying for? Niall wondered, suspecting very well whom, but he had to make sure.

'I urgently need some information. I think your government is investigating me,' Niall said into his phone.

'Uhm,' Nikolai grunted. 'What makes you think that?'

Having been given a rundown of what happened, Nikolai replied, 'Sounds possible. Leave it to me. I'll see what I can find out. But she may work for Interpol; you better check with them. In the meantime, sterilise your house.'

'I thought as much,' Niall replied, trusting that Nikolai's vast Russian Mafia network operating in St. Petersburg and Moscow would deliver on time. 'And the usual fee applies?'

'Absolutely.'

Despite Niall's warning not to be taken in by Irina's petite appearance, catching her turned into a disaster.

Two of his men were severely concussed, felled by lightning fast wheel-kicks to their heads. One man died with a Hiraken Jodan to his throat with no one to clear the crushed airway in time. The fourth man had brought her resistance to an abrupt end with a bullet piercing her right arm's biceps. Thrown off balance, and joined by four more men, they had pinned her down, flipped her on to her stomach, and secured her hands behind her back.

Fighting the pain and nausea, and severely hampered by the rope tied around her neck and feet, Irina slowly climbed the steps back to where Niall was waiting for her.

'Don't touch me again,' she hissed, being shoved in the back for the umpteenth time.

'Shut up!' the offender shouted and gave her another push with the rifle's butt.

Covered in blood, and with her head hung low, she did not retaliate: there was no point in getting killed on these steps by his men. She would let Niall do the honours himself as that would also be the last thing he'd ever do on this earth, of that she was certain. She would not die alone. No.

Angered by her own failure, she shook her head annoyed, remembering the gnawing fear as she had said goodbye to her family in Moscow. The fear of never seeing her home again, of never seeing her parents again, of never holding her beautiful baby girl in her arms again.

And now it was happening. For her, it would soon be over.

CHAPTER 84

Caribbean
Tuesday Morning

Pacing, Niall became increasingly distracted by the parcel perched on top of the mantelpiece. He reached out, wanting to discard it, but his curiosity got the better of him. He paused, and with a sense of foreboding removed the wrapping, uncovering a white shoebox.

Lying on top of a pile of letters was a small pink book titled: "My First Diary" – Maura.

Intrigued he sat down and with great care turned the pages. He could not help but smile as he read about his sister's childhood fantasies of boyfriends and someday travelling the world. Describing how wonderful her thirteenth birthday had been and how much she loved her family.

As he flipped through the pages her writing matured – the girlish over-rounded letters and twirls were replaced by confident strokes. There was nothing which concerned him. He lost interest thumbing through some more pages. Then a subtle change, her writing became unsteady, wavering, the words sombre, filled with anguish. She made a bizarre claim of her dad having touched her in a way she thought inappropriate!

Niall stood up. He felt uncomfortable, things did not add up …

He continued to read, paying close attention to every

word, to every nuance.

Unfolding on the pink pages was the true story of the last year of Maura's life, a life tormented by her *beloved* father. After the first touch he had continued regularly violating her young body. Nights she would lay awake fearing his footsteps, his warm breath on her neck. She could not bear it any longer.

A cold tremor ran down Niall's spine. *It can't be!*

The image Maura painted was that of a selfish monster, one who had ignored her pleas, acting only for his own self-gratification. It was the shocking truth about the man he had worshipped. Of the man, he had without question revered all his life.

'… I could not stop myself as I plunged the knife into your neck. And when you begged me to stop, I could not … The blood poured from your mouth, throat, covering my face, my hair. It was terrible … but I couldn't stop. When you were already dead, I continued to drive the blade into your back. You did not stop when I had begged you to. No, you had ignored me, grunting like a pig, telling me you love me! God knows how I hated you. And now, you know, Daddy, I'm sorry. I hated you … but now, strangely, I miss you … Daddy, I'm so very, very sorry …'

Their mother had rushed in too late, finding her naked husband on top of Maura who had continued to plunge the knife into his body.

Niall dropped the book as if it was a red-hot ember. 'My God, no!' His heart raced. His ears buzzed. He needed air. He could not believe the words written by the only person who had nothing to gain by lying.

The past flashed by – a road littered with the mangled bodies of young women. Consumed by self-pity, he had never tried to understand, or question, his mother's motive nor bothered to listen to her confession of a crime she never committed.

'But why?' he groaned, struggling to digest the truth – the cruelty of his father, the display of selfless love by his mother. Nothing made sense. Was this sacrifice to protect her children? Not to ruin the legacy of the man she had once loved, neither destroy a son's adoration of his father?

'Stupid woman!' Niall shouted.

For half an hour he remained locked in his suite not wanting to see anyone. Ultimately, he shoved his guilt aside, blaming his mother for the murders and the crimes he had committed.

Tied up and bleeding, Irina looked defiantly at Niall who was deep in thought, seated in front of the large expanse of glass. Ignoring her, he stared out over the sea, at the unfolding dawn. She frowned, somewhat puzzled by the deranged look on his face – her executioner face.

'I'm here,' she said.

'Sit down,' he offered, fighting the animosity in his voice, indicating the seat next to him.

'I'm fine where I am,' she said, resenting being in the same room, let alone sit near him.

'Suit yourself. Thought I'll share some news while you're still with us,' he said, his voice hollow.

She did not respond. She did not move as she fought the dizziness washing over her.

He held up a pink book, and said, 'My sister's diary which I've read. That was after I watched your antics on the security footage. But I'll get to that in a minute. You were right; the parcel did reveal an important fact: my mother did not kill my father, my sister did. Quite astonishing, actually. If I had read her letters earlier, life might have been very different.'

'I thought as much,' Irina said, not surprised by the news, having never believed his version of events regarding his father's death.

'Right, right, I might have made a mistake, but bottom line: she's to blame. Why did she not just tell the truth? Did she think I could not handle it? Goddamn women, always thinking with their bleeding little hearts! The way I see it, I don't owe anyone an apology. The one who does is my mother. And she's dead. So, we'll just have to live with it and move on. As far as I'm concerned, I did nothing wrong.'

'If you really think that, then you're crazier than I thought. How can you sleep at night? How do you do it? Explain why you—'

A loud whoop-whoop noise cut her off, followed by short bursts of gunfire.

Niall jumped up, cautioned her to stay where she was and rushed out of the room.

A few seconds later he returned carrying a briefcase and a revolver. He stopped at the coffee table and activated the direct line to his security room. 'What the hell's happening?'

'We're under attack. I think, Russian Special Forces!' the guard shouted.

'Got it! You hold them off, ten minutes. Tell Karl to meet me at the plane. Now!' he ordered and slammed the phone down.

'Who are they?' Niall asked, beside himself.

'Friends.'

'Really! Then here's a parting gift to remember me by,' he barked and fired his revolver just as she started to move.

The force of the bullet slamming into her shoulder sent her crashing to the floor. She did not move, her eyes wide with shock.

'Rot in hell!' he shouted as he fled through a secret passage in the wooden panel.

Mustering all her strength and ignoring the excruciating pain in her shoulder, arm and side, she dragged herself towards the window. Pushing herself upright against the glass wall, she prayed someone would see her.

All of a sudden, the gunfire fell silent, followed by loud shouting reverberating throughout the empty house.

Her eyelids felt heavy as she focused on the three Futura Commando zodiacs racing across the surf, each carrying ten armed marines. In the background the dark shape of a submarine drew nearer.

Her eyes closed.

Her head lolled to the side.

She was no longer aware of the twenty-four-armed men in camouflage gear herding Niall's inferior force into a small huddle in the garden. Marines, who, under cover of darkness, had abseiled from the top of the cliff and struck with lightning speed in neutralising any resistance. The operation had lasted less than eight minutes.

The "All Go" for extraction had been issued to the elite unit of Alfa Force when Irina had failed to rendezvous on time. The memo sent to FSB HQ from Niall's computer at 03h45 had been explicit. It was what the team in Moscow had been waiting for: "Mission accomplished, rendezvous 04h30, the pier. Codename: Nemesis".

Since Irina's urgent call from inside the ladies' restroom in Niall's restaurant on the Friday evening, the FSB's local unit had been standing by for her immediate extraction. And when she had activated the powerful homing device fitted into the lining of her suitcase on the Saturday morning, Alfa Force had taken over. Tracking her signal by satellite, the FSB had always known her location except for the period when she had vanished into the Atlas Mountains.

The instant Niall's plane had touched down on the island, orders were issued to one of the Akula II nuclear submarines patrolling the East Coast of America to take up a position five kilometres off Niall's island. Having covered the distance to the island at a maximum submerged speed of thirty-five knots, it had rendezvoused with the Alfa Force members flown in from Russia. The remaining two hours sailing was completed by Monday noon.

Since then the U-boat had been in position at periscope depth, waiting for final orders.

Gripping the polished stainless-steel handrail, Niall flew down the stairs, reaching the hangar bay within minutes. A few seconds later a slightly out of breath Karl stepped out of the elevator.

In the still of the early morning the thunder of the

393

powerful jet engines travelled to the Alfa Unit searching for the man guilty of countless crimes against their country. Clearing the trees, Karl taxied to the end of the runway. Ready for take-off, he released the brakes, catapulting the plane forward.

The next instant the sky turned dark as the rising sun was obliterated by a cloud of flying grit and dirt. Flabbergasted, Niall stared at the sods of grass and dirt hanging in mid-air before crashing back into the newly-formed crater.

The second explosion struck even closer, repeating the same display of destruction to the runway.

Instinctively, Karl dropped the power, terminating the forward thrust, and braked hard. Veering off the runway they narrowly avoided the first crater. With the wheels sinking into the soft sand the plane came to an abrupt halt.

Niall knew there was nothing he could do. Even if they somehow managed to get into the air, a surface-to-air missile would undoubtedly bring their journey to an end.

'Well, Karl, I'm afraid this is it,' Niall said. Noticing the state of shock, the pilot was in, he added, 'Don't worry, you'll be fine. It's me they're after. One more favour, I promise it will be worth it. Are you up for it? Karl, listen to me!'

'Yes, OK. What?'

'Inside this briefcase along with my passport and cash are a few documents, decoys, rubbish, except for this one,' Niall said and fished out a folded travel brochure advertising the Caribbean. 'Let them have the case. They'll think they'll have everything. But this brochure, whatever you do, don't lose it. It contains coded information … Karl, are you listening?'

'Yes, I am … coded information, sure. And?'

'To decipher this, you must access the following email: ballinagee1@hotmail.com password, *llain69*. Open the letter in the draft file, subject, "Washington DC". The information contained in the draft letter will decipher this brochure. You've got it? It will put you in touch with some very powerful friends of mine, and funds. These are men who can, and will help.'

'Got it.' Having memorised the details, Karl placed the brochure into the side pocket of his seat.

'I'll contact you, although when is anyone's guess. If you hear nothing from me by the end of twelve months, then assume I'm dead.'

Looking out of the cockpit window, three black rubber boats beached themselves at breakneck speed next to the stranded plane. Before coming to a stop, thirty armed men jumped out and surrounded them. Pointing with his assault rifle, a young captain indicated for Niall and Karl to get out.

'Karl … thanks. Hopefully, we'll meet again soon,' Niall said, leading the way to the waiting marines.

Identified as Niall McGuire, his hands were cuffed behind his back. With the butts of their assault rifles he was herded along like a stubborn bull. The cold intimidating stares of the Russian troops said it all: if they could have things their way, he would not survive another second.

During the short journey across the water to the black shape looming up ahead, Niall said nothing. Looking over his shoulder he saw Karl enter the plane unharmed, but without the briefcase.

Good, at least he's free, Niall thought.

With the boat steadied against the black hull of the submarine, the marines manhandled Niall up the wet steel rings. And much to their amusement, he slipped, grazing his hands badly.

Inside the control room, the U-boat captain confronted him with the small memory stick Irina had retrieved from his computer.

'See this? You shall pay for what you've done,' the captain said. 'If I had things my way, I'd shoot you on the spot, and dump your body overboard. But I must be content in doing my duty. Therefore, I now inform you that you have been charged and found guilty of crimes against the state and people of Russia. Your sentence is to be carried out immediately, by order of the Supreme Court of Russia.'

Niall burst out laughing at the absurdity of it all; under

international law he had his rights. No one could touch him! But his laughter and protestations died in his throat the instant a rifle-butt knocked him unconscious.

CHAPTER 85

Caribbean
Wednesday

At the turn of the key, Niall looked up. Framed in the doorway was Irina with two armed guards by her side.

'You! For Christ's sake, why won't you just die!' Niall shouted. For twenty-four hours he had been locked up in the cell, not having spoken, or seen anyone.

'Temper, temper,' Irina said with a scornful smile. 'Thought you were rid of me. Well, next time, aim better.'

Dressed in Alfa Force combat fatigues, pistol in one hand, her one shoulder bandaged and the other arm in a sling, she looked anything but *a young peasant girl*. Despite her serious wounds she sat up straight in the wheelchair with her head held high: confident, beautiful and extremely dangerous. The real Irina.

One of the guards handed him a mug of coffee.

'Thanks, about bloody time.'

'Shut … fuck up!' the Russian marine snarled.

With their weapons trained on him not another word was said as Niall sipped his coffee.

Irina looked at him pensively, at his glowering defiance: although vanquished, defeated he was not. Even in captivity he remained a threat.

Having finished his coffee, he put the empty mug down and asked, 'Who are you?

'I'll tell you who I am and why I'm here,' she said and turned to the marines. 'Please, wait outside.'

Alone with him – confident the information she was about to share would never be repeated as he was destined to die a slow and lonely death – she said, 'I'm an agent with the Federal'naya Sluzhba Bezopasnosti – the FSB. And as it turned out, you are the reason I joined.'

'Really, I didn't know I've done anything that was any of your business,' Niall said scornfully.

'That's where you're wrong. I joined the FSB to find the person responsible for the death of a young woman named Evgeniya Nikolaeva. And realising no one had any interest in catching her murderer, I soon transferred to Counter-Intelligence, the SKR, where I had access to her file. And that's where I found the names of your Ciarán and Larry O'Rourke. From then on, I made it my business to know everything there was to know about them. Did they work alone? If not, then for whom? I wanted to know the truth. And I found you.'

Niall stared at her, stunned. 'Who the—'

She lifted a hand, stopping him short.

'About a year ago, arms which were recorded as *mothballed* in Russia, turned up in Somalia. The supplier was only a middleman and therefore of little value. But subsequently, you had been named as the possible mastermind in this network of smugglers. Also, someone other than the usual foreign government agencies was hacking into our secret weapons programmes. A possible link was traced back to you, but nothing concrete. Therefore, an agent was inserted on your estate. But other than your involvement in the sex and drug-industries, nothing else was found. Proof, as well as all names of those involved in this network, was needed. My superiors changed tact; someone had to infiltrate your inner circle. So, when I was approached, I jumped at the opportunity. Well, that is one reason why I'm here.'

Niall looked at her stone-faced. 'And what may I ask is the second reason?'

She ignored him, and said, 'I'm sure all the details of your partners and your smuggling operations, ranging from small arms, anti-tank guided missiles, ground-to-air missiles, air-to-air missiles, and even stealing the blueprints of the new T-1 Ural tank, are all recorded on the USB key. Be assured, like you, your friends will receive no mercy.'

'Hurrah! You've done magnificent work. Well done! I'm sure you'll get a medal for this. Right, I get it; you want to be famous and now you'll definitely be. Good for you. Now just get the fuck out. Leave!' Niall growled.

'I'll leave when I've finished. So be quiet and listen.'

'Right, yes, of course, you've got the gun. I'm all ears.'

'The second reason why I'm here, in case you haven't worked it out yet, is personal. I came to Ireland to avenge my sister's death. My name is Svetlana Nikolaeva, the younger sister of Evgeniya Nikolaeva. Still doesn't ring a bell, no? By the look on your face I guess it doesn't, although it should. Or were there just too many killed by Ciarán and Larry to remember?'

How many days and nights she had wished to see the man in front of her suffer, pay for his sins. Thankfully, Ciarán was dead, and Larry she would find soon.

'I have no idea who you're talking about, *Svetlana*,' Niall said sarcastically. 'And, I'm really *sorry* if I have hurt yours or your little sister's feelings. But truth is, I don't care, and you need to grow up and get a fucking life!' He wanted to jump up and strangle her. But his legs did not move, neither did his arms respond. He felt sleepy. A strange lethargy spread through his body with the drug in the coffee taking effect.

'You had my sister killed, you bastard! You had my beautiful sister thrown into a skip like a piece of garbage for the rats to feed on, somewhere in the filthy East End of London. Do you recall now?!'

He did not respond and looked at her, amused.

'My God, how many did you kill that you cannot remember? Those poor young girls in your despicable brothels, just how many died at your hands?' she asked, furious. 'How I wish to see you dead, but that would be too easy. No, maybe their way is much better. You will suffer like those you have destroyed. You will learn what pain is, what loneliness is long before you die!'

'And knowing this about me, you actually seduced and slept with me. Incredible! You're nothing but a slut, a whore!' Niall harangued.

'A little secret; if that's what it takes to get my sister's killer, I'll do it again. Seducing you was part of the plan. Not only seducing, but getting you emotionally involved. And you fell for it. You fell in love! How unbelievably naïve you are. You think you are better … smarter than most men, but you're not. You're no different to them: utterly predictable, weak, pathetic! The truth is you make me sick. My skin crawls just at the mere thought of you having touched me. How many hours I've scrubbed myself nearly raw trying to remove your stench! And you thought I loved you? How infantile! But know this, what I suffered was nothing, as the result is everything. And I never compromise, never,' she said, her voice filled with disdain.

'If you're still wondering about the bugs in your house, well, I planted them. Everything you had discussed in private is on record and now in the hands of the Garda. You are finished. Even, if by some miracle you survive what is ahead of you, you can never go back.'

She fell silent and wheeled her chair around. She took one last look at his distraught face, beaten, his fiery spirit finally extinguished.

400

CHAPTER 86

Caribbean
Thursday

Confused, Niall sat up and rubbed his eyes. The moving sensation had stopped although the bunk bed felt the same, hard and uncomfortable. The sedative Svetlana had slipped into his coffee had finally worn off. He blinked and stared at the four graffiti-scribbled walls. The putrid stench of excrement was enough to make him vomit. Scrambling to the door he peered through the small grated opening in the steel panel. Realising this tiny aperture was to be his only glimpse of the outside world – a desolate semi-dark corridor – he sank to the floor filled with dismay, appalled.

He was locked inside the solitary confinement cellblock "H" in Havana's high-security prison. As ordained between the Russian and Cuban governments, this was to be his home until the last breath would escape his tired, frail old body.

Niall fought the waves of despair which threatened to engulf him. Alone with only his thoughts and memories as companion, he now fully grasped the meaning of Irina's parting words, "You will suffer like those you have destroyed. You will learn what pain is, what loneliness is, long before you die."

But she was wrong!

As long as there was life in him, a small flame of hope flickered: the will to survive. Possessing the power to change people, especially those who did not share in his good fortune such as the penniless guards, he would find a way out. It was only a matter of time. They had miscalculated.

Irina, you'll regret this! You should have killed me when you had the chance.

CHAPTER 87

Haute-Savoie
France
Thursday

Vera still reeled from the emotional rollercoaster ride she had withstood over the last number of days. One moment she had faced execution and was rescued by someone she hardly knew. And twenty minutes later, once more facing certain death, she was again saved by the same man.

Michael should have died there and then. But he had stoically clung to life until she had been safe. Only then did he slip away in her arms. Trying to find a pulse had been to no avail. Alone, covered in his blood, she had listened to his stilled breathing …

Defeated, she had lacked the will to carry on.

Stavros and his friends had come for him.

They had found a faint pulse …

By some miracle, the young surgeon had pulled Michael from the clutches of death. Whisked off to a private clinic in Mykonos, the bullet had been successfully removed.

Throughout this traumatic experience, Vera had remained by his side while Stavros had guarded over them, sealing their newly-formed friendship.

Skimming over a snow-covered Mont Blanc, Vera held Michael's hand, and asked, 'How you're feeling, still dizzy?'

'Could be better … I reckon. But hey, I'm alive and have you to help me get back on my feet. Therefore, I've nothing to complain about,' Michael said and gave a weak smile.

'Glad you think so. But what makes you so sure I want to help?' she teased and gently squeezed his hand.

'Don't worry, I won't break,' Michael chuckled and squeezed her hand hard.

'Ouch!'

'Oops … sorry.'

'Better be, or I'll disappear.'

'No, you won't. I'm not letting you out of my sight. So, you're stuck with me, I'm afraid.'

'OK … OK, you win!' she said smiling warmly.

'That was easy!'

'Confession. I would love to be your *prisoner,* but on one condition.'

'Really, and what is that, may I ask?'

'Once you're well, you promise, no more hero stuff.' Her eyes twinkled as she kissed him.

'Sorry, can't do,' he replied sternly.

'Oh dear, that sounds serious. And why not?'

'Because I'll never let anyone harm you again. Now that, I can promise you.'

'Buckle up we're coming in to land,' Stavros' voice announced over the speaker, interrupting their little *tête-à-tête.*

Below them, the crystal-clear water of Lake Annecy shimmered like a pearl in the bright sunlight. Descending below the granite peaks of the surrounding mountains they made their final approach to Annecy Airport, gateway to the French Alps.

Parting company, Vera ignored Stavros' protestations as she proffered a fistful of diamonds into his hand to help him start a new life as a free man.

'Walk away from this business, Stavros, or you'll go down with Dimitris. Please follow my advice,' Michael insisted.

'Will do so, my friend, will do! Believe me, it's been a dream of mine for far too long.'

404

'Good. You have our number. If you need anything, just call. Better still, I'll give you a call once I'm up and about,' Michael said, thinking of putting Stavros to good use.

Smiling, Stavros looked at the couple, and said, 'Vera, if you ever get bored of him, remember I'm waiting! Now go before I embarrass myself. Take care, my friends.'

Ensconced high in the Aravis Mountains above the picturesque ski resort of La Clusaz, their chalet was the perfect hideaway, destined to remain a closely guarded secret. Pushed to the foot of the bed was the newspaper article depicting the international criminal Niall McGuire's demise. Seemingly, he had died five days ago somewhere in the Caribbean Sea while trying to escape the Russian FSB.

'Please let it go. It belongs to the past,' Michael whispered, holding Vera, his lips brushing her ear. Although he knew these words were not quite true. Yes, Niall might be dead, but the chances were very real that some of his friends would come looking for her … for the diamonds.

'No, please I have to … I want us to have no secrets,' Vera insisted. Pulling away from him, she sat up against the pillow and tucked her knees in under her chin. In a soft melodious voice, she relayed the story of her life, her youth … the reason for having fled to the West.

When she finished, Michael said, 'Vera, know this: I love you for who you are and not for what you have or have not done. I shall never judge you … and as we shall have no secrets, then I must tell you my own little secret, one you can never repeat. Promise?'

'My lips are sealed, cross my heart,' she said with a slight concerned frown.

'I'm a deep undercover agent with Interpol. I joined up after my madness as a mercenary had run its cause. And my current assignment is to catch Niall and his buddies. He's been under investigation for quite some time now.'

Dumbfounded, unable to believe what she just heard, she exclaimed, 'And I thought you were one of them! Oh dear, what a fool I've been! Are you going to arrest me now?'

'Oh, yes! Definitely house arrest. You'll have to stay right here, handcuffed to the cooker, the sink, the iron and, of course, don't forget the bed!'

'Sounds like life in the Gulag would have been a picnic. Maybe I should just hand myself in,' she laughed.

Michael pulled her close, for a moment pushing the banter aside. 'As I've told you before, I'll not let anyone ever hurt you again. And what happened in Russia will be cleared, that I guarantee you. And the diamonds? Well, to tell the truth, I never saw them. Therefore, I cannot report on something I haven't seen. Can I now? Sean's version of events will have to do, and will be in my official report.'

'Any more secrets?' she teased.

'Not that I can think of right now. But there's one more issue we have to deal with.'

'And that is?'

'Your safety. We must make sure no one can ever find you. So, I was thinking … maybe best you begin a new life, one with a new identity? What about as Mrs Mahoney? Well, that's if the name appeals to you?'

'Are you by any chance proposing?' Vera asked, unable to mask her pleasure.

'Hmm … what do you reckon, yes or no?' he beamed, expectantly.

Tenderly, she cupped his face in her hands and looked deep into his eyes. Fighting her tears, she kissed him longingly, and whispered softly, 'Yes.'

Athens, Greece

Sinead looked pale. Comatose, she had been in her own world for five days. The head wound was far worse than originally thought. And the medical personnel had no idea how long her condition would last. But they remained hopeful she would make a full recovery.

Fidgeting by her side, Sean got up every now and then

and strolled outside, agonising over his sister. He knew he could not remain in Athens forever; he had to return to Dublin.

The young Greek nurse who had been on duty for the last eight hours pitied Sean. Touching him on the shoulder the nurse said, 'Sean, don't worry, we'll take care of her. Do what you must. She'll be fine.'

'Thank you.'

After a few more minutes of silence, he stood up and kissed Sinead on the cheek. 'Sis, I have to go and help Ronan; I have to clear our names … But don't worry, I'll be back,' he promised, dragging himself away, leaving his sister on her own in the care of strangers.

Unknown to him only a few members of the Greek police, Irina, Michael and Vera knew the location of the clinic where Sinead had been transferred under a cloak of secrecy five days earlier. As far as the world was concerned, Sinead had vanished without a trace.

And it would seem, Irina as well. Despite her promise to contact him as soon as she was safe, Sean had heard nothing, not a word.

Arriving at Dublin airport he was surprised not to be arrested as feared. Unknown to him, the Garda had no further interest in either him or Ronan, having been supplied with the facts of the case by Irina's and Michael's offices.

The man they were looking for, Niall McGuire, was dead.

But for Sean it was not over; he had to find Irina. There were too many unanswered questions. Was she even still alive? He would start at the Russian Embassy.

CHAPTER 88

Moscow

In Moscow, Svetlana – alias Irina – proceeded with her own agenda: the immediate dismantling of Niall's brothels and sex-trafficking network spread all over Europe. Her determined actions managed to rescue over two thousand girls, returning them to their families in Eastern Europe, India, Africa and the Far East.

Granted leave to recuperate, Svetlana travelled with her two-year-old daughter, Dasha, to her parents in Kursk. Having left Dasha in their care, she drove to the small village of Sokol'e, east of Kursk near the Ukrainian border.

Parking the car outside her late grandparents' cottage, she noticed the garden had been weeded recently. The picket fence, wooden windows and shutters had been refreshed with a new coat of paint. She recognised her parents' handiwork; they loved spending their free time in the tranquillity of the small house in the country away from the drabness of Kursk.

She turned and followed the familiar road, longing for the many carefree days she and her sister had spent here with friends and family, amongst those who had loved them, who had meant so much to them. She sighed at the memory of her *babushka's* warm welcoming smile.

It was such a long time ago.

But since then nothing much had changed, except for the old faces having grown older, and those few not seen anymore, replaced by younger ones.

A group of small children, young and innocent, brushed past her. Laughing, they shouted a friendly greeting and continued down the narrow trail towards the lake.

Further along the road she stopped and watched the sun's rays filter through the forest's umbrella of leaves, the slender trunks rooted in an endless sea of flowers. Entering the woods, she trod with great care in avoiding the clusters of small white blossoms. Ignoring the pain in her side, she knelt down and picked a handful of flowers. Aimlessly, her gaze drifted deeper in amongst the trees, lost in a mystical world of long-forgotten memories.

As the damp stung her knees, she got up and returned to the road.

Walking along the grey unyielding surface, her heart saddened at the sight of the lifeless graves. With a grating sound the wrought iron bolt slid back. Hesitantly, she pushed the gate open and entered the solitude of the cemetery. The mere thought of the ferocious arctic winds which swept freely across the graves during winter made her shiver.

Standing inside the family plot she felt incredibly lonely.

At her feet, the shadows cast by the leaves of the silver birch trees stole over the cold granite stones. A warm, colourful blanket of violets, daisies and forget-me-nots covered the small patch of earth where her grandparents and Evgeniya lay side by side, their final resting place.

Wiping the tears from her cheeks, she placed the bouquet of Lilies of the Valley next to the headstone as their sweet fragrance filled the air. It had been Evgeniya's childhood dream to one day hold these tiny flowers on her wedding day – a dream never fulfilled.

Svetlana sat down on the old wooden bench and listened to the light rustle of the leaves, allowing the silent hush of the late afternoon to cleanse her soul, ridding her of the demons she had braved for so long.

As the light faltered and the shadows deepened, she placed a piece of bread next to the garland of fresh white lilies.

Carefully, she poured some vodka into two small glasses. The contents of the one she discarded on the ground next to the bread. And the other, she drank, and whispered, '*Spi spokoyno sestrenka.*' (Sleep peacefully my dearest sister; it is over.)

AUTHOR'S NOTE

Sex Slavery/Trafficking

The following is an extract of a white paper on Sex Slavery/Trafficking as compiled by SOROPTIMIST INTERNATIONAL (published here with their permission granted on the 15th February, 2010). SOROPTIMIST INTERNATIONAL is a volunteer organisation for business and professional women who work globally to improve the lives of women and girls:

Sex Trafficking is a $32 billion annual industry. Trafficking is a type of slavery that involves the transport or trade of people for the purpose of work. According to the U.N., about 2.5 million people around the world are ensnared in the web of human trafficking at any given time.

Trafficking impacts people of all backgrounds and people are trafficked for a variety of purposes. Men are often trafficked into hard labour jobs, while children are trafficked into labour positions in textile, agriculture and fishing industries. Women and girls are typically trafficked into the commercial sex industry, i.e. prostitution or other forms of sexual exploitation.

Not all slaves are trafficked, but all trafficking victims are victims of slavery. Trafficking is a particularly cruel type of slavery because it removes the victim from all that is familiar to her, rendering her completely isolated and alone, often unable to speak the language of her captors or fellow victims.

Sex trafficking or slavery is the exploitation of women and children, within national or across international borders, for the purposes of forced sex work. Commercial sexual exploitation includes pornography, prostitution and sex trafficking of women and girls, and is characterized by the exploitation of a human being in exchange for goods or money. Each year, an estimated 800,000 women and children are trafficked across international borders—though additional numbers of women and girls are trafficked within countries.

Some sex trafficking is visible, such as street prostitution. But many trafficking victims remain unseen, operating out of unmarked brothels in unsuspecting — and sometimes suburban —neighbourhoods. Sex traffickers may also operate out of a variety of public and private locations, such as massage parlours, spas and strip clubs.

Adult women make up the largest group of sex trafficking victims, followed by girl children, although a small percentage of men and boys are trafficked into the sex industry as well.

Trafficking migration patterns tend to flow from East to West, but women may be trafficked from any country to another country at any given time and trafficking victims exist everywhere. Many of the poorest and most unstable countries have the highest incidences of trafficking, and extreme poverty is a common bond among trafficking victims. Where economic alternatives do not exist, women and girls are more vulnerable to being tricked and coerced into sexual servitude. Increased unemployment and the loss of job security have undermined women's incomes and economic position. A stalled gender wage gap, as well as an increase in women's part-time and informal sector work, push women into poorly paid jobs and long-term and hidden unemployment, which leaves women vulnerable to traffickers.

According to the United Nations Office on Drugs and Crime (UNODC), Thailand, China, Nigeria, Albania, Bulgaria, Belarus, Moldova and Ukraine are among the countries that are the greatest sources of trafficked persons. The UNODC cites Thailand, Japan, Israel, Belgium, the Netherlands, Germany, Italy and the United States as common destination countries of trafficked women and girls.

Organized crime is largely responsible for the spread of international human trafficking. Sex trafficking — along with its correlative elements, kidnapping, rape, prostitution and physical abuse — is illegal in nearly every country in the world. However, widespread corruption and greed make it possible for sex trafficking to proliferate quickly and easily. Though national and international institutions may attempt to regulate and enforce anti trafficking legislation, local governments and police forces may, in fact, be participating in sex trafficking rings.

Why do traffickers traffic? Because sex trafficking can be extremely lucrative, especially in areas where opportunities for education and legitimate employment may be limited. According to the United Nations Office on Drugs and Crime (UNODC), the greatest numbers of traffickers are from Asia, followed by Central and South-eastern Europe, and Western Europe. Crime groups involved in the sex trafficking of women and girls are also often involved in the transnational trafficking of drugs and firearms, and frequently use violence as a means of carrying out their activities.

One overriding factor in the proliferation of trafficking is the fundamental belief that the lives of women and girls are expendable. In societies where women and girls are undervalued or not valued at all, women are at greater risk for being abused, trafficked, and coerced into sex slavery. If women experienced improved economic and social status, trafficking would in large part be eradicated.

Women and girls are ensnared in sex trafficking in a variety of ways. Some are lured by offers of legitimate and legal work as shop assistants or waitresses. Others are promised marriage, educational opportunities and a better life. Still, others are sold into trafficking by boyfriends, friends, neighbours or even parents.

Trafficking victims often pass among multiple traffickers, moving further and further from their home countries. Women often travel through multiple countries before ending at their final destination. For example, a woman from the Ukraine may be sold to a trafficker in Turkey, who then passes her on to a trafficker in Thailand. Along the way she becomes confused and disoriented.

Typically, once in the custody of traffickers, a victim's passport and official papers are confiscated and held. Victims are told they are in the destination country illegally, which increases victims' dependence on their traffickers. Victims are often kept in captivity and also trapped into debt bondage, whereby they are obliged to pay back large recruitment and transportation fees before being released from their traffickers. Many victims report being charged additional fines or fees while under bondage, requiring them to work longer to pay off their debts.

Trafficking victims experience various stages of degradation and physical and psychological torture. Victims are often deprived of food and sleep, are unable to move about freely, and are physically tortured. In order to keep women captive, victims are told their families and their children will be harmed or murdered if they (the women) try to escape or tell anyone about their situation. Because victims rarely understand the culture and language of the country into which they have been trafficked, they experience another layer of psychological stress and frustration.

Often, before servicing clients, women are forcibly raped by the traffickers themselves, in order to initiate the cycle of abuse and degradation. Some women are drugged in order to prevent them from escaping. Once 'broken in,' sex trafficked victims might service up to 30 men a day, and are vulnerable to sexually transmitted diseases, HIV infection and unwanted pregnancy.

Many believe that sex trafficking is something that occurs 'somewhere else.' However, many of the biggest trafficking consumers are developed nations, and men from all sectors of society support the trafficking industry. There is no one profile that encapsulates the 'typical' client. Rather, men who purchase trafficked women are both rich and poor, Eastern and Western. Many are married and have children, and in some cases, as was reported in one New York Times article, men have sex with trafficked girls in lieu of abusing their own young children.

One reason for the proliferation of sex trafficking is because in many parts of the world there is little to no perceived stigma to purchasing sexual favours for money, and prostitution is viewed as a victimless crime. Because women are culturally and socially devalued in so many societies, there is little conflict with the purchasing of women and girls for sexual services. Further, few realize the explicit connection between the commercial sex trade and the trafficking of women and girls and the illegal slave trade. In western society, in particular, there is a commonly held perception that women choose to enter into the commercial sex trade. However, for the majority of women in the sex trade, and specifically in the case of trafficked women and girls who are coerced or forced into servitude, this is simply not the case.

415

In addition, sex tourism — that is, the practice of travelling or vacationing for the purpose of having sex — is a billion-dollar industry that further encourages the sexual exploitation of women and girls. Many sex tours explicitly feature young girls. The tours are marketed specifically to paedophiles who prey on young children, and men who believe that having sex with virgins or young girls will cure sexually transmitted diseases (STDs). Often, these men spread HIV and other STDs to their young victims, creating localized disease epidemics. Trafficking has a harrowing effect on the mental, emotional and physical well-being of the women and girls ensnared in its web. Beyond the physical abuse, trafficked women suffer extreme emotional stress, including shame, grief, fear, distrust and suicidal thoughts. Victims often experience posttraumatic stress disorder, and with that, acute anxiety, depression and insomnia. Many victims turn to drugs and alcohol to numb the pain.

Sex trafficking promotes societal breakdown by removing women and girls from their families and communities. Trafficking fuels organised crime groups that usually participate in many other illegal activities, including drug and weapons trafficking and money laundering. It negatively impacts local and national labour markets, due to the loss of human resources. Sex trafficking burdens public health systems. And trafficking erodes government authority, encourages widespread corruption, and threatens the security of vulnerable populations.

For an excerpt of Silent Screams' exciting

fast-paced sequel

VEINS OF DEATH

By

JAMES LEONARD

Please turn the page

CHAPTER 1

East Berlin

March 1985

Furious, Lieutenant General Petr Ivanov let out a curse and immediately dropped to the ground, ignoring the sting of the cold wet snow. Sheltered by the flaky wall, he stared at the hovering blinding light blocking their path, meticulously searching the dark crevices of the bare ruins.

Behind him the three petrified shadows pressed their bodies against the wall. Wide-eyed, they waited for him to move, instruct them what to do next. The nervous puffs escaping their clenched teeth were swiftly whisked away by the freezing wind as if expunging their last breaths. Above them the windowless openings glared down, howling accusingly, "Traitors, fleeing like thieves in the night!"

Lt Gen Ivanov remained motionless, expecting the worst: vicious dogs snapping at the still shadows, soldiers charging, shots ringing out. But the only movement was the flurry of snowflakes swirling aimlessly in the bright light.

For the umpteenth time, Lt Gen Ivanov questioned his own wisdom, having made a deal with those he despised. *Did we walk into a trap the minute we stepped outside our apartment? What if he was … Stop, enough!* It was far too late for regrets, for self-remonstration.

The simple truth was, if it was a trap, he would be solely to blame.

United in their anger, convincing them to escape the pervasive evil ruling their country was easy – he had known his wife and children would follow him into hell itself, if need be.

But facing the reality, staring defeat in the eyes, the very real prospect of witnessing those he loved, killed, was very different. With their bodies removed from the cold barren snow, the dark crimson stain would be the only proof of their existence, soon to be washed away by the first thaw.

Recalling the Politburo Chairman's words, he angrily crunched his fist in the snow as if squashing a vile insect. The rasping voice of the bastard still rung painfully in his ears: "Your son's cowardly act was an admission of guilt. I suggest you accept this fact. Forget him. He was a traitor to our Motherland!" None of them would ever forget these slanderous words, and could never accept them.

Enraged, he watched the searchlight linger as the minutes ticked slowly by until, at last, the comforting darkness engulfed them once more, returning the rugged cold walls to their deceiving calm slumber.

How many eyes were watching? Lt Gen Ivanov could only imagine. Wiping the fresh snow off his brow and trimmed grey beard, he squinted into the blizzard, waiting for the signal. His gloved hand touched the loaded pistol on his hip. If they had been betrayed, he would spare his family a slow and painful death. Impatiently, he shifted his weight, fighting the creeping numbness in his toes.

Fifty metres to his left stood the four-metre high concrete wall, and on top of it guard-towers were dotted as far as the eye could see. In front of this synthetic scar drawn across the face of Mother Earth was a 2.4 metre-high chain-link fence adorned with coils of razor-sharp wire. The restricted zone. Littered with antipersonnel-mines and rows of anchored Czech hedgehog anti-tank barriers, any attempt to traverse this man-made barrier would be suicide.

Suddenly, across the fifteen-metre gap in the wall, a barely visible red blip caught his eye. *At last!* Preparing to move, the general's fingers inched along the wall as the red light flashed again.

Risking a quick glance over the wall, he whispered to his wife Elena by his side, 'It's time.' The way was clear. He gently squeezed her hand, and said, 'Follow at one-minute intervals.' Without another word he raced across the opening.

Beneath the dilapidated porch, with Elena, Klara and Sergei by his side, he faced Captain Kirill Abramovich. Dressed in soviet army combat fatigues the man studied the family with cold eyes. 'You're all here. Then let's go. Hurry, and no sound!' he hissed.

The absence of a salute by the junior officer as dictated by military protocol was not lost on the general. But he understood; he was no longer to be respected, instead, he was to be despised. He was a disgrace to the uniform he still wore. The general's tall frame slumped despite the desire to remain erect, tall and proud. Reluctantly, he accepted his new status of traitor.

Abruptly the young captain turned away. Having traversed a hundred metres through the ruins, he stopped in front of a pile of snow. With his boots he cleared a path, exposing a flight of steps leading down into a basement.

'This way,' he said, and climbed over the scattered debris.

The putrid stench of stale water and fermenting waste was unbearable. Wading waist-deep through the icy filth, Klara cried out, 'Mama, it's freezing!' Her young body shook

421

uncontrollably. 'Papa, I can't do this. It's … it's t … t … too cold!' she moaned through clattering teeth.

'Shut up or you'll get us all killed!' the captain snarled from inside the dark.

Behind her, Sergei whispered, 'Sssh … it's ok.' Reaching out, he held her timid shoulders and gently steered her forward.

The crack of a blue night-light lifted the oppressing blackness, exposing four mould-covered walls. Guided by the light, they hurried along and scrambled on to a raised concrete platform.

'Come!' the captain barked.

Filing into the adjoining room they faced a dead-end. Except for a pile of builder's rubble stacked against the far wall, the room was empty with no sign of an exit. Lt Gen Ivanov drew his pistol and took aim at the captain's head, snarling, 'What the hell is this?' At only two metres, he would not miss.

'Put your gun away, old man. Stop acting like a buffoon and give me a hand,' the captain mocked. Ignoring the weapon, he started to remove the pile of stacked timbers and rubble revealing a solid steel door. Unlocking it, he said, 'Don't worry, the alarm has been deactivated and will remain so for another forty minutes.'

'Is that enough time?' the general asked, concerned.

'*Da, moy General.* It's all I could manage. Show some faith and stop wasting time,' he said scathingly and entered a small hall accessing the bowels of the earth. His gloved hand gripped the metal rail, rattling the rickety spiral staircase, as he started to descend.

Familiar with some of the routes to the West - Checkpoint Charlie, the underground train tunnels and the secret passageways - the general had opted for the latter being the safest option. The tunnel they found themselves in was one of the last still used by the Soviet Security Forces for covert operations. Therefore, all movement in and out was constantly monitored. The difference this time: theirs was anything but an authorised covert operation.

Standing in front of the rusty door nine storeys below the ground, the captain said, 'This is as far as I go. From here, you're on your own. *Dosvidaniya*.'

Soundlessly, the door swung open on its well-oiled hinges. The blinking overhead security camera gave no indication whether they were being watched or not.

'Take this and leave it in the lock. We'll secure the tunnel once you're through,' the captain instructed, handing the general a small key. Looking at his watch, he sneered, 'You still have thirty-three minutes to reach the security screen on the far side before it shuts. If you don't make it, then the only way out is this way. And believe me, you don't want that.' A faint twitch tugged at the corner of his eye.

Lt Gen Ivanov suppressed a powerful urge to punch the captain. Instead, he switched the flashlight on, took the small key, and led his family into the cramped musty tunnel.

'Remember, you fled via the underground rail line, having bribed the men on duty to look the other way. If the Americans discover this tunnel, we'll know about it and we shall find you,' the captain warned.

The general did not waste another second and shut the door. Setting off at a brisk pace, his two-metre-tall frame seemed oblivious to the forty kilograms strapped to his back. Behind him, his wife and daughter struggled to keep up, burdened by their packs filled with everything they needed for a new life in the West – some clothes and a few personal memorabilia. After two hundred metres of twists and turns the general stopped, giving his family a chance to catch their breaths.

'Something's wrong,' he whispered to his wife.

'What do you mean, Petr?' Elena asked.

'I don't trust the captain.'

'Yes, I agree. I didn't like him either.'

Turning towards his eighteen-year-old son, he gave him the key and said, 'Sergei, take your mother and sister to safety. I'll wait here to make sure no one follows. When you reach the gate you stay five minutes, no more. If I don't show by then, you run. And if you hear any noises, no matter what, you run. You get out and you don't come back. Understood?'

'Yes, Papa,' Sergei replied without question.

In the dim light, Lt Gen Ivanov's grey eyes shone as he embraced his wife, kissing her gently. Tasting her tears, he swallowed hard, struggling to control his welling sadness. *Will I ever see you … our children again?* 'Remember Andrei; never forget why we had to do this. I'll be with you shortly.' Releasing himself from her embrace, he briefly hugged and kissed his two children. 'Now, please, go.'

'Petr … please come with us,' Elena pleaded.

'I'll be with you in a few minutes.'

Taking his mother by her hand, Sergei led her away.

Lt Gen Ivanov watched the three figures stagger forward, framed by the soft yellow light which bounced off the rough surface of the tunnel. 'God be with you,' he whispered.

Having found cover behind a wooden prop, he wiped the moisture from his eyes. Despite his wretched state, his senses remained alert. With ruthless determination, he gripped the pistol in both hands and took aim in the dark, at the unseen enemy he knew were there.

With every step taken, Sergei was becoming disorientated; there had been too many twists and turns. *Were they heading to safety, or not?*

Once more water soaked his shoes; at least it was not freezing. Rushing forward his right foot skidded, sending him crashing into the tunnel wall. Having regained his balance, he warned his mother and sister panting a few paces behind him, 'Be careful, it's very slippery.'

The warning had hardly left his lips when the clapping of gunfire echoed in the distance.

They froze.

Elena was first to react.

She started to turn back, crying out, 'Petr … Petr!'

'Mama, no!' Sergei shouted. Storming past his sister, he grabbed his mother by the arm. 'Please, there's no point; you heard what Papa said, we must continue.'

'No, you go. Take Klara … take care of her. I can't, not without him. Please, Sergei, just let me go.'

'No, I won't. We need you,' he replied adamant, and forced her to continue.

As they started to run the gunfire flared up again. There were too many shots, too many men in the tunnel for their father to survive; he would die deep underground, and alone.

'Hurry! Papa will be fine, hurry!' Sergei urged them on, trying to remain strong despite his words ringing hollow in his own ears.

Driven by the approaching shouts and gunfire, they rushed through the water and as the floor of the tunnel rose steeply, they stumbled on to dry land.

They paused.

Behind them there was only silence.

Sergei shook his head in dismay, fully understanding why no one was chasing them. *Why bother when the security gate is still shut. And this key? Lying pig! There was never to be any escape. If we're forced back, they'll kill us!*

Despite this feeling of defeat, he pushed ahead.

Soon the tunnel levelled out, becoming firm underfoot. Concrete. In the dim light he noticed the metal supports of the security gate, and much to his surprise it was open!

Having ushered his mother and sister through, he jammed his backpack firmly underneath the metal frame, preventing it from shutting, just in case his dad was still alive.

Forced to crouch and feeling her way in the dark, Klara bumped her head into a solid wall. 'Ouch! This is a dead-end!' she groaned. Desperate, she searched for a handle, a door, a way out.

'No, it can't be. Keep looking,' Sergei said, remaining hopeful. Reaching Klara, he swept the flashlight from side to side: four walls cut into solid rock – a small chamber. The beam crept along the low ceiling and came to rest on a door handle, which when tested, turned with ease. He pushed upwards, but the door would not budge. Deftly, he inserted the key into the lock and turned till he heard the soft click. Again he tried, but found it too heavy to lift. Positioning himself beneath the trapdoor, he straightened his legs and heaved upwards, opening it. Popping his head through the hatch, he noticed two large wooden crates strapped on top, concealing the entrance.

'Klara, you first, give me your foot,' Sergei said. Kneeling, he catapulted his sister, and then his mother, into the room above.

'Quick, hand me those timbers,' Sergei said, pointing with his flashlight at the two short, solid timber joists.

Grabbing the timbers, he once more disappeared back down the tunnel. At the security gate he jammed the timbers underneath the bottom bar of the frame. Having retrieved his backpack, he raced to join his mother and sister. Reaching them, he sneered sceptically, 'I suppose this is either the West, or the platform to the Gulag?'

His mother, in a state of shock with the loss of her husband, did not appreciate his glib comment. The price to reach their goal had been too high. She dreaded to continue without him, but she could not give up, not now – if she did, his death would have been in vain. But what if Sergei's words proved to be correct? She knew they would be killed. Then so be it! Stubbornly, she climbed over the timbers and boxes.

Not unlike his mother, Sergei also suffered the loss of a loved one. *And for what?* he seethed. He hated himself for having left without saying goodbye … for having left without her, period! And worse, for having made a promise he could never keep: he would most likely never see her again, his first and only love. Without her, there was very little sense in going on … life seemed meaningless.

Approaching the sound of wailing sirens piercing the night, he kicked angrily at the filthy rats loitering on the cold slab of steps.

How could he ever forget her? Her radiant smile, her gentle, hazel-green eyes. She had captivated his soul the moment he had laid eyes on her nine years ago. Her unaffected beauty, her innocence, had been like a powerful magnet, sucking in the shredded remains of a young schoolboy's frayed heart. Fearing rejection, he had harboured these feelings for years while his love-forlorn eyes followed her from classroom to classroom, from day to day …

Cautiously, he opened the basement door, letting in a gush of freezing air. He poked his head outside. Seeing no one, he quickly climbed the short flight of steps towards the empty road above. To his left, floodlights danced menacingly, as if

427

choreographed, over the graffiti-covered concrete wall. He had no more doubts: they were in the West.

At last they were safe.

With his mother and sister by his side, he staggered forlornly, aimlessly, into the night, trudging through fresh snow, deeper into West Berlin. Elena sagged on to her knees, unable to bear her anguish any longer. Sergei, joined by Klara, crouched down beside her. Cradling them both, his courage waned, feeling far too young, too inapt to lead them into a world he knew nothing about.

Caught up in their grief, none saw the tall figure approach. Without a sound the shadow reached out and touched Elena, his fingers pressing gently on her shoulder. 'Shhh … it's all right,' he whispered.

Recognising the familiar voice, Elena looked up at the silhouette towering over her. 'Petr!' she cried out.

Ignoring the burning pain in his side, Lt Gen Ivanov lifted his wife into his arms. As they embraced, shutting out the world around them, they were oblivious of the scarlet stain which seeped into the snow at their feet.

The telescopic sights guided the two red dots' relentless creep towards the four figures huddled together in the dark.

For twenty minutes the snipers had followed the hapless family, waiting for the right moment. Their orders had been simple: "Kill anyone who survives the tunnel, but only once they're well clear of the basement."

The trap set for the Ivanov family was about to shut close. They were to join the many other delusional traitors who had dreamed of fleeing the Motherland. Assisted by *dissidents* inside the Russian military apparatus, these defectors never survived, never lived to tell their tale. For them, their road to freedom always ended in the same way.

In horror, Sergei noticed the red dots crawl up his parents' winter coats. 'Mama, Papa!' he shouted and jumped up. With all his strength, he crashed into them the instant two muffled shots rang out in the dark.

Having re-acquired their targets a second volley thundered in the silence …

42608774R00256

Printed in Poland
by Amazon Fulfillment
Poland Sp. z o.o., Wrocław

Silent Screams

by

James Leonard

First published 2019

CIDE Publishers, Co. Cork, Ireland

ISBN 9781793221346

Copy-Editor and Proofreader:
Christina Hitchcock of Hitchcock Editing

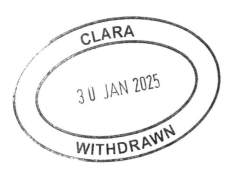